NIGHT [illegible]ER

Ken Follett was only twenty-seven when he wrote the award-winning novel *Eye of the Needle*, which became an international bestseller. He has since written several equally successful novels, including, most recently, *World Without End*, the bestselling sequel to *The Pillars of the Earth*. He is also author of the non-fiction bestseller *On Wings of Eagles*. Ken Follett lives with his family in London and Hertfordshire.

Visit the Ken Follett website at www.ken-follett.com

Also by Ken Follett

THE MODIGLIANI SCANDAL
PAPER MONEY
EYE OF THE NEEDLE
TRIPLE
THE KEY TO REBECCA
THE MAN FROM ST PETERSBURG
ON WINGS OF EAGLES
LIE DOWN WITH LIONS
THE PILLARS OF THE EARTH
A DANGEROUS FORTUNE
A PLACE CALLED FREEDOM
THE THIRD TWIN
THE HAMMER OF EDEN
CODE TO ZERO
JACKDAWS
HORNET FLIGHT
WHITEOUT
WORLD WITHOUT END

KEN FOLLETT

NIGHT OVER WATER

PAN BOOKS

First published 1991 in Great Britain by Macmillan

This edition published 1992 by Pan Books
an imprint of Pan Macmillan, a division of Macmillan Publishers Limited
Pan Macmillan, 20 New Wharf Road, London N1 9RR
Basingstoke and Oxford
Associated companies throughout the world
www.panmacmillan.com

ISBN 978-0-330-53316-4

1 3 5 7 9 8 6 4 2

A CIP catalogue record for this book is available from the British Library.

Typeset by SetSystems Ltd, Saffron Walden, Essex
Printed and bound in the UK by
CPI Mackays, Chatham ME5 8TD

To my sister Hannah with love

PASSENGER DECK PLAN
PAN AMERICAN AIRWAYS SUPER-CLASS

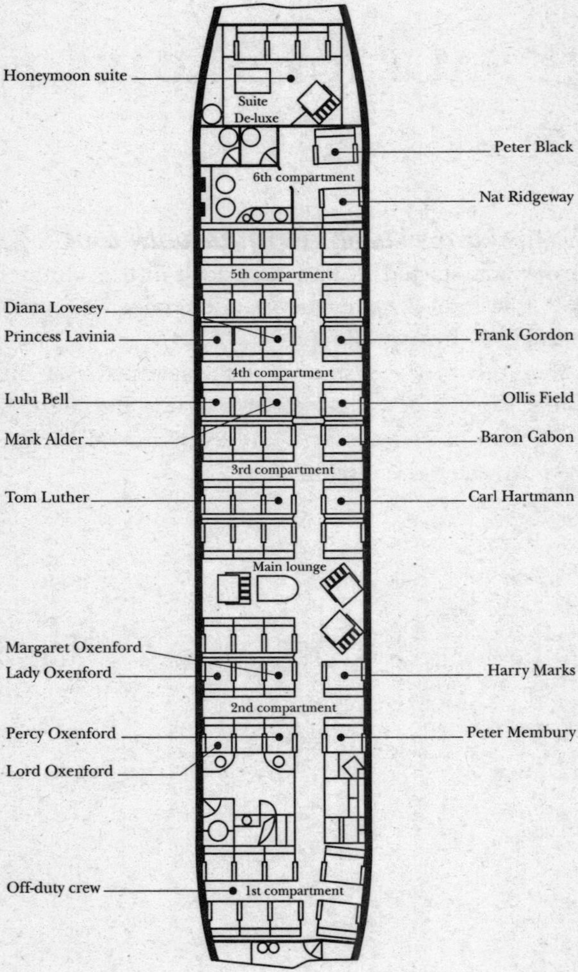

AUTHOR'S NOTE

The first air passenger service between the USA and Europe was started by Pan American in the summer of 1939. It lasted only a few weeks: the service was curtailed when Hitler invaded Poland.

This novel is the story of an imaginary last flight, taking place a few days after war was declared. The flight, the passengers and the crew are all fictional. However, the plane itself is real.

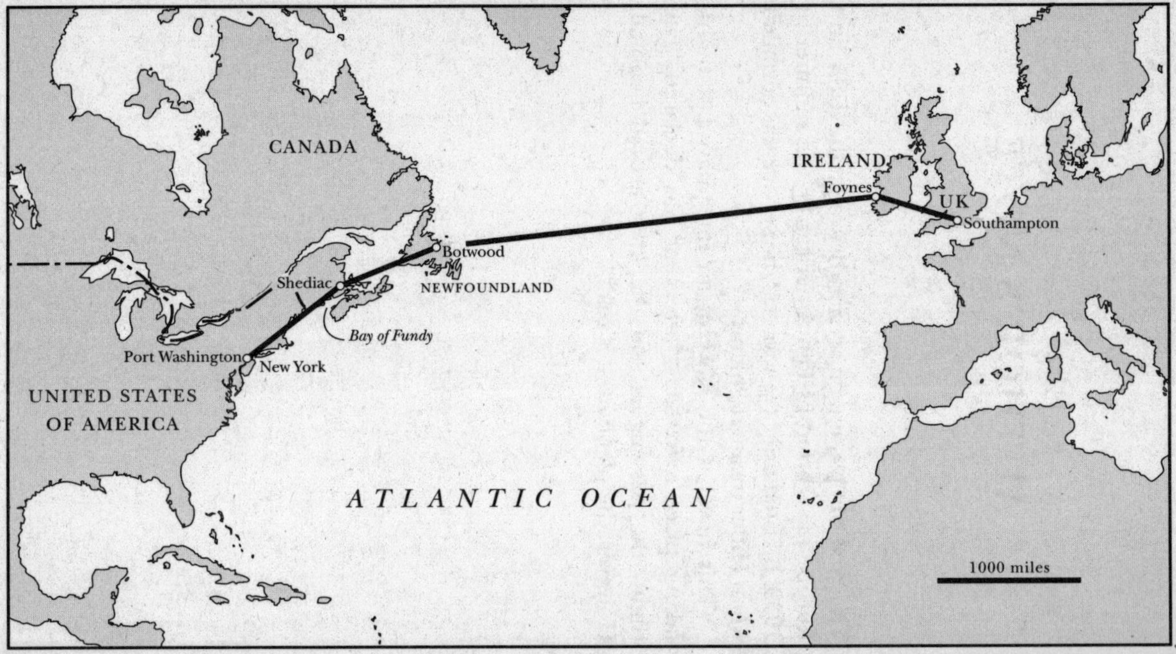
CANADA
UNITED STATES
OF AMERICA
Port Washington
New York
Shediac
Bay of Fundy
Botwood
NEWFOUNDLAND
IRELAND
Foynes
UK
Southampton
ATLANTIC OCEAN
1000 miles

Part One

England

CHAPTER ONE

IT WAS the most romantic plane ever made.

Standing on the dock at Southampton, at half-past twelve on the day war was declared, Tom Luther peered into the sky, waiting for the plane with a heart full of eagerness and dread. Under his breath he hummed a few bars of Beethoven over and over again: the first movement of the 'Emperor' concerto, a stirring tune, appropriately warlike.

There was a crowd of sightseers around him: aircraft enthusiasts with binoculars, small boys and curiosity seekers. Luther reckoned this must be the ninth time the Pan American Clipper had landed on Southampton Water, but the novelty had not worn off. The plane was so fascinating, so enchanting, that people flocked to look at it even on the day their country went to war. Beside the same dock were two magnificent ocean liners, towering over people's heads, but the floating hotels had lost their magic: everyone was looking at the sky.

However, while they waited they were all talking about the war in their English accents. The children were excited by the prospect; the men spoke knowingly in low tones about tanks and artillery; the women just looked grim. Luther was an American, and he hoped his country would stay out of the war: it was none of their business. Besides, one thing you could say for the Nazis, they were tough on Communism.

Luther was a businessman, manufacturing wool cloth, and he had had a lot of trouble with reds in his mills at one time. He had been at their mercy: they had almost ruined him. He still felt bitter about it. His father's menswear store had been run into the ground by Jews setting up in competition, and then Luther Woolens was threatened by the Commies – most of whom were Jews! Then Luther had met Ray Patriarca, and his life had changed. Patriarca's people knew what to do about Communists. There were some accidents. One hothead got his hand caught in a loom. A union recruiter was killed in a hit-and-run. Two men who complained about breaches of the safety regulations got into a fight in a bar and finished up in hospital. A woman troublemaker dropped her lawsuit against the company after her house burned down. It only took a few weeks. Since then there had been no unrest. Patriarca knew what Hitler knew: the way to deal with Communists was to crush them like cockroaches. Luther stamped his foot, still humming Beethoven.

A launch put out from the Imperial Airways flying-boat dock, across the estuary at Hythe, and made several passes along the splashdown zone, checking for floating debris. An eager murmur went up from the crowd: the plane must be approaching.

The first to spot it was a small boy with large new boots. He had no binoculars, but his eleven-year-old eyesight was better than lenses. 'Here it comes!' he shrilled. 'Here comes the Clipper!' He pointed south-west. Everyone looked that way. At first Luther could see only a vague shape that might have been a bird, but soon its outline resolved and a buzz of excitement spread through the crowd as people told one another that the boy was right.

Everyone called it the Clipper, but technically it was a Boeing B-314. Pan American had commissioned Boeing to build a plane capable of carrying passengers across the Atlantic Ocean in total luxury, and this was the result: enormous, majestic, unbelievably powerful, an airborne palace. The airline had taken delivery of six and ordered another six. In comfort and elegance they were equal to the fabulous ocean liners which docked at Southampton, but the ships took four or five days to cross the Atlantic whereas the Clipper could make the trip in twenty-five to thirty hours.

It looked like a winged whale, Luther thought as the plane came closer. It had a big blunt whale-like snout, a massive body, and a tapering rear which culminated in twin high-mounted tailfins. The huge engines were built into the wings. Below the wings was a pair of stubby sea-wings which served to stabilize the aircraft when it was in the water. The bottom of the plane had a sharp knife-edge like the hull of a fast ship.

Soon Luther could make out the big rectangular windows, in two irregular rows marking upper and lower decks. He had come to England on the Clipper exactly a week earlier, so he was familiar with its lay-out. The upper deck comprised the flight cabin and baggage holds and the lower was the passenger deck. Instead of seat rows, the passenger deck had a series of lounges with davenport couches. At mealtimes the main lounge became the dining room, and at night the couches were converted into beds.

Everything was done to insulate the passengers from the world and the weather outside the windows. There were thick carpets, soft lighting, velvet fabrics, soothing colours and deep upholstery. The heavy soundproofing reduced the roar of the mighty engines to a distant, reassuring hum. The Captain was calmly authoritative, the crew clean-cut and smart in their Pan American uniforms, the stewards ever-attentive. Every need was catered for: there was constant food and drink; whatever you wanted appeared as if by magic, just when you wanted it – curtained bunks at bedtime, fresh strawberries at breakfast. The world outside started to appear unreal, like a film projected on to the windows, and the interior of the aircraft seemed like the whole universe.

Such comfort did not come cheap. The round trip fare was $675, half the price of a small house. The passengers were royalty, movie stars, chairmen of large corporations and presidents of small countries.

Tom Luther was none of those things. He was rich, but he had worked hard for his money and he would not normally have squandered it on luxury. However, he had needed to familiarize himself with the plane. He had been asked to do a dangerous job for a powerful man – very powerful indeed. He would not be paid for his work, but to be owed a favour by such a man was better than money.

The whole thing might yet be called off: Luther was waiting for a message giving him the final go-ahead. Half the time he was eager to get on with it; the other half, he hoped he would not have to do it.

The plane came down at an angle, its tail lower than its nose. It was quite close now, and Luther was struck again by its tremendous size. He knew that it was 109 feet long, and 152 feet from one wing tip to the other, but the measurements were just numbers until you actually saw the goddamn thing floating through the air.

For a moment it looked as if it was not flying but falling, and would crash into the sea like a dropped stone and sink to the bottom. Then it seemed to hang in the air, just above the surface, as if suspended on a string, for a long moment of suspense. At last it touched the water, skipping the surface, splashing across the tops of the waves like a stone thrown skimwise, sending up small explosions of foam. But there was very little swell in the sheltered estuary, and a moment later, with an explosion of spray like the smoke from a bomb, the hull plunged into the water.

It cleaved the surface, ploughing a white furrow in the green, sending twin curves of spray high in the air on either side: Luther thought of a mallard coming down on a lake with spread wings and folded feet. The hull sank lower, enlarging the sail-shaped curtains of spray that flew up to left and right; then it began to tilt forward. The spray increased as the plane levelled out, submerging more and more of its belly. Then at last its nose was down. Its speed slowed suddenly, the spray diminished to a wash, and the aircraft sailed the sea like the ship it was, as calmly as if it had never dared to reach for the sky.

Luther realized he had been holding his breath, and let it out in a long relieved sigh. He started humming again.

The plane taxied towards its berth, where Luther had disembarked a week ago. The dock was a specially designed raft with twin piers. In a few minutes, ropes would be attached to stanchions at the front and rear of the plane and it would be winched in, backwards, to its parking slot between the piers. Then the privileged passengers would emerge, stepping from the door on to the broad surface of the sea-wing, then on to the raft, and from there up a gangway to dry land.

Luther turned away, then stopped suddenly. Standing at his shoulder was someone he had not seen before: a man of about his own height, dressed in a dark grey suit and a bowler hat, like a clerk on his way to the office. Luther was about to pass on, then he looked again. The face beneath the bowler hat was not that of a clerk. The man had a high forehead, bright blue eyes, a long jaw and a thin, cruel mouth. He was older than Luther, about forty, but he was broad-shouldered and seemed fit. He looked handsome and dangerous. He stared into Luther's eyes.

Luther stopped humming.

The man said, 'I am Henry Faber.'

'Tom Luther.'

'I have a message for you.'

Luther's heart skipped a beat. He tried to hide his

excitement, and spoke in the same clipped tones as the other man. 'Good. Go ahead.'

'The man you're so interested in will be on this plane on Wednesday when it leaves for New York.'

'You're sure?'

The man looked hard at Luther and did not answer.

Luther nodded grimly. So the job was on. At least the suspense was over. 'Thank you,' he said.

'There's more.'

'I'm listening.'

'The second part of the message is: Don't let us down.'

Luther took a deep breath. 'Tell them not to worry,' he said, with more confidence than he really felt. 'The guy may leave Southampton, but he'll never reach New York.'

Imperial Airways had a flying-boat facility just across the estuary from Southampton docks. Imperial's mechanics serviced the Clipper, supervised by the Pan American flight engineer. On this trip the engineer was Eddie Deakin.

It was a big job, but they had three days. After discharging its passengers at Berth 108, the Clipper taxied across to Hythe. There, in the water, it was manoeuvred on to a dolly, then it was winched up a slipway and towed, looking like a whale balanced on a baby carriage, into the enormous green hangar.

The transatlantic flight was a punishing task for the engines. On the longest leg, from Newfoundland to

Ireland, the plane was in the air for nine hours and on the return journey, against head winds, the same route took sixteen and a half. Hour after hour the fuel flowed, the plugs sparked, the fourteen cylinders in each enormous engine pumped tirelessly up and down, and the fifteen-foot propellers chopped through clouds and rain and gales.

For Eddie that was the romance of engineering. It was wonderful, it was amazing that men could make engines that would work perfectly and precisely, hour after hour. There were so many things that might have gone wrong, so many moving parts that had to be precision-made and meticulously fitted together so that they would not snap, slip, get blocked or simply wear out while they carried a forty-one-ton airplane over thousands of miles.

By Wednesday morning the Clipper would be ready to do it again.

CHAPTER TWO

THE DAY war broke out was a lovely late-summer Sunday, mild and sunny.

A few minutes before the news was broadcast on the wireless, Margaret Oxenford was outside the sprawling brick mansion that was her family home, perspiring gently in a hat and coat, and fuming because she was forced to go to church. On the far side of the village the single bell in the church tower tolled a monotonous note.

Margaret hated church, but her father would not let her miss the service, even though she was nineteen and old enough to make up her own mind about religion. A year or so ago she had summoned up the nerve to tell him that she did not want to go, but he had refused to listen. Margaret had said, 'Don't you think it's hypocritical for me to go to church when I don't believe in God?' Father had replied, 'Don't be ridiculous.' Defeated and angry, she had told her mother that when she was of age she would never go to church again. Mother had said, 'That will be up to your husband, dear.' As far as they were concerned the argument was over, but Margaret had seethed with resentment every Sunday morning since then.

Her sister and brother came out of the house. Elizabeth was twenty-one. She was tall and clumsy and not very pretty. Once upon a time the two sisters had known everything about one another. As girls they had been together constantly for years, for they never went to school, but got a haphazard education at home from governesses and tutors. They had always shared one another's secrets. But lately they had grown apart. In adolescence, Elizabeth had embraced their parents' rigid traditional values: she was ultra-conservative, fervently royalist, blind to new ideas and hostile to change. Margaret had taken the opposite path. She was a feminist and a socialist, interested in jazz music, cubist painting and free verse. Elizabeth felt Margaret was disloyal to her family in adopting radical ideas. Margaret was irritated by her sister's foolishness, but she was also sad that they were no longer intimate friends. She did not have many intimate friends.

Percy was fourteen. He was neither for nor against radical ideas, but he was naturally mischievous, and he empathized with Margaret's rebelliousness. Fellow-sufferers under their father's tyranny; they gave one another sympathy and support, and Margaret loved him dearly.

Mother and Father came out a moment later. Father was wearing a hideous orange-and-green tie. He was practically colour-blind, but Mother had probably bought it for him. Mother had red hair and sea-green eyes and pale, creamy skin, and she looked radiant in colours like orange and green. But Father had black hair going grey and a flushed complexion; on him the tie looked like a warning against something dangerous.

Elizabeth resembled Father, with dark hair and irregular features. Margaret had Mother's colouring: she would have liked a scarf in the silk of Father's tie. Percy was changing so rapidly that no one could tell whom he would eventually take after.

They walked down the long drive to the little village outside the gates. Father owned most of the houses and all the farmland for miles around. He had done nothing to earn such wealth: a series of marriages in the early nineteenth century had united the three most important landowning families in the county, and the resulting huge estate had been handed down intact from generation to generation.

They walked along the village street and across the green to the grey stone church. They entered in procession: Father and Mother first; Margaret behind with Elizabeth; and Percy bringing up the rear. The villagers in the congregation touched their forelocks as the Oxenfords made their way down the aisle to the family pew. The wealthier farmers, all of whom rented their land from Father, inclined their heads in polite bows; and the middle classes, Dr Rowan and Colonel Smythe and Sir Alfred, nodded respectfully. This ludicrous feudal ritual made Margaret cringe with embarrassment every time it happened. All men were supposed to be equal before God, weren't they? She wanted to shout out, 'My father is no better than any of you, and a lot worse than most!' One of these days perhaps she would have the courage. If she made a scene in church she might never have to go back. But she was too scared of what Father would do.

Just as they were entering their pew, with all eyes on them, Percy said in a loud stage whisper, 'Nice tie, Father.' Margaret suppressed a laugh and was seized by a fit of the giggles. She and Percy sat down quickly and hid their faces, pretending to pray, until the fit passed. After that Margaret felt better.

The vicar preached a sermon about the Prodigal Son. Margaret thought the silly old duffer might have chosen a topic more relevant to what was on everyone's mind: the likelihood of war. The Prime Minister had sent Hitler an ultimatum, which the Führer had ignored, and a declaration of war was expected at any moment.

Margaret dreaded war. A boy she loved had died in the Spanish Civil War. It was just over a year ago, but she still cried sometimes at night. To her, war meant that thousands more girls would know the grief she had suffered. The thought was almost unbearable.

And yet another part of her wanted war. For years she had felt strongly about Britain's cowardice during the Spanish war. Her country had stood by and watched while the elected socialist government was overthrown by a gang of bullies armed by Hitler and Mussolini. Hundreds of idealistic young men from all over Europe had gone to Spain to fight for democracy. But they lacked weapons, and the democratic governments of the world had refused to supply them, so the young men had lost their lives, and people such as Margaret had felt angry and helpless and ashamed. If Britain would now take a stand against the Fascists she could begin to feel proud of her country again.

There was another reason why her heart leaped at the prospect of war. It would surely mean the end of the narrow, suffocating life she lived with her parents. She was bored, cramped and frustrated by their unvarying rituals and their pointless social life. She longed to escape and have a life of her own, but it seemed impossible: she was under age, she had no money, and there was no kind of work that she was fit for. But, she thought eagerly, surely everything would be different in wartime?

She had read with fascination how in the last war women had put on trousers and gone to work in factories. Nowadays there were female branches of the army, navy and air force. Margaret dreamed of volunteering for the Auxiliary Territorial Service, the women's army. One of the few practical skills she possessed was that she could drive. Father's chauffeur, Digby, had taught her on the Rolls, and Ian, the boy who died, had let her ride his motorcycle. She could even handle a motor boat, for Father kept a small yacht at Nice. The ATS needed ambulance drivers and dispatch riders. She saw herself in uniform, wearing a helmet, astride a motorcycle, carrying urgent reports from one battlefield to another at top speed, with a photograph of Ian in the breast pocket of her khaki jacket. She felt sure she could be brave, given the chance.

War was actually declared during the service, they

found out later. There was even an air-raid warning at twenty-eight minutes past eleven, in the middle of the sermon, but it did not reach their village, and anyway it was a false alarm. So the Oxenford family walked home from church unaware that they were at war with Germany.

Percy wanted to take a gun and go after rabbits. They could all shoot: it was a family pastime, almost an obsession. But of course Father turned down Percy's request, for it was not done to shoot on Sundays. Percy was disappointed, but he would obey. Although he was full of devilment, he was not yet man enough to defy Father openly.

Margaret loved her brother's impishness. He was the only ray of sunshine in the gloom of her life. She often wished that she could mock Father as Percy did, and laugh behind his back, but she got too cross to joke about it.

At home they were astonished to find a barefoot parlourmaid watering flowers in the hall. Father did not recognize her. 'Who are you?' he said abruptly.

Mother said in her soft American voice, 'Her name is Jenkins, she started this week.'

The girl dropped a curtsy.

Father went on, 'And where the devil are her shoes?'

An expression of suspicion crossed the girl's face and she shot an accusing look at Percy. 'Please, your lordship, it was young Lord Isley.' Percy was the Earl of Isley. 'He told me parlourmaids must go barefoot on Sunday out of respect.'

Mother sighed and Father gave an exasperated

grunt. Margaret could not help giggling. This was Percy's favourite trick: telling new servants of imaginary house rules. He could say ridiculous things with a dead straight face, and the family had such a reputation for eccentricity that people would believe anything of them.

Percy often made Margaret laugh, but now she was sorry for the poor parlourmaid, standing barefoot in the hall and feeling foolish.

'Go and put your shoes on,' Mother said.

Margaret added, 'And never believe Lord Isley.'

They took off their hats and went into the morning room. Margaret pulled Percy's hair and hissed, 'That was a mean thing to do.' Percy just grinned: he was incorrigible. He had once told the vicar that Father had died of a heart attack in the night, and the whole village went into mourning before they found out it was not true.

Father turned on the wireless, and it was then that they heard the news: Britain had declared war on Germany.

Margaret felt a kind of savage glee rising in her breast, like the excitement of driving too fast or climbing to the top of a tall tree. There was no longer any point in agonizing over it: there would be tragedy and bereavement, pain and grief, but now these things could not be avoided, the die was cast and the only thing to do was fight. The thought made her heart beat faster. Everything would be different. Social conventions would be abandoned, women would join in the struggle, class barriers would break down, everyone would work together. She could taste the air of freedom already. And they would be at war with the Fascists, the very people who had killed poor Ian and thousands more fine young men. Margaret did not believe she was a vindictive person, but when she thought about fighting the Nazis she felt vengeful. The feeling was unfamiliar, frightening and thrilling.

Father was furious. He was already portly and red-faced, and when he got angry he always looked as if he might burst. 'Damn Chamberlain!' he said. 'Damn and blast the wretched man!'

'Algernon, please,' Mother said, reproving him for his intemperate language.

Father had been one of the founders of the British Union of Fascists. He had been a different person then: not just younger, but slimmer, more handsome, and less irritable. He had charmed people and won their loyalty. He had written a controversial book called *Mongrel Men: The Threat of Racial Pollution*, about how civilization had gone downhill since white people started to interbreed with Jews, Asians, Orientals and even Negroes. He had corresponded with Adolf Hitler, who he thought to be the greatest statesman since Napoleon. There had been big house parties here every weekend, with politicians, foreign statesmen sometimes, and – on one unforgettable occasion – the King. The discussions went on far into the night, the butler bringing up more brandy from the cellar while the footmen yawned in the hall. All through the Depression, Father had waited for the country to call him to its rescue in its hour of need, and ask him to be

Prime Minister in a government of national reconstruction. But the call never came. The weekend parties got fewer and smaller; the more distinguished guests found ways to dissociate themselves publicly from the British Union of Fascists; and Father became a bitter, disappointed man. His charm went with his confidence. His good looks were ruined by resentment, boredom and drink. His intellect had never been real: Margaret had read his book and had been shocked to find that it was not just wrong, but foolish.

In recent years his platform had shrunk to one obsessive idea: that Britain and Germany should unite against the Soviet Union. He had advocated this in magazine articles and letters to the newspapers, and on the increasingly rare occasions when he was invited to speak at political meetings and university debating societies. He held on to the idea defiantly as events in Europe made his policy more and more unrealistic. With the declaration of war between Britain and Germany his hopes were finally dashed and Margaret found in her heart a little pity for him among all her other tumultuous emotions.

'Britain and Germany will wipe one another out and leave Europe to be dominated by atheistical Communism!' he said.

The reference to atheism reminded Margaret of being forced to go to church, and she said, 'I don't mind, I'm an atheist.'

Mother said, 'You can't be, dear, you're Church of England.'

Margaret could not help laughing. Elizabeth, who

was close to tears, said, 'How can you laugh? It's a tragedy!'

Elizabeth was a great admirer of the Nazis. She spoke German – they both did, thanks to a German governess who had lasted longer than most – and she had been to Berlin several times and twice dined with the Führer himself. Margaret suspected the Nazis were snobs who liked to bask in the approval of an English aristocrat.

Now Margaret turned to Elizabeth and said, 'It's time we stood up to those bullies.'

'They aren't bullies,' Elizabeth spoke indignantly. 'They're proud, strong, pure-bred Aryans, and it's a tragedy that our country is at war with them. Father's right – the white people will wipe each other out and the world will be left to the mongrels and the Jews.'

Margaret had no patience with this kind of drivel. 'There's nothing wrong with Jews!' she said hotly.

Father held a finger up in the air. 'There's nothing wrong with the Jew – *in his place*.'

'Which is under the heel of the jackboot, in your – your Fascist system.' She had been on the point of saying 'your filthy system' but she suddenly became scared and bit back the insult: it was dangerous to make Father too angry.

Elizabeth said, 'And in your Bolshevik system the Jews rule the roost!'

'I'm not a Bolshevik, I'm a socialist.'

Percy imitated Mother's accent. 'You can't be, dear, you're Church of England.'

Margaret laughed despite herself, and once again her laughter infuriated her sister. Elizabeth said bitterly, 'You just want to destroy everything that's fine and pure, and then laugh about it afterwards.'

That was hardly worth a response but Margaret still wanted to make her point. She turned to Father and said, 'Well, I agree with you about Neville Chamberlain, anyway. He's made our military position far worse by letting the Fascists take over Spain. Now the enemy is in the west as well as the east.'

'Chamberlain did not let the Fascists take over Spain,' Father said. 'Britain made a non-intervention pact with Germany, Italy and France. All we did was keep our word.'

This was completely hypocritical, and he knew it. Margaret felt herself flush with indignation. 'We kept our word while the Italians and the Germans broke theirs!' she protested. 'So the Fascists got guns and the democrats got nothing . . . but heroes.'

There was a moment of embarrassed silence.

Mother said, 'I'm truly sorry that Ian died, dear, but he was a very bad influence on you.'

Suddenly Margaret wanted to cry.

Ian Rochdale was the best thing that ever happened to her, and the pain of his death could still make her gasp.

For years she had been dancing at hunt balls with empty-headed young members of the squirearchy, boys who had nothing on their minds but drinking and hunting, and she had despaired of ever meeting a man of her own age who interested her. Ian had come into her life like the light of reason and since he died she had been living in the dark.

He had been in his final year at Oxford. Margaret would have loved to go to university, but there was no possibility of her qualifying: she had never gone to school. However, she had read widely – there was nothing else to do! – and she was thrilled to find someone like herself, who liked talking about ideas. He was the only man who could explain things to her without condescension. Ian was the most clear-thinking person she had ever come across; he had endless patience in discussion and he was quite without intellectual vanity – he never pretended to understand when he did not. She adored him from the very start.

For a long time she did not think of it as love. But one day he confessed, awkwardly and with great embarrassment, uncharacteristically struggling to find the right words, finally saying, 'I think I must have fallen in love with you – will it spoil everything?' And then she realized joyfully that she too was in love.

He changed her life. It was as if she had moved to another country, where everything was different: the landscape, the weather, the people, the food. She enjoyed everything. The constraints and irritations of living with her parents came to seem minor.

Even after he joined the International Brigade and went to Spain to fight for the elected socialist government against the Fascist rebels, he continued to light up her life. She was proud of him because he had the courage of his convictions and was ready to risk death for the cause he believed in. Sometimes she would get a letter from him. Once he sent a poem. Then came the note that said he was dead, blown to bits by a direct hit from a shell, and Margaret felt that her life had come to an end.

'A bad influence,' she echoed bitterly. 'Yes. He taught me to question dogma, to disbelieve lies, to hate ignorance and to despise hypocrisy. As a result, I'm hardly fit for civilized society.'

Father, Mother and Elizabeth all started talking at once, then stopped because none of them could be heard, and Percy spoke into the sudden silence. 'Talking of Jews,' he said, 'I came across a curious picture in the cellar, in one of those old suitcases from Stamford.' Stamford, Connecticut, was where Mother's family lived. Percy took from his shirt pocket a creased and faded sepia photograph. 'I did have a great-grandmother called Ruth Glencarry, didn't I?'

Mother answered, 'Yes – she was my mother's mother. Why, dear, what have you found?'

Percy gave the photograph to Father and the others crowded around to look at it. It showed a street scene in an American city, probably New York, about seventy years ago. In the foreground was a Jewish man of about thirty with a black beard, dressed in rough working-men's clothes and a hat. He stood by a handcart bearing a grinding-wheel. The cart was clearly lettered with the words 'Reuben Fishbein – Grinder'. Beside the man stood a girl about ten years old in a shabby cotton dress and heavy boots.

Father asked, 'What is this, Percy? Who are these wretched people?'

'Turn it over,' said Percy.

Father turned the picture over. On the back was written: 'Ruthie Glencarry, née Fishbein, aged 10.'

Margaret looked at Father. He was utterly horrified.

Percy went on, 'Interesting that Mother's grandfather should marry the daughter of an itinerant Jewish knife-grinder, but they say America's like that.'

'This is impossible!' Father said, but his voice was shaky and Margaret guessed that he thought it was all too possible.

Percy went on blithely, 'Anyway, Jewishness descends through the female, so as my mother's mother was Jewish, that makes me a Jew.'

Father had gone quite pale. Mother looked mystified, a slight frown creasing her brow.

Percy said, 'I do hope the Germans don't win this war. I shan't be allowed to go to the cinema and Mother will have to sew yellow stars on all her ball-gowns.'

This was sounding too good to be true. Margaret peered intently at the words written on the back of the picture, and the truth dawned. 'Percy!' she said delightedly. 'That's *your* handwriting!'

'No, it's not!' said Percy.

But everyone could see that it was. Margaret laughed gleefully. Percy had found this old picture of a little Jewish girl somewhere and had faked the inscription on the back to fool Father. Father had fallen for it, too, and no wonder: it must be the ultimate nightmare of every racist to find that he has mixed ancestry. Serve him right.

Father said,'Bah!' and threw the picture down on a table.

Mother said, 'Percy, really,' in an aggrieved voice. They might have said more, but at that moment the door opened and Bates, the bad-tempered butler, said, 'Luncheon is served, my lady.'

They left the morning room and crossed the hall to the small dining room. There would be overdone roast beef, as always on Sundays. Mother would have a salad: she never ate cooked food, believing that the heat destroyed the goodness.

Father said grace and they sat down. Bates offered Mother the smoked salmon. Smoked, pickled or otherwise preserved foods were all right, according to her theory.

'Of course, there's only one thing to be done,' Mother said as she helped herself from the proffered plate. She spoke in the offhand tone of one who merely draws attention to the obvious. 'We must all go and live in America until this silly war is over.'

There was a moment of shocked silence.

Margaret, horrified, burst out, 'No!'

Mother said, 'Now, I think we've had quite enough squabbling for one day. Please let us have lunch in peace and harmony.'

'No!' Margaret repeated. She was almost speechless with outrage. 'You – you can't do this, it's – it's—' She wanted to rail and storm at them, to accuse them of treason and cowardice, to shout her contempt and defiance out loud, but the words would not come, and all she could say was, 'It's not fair!'

Even that was too much. Father said, 'If you can't hold your tongue you'd better leave us.'

Margaret put her napkin to her mouth to choke down a sob, pushed her chair back, stood up and fled the room.

They had been planning this for months, of course.

Percy came to Margaret's room after lunch and told her the details. The house was to be closed up, the furniture covered with dust sheets and the servants dismissed. The estate would be left in the hands of Father's business manager, who would collect the rents. The money would pile up in the bank: it could not be sent to America because of wartime exchange control rules. The horses would be sold, the blankets mothballed, the silver locked away.

Elizabeth, Margaret and Percy were to pack one suitcase each: the rest of their belongings would be forwarded by a removal company. Father had booked tickets for all of them on the Pan American Clipper and they were to leave on Wednesday.

Percy was wild with excitement. He had flown once or twice before, but the Clipper was different. The plane was huge and opulent: the newspapers had been full of it when the service was inaugurated just a few weeks ago. The flight to New York took twenty-nine hours, and everyone went to bed at night over the Atlantic Ocean.

It was disgustingly appropriate, Margaret thought, that they should depart in cosseted luxury, when they were leaving their countrymen to deprivation, hardship and war.

Percy left to pack his case and Margaret lay on her bed, staring at the ceiling, bitterly disappointed, boiling with rage, crying with frustration, powerless to do anything about her fate.

She stayed in her room until bedtime.

On Monday morning, while she was still in bed, Mother came to her room. Margaret sat up and gave her a hostile stare. Mother sat at the dressing-table and looked at Margaret in the mirror. 'Please don't make trouble with your father over this,' she said.

Margaret realized that her mother was nervous. In other circumstances this might have caused Margaret to soften her tone but she was too upset to sympathize. 'It's so cowardly!' she burst out.

Mother paled. 'We're not being cowardly.'

'But to run away from your country when a war begins!'

'We have no choice. We have to go.'

Margaret was perplexed. 'Why?'

Mother turned from the mirror and looked directly at her. 'Otherwise they will put your father in prison.'

Margaret was taken completely by surprise. 'How can they do that? It's not a crime to be a Fascist.'

'They have Emergency Powers. Does it matter? A sympathizer in the Home Office warned us. Father will be arrested if he's still in Britain at the end of the week.'

Margaret could hardly believe that they wanted to put her father in jail like a thief. She felt foolish: she had not thought about how much difference war would make to everyday life.

'But they won't let us take any money with us,' Mother said bitterly. 'So much for the British sense of fair play.'

Money was the last thing Margaret cared about right now. Her whole life was in the balance. She felt a sudden access of bravery, and she made up her mind to tell her mother the truth. Before she had time to lose her nerve, she took a deep breath and said, 'Mother, I don't want to go with you.'

Mother displayed no surprise. Perhaps she had even expected something like this. In the mild, vague tone she used when trying to avoid an argument, she said, 'You have to come, dear.'

'They're not going to put *me* in jail. I can live with Aunt Martha, or even Cousin Catherine. Won't you talk to Father?'

Suddenly Mother looked uncharacteristically fierce. I gave birth to you in pain and suffering, and I'm not going to let you risk your life while I can prevent it.'

For a moment Margaret was taken aback by her mother's naked emotion. Then she protested, 'I ought to have a say in it – it's my life!'

Mother sighed and reverted to her normal languorous manner. 'It makes no difference what you and I think. Your father won't let you stay behind, whatever we say.'

Her passivity annoyed Margaret, and she resolved to take action. 'I shall ask him directly.'

'I wish you wouldn't,' Mother said, and now there was a pleading note in her voice. 'This is awfully hard for him as it is. He loves England, you know. In any other circumstances he'd be telephoning to the War Office trying to get a job. It's breaking his heart.'

'What about my heart?'

'It's not the same for you. You're young, your life is in front of you. For him this is the end of all hope.'

'It's not my fault he's a Fascist,' Margaret retorted harshly.

Mother stood up. 'I hoped you'd be kinder,' she said quietly, and she went out.

Margaret felt guilty and indignant at the same time. It was so unfair! Her father had been pouring scorn on her opinions ever since she had had any, and now that events had proved him wrong she was being asked to sympathize.

She sighed. Her mother was beautiful, eccentric and vague. She had been born rich and determined. Her eccentricities were the result of a strong will with no education to help her discriminate between sense and nonsense. The vagueness was a strong woman's way of coping with masculine dominance: she was not allowed to confront her husband, so the only way she could escape his control was by pretending not to understand him. Margaret loved her mother and regarded her peculiarities with a fond tolerance – but she was determined not to be like her, despite their physical resemblance. If others refused to educate her she would jolly well teach herself; and she would rather be an old spinster than marry some pig who thought he had the right to boss her around like an underhouse parlourmaid.

Sometimes she longed for a different kind of relationship with her mother. She wanted to confide in her, gain her sympathy, ask her advice. They could be allies, struggling together for freedom against a world that wanted to treat them as ornaments. But Mother had given up that struggle long ago, and she wanted Margaret to do the same. It was not going to happen. Margaret was going to be herself: she was absolutely set on it. But how?

All day Monday she felt unable to eat. She drank endless cups of tea while the servants went about the business of closing up the house. On Tuesday, when Mother realized that Margaret was not going to pack, she told the new maid, Jenkins, to do it for her. Of course, Jenkins did not know what to pack, and Margaret had to help her; so in the end Mother got her way, as she so often did.

Margaret said to the girl, 'It's bad luck for you that we decided to close up the house the week after you started work here.'

'There'll be no shortage of work now, m'lady,' Jenkins said. 'Our dad says there's no unemployment in wartime.'

'What will you do – work in a factory?'

'I'm going to join up. It said on the wireless that seventeen thousand women joined the ATS yesterday. There's queues outside every town hall in the country – I seen a picture in the paper.'

'Lucky you,' Margaret said despondently. 'The only thing I'll be queuing for is a plane to America.'

'You've got to do what the Marquess wants,' Jenkins said.

'What does your dad say about you joining up?'

'I shan't tell him – just do it.'

'But what if he takes you back?'

'He can't do that. I'm eighteen. Once you've signed on, that's it. Provided you're old enough there's nothing your parents can do about it.'

Margaret was startled. 'Are you sure?'

'Course. Everyone knows.'

'I didn't,' Margaret said thoughtfully.

Jenkins took Margaret's case down to the hall. They would be leaving very early on Wednesday morning. Seeing the cases lined up, Margaret realized that she was going to spend the war in Connecticut unless she did something other than sulk. Despite Mother's plea not to make a fuss, she had to confront her father.

The very thought made her feel shaky. She went back to her room to steel her nerves and consider what she might say. She would have to be calm. Tears would not move him and anger would only provoke his scorn. She should appear sensible, responsible, mature. She should not be argumentative, for that would enrage him, and then he would frighten her so much that she would be unable to go on.

How should she begin? 'I think I have a right to say something about my own future.'

No, that was no good. He would reply, 'I am responsible for you so I must decide.'

Perhaps she should begin, 'May I talk to you about going to America?'

He would probably say, 'There is nothing to discuss.'

Her opening had to be so inoffensive that even he would not be able to rebuff it. She decided she would try, 'Can I ask you something?' He would have to agree to that.

Then what? How could she approach the subject without provoking one of his dreadful rages? She might say, 'You were in the army in the last war, weren't you?' She knew he had seen action in France. Then she would ask, 'Was Mother involved?' She knew the answer to this, too: Mother had been a volunteer nurse in London, caring for wounded American officers. Finally she would end, 'You both served your countries, so I know you'll understand why I want to do the same.' Now surely that was irresistible.

If only he would concede the principle, she could deal with his other objections, she felt. She could live with relatives until she joined up, which would be a matter of days. She was nineteen: many girls of that age had been working full time for six years. She was old enough to get married, drive a car, and go to jail. There was no reason why she should not be allowed to stay in England.

That made sense. Now all she needed was courage.

Father would be in his study with his business manager. Margaret left her room. On the landing outside her bedroom door she suddenly felt weak with fear. It infuriated him to be opposed. His rages were terrible and his punishments cruel. When she was eleven she had been made to stand in the corner of his study, facing the wall, for an entire day after being rude to a house-guest; he had taken away her teddy bear as a punishment for bed-wetting at the age of seven; once, in a fury, he had thrown a cat out of an upstairs window. What would he do now when she told him she wanted to stay in England and fight against the Nazis?

She forced herself to go down the stairs, but as she approached his study her fears grew. She visualized him getting angry, his face reddening and his eyes bulging, and she felt terrified. She tried to calm her racing pulse by asking herself whether there was really anything to be afraid of. He could no longer break her heart by taking away her teddy bear. But she knew deep down that he could still find ways of making her wish she were dead.

As she stood outside the study door, trembling, the housekeeper rustled across the hall in her black silk dress. Mrs Allen ruled the female staff of the household strictly, but she had always been indulgent towards the children. She was fond of the family and was upset that they were leaving: it was the end of a way of life for her. She gave Margaret a tearful smile.

Looking at her, Margaret was struck by a heart-stopping notion.

An entire plan of escape came full-blown into her head. She would borrow money from Mrs Allen, leave the house now, catch the four fifty-five train to London, stay overnight at her cousin Catherine's flat, and join the ATS first thing in the morning. By the time Father caught up with her it would be too late.

It was so simple and daring that she could hardly believe it might be possible. But before she could think twice about it she found herself saying, 'Oh, Mrs Allen, would you give me some money? I've got to do some last-minute shopping and I don't want to disturb Father, he's so busy.'

Mrs Allen did not hesitate. 'Of course, my lady. How much do you need?'

Margaret did not know what the train fare to London was: she had never bought her own ticket. Guessing wildly, she said, 'Oh, a pound should be enough.' She was thinking: Am I really doing this?

Mrs Allen took two ten-shilling notes from her purse. She would probably have handed over her life savings if asked.

Margaret took the money with trembling fingers. This could be my ticket to freedom, she thought and, frightened as she was, a small flame of joyful hope flickered in her breast.

Mrs Allen, thinking she was upset about emigrating, squeezed her hand. 'This is a sad day, Lady Margaret,' she said. 'A sad day for us all.' Shaking her grey head dismally she disappeared into the back of the house.

Margaret looked around frenziedly. No one was in sight. Her heart was fluttering like a trapped bird and her breath came in shallow gasps. She knew that if she hesitated she would lose her nerve. She did not dare wait long enough to put on a coat. Clutching the money in her hand she walked out of the front door.

The station was two miles away in the next village. At every step along the road Margaret expected to hear

Father's Rolls-Royce purring up behind her. But how could he know what she had done? It was unlikely that anyone would notice her absence before dinner time and if they did they would assume she had gone shopping as she had told Mrs Allen. All the same, she was in a constant fever of apprehension.

She got to the station in plenty of time, bought her ticket – she had more than enough money – and sat in the ladies' waiting room watching the hands of the big clock on the wall.

The train was late.

Four fifty-five came around, then five o'clock, then five past five. By this time Margaret was so frightened that she felt like giving up and returning home just to escape the tension.

The train came in at fourteen minutes past five, and still Father had not come.

Margaret boarded with her heart in her mouth.

She stood at the window, staring at the ticket barrier, expecting to see him arrive at the last minute to catch her.

At last the train moved.

She could hardly believe that she was getting away.

The train picked up speed and the first faint tremors of elation stirred in her heart. A few seconds later it was out of the station. Margaret watched the village recede, and her heart filled with triumph. She had done it – she had escaped!

Suddenly she felt weak-kneed. She looked around for a seat, and realized for the first time that the train was full. Every seat was taken, even in this first-class carriage, and there were soldiers sitting on the floor. She remained standing.

Her euphoria did not diminish even though the journey was, by normal standards, something of a nightmare. More people crowded into the carriages at each station. The train was delayed for three hours outside Reading. All the light bulbs had been removed because of the blackout, so after nightfall the train was in total darkness, except for the occasional flash of the guard's torch as he patrolled, picking his way over passengers sitting and lying on the floor. When Margaret could stand no longer she too sat on the floor. This sort of thing did not matter any more, she told herself. Her dress would get filthy but tomorrow she would be in uniform. Everything was different: there was a war on.

Margaret wondered whether Father might have learned she was missing, found out that she caught the train, and driven at top speed to London to intercept her at Paddington station. It was unlikely, but possible, and her heart filled with dread as the train pulled into the station.

However, when at last she got off he was nowhere to be seen, and she felt another thrill of triumph. He was not omnipotent after all! She managed to find a taxi in the cavernous gloom of the station. It took her to Bayswater using only its sidelights. The driver used a torch to light her to the apartment building in which Catherine had a flat.

The building's windows were all blacked out, but the hall was a blaze of light. The porter had gone off duty

– it was now almost midnight – but Margaret knew her way. She went up the stairs and rang the bell.

There was no reply.

Her heart sank.

She rang again, but she knew it was pointless: the flat was small and the bell was loud. Catherine was not there.

It was hardly surprising: Catherine lived with her parents in Kent, and used the flat as a *pied-à-terre.* London social life had come to a halt, of course, so Catherine would have no reason to be here. Margaret had not thought of that.

She was not dashed, but she was disappointed. She had been looking forward to sitting down with Catherine, drinking cocoa and sharing with her the details of her great adventure. However, that would have to wait. She considered what she should do next. She had several relatives in London, but if she went to them they would telephone Father. Catherine would have been a willing co-conspirator, but she could not trust any of her other relations.

Then she remembered that Aunt Martha did not have a telephone.

She was a great-aunt, in fact; a fractious spinster of about seventy. She lived less than a mile away. She would be fast asleep by now, and it would make her furious to be wakened, but that could not be helped. The important thing was that she would have no way of alerting Father to Margaret's whereabouts.

Margaret went back down the stairs and out into the street – to find herself in total darkness.

The blackout was quite scary. She stood outside the door and looked around, her eyes wide open and staring, seeing nothing. It gave her a queer feeling in her tummy, like being dizzy.

She closed her eyes and pictured the familiar street scene as it ought to be. Behind her was Ovington House where Catherine lived. Normally there would be lights in several windows and a splash of brilliance from the lamp over the door. On the corner to her left was a small church whose portico was always floodlit. The pavement was lined with lamp-posts, each of which should cast a little circle of light, and the road should be lit by the headlamps of buses, taxis and cars.

She opened her eyes again, and saw nothing.

It was unnerving. For a moment she imagined that there was nothing around her: the street had disappeared and she was in limbo, falling through a void. She felt suddenly seasick. Then she pulled herself together and visualized the route to Aunt Martha's house.

I head east from here, she thought, and go left at the second turning, and Aunt Martha's place is at the end of that block. It should be easy enough, even in the dark.

She longed for some relief: a lighted taxi, a full moon, or a helpful policeman. After a moment her wish was granted: a car came creeping along, its faint sidelights like the eyes of a cat in the heavy gloom, and suddenly she could see the line of the kerb all the way to the street corner.

She began to walk.

The car passed on, its red rear lights receding into the dark distance. Margaret thought she was still three or four steps from the corner when she stumbled down the kerb. She crossed the road and found the opposite pavement without falling over it. That encouraged her and she walked on more confidently.

Suddenly something hard smacked into her face with agonizing violence.

She cried out in pain and sudden fear. For a moment she was in a blind panic and wanted to turn and run. With an effort she calmed herself. Her hand went to her cheek and rubbed where it hurt. What on earth had happened? What was there to hit her at face level in the middle of the pavement? She reached out with both hands. She felt something almost immediately, and jerked her hands back fearfully; then she gritted her teeth and reached out again. She was touching something cold and hard and round, like an oversize pie dish floating in mid-air. Exploring it further, she felt a round column with a rectangular hole and an out-jutting top. When she realized what it was she laughed despite her sore face. She had been attacked by a pillar-box.

She felt her way round it, then walked on with both arms stretched out in front of her.

After a while she stumbled down another kerb. Regaining her balance, she felt relieved: she had reached Aunt Martha's street. She turned left.

It occurred to her that Aunt Martha might not hear the doorbell. She lived alone: there was no one else to answer. If that happened, Margaret would have to make her way back to Catherine's building and sleep in the corridor. She could cope with sleeping on the floor, but she dreaded another walk through the blackout. Perhaps she would simply curl up on Aunt Martha's doorstep and wait for daylight.

Aunt Martha's small house was at the far end of a long block. Margaret walked slowly. The city was dark but not silent. She could hear the occasional car in the distance. Dogs barked as she passed their doors and a pair of cats howled oblivious of her. Once she heard the tinkling music of a late party. A little farther on she picked up the muffled shouts of a domestic row behind the blackout curtains. She found herself longing to be inside a house with lamps and a fireplace and a teapot.

The block seemed longer than Margaret remembered. However, she could not possibly have gone wrong: she had turned left at the second cross-street. Nevertheless, the suspicion that she was lost grew relentlessly. Her sense of time failed her: had she been walking along this block for five minutes, twenty minutes, two hours or all night? Suddenly she was not even sure whether there were any houses near by. She could be in the middle of Hyde Park, having wandered through the entrance by blind chance. She began to feel that there were creatures all around her in the darkness, watching her with cat-like night vision, waiting for her to stumble into them so they could grab her. A scream started low in her throat and she pushed it back.

She made herself think. Where could she have gone

wrong? She knew there was a cross-street when she stumbled down a kerb. But, she now recalled, as well as the main cross-streets there were little alleys and mews. She might have turned down one of those. By now she could have walked a mile or more in the wrong direction.

She tried to recall the heady feeling of excitement and triumph she had felt on the train, but it had gone, and now she just felt alone and afraid.

She decided to stop and stand quite still. No harm could come to her like that.

She stayed still for a long time: after a while she could not tell how long. Now she was afraid to move: fear had paralysed her. She thought she would stand upright until she fainted with exhaustion, or until morning.

Then a car appeared.

Its dim sidelights gave very little illumination, but by comparison with the previous pitch blackness it seemed like daylight. She saw that she was, indeed, standing in the middle of the road, and she scurried to the pavement to get out of the way of the car. She was in a square that seemed vaguely familiar. The car passed her and turned a corner, and she hurried after it, hoping to see a landmark that would tell her where she was. Reaching the corner, she saw the car at the far end of a short, narrow street of small shops, one of which was a milliner's patronized by Mother, and she realized she was just a few yards from Marble Arch.

She could have wept with relief.

At the next corner she waited for another car to light up the way ahead; then she walked on into Mayfair.

A few minutes later she stood outside Claridge's Hotel. The building was blacked out, of course, but she was able to locate the door, and she wondered whether to go in.

She did not think she had enough money to pay for a room, but her recollection was that people did not pay their hotel bill until they left. She could take a room for two nights, go out tomorrow as if she expected to return later, join the ATS, then phone the hotel and tell them to send the bill to Father's lawyer.

She took a deep breath and pushed open the door.

Like most public buildings that were open at night, the hotel had rigged up a double door, like an air-lock, so that people could go in and out without the interior lights showing on the outside. Margaret let the outer door close behind her, then went through the second door and into the grateful light of the hotel foyer. She felt a tremendous surge of relief. This was normality: the nightmare was over.

A young night porter was dozing at the desk. Margaret coughed, and he woke up, startled and confused. Margaret said, 'I need a room.'

'At this time of night?' the man blurted.

'I got caught in the blackout,' Margaret explained. 'Now I can't get home.'

The man began to gather his wits. 'No luggage?'

'No,' Margaret said guiltily. Then she was struck by

a thought, and added, 'Of course not – I didn't *plan* to get stranded.'

He looked at her rather strangely. Surely, Margaret thought, he could not refuse her? He swallowed, rubbed his face, and pretended to consult a book. What was the matter with the man? Making up his mind, he closed the book and said, 'We're full.'

'Oh, come on, you must have *something*—'

'You've had a fight with your old man, haven't you?' he said with a wink.

Margaret could hardly believe this was happening. 'I can't get home,' she repeated, as the man had obviously failed to understand her the first time.

'I can't help that,' he said. With a sudden access of wit he added, 'Blame Hitler.'

He was rather young. 'Where is your supervisor?' she said.

He looked offended. 'I'm in charge until six o'clock.'

Margaret looked around. 'I'll just have to sit in the lounge until morning,' she said wearily.

'You can't do that!' the porter said, looking scared. 'A young girl alone, with no luggage, spending the night in the lounge? It's more than my job's worth.'

'I'm not a *young girl*,' she said angrily. 'I'm Lady Margaret Oxenford.' She hated to use her title but she was desperate.

However, it did no good. The porter gave her a hard, insolent look, and said, 'Oh, yeah?'

Margaret was about to shout at him when she caught sight of her reflection in the glass of the door, and realized she had a black eye. On top of that her hands were filthy and her dress was torn. She recalled that she had bumped into a pillar-box and sat on the floor of a train. No wonder the porter would not give her a room. She said desperately, 'But you can't turn me out into the blackout!'

'I can't do anything else!' the porter said.

Margaret wondered how he would react if she simply sat down and refused to move. That was what she felt like doing: she was bone tired and weak with strain. But she had been through so much that she had no energy left for a confrontation. Besides, it was late and they were alone: there was no telling what the man might do if she gave him an excuse to lay hands on her.

Wearily, she turned her back on him and went out, bitterly disappointed, into the night.

Even as she walked away from the hotel she wished she had put up more of a fight. Why was it that her intentions were always so much more fierce than her actions? Now that she had given in, she was angry enough to defy the porter. She was almost ready to turn back. But she kept on walking: it seemed easier.

She had nowhere to go. She would not be able to find Catherine's building again; she had never succeeded in finding Aunt Martha's house; she could not trust any other relatives and she was too dirty to get a hotel room.

She would just have to wander around until it got light. The weather was fine: there was no rain and the night air was only slightly chilly. If she kept moving she would not even feel cold. She could see where she was going now: there were plenty of traffic lights in the West End, and a car passed every minute or two. She could hear music and noise from the nightclubs, and now and again she would see people of her own class, the women in gorgeous gowns and the men wearing white-tie-and-tails, arriving home in their chauffeur-driven cars after a late party. In one street, rather curiously, she saw three other solitary women: one standing in a doorway, one leaning on a lamp-post and one sitting in a car. They were all smoking and apparently waiting for people. She wondered if they were what Mother called Fallen Women.

She began to feel tired. She was still wearing the light indoor shoes she had had on when she made her escape from home. On impulse she sat down on a doorstep, took off her shoes, and rubbed her aching feet.

Looking up, she could make out the vague shape of the buildings on the other side of the street. Was it getting light at last? Perhaps she would find a workman's café that opened early. She could order breakfast and wait there until the recruiting offices opened. She had eaten next to nothing for two days, and the thought of bacon and eggs made her mouth water.

Suddenly there was a white face hovering in the air in front of her. She let out a little cry of fright. The face came closer and she saw a youngish man in evening dress. He said, 'Hello, beautiful.'

Margaret scrambled to her feet quickly. She hated

drunks – they were so undignified. 'Please go away,' she said. She tried to sound firm but there was a tremor in her voice.

He staggered closer. 'Give us a kiss, then.'

'Certainly not!' she said, horrified. She took a step back, stumbled, and dropped her shoes. Somehow the loss of her shoes made her feel helplessly vulnerable. She turned around and bent down to grope for them. He chuckled fruitily, then to her horror she felt his hand between her thighs, fumbling with painful clumsiness. She straightened up instantly, without finding her shoes, and stepped away from him. Turning to face him, she shouted, 'Get away from me!'

He laughed again and said, 'That's right, go on, I like a bit of resistance.' With surprising agility he grabbed her by the shoulders and pulled her to him. His alcoholic breath blew over her face in a nauseating fog and suddenly he was kissing her mouth.

It was unspeakably disgusting, and she felt quite sick, but his embrace was so strong that she could hardly breathe, let alone protest. She squirmed ineffectually while he slobbered over her. Then he took one hand from her shoulder to grasp her breast. He squeezed brutally hard and she gasped with pain. But because he had let go of her shoulder she was mercifully able to half-turn away from him and start to scream.

She screamed loud and long.

She could vaguely hear him saying, in a worried voice, 'All right, all right, don't take on so, I didn't mean any harm,' but she was too scared to be reasoned with and she just carried on screaming. Faces materialized out of the darkness: a passer-by in workman's clothes, a Fallen Woman with cigarette and handbag, and a head at a window in the house behind them. The drunk vanished into the night, and Margaret stopped screaming and began to cry. Then there was the sound of running boots, the narrow beam of a masked flashlight, and a policeman's helmet.

The policeman shone his light on Margaret's face.

The woman muttered, 'She ain't one of us, Steve.'

The policeman called Steve said, 'What's your name, girl?'

'Margaret Oxenford.'

The man in work clothes said, 'A toff took her for a tart, that's what happened.' Satisfied, he went off.

The policeman said, 'Would that be *Lady* Margaret Oxenford?'

Margaret sniffed miserably and nodded.

The woman said, 'I told you she weren't one of us.' With that she drew on her cigarette, dropped the end, trod on it and disappeared.

The policeman said, 'You come with me, my Lady, you'll be all right now.'

Margaret wiped her face with her sleeve. The policeman offered her his arm. She took it. He shone his torch on the pavement in front of her and they began to walk.

After a moment Margaret shuddered and said, 'That frightful man.'

The policeman was briskly unsympathetic. 'Can't

really blame him,' he said cheerfully. 'This is the most notorious street in London. It's a fair assumption that a girl alone here at this hour is a Lady of the Night.'

Margaret supposed he was right, although it seemed rather unfair.

The familiar blue lamp of a police station appeared in the morning twilight. The policeman said, 'You have a nice cup of tea and you'll feel better.'

They went inside. Two policemen stood behind a counter, one middle-aged and stocky and the other young and thin. On each side of the hall was a plain wooden bench up against the wall. There was only one other person in the hall: a pale woman with her hair in a scarf and house slippers on her feet, sitting on one of the benches, waiting with tired patience.

Margaret's rescuer directed her to the opposite bench, saying. 'Sit yourself down there for a minute.' Margaret did as she was told. The constable went up to the desk and spoke to the older man. 'Sarge, that's Lady Margaret Oxenford. Had a run-in with a drunk in Bolting Lane.'

'I suppose he thought she was on the game.'

Margaret was struck by the variety of euphemisms for prostitution. People seemed to have a horror of calling it what it was and had to refer to it obliquely. She herself had known about it only in the vaguest possible way, indeed she had not really believed it went on, until tonight. But there had been nothing vague about the intentions of the young man in evening dress.

The sergeant looked over at Margaret in an

interested way, then said something in a low voice that she could not hear. Steve nodded and disappeared into the back of the building.

Margaret realized she had left her shoes on that doorstep. Now there were holes in the feet of her stockings. She began to worry: she could hardly turn up at the recruiting station in this state. Perhaps she could go back for her shoes in daylight. But they might no longer be there. And she badly needed a wash and a clean dress, too. It would be heartbreaking to be turned down for the ATS after all this. But where could she go to tidy herself? By morning even Aunt Martha's house would not be safe: Father might turn up there, searching for her. Surely, she thought with anguish, her whole plan was not going to fall apart because of a pair of shoes?

Her policeman came back with tea in a thick earthenware mug. It was weak and had too much sugar in it, but Margaret sipped it gratefully. It restored her resolve. She *could* overcome her problems. She would leave as soon as she had finished her tea. She would go to a poor district and find a shop selling cheap clothes – she still had a few shillings. She would buy a dress, a pair of sandals and a set of clean underwear. She would go to a public bathhouse and wash and change. Then she would be ready for the army.

While she was elaborating this plan, there was a noise outside the door and a group of young men burst in. They were well dressed, some in evening clothes and others in lounge suits. After a moment

Margaret realized they were dragging with them an unwilling companion. One of the men started to shout at the sergeant behind the counter.

The sergeant interrupted him. 'All right, all right, quieten down!' he said in a commanding voice. 'You're not on the rugby field now, you know – this is a police station.' The noise muted somewhat, but not enough for the sergeant. 'If you don't behave yourselves I'll clap the lot of you in the bleedin' cells,' he shouted. 'Now bloody well SHUT UP!'

They became quiet and released their prisoner, who stood there looking sulky. The sergeant pointed at one of the men, a dark-haired fellow of about Margaret's age. 'Right – you. Tell me what all the fuss is about.'

The young man pointed at the prisoner. 'This blighter took my sister to a restaurant then sneaked off without paying!' he said indignantly. He spoke with an upper-class accent, and his face was vaguely familiar to Margaret. She hoped he would not recognize her: it would be too humiliating for people to know that she had had to be rescued by a policeman after running away from home.

A younger man in a striped suit added, 'His name's Harry Marks and he ought to be locked up.'

Margaret looked with interest at Harry Marks. He was a strikingly handsome man of twenty-two or twenty-three, with blond hair and regular features. Although he was rather rumpled, he wore his double-breasted dinner jacket with easy elegance. He looked around contemptuously and said, 'These fellows are drunk.'

The young man in the striped suit burst out, 'We

may be drunk but he's a cad – and a thief. Look what we found in his pocket.' He threw something down on the counter. 'These cufflinks were stolen earlier in the evening from Sir Simon Monkford.'

'All right,' said the sergeant. 'So you're accusing him of obtaining a pecuniary advantage by deception – that's not paying his restaurant bill – *and* of stealing. Anything else?'

The wearer of the striped suit laughed scornfully and said, 'Isn't that enough for you?'

The sergeant pointed his pencil at him. 'You remember where you bloody well are, son. You may have been born with a silver spoon in your mouth but this is a police station and if you don't speak politely you'll spend the rest of the night in a bleedin' cell.'

The young man looked foolish and said no more.

The sergeant turned his attention back to the first speaker. 'Now, can you supply all the details of both accusations? I need the name and address of the restaurant, your sister's name and address, plus the name and address of the party that owns the cufflinks.'

'Yes, I can give you all that. The restaurant—'

'Good. You stay here.' He pointed at the accused man. 'You sit down.' He waved his hand at the crowd of young men. 'The rest of you can go home.'

They all looked rather nonplussed. Their great adventure had ended in anticlimax. For a moment none of them moved.

The sergeant said, 'Go on, bugger off, the lot of you!'

Margaret had never heard so much swearing in one day.

The young men moved off, muttering. The boy in the striped suit said, 'You bring a thief to justice and you get treated as if you were a criminal yourself!' But he was passing through the door before he finished the sentence.

The sergeant began to question the dark-haired boy, making notes. Harry Marks stood beside him for a moment, then turned away impatiently. He spotted Margaret, threw her a sunny grin, and sat down next to her. He said, 'All right, girl? What you doing here, then, this time o' night?'

Margaret was bewildered. He was quite transformed. His haughty manner and refined speech had gone, and he spoke with the same accent as the sergeant. For a moment she was too surprised to reply.

Harry threw an appraising glance at the doorway, as if he might be thinking of making a dash for it; then he looked back at the desk and saw the younger policeman, who had not yet said a word, staring at him watchfully. He seemed to give up the idea of escape. He turned back to Margaret. 'Who give you that black eye – your old man?'

Margaret found her voice and said, 'I got lost in the blackout and bumped into a pillar-box.'

It was his turn to be surprised. He had taken her for a working-class girl. Now, hearing her accent, he realized his mistake. Without a blink he reverted to his former persona. 'I say, what jolly bad luck!'

Margaret was fascinated. Which was his real self? He smelled of cologne. His hair was well cut, if a fraction too long. He wore a midnight-blue evening suit in the fashion set by Edward VIII, with silk socks and patent-leather shoes. His jewellery was very good: diamond studs in his shirt-front with matching cufflinks, a gold wristwatch with a black crocodile strap, and a signet ring on the little finger of his left hand. His hands were large and strong-looking, but his fingernails were perfectly clean.

In a low voice she said, 'Did you really leave the restaurant without paying?'

He looked at her appraisingly, then seemed to reach a decision. 'Actually, I did,' he said in a conspiratorial tone.

'But why?'

'Because, if I'd listened for one more minute to Rebecca Maugham-Flint talking about her blasted horses, I should have been unable to resist the urge to take her by the throat and strangle her.'

Margaret giggled. She knew Rebecca Maugham-Flint, who was a large, plain girl, the daughter of a general, with her father's hearty manner and parade-ground voice. 'I can just imagine it,' she said. It would be hard to think of a more unsuitable dinner companion for the attractive Mr Marks.

Constable Steve appeared and picked up her empty mug. 'Feeling better, Lady Margaret?'

Out of the corner of her eye she saw Harry Marks react to her title. 'Much better, thank you,' she said. For a moment she had forgotten her own troubles in talking to Harry, but now she remembered all she had to do. 'You've been so kind,' she went on. 'Now I'm going to leave you to get on with more important things.'

'No need for you to rush off,' the constable said. 'Your father, the Marquess, is on his way to fetch you.'

Margaret's heart stopped. How could this be? She had been so convinced that she was safe – she had underestimated her father! Now she was as frightened as she had been walking along the road to the railway station. He was after her, on his way here at this very minute! She felt shaky. 'How does he know where I am?' she said in a high, strained voice.

The young policeman looked proud. 'Your description was circulated late yesterday evening, and I read it when I come on duty. I never recognized you in the blackout, but I remembered the name. The instruction is to inform the Marquess immediately. As soon as I brought you in here, I rung him up on the telephone.'

Margaret stood up, her heart fluttering wildly. 'I shan't wait for him,' she said. 'It's light now.'

The policeman looked anxious. 'Just a minute,' he said nervously. He turned to the desk. 'Sarge, the lady doesn't want to wait for her father.'

Harry Marks said to Margaret, 'They can't make you stay – running away from home isn't a crime at your age. If you want to go, just walk out.'

Margaret was terrified that they would find some excuse to detain her.

The sergeant got off his seat and came around the counter. 'He's quite right,' the sergeant said. 'You can go any time you like.'

'Oh, thank you,' Margaret said gratefully.

The sergeant smiled. 'But you've got no shoes, and there's holes in your stockings. If you must leave before your father gets here, at least let us call a taxi.'

Margaret thought for a moment. They had phoned Father as soon as she arrived at the police station, but that was less than an hour ago. Father could not possibly get here for another hour or more. 'All right,' she said to the kindly sergeant. 'Thank you.'

He opened a door off the hall. 'You'll be more comfortable in here, while you wait for the taxi.' He switched on the light.

Margaret would have preferred to stay and talk to the fascinating Harry Marks, but she did not want to refuse the sergeant's kindness, especially after he had given in to her. 'Thank you,' she said again.

As she walked to the door she heard Harry say, 'More fool you.'

She stepped into the little room. There were some cheap chairs and a bench, a naked bulb hanging from the ceiling, and a barred window. She could not imagine why the sergeant thought this more comfortable than the hallway. She turned to tell him so.

The door closed in her face. A presentiment of ruin filled her heart with dread. She lunged at the door and grabbed the handle. As she did so her sudden fear was confirmed and she heard a key turn in the lock. She rattled the handle furiously. The door would not open.

She slumped in despair with her head against the wood.

From outside she heard a low laugh, then Harry's voice, muffled but comprehensible, saying, 'You bastard.'

The sergeant's voice was now anything but kindly. 'You shut your hole,' he said crudely.

'You've got no right, you know that.'

'Her father's a bloody marquess, and that's all the right I need.'

No more was said.

Margaret realized bitterly that she had lost. Her great escape had failed. She had been betrayed by the very people she thought were helping her. For a little while she had been free, but now it was over. She would not be joining the ATS today, she thought miserably, she would be boarding the Pan American Clipper and flying to New York, running away from the war. After all she had been through her fate was unchanged. It seemed so desperately unfair.

After a long moment she turned from the door and walked the few steps to the window. She could see an empty yard and a brick wall. She stood there, defeated and helpless, looking through the bars at the brightening daylight, waiting for her father.

Eddie Deakin gave the Pan American Clipper a final once-over. The four Wright Cyclone 1500-horsepower engines gleamed with oil. Each engine was as high as a man. All fifty-six spark plugs had been replaced. On impulse, Eddie took a feeler from his overalls pocket and slid it into an engine mount between the rubber and the metal to test the bond. The pounding vibration of the long flight put a terrific strain on the adhesive.

But Eddie's feeler would not go in even a quarter of an inch. The mounts were holding.

He closed the hatch and climbed down the ladder. While the plane was being eased back into the water he would change out of his overalls, get cleaned up, and put on his black Pan American flight uniform.

The sun was shining as he left the dock and strolled up the hill towards the hotel where the crew stayed during the layover. He was proud of the plane and the job he did. The Clipper crews were an élite, the best men the airline had, for the new transatlantic service was the most prestigious route. All his life he would be able to say he had flown the Atlantic in the early days.

However, he was planning to give it up soon. He was thirty years old, he had been married for a year, and Carol-Ann was pregnant. Flying was all right for a single man but he was not going to spend his life away from his wife and children. He had been saving money and he had almost enough to start a business. He had an option on a site near Bangor, Maine, that would make a perfect airfield. He would service planes and sell fuel, and eventually have an aircraft for charter. Secretly he dreamed that one day he might have an airline of his own, like the pioneering Juan Trippe, founder of Pan American.

He entered the grounds of the Langdown Lawn Hotel. It was a piece of luck for Pan American crew that there was such a pleasant hotel a mile or so from the Imperial Airways complex. The place was a typical English country house, run by a gracious couple who charmed everyone and served tea on the lawn on sunny afternoons.

He went inside. In the hall he ran into his assistant engineer, Desmond Finn – known, inevitably, as Mickey. Mickey reminded Eddie of the Jimmy Olsen character in the Superman comics: he was a happy-go-lucky type with a big toothy grin and a propensity to hero-worship Eddie, who found such adoration embarrassing. He was speaking into the telephone and now, when he saw Eddie, he said, 'Oh, wait, you're lucky, he just walked in.' He handed the earpiece to Eddie and said, 'A phone call for you.' Then he went upstairs, politely leaving Eddie alone.

Eddie spoke into the phone. 'Hello?'

'Is this Edward Deakin?'

Eddie frowned. The voice was unfamiliar, and nobody called him Edward. He said, 'Yes, I'm Eddie Deakin. Who are you?'

'Wait, I have your wife on the line.'

Eddie's heart lurched. Why was Carol-Ann calling him from the States? Something was wrong.

A moment later he heard her voice. 'Eddie?'

'Hi, honey, what's up?'

She burst into tears.

A whole series of awful explanations came to mind: the house had burned down, someone had died, she had hurt herself in some kind of accident, she had suffered a miscarriage—

'Carol-Ann, calm down, are you all right?'

She spoke through sobs. 'I'm – not – hurt—'

'What, then?' he said fearfully. 'What's happened? Try to tell me, babe.'

'These men – came to the house.'

Eddie went cold with dread. 'What men? What did they do?'

'They made me get into a car.'

'Jesus God, who are they?' The anger was like a pain in his chest and he had to fight for breath. 'Did they hurt you?'

'I'm all right . . . but Eddie, I'm so scared.'

He did not know what to say next. Too many questions came to his lips. Men had gone to his house and forced Carol-Ann to get into a car! What was happening? Finally he said, 'But why?'

'They won't tell me.'

'What did they say?'

'Eddie, you have to do what they want, that's all I know.'

Even in his anger and fear, Eddie heard Pop say *Never sign a blank cheque.* All the same he did not hesitate. 'I'll do it, but what—'

'Promise!'

'I promise!'

'Thank God.'

'When did this happen?'

'A couple of hours ago.'

'Where are you now?'

'We're in a house not far—' Her speech turned into a shocked cry.

'Carol-Ann! What's happening? Are you okay?'

There was no response. Furious, frightened and impotent, Eddie squeezed the phone until his knuckles turned white.

Then the original male voice returned. 'Listen to me very carefully, Edward.'

'No, you listen to me, shitheel,' Eddie raged. 'If you hurt her I'll kill you, I swear to God, I'll track you down if it takes as long as I live and when I find you, you punk, I'll tear your head off your neck with my hands, now do you read me loud and clear?'

There was a moment's hesitation, as if the man at the other end of the line had not expected such a tirade. Then he said, 'Don't act tough, you're too far away.' He sounded a little shook, but he was right: Eddie could do nothing. The man went on: 'Just pay attention.'

Eddie held his tongue with an effort.

'You'll get your instructions on the plane from a man called Tom Luther.'

On the plane! What did that mean? Would this Tom Luther be a passenger, or what? Eddie said, 'But what do you want me to do?'

'Shut up. Luther will tell you. And you'd better follow his orders to the letter if you want to see your wife again.'

'How do I know—'

'And one more thing. Don't call the police. It won't do you any good. But if you do call them, I'll fuck her just to be mean.'

'You bastard, I'll—'

The line went dead.

CHAPTER THREE

HARRY MARKS was the luckiest man alive.

His mother had always told him he was lucky. Although his father had been killed in the Great War, he was lucky to have a strong and capable mother to bring him up. She cleaned offices for a living, and all through the slump she had never been out of work. They lived in a tenement in Battersea, with a cold-water tap on each landing and outside toilets, but they were surrounded by good neighbours, people who helped one another through times of trouble. Harry had a knack of escaping from trouble. When boys were being thrashed at school, the teacher's cane would break just before he got to Harry. Harry could fall under a horse and cart and have them pass over him without touching him.

It was his love of jewellery that had made him a thief.

As an adolescent he had loved to walk along the opulent shopping streets of the West End and look in the windows of jewellers' shops. He was enraptured by the diamonds and precious stones glinting on dark velvet pads under the bright display lights. He liked them for their beauty, but also because they symbolized a kind of life he had read about in books, a life of spacious country houses with broad green lawns, where pretty girls with names like Lady Penelope and Jessica Chumley played tennis all afternoon and came in panting for tea.

He had been apprenticed to a jeweller, but he had been bored and restless, and he left after six months. Mending broken watch straps and enlarging wedding rings for overweight wives had no glamour. But he had learned to tell a ruby from a red garnet, a natural pearl from a cultured one, and a modern brilliant-cut diamond from a nineteenth-century old mine cut. He had also discovered the difference between an appropriate setting and an ugly one, a graceful design and a tasteless piece of ostentation; and the ability to discriminate had further inflamed his lust for beautiful jewellery and his longing for the style of life that went with it.

He eventually found a way to satisfy both desires by making use of girls such as Rebecca Maugham-Flint.

He had met Rebecca at Ascot. He often picked up rich girls at race meetings. The open air and the crowds made it possible for him to hover between two groups of young racegoers in such a way that everyone thought he was part of the other group. Rebecca was a tall girl with a big nose, dreadfully dressed in a ruched jersey frock and a Robin Hood hat with a feather in it. None of the young men around her paid any attention to her, and she was pathetically grateful to Harry for talking to her.

He had not pursued the acquaintanceship right away, for it was best not to seem eager. But when he ran into her a month later, at an art gallery, she greeted him like an old friend and introduced him to her mother.

Girls such as Rebecca were not supposed to go unchaperoned to cinemas and restaurants with boys, of course; only shop-girls and factory workers did that. So they would always pretend to their parents that they were going out in a crowd and, to make it look right, they would generally begin the evening at a cocktail party. Afterwards they could discreetly go off in pairs. This suited Harry ideally: since he was not officially 'courting' Rebecca, her parents saw no need to look closely into his background, and they never questioned the vague stories he told of a country house in Yorkshire, a minor public school in Scotland, an invalid mother living in the South of France and a prospective commission in the Royal Air Force.

Vague stories were common in upper-class society, he had found. They were told by young men who did not want to admit to being desperately poor, or having parents who were hopeless drunks, or coming from families which had disgraced themselves by scandal. No one troubled to pin a fellow down until he showed signs of a serious attachment to a well-bred girl.

In this indefinite way Harry had been going around with Rebecca for three weeks. She had got him invited to a weekend house-party in Kent, where he had played cricket and stolen money from the hosts, who had been too embarrassed to report the theft for fear of offending their guests. She had also taken him to several balls where he had picked pockets and emptied purses. In addition, when calling at her parents' house he had taken small sums of money, some silver cutlery and three interesting Victorian brooches which her mother had not yet missed.

There was nothing immoral in what he did, in his opinion. The people from whom he stole did not deserve their wealth. Most of them had never done a day's work in their lives. Those few who had to have some kind of job used their public-school connections to get overpaid sinecures: they were diplomats, chairmen of companies, judges, or Conservative MPs. Stealing from them was like killing Nazis: a service to the public, not a crime.

He had been doing this for two years, and he knew it could not go on for ever. The world of upper-class English society was large but limited, and eventually someone would find him out. The war had come at a time when he was ready to look for a different way of life.

However, he was not going to join the army as a regular soldier. Bad food, itchy clothes, bullying and military discipline were not for him, and he looked sickly in olive drab. Air Force blue matched his eyes, however, and he could easily see himself as a pilot. So he was going to be an officer in the RAF. He had not yet figured out how, but he would manage it: he was lucky that way.

In the meantime he decided to use Rebecca to get inside one more wealthy home before dropping her.

They began the evening at a reception in the Belgravia home of Sir Simon Monkford, a rich publisher.

Harry spent some time with the Honourable Lydia

Moss, overweight daughter of a Scottish earl. Awkward and lonely, she was just the kind of girl who was most vulnerable to his charm, and he enchanted her for twenty minutes more or less out of habit. Then he talked to Rebecca for a while, to keep her sweet. After that he judged the time was right to make his move.

He excused himself and left the room. The party was going on in the large double drawing room on the first floor. As he crossed the landing and slipped up the stairs he felt the thrilling rush of adrenalin that always came to him when he was about to do a job. The knowledge that he was going to steal from his hosts, and risk being caught red-handed and shown up as a fraud, filled him with fear and excitement.

He reached the next floor and followed the corridor to the front of the house. The farthest door probably led to the master bedroom suite, he thought. He opened it and saw a large bedroom with flowered curtains and a pink bedspread. He was about to step inside when another door opened and a challenging voice called out, 'I say!'

Harry turned around, his tension drawing tighter. He saw a man of about his own age step into the corridor and look curiously at him.

As always, the right words came to him when he needed them. 'Ah, is it in there?' he said.

'What?'

'Is that the lav?'

The young man's face cleared. 'Oh, I see. You want the green door at the other end of the corridor.'

'Thanks awfully.'

'Not at all.'

Harry went along the corridor. 'Lovely house,' he remarked.

'Isn't it.' The man descended the staircase and disappeared.

Harry allowed himself a pleased grin. People could be so gullible.

He retraced his steps and went into the pink bedroom. As usual, there was a suite of rooms. The colour scheme indicated that this was Lady Monkford's room. A rapid survey revealed a small dressing room off to one side, also decorated in pink; an adjoining, smaller bedroom, with green leather chairs and striped wallpaper; and a gentleman's dressing room off that. Upper-class couples often slept separately, Harry had learned. He had not yet decided whether that was because they were less randy than the working class, or because they felt obliged to make use of all the many rooms in their vast houses.

Sir Simon's dressing room was furnished with a heavy mahogany wardrobe and matching chest. Harry opened the top drawer of the chest. There, inside a small leather jewel box, was an assortment of studs, collar stiffeners and cufflinks, not neatly arranged but tumbled about haphazardly. Most of them were rather ordinary, but Harry's discriminating eye lit on a charming pair of gold cufflinks with small rubies inset. He put them in his pocket. Next to the jewel box was a soft leather wallet containing about fifty pounds in five-pound notes. Harry took twenty pounds and felt pleased with himself. Easy, he thought. It would take most people two months' hard work in a dirty factory to earn twenty pounds.

He never stole everything. Taking just a few items created a doubt. People thought they might have mislaid the jewellery or made a mistake about how much was in the wallet, so they hesitated to report the theft.

He closed the drawer and moved into Lady Monkford's bedroom. He was tempted to get out now with the useful haul he had already made, but he decided to risk a few minutes more. Women generally had better jewellery than their husbands. Lady Monkford might have sapphires. Harry loved sapphires.

It was a fine evening, and a window was open wide. Harry glanced through it and saw a small balcony with a wrought-iron balustrade. He went quickly into the dressing room and sat at the dressing-table. He opened all the drawers and found several boxes and trays of jewellery. He began to go through them rapidly, listening warily for the sound of the door opening.

Lady Monkford did not have good taste. She was a pretty woman who had struck Harry as rather ineffectual, and she – or her husband – chose showy, rather cheap jewellery. Her pearls were ill-matched, her brooches big and ugly, her earrings clumsy and her bracelets flashy. He was disappointed.

He was hesitating over an almost-attractive pendant when he heard the bedroom door open.

He froze, stomach in a knot, thinking fast.

The only door out of the dressing room led to the bedroom. There was a small window, but it was firmly closed and he probably could not open it quickly or silently enough. He wondered if he had time to hide in the wardrobe.

From where he stood he could not quite see the bedroom door. He heard it close again, then there was a feminine cough and light footsteps on the carpet. He leaned towards the mirror and found he could see into the bedroom. Lady Monkford had come in and she was heading for the dressing room. There was not even time to close the drawers.

His breath came fast. He was taut with fear, but he had been in spots like this before. He paused for one more moment, forcing himself to breathe evenly, calming his mind. Then he moved.

He stood up, stepped quickly through the door into the bedroom, and said, 'I say!'

Lady Monkford was brought up short in the middle of the room. She put her hand to her mouth and let out a tiny scream.

A flowered curtain flapped in the breeze from the open window, and Harry was inspired.

'I say,' he repeated, deliberately sounding a bit stupefied. 'I've just seen someone jump out of your window.'

She found her voice. 'What on earth do you mean?' she said. 'And what are you doing in my bedroom?'

Acting the part, Harry strode to the window and looked out. 'Gone already!' he said.

'Please explain yourself!'

Harry took a deep breath, as if marshalling his thoughts. Lady Monkford was about forty, a fluttery woman in a green silk dress. If he kept his nerve he could deal with her. He smiled winningly, assumed the persona of a hearty, rugby-playing, overgrown schoolboy – a type that must be familiar to her – and began to pull the wool over her eyes.

'It's the oddest thing I ever saw,' he said. 'I was in the corridor when a strange-looking cove peeped out of this room. He caught my eye and ducked back in again. I knew it was your bedroom, because I had looked in here myself when I was hunting for the bathroom. I wondered what the chap was up to – he didn't look like one of your servants and he certainly wasn't a guest. So I came along to ask him. When I opened the door he jumped out of the window.' Then, to account for the still-open drawers of the dressing-table, he added, 'I've just looked into your dressing room, and I'm afraid there's no doubt he was after your jewellery.'

That was brilliant, he said admiringly to himself. I should be on the bleedin' wireless.

She put her hand to her forehead. 'Oh, what a dreadful thing,' she said weakly.

'You'd better sit down,' Harry said solicitously. He helped her to a small pink chair.

'To think!' she said. 'If you hadn't chased him off, he would have been here when I walked in! I'm afraid I shall faint.' She grasped Harry's hand and held it tightly. 'I'm so grateful to you.'

Harry smothered a grin. He had got away with it again.

He thought ahead for a moment. He did not want

her to make too much fuss. Ideally he would like her to keep the whole thing to herself. 'Look, don't tell Rebecca what's happened, will you?' he said as a first step. 'She's got a nervous disposition and something like this could lay her low for weeks.'

'Me, too,' said Lady Monkford. 'Weeks!' She was too upset to reflect that the muscular, hearty Rebecca was hardly the type to have a nervous disposition.

'You'll probably have to call the police, and so on, but it will spoil the party,' he went on.

'Oh dear – that would be too dreadful. Do we *have* to call them?'

'Well . . .' Harry concealed his satisfaction. 'It rather depends on what the blighter stole. Why don't you have a quick look?'

'Oh, goodness, yes, I'd better.'

Harry squeezed her hand for encouragement then helped her up. They went into the dressing room. She gasped when she saw all the drawers open. Harry handed her to her chair. She sat down and started looking through her jewellery. After a moment she said, 'I don't think he can have taken much.'

'Perhaps I surprised him before he got started,' Harry said.

She continued sorting through the necklaces, bracelets and brooches. 'I think you must have,' she said. 'How wonderful you are.'

'If you haven't lost anything, you don't really have to tell anyone.'

'Except Sir Simon, of course,' she said.

'Of course,' Harry said, although he had hoped otherwise. 'You could tell him after the party's over. That way at least you won't spoil his evening.'

'What a good idea,' she said gratefully.

This was very satisfactory. Harry was immensely relieved. He decided to quit while he was so far ahead. 'I'd better go down,' he said. 'I'll leave you to catch your breath.' He bent swiftly and kissed her cheek. She was taken by surprise, and she blushed. He whispered in her ear, 'I think you're terribly brave.' With that he went out.

Middle-aged women were even easier than their daughters, he thought. In the empty corridor he caught sight of himself in a mirror. He stopped to adjust his bow tie and grinned triumphantly at his reflection. 'You are a devil, Harold,' he murmured.

The party was coming to an end. When Harry re-entered the drawing room, Rebecca said irritably, 'Where have you been?'

'Talking to our hostess,' he replied. 'Sorry. Shall we take our leave?'

He walked out of the house with his host's cufflinks and twenty pounds in his pocket.

They got a cab in Belgrave Square and rode to a restaurant in Piccadilly. Harry loved good restaurants: he got a deep sense of well-being from the crisp napkins, the polished glasses, the menus in French and the deferential waiters. His father had never seen the inside of such a place. His mother might have, if she had come in to clean it. He ordered a bottle of champagne, consulting the list carefully and choosing a vintage he knew to be good but not rare, so that the price was not too high.

When he first started taking girls to restaurants he had made a few mistakes, but he was a quick learner. One useful trick had been to leave the menu unopened, and say, 'I'd like a sole, have you got any?' The waiter would open the menu and show him where it said *Sole meunière, Les goujons de sole avec sauce tartare,* and *Sole grillée,* and then, seeing him hesitate, would probably say, 'The goujons are very nice, sir.' Harry soon learned the French for all the basic dishes. He also noticed that people who frequently ate in such places quite often asked the waiter what a particular dish was: wealthy English people did not necessarily understand French. Thereafter he made a point of asking for the translation of one dish every time he ate in a fancy restaurant, and now he could read a menu better than most rich boys of his age. Wine was no problem, either. Sommeliers were normally pleased to be asked for a recommendation, and they did not expect a young man to be familiar with all the châteaux and communes and the different vintages. The trick, in restaurants as in life, was to appear at ease, especially when you were not.

The champagne he chose was good, but there was something wrong with his mood tonight, and he soon figured out that the problem was Rebecca. He kept thinking how delightful it would be to bring a *pretty* girl to a place like this. He always went out with unattractive girls: plain girls, fat girls, spotty girls, silly girls. They were easy to get acquainted with and then, once they had fallen for him, they were eager to take him at face value, reluctant to question him in case they should lose him. As a strategy for getting inside wealthy homes it was matchless. The snag was that he spent all his time with girls he did not like. One day, perhaps . . .

Rebecca was sullen tonight. She was discontented about something. Perhaps after seeing Harry regularly for three weeks she was wondering why he still had not attempted to 'go too far', by which she would mean touching her breasts. The truth was he could not pretend to lust after her. He could charm her, romance her, make her laugh, and make her love him, but he could not desire her. On one excruciating occasion he had found himself in a hay loft with a skinny, depressed girl set on losing her virginity, and he had tried to force himself; but his body had refused to co-operate, and he still squirmed with embarrassment every time he thought of it.

His sexual experience, such as it was, was mostly with girls of his own class, and none of those relationships had lasted. He had had just one deeply satisfying love affair. At the age of eighteen he had been shamelessly picked up in Bond Street by an older woman, the bored wife of a busy solicitor, and they had been lovers for two years. He had learned a lot from Marjorie – about making love, which she taught him enthusiastically; about upper-class manners, which he picked up surreptitiously; and about poetry, which they read and discussed in bed together. Harry had been deeply fond of her. She ended the affair instantly and brutally when her husband found out that she had a lover (he never knew who). Since then Harry had seen them both several times: the woman always looked at him as if he were not there. Harry found this cruel. She had meant a lot to him, and she had seemed to care for him. Was she strong-willed, or just heartless? He would probably never know.

The champagne and the good food were not lifting Harry's spirits or Rebecca's. He began to feel restless. He had been planning to drop her gently after tonight, but suddenly he could not bear the thought of spending even the rest of this evening with her. He wished he had not wasted money on dinner for her. He looked at her grumpy face, bare of make-up and squashed beneath a silly little hat with a feather, and he began to hate her.

When they had finished dessert he ordered coffee and went to the lavatory. The cloakroom was right next to the men's room, near the exit door, and not visible from their table. Harry was seized by an irresistible impulse. He collected his hat, tipped the cloakroom attendant, and slipped out of the restaurant.

It was a mild night. The blackout made it very dark, but Harry knew the West End well, and there were traffic lights to navigate by, plus the sparing glow of car sidelights. He felt as if he had been let out of school. He had got rid of Rebecca, saved himself seven or eight pounds and given himself a night off, all at one inspired stroke.

The theatres, cinemas and dance halls had been closed by the government, 'until the scale of the

German attack upon Britain has been judged', they said. But nightclubs always operated on the fringe of the law and there were still plenty open if you knew where to look. Soon Harry was making himself comfortable at a table in a cellar in Soho, sipping whisky and listening to a first-rate American jazz band and toying with the idea of making a play for the cigarette girl.

He was still thinking about it when Rebecca's brother came in.

The following morning he sat in a cell in the basement underneath the courthouse, depressed and remorseful, waiting to be taken before the magistrates. He was in deep trouble.

Walking out of the restaurant like that had been bloody silly. Rebecca was not the type to swallow her pride and pay the bill quietly. She had made a fuss, the manager had called the police, her family had been dragged in . . . It was just the kind of furore Harry was normally so careful to avoid. Even so he would have got away with it, had it not been for the incredible bad luck of running into Rebecca's brother a couple of hours later.

He was in a large cell with fifteen or twenty other prisoners who would be brought before the Bench this morning. There were no windows, and the room was full of cigarette smoke. Harry would not be tried today: this would be a preliminary hearing.

He would eventually be convicted, of course. The evidence against him was indisputable. The head waiter would corroborate Rebecca's complaint, and Sir Simon Monkford would identify the cufflinks as his.

But it was worse than that. Harry had been interviewed by an inspector from the Criminal Investigation Department. The man had been wearing the detective's uniform of serviceable serge suit, plain white shirt and black tie, waistcoat with no watch chain, and highly polished, well-worn boots. He was an experienced policeman with a sharp mind and a wary manner. He had said, 'For the last two or three years we've been getting odd reports, from wealthy houses, of *lost* jewellery. Not *stolen*, of course. Just missing. Bracelets, earrings, pendants, shirt studs . . . The losers are quite sure the stuff can't have been stolen, because the only people who had the opportunity to take it would have been their guests. The only reason they report it is that they want to claim it if it turns up somewhere.'

Harry had kept his mouth shut tight throughout the entire interview, but inside he was feeling sick. He had been sure that his career had gone entirely unnoticed until now. He was shocked to learn the opposite: they had been on to him for some time.

The detective opened a fat file. 'The Earl of Dorset, a Georgian silver bonbonnière and a lacquered snuff box, also Georgian. Mrs Harry Jaspers, a pearl bracelet with ruby clasp by Tiffany's. The Contessa di Malvoli, an art-deco diamond pendant on a silver chain. This man has good taste.' The detective looked pointedly at the diamond studs in Harry's dress shirt.

Harry realized the file must contain details of dozens of crimes committed by him. He knew also that he would eventually be convicted of at least some. This shrewd detective had put together all the basic facts: he could easily gather witnesses to say that Harry had been at each location at the time of the theft. Sooner or later they would search his lodgings and his mother's house. Most of the jewellery had been fenced, but he had kept a few pieces: the shirt studs the detective had noticed had been taken from a sleeping drunk at a ball in Grosvenor Square, and his mother had a brooch he had deftly plucked from the bosom of a countess at a wedding reception in a Surrey garden. And then how would he answer when they asked him what he lived on?

He was headed for a long stretch in jail. And when he got out he would be conscripted into the army, which was more or less the same thing. The thought made his blood run cold.

He steadfastly refused to say a word, even when the detective took him by the lapels of his dinner jacket and slammed him against the wall; but silence would not save him. The law had time on its side.

Harry had only one chance of freedom. He would have to persuade the magistrates to give him bail, then disappear. Suddenly he yearned for freedom as if he had been in jail for years instead of hours.

Disappearing would not be simple, but the alternative made him shiver.

In robbing the rich he had grown accustomed to their style of living. He got up late, drank coffee from a china cup, wore beautiful clothes and ate in expensive restaurants. He still enjoyed returning to his roots, drinking in the pub with old mates or taking his ma to the Odeon. But the thought of prison was unbearable: the dirty clothes, the horrible food, the total lack of privacy, and, worst of all, the grinding boredom of a totally pointless existence.

With a shudder of loathing he concentrated his mind on the problem of getting bail.

The police would oppose bail, of course, but the magistrates would make the decision. Harry had never appeared in court before, but in the streets from which he came people knew these things just as they knew who was eligible for a council house and how to sweep chimneys. Bail was automatically refused only in murder trials. Otherwise it was up to the discretion of the magistrates. Normally they did what the police asked, but not always. Sometimes they could be talked round, by a clever lawyer or by a defendant with a sob story about a sick child. Sometimes, if the police prosecutor was a little too arrogant, they would give bail just to assert their independence. He would have to put up some money, probably twenty-five or fifty pounds. This was no problem. He had plenty of money. He had been allowed to make a phone call, and he had rung the newsagent's shop on the corner of the street where his ma lived and asked Bernie, the proprietor, to send one of the paper-boys to fetch ma to the phone. When finally she got there he told her where to find his money.

'They'll give me bail, Ma,' Harry said cockily.

'I know, son,' his mother said. 'You've always been lucky.'

But if not . . .

I've got out of awkward situations before, he told himself cheerily.

But not this awkward.

A warder shouted out, 'Marks!'

Harry stood up. He had not planned what he would say: he was a spur-of-the-moment improviser. But for once he wished he had something prepared. Let's get it over with, he thought edgily. He buttoned his jacket, adjusted his bow tie and straightened the square of white linen in his breast pocket. He rubbed his chin and wished he had been allowed to shave. At the last minute the germ of a story appeared in his mind, and he took the cufflinks out of his shirt and pocketed them.

The gate was opened and he stepped outside.

He was led up a concrete staircase and emerged in the dock in the middle of the courtroom. In front of him were the lawyers' seats, all empty, the magistrates' clerk, a qualified lawyer, behind his desk, and the Bench, with three non-professional magistrates.

Harry thought, Christ, I hope the bastards let me go.

In the press gallery, to one side, was a young reporter with a notebook. Harry turned round and looked towards the back of the court. There in the public seats he spotted Ma, in her best coat and a new hat. She tapped her pocket significantly: Harry took that to mean that she had the money for his bail. He saw to his horror that she was wearing the brooch he had stolen from the Countess of Eyer.

He faced front and grasped the rail to keep his

hands from trembling. The prosecutor, a bald police inspector with a big nose, was saying, 'Number three on your list, your worships. Theft of twenty pounds in money and a pair of gold cufflinks worth fifteen guineas, the property of Sir Simon Monkford, and obtaining a pecuniary advantage by deception at the Saint Raphael restaurant in Piccadilly. The police are requesting a remand in custody because we are investigating further offences involving large sums of money.'

Harry was studying the magistrates warily. On one side was an old codger with white sideburns and a stiff collar, and on the other a military type in a regimental tie. They both looked down their noses at him, and he guessed they believed that everyone who appeared before them must be guilty of something. He felt hopeless. Then he told himself that stupid prejudice could quickly be turned into equally foolish credulity. Better they should not be too clever, if he was going to pull the wool over their eyes. The chairman, in the middle, was the only one who really counted. He was a middle-aged man with a grey moustache, grey suit and a world-weary air which suggested that in his time he had heard more tall stories and plausible excuses than he cared to remember. He would be the one to watch, Harry thought anxiously.

The chairman now said to Harry, 'Are you asking for bail?'

Harry pretended to be confused. 'Oh! Goodness gracious! I think so. Yes – yes, I am.'

All three magistrates sat up and began to take notice when they heard his upper-class accent. Harry enjoyed the effect. He was proud of his ability to confound people's social expectations. The reaction of the Bench gave him heart. I can fool them, he thought. I bet I can.

The chairman said, 'Well, what have you got to say for yourself?'

Harry was listening carefully to the chairman's accent, trying to place his social class precisely. He decided the man was educated middle class: a pharmacist, perhaps, or a bank manager. He would be shrewd, but he would be in the habit of deferring to the upper classes.

Harry put on an expression of embarrassment, and adopted the tone of a schoolboy addressing a headmaster. 'I'm afraid there's been the most frightful muddle, sir,' he began. The interest of the magistrates went up another notch, and they shifted in their seats and leaned forward interestedly. This was not going to be a run-of-the-mill case, they could see, and they were grateful for some relief from the usual tedium. Harry went on, 'To tell you the truth, some of the fellows drank too much port at the Carlton Club yesterday, and that was really the cause of it all.' He paused, as if that might be all he had to say, and looked expectantly at the Bench.

The military magistrate said: 'The Carlton Club!' His expression said it was not often that members of that august institution appeared before the Bench.

Harry wondered if he had gone too far. Perhaps they would refuse to believe that he was a member. He hurried on, 'It's dreadfully embarrassing, but I shall go round and apologize *immediately* to all concerned and get the whole thing straightened out without delay . . .' He pretended to remember suddenly that he was wearing evening dress. 'That is, as soon as I've changed.'

The old codger said, 'Are you saying you didn't *intend* to take twenty pounds and a pair of cufflinks?'

His tone was incredulous, but nevertheless it was a good sign that they were asking questions. It meant they were not dismissing his story out of hand. If they had not believed a word of what he was saying they would not have bothered to challenge him on the details. His heart lifted: perhaps he would be freed!

He said, 'I did borrow the cufflinks – I had come out without my own.' He held up his arms to show the unfastened cuffs of his dress shirt sticking out from the sleeves of his jacket. His cufflinks were in his pocket.

The old codger asked, 'And what about the twenty pounds?'

That was a more difficult question, Harry realized anxiously. No plausible excuse came to mind. You might forget your cufflinks and casually borrow someone else's, but borrowing money without permission was the same as stealing. He was on the edge of panic when inspiration rescued him once again. 'I do think Sir Simon might have been mistaken about how much there was in his wallet originally.' Harry lowered his voice, as if to say something to the magistrates that the common people in the court ought not to hear. 'He is frightfully rich, sir.'

The chairman said, 'He didn't get rich by forgetting

how much money he had.' There was a ripple of laughter from the people in the court. A sense of humour might have been an encouraging sign, but the chairman did not crack a smile: he had not intended to be funny. He's a bank manager, Harry thought; money's no joking matter. The magistrate went on, 'And why did you not pay your bill at the restaurant?'

'I say, I am most awfully sorry about that. I had the most appalling row with – with my dining partner.' Harry ostentatiously refrained from saying who he was dining with: it was bad form, among public-school boys, to bandy a woman's name about, and the magistrates would know that. 'I'm afraid I sort of stormed out, completely forgetting about the bill.'

The chairman looked over the top of his spectacles and fixed Harry with a hard stare. Harry felt he had gone wrong somewhere. His heart sank. What had he said? It occurred to him that he had displayed a casual attitude towards a debt. This was normal among the upper classes but a deadly sin to a bank manager. Panic seized him and he felt he was about to lose everything by a small error of judgement. Quickly he blurted out, 'Fearfully irresponsible of me, sir, and I shall go round there this lunchtime and settle up, of course. That is, if you let me go.'

He could not tell whether the chairman was mollified or not. 'So you're telling me that when you have made your explanations the charges against you are likely to be dropped?'

Harry decided he ought to guard against appearing to have a glib answer to every question. He hung his head and looked foolish. 'I suppose it would serve me bally well right if people refused to drop the charges.'

'It probably would,' the chairman said sternly.

You pompous old fart, Harry thought, but he knew that this kind of thing, though humiliating, was good for his case. The more they scolded him, the less likely they were to send him back to jail.

'Is there anything else you would like to say?' the chairman asked.

In a low voice Harry replied, 'Only that I'm most frightfully ashamed of myself, sir.'

'Hm.' The chairman grunted sceptically, but the military man nodded approvingly.

The three magistrates conferred in murmurs for a while. After a while Harry realized he was holding his breath, and forced himself to let it out. It was unbearable that his whole future should be in the hands of these old duffers. He wished they would hurry up and make up their minds; then when they all nodded in unison he wished they would postpone the awful moment.

The chairman looked up. 'I hope a night in the cells has taught you a lesson,' he said.

Oh, God, I think he's going to let me go, Harry thought. He swallowed and said, 'Absolutely, sir. I never want to go back there again, ever.'

'Make sure of it.'

There was another pause, then the chairman looked away from Harry and addressed the court. 'I'm not saying we believe everything we've heard, but we don't think this is a case for a custodial remand.'

A wave of relief washed over Harry, and his legs went weak.

The chairman said, 'Remanded for seven days. Bail in the sum of fifty pounds.'

Harry was free.

He saw the streets with new eyes, as if he had been in prison for a year instead of a few hours. London was getting ready for war. Dozens of huge silver balloons floated high in the skies to obstruct German planes. Shops and public buildings were surrounded by sandbags to protect them from bomb damage. There were new air-raid shelters in the parks and everyone carried a gas-mask. People felt they might be wiped out at any minute, and this caused them to drop their reserve and converse amiably with total strangers.

Harry had no memory of the Great War – he had been two years old when it ended. As a little boy he had thought 'the War' was a place, for everyone said to him, 'Your father was killed in the War,' like they said, 'Go and play in the Park, don't fall in the River, Ma's going to the Pub.' Later, when he was old enough to understand what he had lost, any mention of the War was painful to him. With Marjorie, the solicitor's wife who had been his lover for two years, he had read the poetry of the Great War and for a while he had called himself a pacifist. Then he had seen the Blackshirts marching in London and the scared faces of the old Jews as they watched, and he had decided some wars might be worth fighting. In the last few years he had been disgusted at the way the British government turned a blind eye to what was happening in Germany, just because they hoped Hitler would destroy the Soviet Union. But now that war had actually broken out, he thought only of all the small boys who would live, as he had, with a hole in their lives where a father should be.

But the bombers had not yet come, and it was another sunny day.

Harry decided not to go to his lodgings. The police would be furious about his getting bail and they would want to re-arrest him at the first opportunity. He had better lie low for a while. But how long would he have to keep looking back over his shoulder? Could he evade the police for ever? And if not, what would he do?

He got on the bus with his ma. He would go to her place in Battersea for the moment.

Ma looked sad. She knew how he made his living, although they had never talked about it. Now she said thoughtfully, 'I could never give you nothing.'

'You gave me everything, Ma,' he protested.

'No, I didn't, otherwise why would you need to steal?'

He did not have an answer to that.

When they got off the bus he went into the corner newsagent's, thanked Bernie for calling Ma to the phone earlier and bought the *Daily Express*. The headline said POLES BOMB BERLIN. As he came out he saw a bobby cycling along the road, and he felt a moment of foolish panic. He almost turned and ran before he got himself under control and remembered they always sent two people to arrest you.

I can't live like this, he thought.

They went to Ma's building and climbed the stone staircase to the fourth floor. Ma put the kettle on and said, 'I've pressed your blue suit – you can change into that.' She still took care of his clothes, sewing on buttons and darning his silk socks. Harry went into the bedroom, dragged his case from under the bed and counted his money.

After two years of thieving he had two hundred and forty-seven pounds. I must have pinched four times that much, he thought. I wonder what I spent the rest on?

He also had an American passport.

He flicked through it thoughtfully. He remembered finding it in a bureau at the home of a diplomat in Kensington. He had noticed that the owner's name was Harold and the picture looked a little like himself, so he had pocketed it.

America, he thought.

He could do an American accent. In fact, he knew something most British people did not – that there were several different American accents, some of which were posher than others. Take the word *Boston.* People from Boston would say *Baston.* People from New York would say *Bawston.* The more English you sounded, the more upper class you were in America – and there were millions of rich American girls just waiting to be romanced.

Whereas in this country there was nothing for him but jail and the army.

He had a passport and a pocketful of money. He had a clean suit in his mother's wardrobe and he could buy a few shirts and a suitcase. He was seventy-five miles from Southampton.

He could be gone today.

It was like a dream.

His mother woke him up by calling from the kitchen, 'Harry, d'you want a bacon sandwich?'

'Yes, please.'

He went into the kitchen and sat at the table. She put a sandwich in front of him but he did not pick it up. 'Let's go to America, Ma,' he said.

She burst out laughing. 'Me? America? I should cocoa!'

'I mean it. I'm going.'

She became solemn. 'It's not for me, son. I'm too old to emigrate.'

'But there's going to be a war.'

'I've lived here through one war, and a general strike and a slump.' She looked around at the tiny kitchen. 'It ain't much but it's what I know.'

Harry had not really expected her to agree, but now that she had said it he felt despondent. His mother was all he had.

She said, 'What'll you do there, anyway?'

'Are you worried about me thieving?'

'It always ends up the same way, thieving. I never heard of a tea-leaf that wasn't collared sooner or later.'

A tea-leaf was a thief, in rhyming slang. Harry said, 'I'd like to join the air force and learn to fly.'

'Would you be allowed?'

'Over there they don't care if you're working class, so long as you've got the brains.'

She looked more cheerful then. She sat down and sipped her tea while Harry ate his bacon sandwich. When he had finished he took out his money and counted out fifty pounds.

'What's that for?' she said. It was as much money as she earned in two years of cleaning offices.

'It'll come in handy,' he said. 'Take it, Ma. I want you to have it.'

She took the money. 'You're really going, then.'

'I'm going to borrow Sid Brennan's motorbike and drive to Southampton today and get a ship.'

She reached across the little table and took his hand. 'Good luck to you, son.'

He squeezed her hand gently. 'I'll send you more money from America.'

'No need, unless you've got it to spare. I'd rather you send me a letter now and again, so I know how you're going on.'

'Yeah. I'll write.'

Her eyes filled with tears. 'Come back and see your old ma one day, won't you?'

He squeezed her hand. 'Course I will, Ma. I'll be back.'

Harry looked at himself in the barber's mirror. The blue suit which had cost him thirteen pounds in Savile Row, fitted beautifully and went well with his blue eyes. The soft collar of his new shirt looked American. The barber brushed the padded shoulders of the double-breasted jacket, and Harry tipped him and left.

He went up the marble staircase from the basement and emerged in the ornate lobby of the South-Western Hotel. It was thronged with people. This was the departure point for most transatlantic crossings, and thousands of people were trying to leave England.

Harry had discovered how many when he tried to get a berth on a liner. All the ships were booked up for weeks ahead. Some of the shipping lines had closed their offices rather than waste staff time turning people away. For a while it had looked impossible. He had been ready to give up, and start thinking of another plan, when a travel agent had mentioned the Pan American Clipper.

He had read about the Clipper in the newspapers. The service had started in the summer. You could fly to New York in less than thirty hours, instead of four or five days on a ship. But a one-way ticket cost ninety pounds. Ninety pounds! You could almost buy a new car for that.

Harry had spent the money. It was mad, but now that he had made up his mind to go he would pay any price to get out of the country. And the plane was seductively luxurious: it would be champagne all the way to New York. This was the kind of insane extravagance that Harry loved.

He was no longer jumping every time he saw a copper: there was no way the Southampton police could know about him. However, he had never flown before, and now he was feeling nervous about that.

He checked his wristwatch, a Patek Philippe stolen

from a royal equerry. He had time for a quick cup of coffee to settle his stomach. He went into the lounge.

While he was sipping his coffee a stunningly beautiful woman walked in. She was a perfect blonde, and she wore a wasp-waisted dress of cream silk with orange-red polka dots. She was in her early thirties, about ten years older than Harry, but that did not stop him smiling when he caught her eye.

She sat at the next table, sideways-on to Harry, and he studied the way the spotted silk clung to her bosom and draped her knees. She had cream shoes and a straw hat, and she put a small handbag on the table.

After a moment she was joined by a man in a blazer. Hearing them speak, Harry discovered that she was English but he was American. Harry listened carefully, brushing up his accent. Her name was Diana; the man was Mark. He saw the man touch her arm. She leaned closer. They were in love and saw no one but each other: the room might have been empty.

Harry felt a pang of envy.

He looked away. He still felt queasy. He was about to fly all the way across the Atlantic. It seemed a long way to go with no land beneath. He had never understood the principle of air travel, anyway: the propellers went round and round, so how come the plane went up?

While he listened to Mark and Diana, he practised looking nonchalant. He did not want the other passengers on the Clipper to know he was nervous. I'm Harry Vandenpost, he thought, a well-off young American returning home because of the war in Europe.

Pronounced Yurrup. I don't have a job, just now, but I suppose I'll have to settle down to something soon. My father has investments. My mother, God rest her soul, was English and I went to school over there. I didn't go to university – never did like swotting. (Did Americans say 'swotting'? He was not sure.) I've spent so much time in England that I've picked up some of the local lingo. I've flown a few times, sure, but this is my first flight across the Atlantic Ocean, you bet. I'm *really* looking forward to it!

By the time he finished his coffee he was hardly scared at all.

Eddie Deakin hung up. He looked around the hall: it was empty. No one had overheard. He stared at the phone that had plunged him into horror, hating it, as if he might end the nightmare by smashing the instrument. Then he slowly turned away.

Who were they? Where had they taken Carol-Ann? Why had they kidnapped her? What could they possibly want from him? The questions buzzed in his head like flies in a jar. He tried to think. He forced himself to concentrate on one question at a time.

Who *were* they? Could they be simple lunatics? No. They were too well organized: crazy people might manage a kidnap, but it had taken careful planning to find out where Eddie would be immediately after the snatch and get him on the phone with Carol-Ann at the right moment. They were rational people, then, but they were prepared to break the law. They might be anarchists of some kind, but most likely he was dealing with gangsters.

Where had they taken Carol-Ann? She had said she was in a house. It might belong to one of the kidnappers, but more likely they had taken over or rented an empty house in a lonely spot. Carol-Ann had said it had happened a couple of hours ago, so the house could not be more than sixty or seventy miles from Bangor.

Why had they kidnapped her? They wanted something from him, something he would not give voluntarily, something he would not do for money – something, he guessed, that he would want to refuse them. But what? He had no money, he knew no secrets, and no one was in his power.

It had to be something to do with the Clipper.

He would get his instructions on the plane, they had said, from a man called Tom Luther. Might Luther be working for someone who wanted details of the construction and operation of the plane? Another airline, perhaps, or a foreign country? It was possible. The Germans or the Japanese might be hoping to build a copy to use as a bomber. But there had to be easier ways for them to get blueprints. Hundreds of people, maybe thousands, could supply such information: Pan American employees, Boeing employees, even the Imperial Airways mechanics who serviced the engines here at Hythe. Kidnapping was not necessary. Hell, enough technical details had been published in the magazines.

Might someone want to steal the plane? It was hard to imagine.

The likeliest explanation was that they wanted Eddie to co-operate in smuggling something, or somebody, into the United States.

Well, that was as much as he knew or could guess. What was he going to do?

He was a law-abiding citizen and the victim of a crime, and he wanted with all his heart to call the police.

But he was terrified.

He had never been so scared in his life. As a boy he had been frightened of Pop and the Devil, but since then nothing had really petrified him. Now he was helpless and rigid with fear. He felt paralysed: for a moment he could not even move from where he stood.

He thought of the police.

He was in goddamn England, there was no point in talking to their bicycling local cops. But he could try to put a telephone call through to the county sheriff back home, or the Maine State Police, or even the FBI, and get them to start searching for an isolated house that had recently been rented by a man—

Don't call the police, it won't do you any good, the voice on the phone had said. *But if you do call them, I'll fuck her just to be mean.*

Eddie believed him. There had been a note of longing in the spiteful voice, as if the man was half hoping for an excuse to rape her. With her rounded belly and swollen breasts she had a lush, ripe look that—

He clenched his fist, but there was nothing to punch but the wall. With a groan of despair he stumbled out through the front door. Not looking where he was going, he crossed the lawn. He came to a stand of trees, stopped and leaned his forehead against the furrowed bark of an oak.

Eddie was a simple man. He had been born in a farmhouse a few miles out of Bangor. His father was a poor farmer, with a few acres of potato fields, some chickens, a cow and a vegetable patch. New England was a bad place to be poor: the winters were long and bitterly cold. Mom and Pop believed that everything was the will of God. Even when Eddie's baby sister caught pneumonia and died, Pop said God had a purpose in it, 'too deep for us to comprehend'. In those days Eddie daydreamed about finding buried treasure in the woods: a brass-bound pirate's chest full of gold and precious gems like in the stories. In his fantasy he took a gold coin into Bangor and bought big soft beds, a truckload of firewood, pretty china for his mother, sheepskin coats for all the family, thick steaks and an icebox full of ice cream and a pineapple. The dismal, ramshackle farmhouse was transformed into a place of warmth, comfort and happiness.

He never found buried treasure, but he got education, walking the six miles to school every day. He liked it because the schoolroom was warmer than his home, and Mrs Maple liked him because he always asked how things worked.

Years later it was Mrs Maple who wrote to the congressman who got Eddie a chance to take the entrance examination for Annapolis.

He thought the Naval Academy was paradise. There were blankets and good clothes and all the food you could eat: he had never imagined such plenty. The tough physical regime was easy to him; the bullshit was no worse than he had listened to in chapel all his life; and the 'hazing' was petty harassment by comparison with the beatings his father handed out.

It was at Annapolis that he first became aware of how he appeared to other people. He learned that he was earnest, dogged, inflexible and hard-working. Even though he was skinny, bullies rarely picked on him: there was a look in his eye that scared them off. People liked him because they could rely on him to do what he promised, but nobody ever cried on his shoulder.

He was surprised to be praised as a hard worker. Both Pop and Mrs Maple had taught him that you could get what you wanted by working for it, and Eddie had never conceived of any other way. All the same the compliment pleased him. His father's highest term of praise had been to call someone a 'driver', the Maine dialect word for a hard worker.

He was commissioned an ensign and assigned to aviation training on flying boats. Annapolis had been comfortable, by comparison with his home, but the US Navy was positively luxurious. He was able to send money home to his parents, for them to fix the farmhouse roof and buy a new stove.

He had been four years in the Navy when Mom died, and Pop went just five months later. Their few acres were absorbed into the neighbouring farm, but Eddie was able to buy the house and the woodland for a song. He resigned from the Navy and got a well-paid job with Pan American Airways System.

In between flights he worked on the old house, installing plumbing and electricity and a water heater, doing the work himself and paying for the materials out of his engineer's wages. He got electric heaters for the bedrooms, a radio and even a telephone. Then he found Carol-Ann. Soon, he had thought, the house would be filled with the laughter of children, and then his dream would have come true.

Instead it had turned into a nightmare.

CHAPTER FOUR

THE FIRST words Mark Alder said to Diana Lovesey were, 'My goodness, you're the nicest thing I've seen all day.'

People said that sort of thing to her all the time. She was pretty and vivacious, and she loved to dress well. That night she was wearing a long turquoise dress with little lapels, a shirred bodice and short sleeves gathered at the elbow, and she knew she looked wonderful.

She was at the Midland Hotel in Manchester, attending a dinner-dance. She was not sure whether it was the Chamber of Commerce, the Freemasons' ladies' night, or the Red Cross fund-raiser: the same people were at all such functions. She had danced with most of her husband Mervyn's business associates, who had held her too close and trodden on her toes, and all of their wives had glared daggers at her. It was strange, Diana thought, that when a man made a bit of a fool of himself over a pretty girl, his wife always hated the girl for it, not the man. It was not as if Diana had designs on any of their pompous, whisky-soaked husbands.

She had scandalized them all and embarrassed her husband by teaching the deputy mayor to jitterbug.

Now, feeling the need of a break, she had slipped into the hotel bar on the pretence of buying cigarettes.

He was there alone, sipping a small cognac, and he looked up at her as though she had brought sunshine into the room. He was a small, neat man with a boyish smile and an American accent. His remark seemed spontaneous and he had a charming manner, so she smiled radiantly at him, but she did not speak. She bought cigarettes and drank a glass of iced water, then returned to the dance.

He must have asked the barman who she was, and found her address somehow, for the next day she got a note from him, on Midland Hotel writing paper.

Actually, it was a poem.

It began:

> Fixed in my heart, the picture of your smile
> Engraven, ever present to mind's eye
> Not pain, nor years, nor sorrow can defile

It made her cry.

She cried because of everything she had hoped for and never achieved. She cried because she lived in a grimy industrial city with a husband who hated to take holidays. She cried because the poem was the only gracious, romantic thing that had happened to her for five years. And she cried because she was no longer in love with Mervyn.

After that it happened very quickly.

The next day was Sunday. She went into town on the Monday. Normally she would have gone first to Boots to change her book at the Circulating Library, then bought a combined lunch-and-matinée ticket for two shillings and sixpence at the Paramount Cinema in Oxford Street. After the film she would have walked around Lewis's department store and Finnigan's, and bought ribbons, or napkins, or gifts for her sister's children. She might have gone to one of the little shops in the Shambles to buy some exotic cheese or special ham for Mervyn. Then she would have taken the train back to Altrincham, the suburb where she lived, in time to get the supper.

This time, she had coffee in the bar of the Midland Hotel, lunch in the German restaurant in the basement of the Midland Hotel, and afternoon tea in the lounge of the Midland Hotel. But she did not see the charming man with the American accent.

She went home feeling heartsick. That was ridiculous, she told herself. She had met him for less than a minute and had never said a word to him! He had seemed to symbolize everything she felt was missing from her life. But if she saw him again she would surely discover that he was boorish, insane, diseased, smelly, or all of those things.

She got off the train and walked along the street of large suburban villas where she lived. As she approached her own home, she was shocked and flustered to see him walking towards her, looking at her house with a pretence of idle curiosity.

She flushed scarlet and her heart raced. He, too, was startled. He stopped, but she carried on walking. Then, as she passed him, she said, 'Meet me in the Central Library tomorrow morning!'

She did not expect him to reply, but – she would learn later – he had a quick, humorous mind and he immediately said, 'What section?'

It was a big library, although not so big that two people could lose one another for long; but she said the first thing that came into her mind. 'Biology.' And he laughed.

She entered her house with that laugh in her ears: a warm, relaxed, delighted laugh, the laugh of a man who loved life and felt good about himself.

The house was empty. Mrs Rollins, who did the housework, had already left and Mervyn was not home yet. Diana sat in the modern hygienic kitchen and thought old-fashioned unhygienic thoughts about her humorous American poet.

The next morning she found him sitting at a table under a notice that read SILENCE. When she said, 'Hello,' he put a finger to his lips, pointed to a chair, and wrote her a note.

It said: *I love your hat.*

She had a little hat like an upturned flower-pot with a brim, and she wore it tilted all the way over to one side so that it almost covered her left eye: it was the current fashion, although few women in Manchester had the nerve for it.

She took a little pen from her bag and wrote underneath: *It wouldn't suit you.*

But my geraniums would look perfect in it, he wrote.

She giggled, and he said, 'Shhh!'

Diana thought, Is he mad, or just funny?

She wrote, *I love your poem.*

Then he wrote, *I love you.*

Mad, she thought, but tears came to her eyes. She wrote, *I don't even know your name!*

He gave her a business card. His name was Mark Alder, and he lived in Los Angeles.

California!

They went for early lunch to a VEM restaurant – Vegetables, Eggs and Milk – because she could be sure she would not run into her husband there: wild horses could not have dragged him into a vegetarian restaurant. Then, as it was Tuesday, there was a midday concert at the Houldsworth Hall in Deansgate, with the city's famous Hallé Orchestra and its new conductor, Malcolm Sargent. Diana felt proud that her city could offer such a cultural treat to a visitor.

That day she learned that Mark was a writer of comedy scripts for radio shows. She had never heard of the people he wrote for, but he said they were famous: Jack Benny, Fred Allen, Amos 'n' Andy. He also owned a radio station. He wore a cashmere blazer. He was on an extended holiday, tracing his roots: his family had come originally from Liverpool, the port city a few miles west of Manchester. He was not much taller than Diana, and about her age, with hazel eyes and a few freckles.

And he was pure delight.

He was intelligent, funny and charming. His manners were nice, his fingernails were clean and his clothes were neat. He liked Mozart but he knew about Louis Armstrong. Most of all, he liked Diana.

It was a peculiar thing how few men actually liked women, she thought. The men she knew would fawn on her, try to paw her, suggest discreet assignations when Mervyn's back was turned, and sometimes, when they got maudlin drunk, declare their love for her. But they didn't really like her: their conversation was all banter, they never listened to her and they knew nothing about her. Mark was quite different, as she found out during the following days and weeks.

The day after they met in the library, he rented a car and drove her to the coast where they ate sandwiches on a breezy beach and kissed in the shelter of the dunes.

He had a suite at the Midland, but they could not meet there because Diana was too well known: if she had been seen going upstairs after lunch the news would have been all around town by teatime. However, Mark's inventive mind produced a solution. They drove to the seaside town of Lytham St Anne's, taking a suitcase, and checked into a hotel as Mr and Mrs Alder. They had lunch, then went to bed.

Making love with Mark was such fun.

The first time, he made a pantomime of trying to undress in complete silence, and she was laughing too much to feel shy as she took off her clothes. She did not worry about whether he would like her: he obviously adored her. She was not nervous because he was so nice.

They spent the afternoon in bed, and then checked out, saying they had changed their minds about staying. Mark paid in full for the night so that there was no bad feeling. He dropped her at a station one stop down the line from Altrincham and she arrived home by train just as if she had spent the afternoon in Manchester.

They did this all the blissful summer.

He was supposed to go back to the States at the beginning of August to work on a new show but he stayed and wrote a series of sketches about an American on holiday in Britain, sending his scripts over every week by the new airmail service operated by Pan American.

Despite this reminder that time was running out for them, Diana managed not to think about the future much. Of course Mark would go home one day, but he would still be here tomorrow and that was as far ahead as she cared to look. It was like the war: everyone knew it would be awful, but nobody could tell when it would start, and until it happened there was nothing to do but carry on and try to have a good time.

The day after war broke out he told her he was going home.

She was sitting up in bed with the covers pulled up just under her bust, so that her breasts showed: Mark loved her to sit like that. He thought her breasts were wonderful, although she felt they were too large.

They were having a serious conversation. Britain had declared war on Germany, and even happy lovers had to talk about it. Diana had been following the grisly conflict in China all year, and the thought of war in Europe filled her with dread. Like the Fascists in Spain, the Japanese did not scruple to drop bombs on women and children; and the carnage in Chungking and Ichang had been sickening.

She asked Mark the question that was on everyone's lips. 'What do you think will happen?'

For once he did not have a funny answer. 'I think it's going to be awful,' he said solemnly. 'I believe Europe will be devastated. Maybe this country will survive, being an island. I hope so.'

'Oh,' Diana said. Suddenly, she was frightened. British people were not saying things like that. The newspapers were full of fighting talk, and Mervyn was positively looking forward to war. But Mark was an outsider, and his judgement, delivered in that relaxed American voice, sounded worryingly realistic. Would bombs be dropped on Manchester?

She remembered something Mervyn had said, and repeated it. 'America will have to come into the war sooner or later.'

Mark shocked her by saying, 'Christ, I hope not. This is a European squabble, nothing to do with us. I can just about see why Britain declared war, but I'm damned if I want to see Americans die defending fucking Poland.'

She had never heard him swear like this. Sometimes he whispered obscenities in her ear while they were making love, but that was different. Now he seemed angry. She thought perhaps he was a little frightened.

She knew Mervyn was frightened: in him it came out as reckless optimism. Mark's fear showed as isolationism and cursing.

She was dismayed by his attitude, but she could see his point of view: Why *should* Americans go to war for Poland, or even for Europe? 'But what about me?' she said. She tried for a note of levity. 'You wouldn't like me to be raped by blond Nazis in gleaming jackboots, would you?' It wasn't very funny and she regretted it immediately.

That was when he took an envelope out of his suitcase and handed it to her.

She pulled out a ticket and looked at it. Suddenly she was terrified. 'You're going home!' she cried. It was like the end of the world.

Looking solemn, he said simply, 'There are two tickets.'

She felt as if her heart would stop. 'Two tickets,' she repeated tonelessly. She was disoriented and strangely frightened.

He sat on the bed beside her and took her hand. She knew what he was going to say, and she was at the same time thrilled and terrified.

'Come home with me, Diana,' he said. 'Fly to New York with me. Then come to Reno and get divorced. Then let's go to California and be married. I love you.'

Fly. She could hardly imagine flying across the Atlantic Ocean: such things belonged in fairy tales.

To New York. New York was a dream of skyscrapers and nightclubs, gangsters and millionaires, fashionable heiresses and enormous cars.

And get divorced. And be free of Mervyn!

Then let's go to California. Where movies were made, and oranges grew on trees, and the sun shone every day.

And be married. And have Mark all the time, every day, every night.

She was unable to speak.

Mark said, 'We could have babies.'

She wanted to cry.

'Ask me again,' she whispered.

He said, 'I love you, will you marry me, and have my children?'

'Oh, yes,' she said, and she felt as if she were already flying. 'Yes, yes, yes!'

She had to tell Mervyn that night.

It was Monday. On Tuesday she would have to travel to Southampton with Mark. The Clipper left on Wednesday at 2 p.m.

She was floating on air when she arrived home on Monday afternoon but as soon as she entered the house her euphoria evaporated.

How was she going to tell him?

It was a nice house: a big new villa, white with a red roof. It had four bedrooms, three of which were almost never used, a nice modern bathroom and a kitchen with all the latest gadgets. Now that she was leaving it, she looked at it with nostalgic fondness: it had been her home for five years.

She prepared Mervyn's meals herself. Mrs Rollins

did the cleaning and laundry and if Diana had not cooked she would have had nothing to do. Besides, Mervyn was a working-class boy at heart and he liked his wife to put his meal on the table when he came home. He even called the meal 'tea', and he would drink tea with it, although it was always something substantial – sausages or steak or a meat pie. For Mervyn, 'dinner' was served in hotels. At home you had tea.

What would she say?

Today he would have cold beef, left over from Sunday's roast. Diana put on an apron and began to slice potatoes for frying. When she thought of how angry Mervyn was going to be her hands shook, and she cut her finger with the vegetable knife.

She tried to get a grip on herself as she washed the wound under the cold tap, dried it with a towel and wrapped a bandage round it. What am I afraid of? she asked herself. He won't kill me. He can't stop me: I'm over twenty-one and it's a free country.

The thought did not calm her nerves.

She set the table and washed a lettuce. Although Mervyn worked hard, he almost always came home at the same time. He would say, 'What's the point of being the boss if I have to stop at work when everyone else goes home?' He was an engineer and had a factory that made all kinds of rotors, from small fans for cooling systems to huge screws for ocean liners. Mervyn had always been successful – he was a good businessman – but he hit the jackpot when he started manufacturing propellers for aircraft. Flying was his hobby and he had his own small plane, a Tiger Moth, at an airfield outside town. When the government started to build up the Air Force, two or three years ago, very few people knew how to make curved rotors with mathematical precision but Mervyn was one of those few. Since then, business had boomed.

Diana was his second wife. The first had left him, seven years ago, and run off with another man, taking their two children. Mervyn had divorced her as quickly as he could and had proposed to Diana as soon as the divorce came through. Diana was then twenty-eight and he was thirty-eight. He was attractive, masculine and prosperous, and he worshipped her. His wedding present to her had been a diamond necklace.

A few weeks ago, on their fifth wedding anniversary, he had given her a sewing machine.

Looking back, she could see that the sewing machine had been the last straw. She had been hoping for a car of her own: she could drive and Mervyn could afford it. When she saw the sewing machine she felt she had come to the end of her tether. They had been together for five years and he had not noticed that she never sewed.

She knew that Mervyn loved her, but he did not *see* her. In his vision there was just a person marked 'wife'. She was pretty, she performed her social role adequately, she put his food on the table, and she was always willing in bed. What else should a wife be? He never consulted her about anything. Since she was neither a businessman nor an engineer, it never occurred to him that she had a brain. He talked to the men at his factory more seriously than he talked to her. In his world, men wanted cars and wives wanted sewing machines.

And yet he was very clever. The son of a lathe operator, he had gone to Manchester Grammar School and had studied physics at Manchester University. He had had the opportunity to go on to Cambridge and take his master's degree, but he was not the academic type and he found a job in the design department of a large engineering company. He still followed developments in physics and would talk endlessly to his father – but never to Diana, of course – about atoms and radiation and nuclear fission.

Unfortunately, Diana did not understand physics anyway. She knew a lot about music and literature and a little about history but Mervyn was not much interested in culture, although he liked films and dance music. So they had nothing to talk about.

It might have been different if they had had children. But Mervyn already had two children by his first wife and he did not want any more. Diana had been willing to love them, but she had never been given the chance: their mother had poisoned their minds against Diana, pretending that she had caused the break-up of the marriage. Diana's sister in Liverpool had cute little twin girls with pigtails and Diana lavished all her maternal affection on them.

She was going to miss the twins.

Mervyn enjoyed an energetic social life with the city's leading businessmen and politicians, and for a while Diana enjoyed being his hostess. She had always loved beautiful clothes and she wore them well. But there had to be more to life than that.

For a while she had played the role of the nonconformist of Manchester society – smoking cigars, dressing extravagantly, talking about free love and Communism. She had enjoyed shocking the matrons, but Manchester was not a highly conservative place, and Mervyn and his friends were Liberals, so she had not caused much of a stir.

She was discontented, but she wondered whether she had the right. Most women thought her lucky: she had a sober, reliable, generous husband, a lovely home, and crowds of friends. She told herself she ought to be happy. But she was not – and then Mark came along.

She heard Mervyn's car pull up outside. It was such a familiar noise but tonight it sounded ominous, like the growl of a dangerous beast.

She put the frying-pan on the gas stove with a shaking hand.

Mervyn came into the kitchen.

He was breathtakingly handsome. There was grey in his dark hair now, but it only made him look more distinguished. He was tall and had not got fat like most of his friends. He had no vanity but Diana made him wear well-cut dark suits and expensive white shirts, because she liked him to look as successful as he was.

She was terrified he would see the guilt on her face and demand to know what was the matter.

He kissed her mouth. Full of shame, she kissed him back. Sometimes he would embrace her and press his hand into the cleft of her buttocks, and they would become passionate, so that they had to hurry to the bedroom and leave the food to burn. But that did not happen much any more, and today was no exception, thank God.

He took off his jacket, waistcoat, tie and collar, and rolled up his sleeves; then he washed his hands and face at the kitchen sink. He had broad shoulders and strong arms.

He had not sensed that anything was wrong. He would not, of course: he did not *see* her, she was just there, like the kitchen table. She had no need to worry. He would not know anything until she told him.

I won't tell him yet, she thought.

While the potatoes were frying she buttered the bread and made a pot of tea. She was still shaky, but she hid it. Mervyn read the *Manchester Evening News* and hardly looked at her.

'I've got a bloody troublemaker at the works,' he said as she put the plate in front of him.

I couldn't care less, Diana thought hysterically. I'm nothing to do with you any more.

Then why have I cooked your tea?

'He's a Londoner, from Battersea, and I think he's a Communist. Anyway, he's asking for higher rates for working on the new jig borer. It's not unreasonable, really, but I've priced the job based on the old rates, so he'll have to put up with it.'

Diana screwed up her nerve and said, 'I've got something to tell you.' Then she wished fervently that she could take the words back, but it was too late.

'What did you do to your finger?' he asked, noticing the little bandage.

This commonplace question deflated her. 'Nothing,' she said, slumping into her chair. 'I cut it slicing potatoes.' She picked up her knife and fork.

Mervyn ate heartily. 'I should be more careful who I take on but the trouble is, good toolmakers are hard to come by nowadays.'

She was not expected to respond when he talked about his business. If she made a suggestion, he would give her an irritated look as if she had spoken out of turn. She was there to listen.

While he talked about the new jig borer and the Battersea Communist she remembered their wedding day. Her mother had been alive then. They had got married in Manchester, and the reception had been held at the Midland Hotel. Mervyn in morning dress had been the handsomest man in England. Diana had thought it was for ever. The idea that the marriage might not last had not crossed her mind. She had never met a divorced person before Mervyn. Recalling how she felt then, she wanted to cry.

She also knew that Mervyn would be shattered by her leaving. He had no idea of what was in her mind. The fact that his first wife had left him in exactly the same way made it worse. He was going to be distraught. But first he would be furious.

He finished his beef and poured himself another cup of tea. 'You haven't eaten much,' he said. In fact she had not eaten anything.

'I had a big lunch,' she replied.

'Where did you go?'

The innocent question threw her into a panic. She had eaten sandwiches in bed with Mark at a hotel in Blackpool, and she could not think of a plausible lie. The names of the principal restaurants in Manchester came to mind, but it was possible that Mervyn had had lunch in one of those. After a painful pause she said, 'The Waldorf Café.' There were several Waldorf Cafés – it was a chain of inexpensive restaurants where you could get steak and chips for one shilling and ninepence.

Mervyn did not ask her which one.

She picked up the plates and stood up. Her knees felt so weak she was afraid she would fall down, but she made it to the sink. 'Do you want a sweet?' she asked him.

'Yes, please.'

She went to the pantry and found a can of pears and some condensed milk. She opened the tins and brought his dessert to the table.

Watching him eat canned pears, she was swamped by a sense of the horror of what she was about to do. It seemed unforgivably destructive. Like the coming war, it would smash everything. The life that she and Mervyn had created together in this house, in this city, would be ruined.

She suddenly realized she could not do it.

Mervyn put down his spoon and looked at his fob watch. 'Half-past seven – let's tune in to the news.'

'I can't do it,' Diana said aloud.

'What?'

'I can't do it,' she said again. She would call the whole thing off. She would go and see Mark now and tell him she had changed her mind, she was not going to run away with him after all.

'Why can't you listen to the wireless?' Mervyn asked impatiently.

Diana stared at him. She was tempted to tell him the whole truth, but she did not have the nerve for that either. 'I have to go out,' she said. She cast about frantically for an excuse. 'Doris Williams is in hospital and I ought to visit her.'

'Who's Doris Williams, for heaven's sake?'

There was no such person. 'You have met her,' Diana said, improvising wildly. 'She's had an operation.'

'I don't remember her,' he said, but he was not suspicious: he had a bad memory for casual acquaintances.

Diana was inspired to say, 'Do you want to come with me?'

'Good God, no!' he said, as she had known he would.

'I'll drive myself, then.'

'Don't go too fast in the blackout.' He got up and went through to the sitting room where the wireless was.

Diana stared after him for a moment. He'll never know how close I came to leaving him, she thought with a kind of sadness.

She put on a hat and went out with her coat over her arm. The car started first time, thank God.

She steered out of the drive and turned towards Manchester.

The journey was a nightmare. She was in a desperate rush, but she had to crawl along because her headlights were masked and she could see only a few yards in front – and besides, her vision was blurred because she could not stop crying. If she had not known the road well she would probably have crashed.

The distance was less than ten miles but it took her more than an hour.

When she finally stopped the car outside the Midland she was exhausted. She sat still for a minute, trying to compose herself. She took out her compact and powdered her face to hide the signs of tears.

Mark would be broken-hearted, she knew, but he could bear it. He would soon come to look back on this as a summer romance. It was less cruel to end a short, passionate love affair than to break up a five-year marriage. She and Mark would always look back on the summer of 1939 fondly—

She burst into tears again.

It was no use sitting here thinking about it, she decided after a while. She had to go in and get it over with. She repaired her make-up again and got out of the car.

She walked through the lobby of the hotel and went up the staircase without stopping at the desk. She knew Mark's room number. It was, of course, quite scandalous for a woman alone to go to a single man's hotel room, but she had to take the risk. The alternative would have been to see Mark in the lounge or the bar, and it was unthinkable to give him this kind of news in a public place. She did not look around her, so she did not know whether she had been seen by anyone she knew.

She tapped on his door, praying that he would be there. What if he had decided to go out to a restaurant, or to see a film? There was no reply, and she knocked again, harder. How could he go to the cinema at a time like this?

Then she heard his voice. 'Hello?'

She knocked again and said, 'It's me!'

She heard rapid footsteps. The door was flung open and Mark stood there, looking startled. He smiled happily, drew her inside, closed the door, and embraced her.

Now she felt as disloyal to him as she had to Mervyn earlier. She kissed him guiltily, and the familiar warmth of desire glowed in her veins; but she pulled away and said, 'I can't go with you.'

He paled. 'Don't say that.'

She looked around the suite. He was packing. The wardrobe and drawers were open, his cases were on the floor and everywhere there were folded shirts, tidy piles of underwear and shoes in bags. He was so neat. 'I can't go,' she repeated.

He took her hand and drew her into the bedroom. They sat on the bed. He looked distraught. 'You don't mean this,' he said.

'Mervyn loves me, and we've been together for five years. I can't do this to him.'

'What about me?'

She looked at him. He was wearing a dusty-pink sweater and a bow tie, blue-grey flannel trousers and cordovan shoes. He looked good enough to eat. 'You both love me,' she said. 'But he's my husband.'

'We both love you, but I *like* you,' Mark said.

'Don't you think he likes me?'

'I don't think he even knows you. Listen. I'm thirty-five years old, I've been in love before, I once had an affair that lasted six years. I've never been married but I've been around. I *know* this is right. Nothing has ever felt so right to me. You're beautiful, you're funny, you're unorthodox, you're bright, and you love to make love. I'm cute, I'm funny, I'm unorthodox, I'm bright, and I want to make love to you right now—'

'No,' she said, but she did not mean it.

He drew her to him gently and they kissed.

'We're so right for each other,' he murmured. 'Remember writing notes to one another underneath the SILENCE sign? You understood the game, right away, without explanations. Other women think I'm nuts, but you like me this way.'

It was true, she thought, and when she did odd things, like smoking a pipe, or going out with no panties on, or attending Fascist meetings and sounding the fire alarm, Mervyn became annoyed, whereas Mark laughed delightedly.

He stroked her hair, then her cheek. Slowly her panic subsided and she began to feel soothed. She laid her head on his shoulder and let her lips brush the soft skin of his neck. She felt his fingertips on her leg, beneath her dress, stroking the inside of her thigh where her stockings ended. This was not what was supposed to happen, she thought weakly.

He pushed her gently backwards on the bed, and her hat fell off. 'This isn't right,' she said feebly. He kissed her mouth, nibbling her lips gently with his own. She felt his fingers through the fine silk of her panties, and she shuddered with pleasure. After a moment his hand slid inside.

He knew just what to do.

One day early in the summer, as they lay naked in a hotel bedroom with the sound of the waves coming through the open window, he had said, 'Show me what you do when you touch yourself.'

She had been embarrassed, and pretended not to understand. 'What do you mean?'

'You know. When you touch yourself. Show me. Then I'll know what you like.'

'I don't touch myself,' she lied.

'Well . . . when you were a girl, before you were married – you must have done it then, everyone does. Show me what you used to do.'

She was about to refuse, then she thought how sexy it would be. 'You want me to stimulate myself – down there – while you watch?' she said, and her voice was thick with desire.

He grinned wickedly and nodded.

'You mean . . . all the way?'

'All the way.'

'I couldn't,' she said, but she did.

Now his fingertips touched her knowingly, in exactly the right places, with the same familiar motion and just the right pressure. She closed her eyes and gave herself up to the sensation.

After a while she began to moan softly and raise and lower her hips rhythmically. She felt his warm breath on her face as he leaned closer to her. Then, just as she was losing control, he said urgently, 'Look at me.'

She opened her eyes. He continued to caress her in exactly the same way, just a little faster. 'Don't close your eyes,' he said. Looking into his eyes while he did that was shockingly intimate, a kind of hyper-nakedness. It was as if he could see everything and know everything about her, and she felt an exhilarating freedom because she had nothing left to hide. The climax came, and she forced herself to hold his gaze while her hips jerked and she grimaced and gasped with the spasms of pleasure that shook her body, and he smiled down at her all the while and said, 'I love you, Diana, I love you so much.'

When it was over she grabbed him and held him, panting and shaking with emotion, feeling that she never wanted to let go. She would have wept, but she had no tears left.

She never did tell Mervyn.

Mark's inventive mind came up with the solution, and she rehearsed it as she drove home, calm and collected and quietly determined.

Mervyn was in his pyjamas and dressing-gown, smoking a cigarette and listening to music on the wireless. 'That were a bloody long visit,' he said mildly.

Only a little nervous, Diana said, 'I had to drive terribly slowly.' She swallowed, took a deep breath, and said, 'I'm going away tomorrow.'

He was faintly surprised. 'Where to?'

'I'd like to visit Thea and see the twins. I want to make sure she's all right, and there's no telling when I'll get another chance – the trains are already becoming irregular and petrol rationing starts next week.'

He nodded assent. 'Aye, you're right. Better go now while you can.'

'I'll go up and pack a case.'

'Pack one for me, will you?'

For an awful moment she thought he wanted to go with her. 'What for?' she said, aghast.

'I'll not sleep in an empty house,' he said. 'I'll stop at the Reform Club tomorrow night. You'll be back Wednesday?'

'Yes, Wednesday,' she lied.

'All right.'

She went upstairs. As she put his underwear and socks into a small suitcase, she thought, It's the last time I'll ever do this for him. She folded a white shirt and picked out a silver-grey tie: sombre colours suited his dark hair and brown eyes. She was relieved that he had accepted her story, but she also felt frustrated, as if there were something she had left undone. Although she was terrified of confronting him, she also wanted to explain why she was leaving him. She needed to tell him that he had let her down, he had become overbearing and thoughtless, he no longer cherished her as he once had. But now she never would say those things to him, and she felt oddly disappointed.

She closed his case and began to put make-up and toiletries into her sponge bag. It seemed a funny way to end five years of marriage, packing socks and toothpaste and cold cream.

After a while he came upstairs. The packing was all done and she was in her least attractive nightdress, sitting in front of her dressing-table mirror, taking off her make-up. He came up behind her and grasped her breasts.

Oh, no, she thought, not tonight, please!

Although she was horrified, her body responded immediately and she blushed guiltily. Mervyn's fingers squeezed her swelling nipples and she drew in her breath in a small gasp of pleasure and despair. He took her hands and drew her up. She followed helplessly as he led her to the bed. He turned out the light and they lay down in pitch blackness. He mounted her immediately and made love to her with a kind of furious desperation, almost as if he knew she was going away from him and there was nothing he could do about it. Her body betrayed her and she thrilled with pleasure and shame. She realized with mortification that she would have reached orgasm with two men in two hours, and she tried to stop herself, but she could not.

When she came, she cried.

Fortunately, Mervyn did not notice.

*

Sitting in the elegant lounge of the South-Western Hotel on Wednesday morning, waiting for a taxi to take her and Mark to Berth 108 in Southampton Docks to board the Pan American Clipper, she felt triumphant and free.

Everyone in the room was either looking at her or trying not to look at her. She was getting a particularly hard stare from a handsome man in a blue suit who must be ten years younger than she was. But she was used to that. It always happened when she looked good, and today she was stunning. Her cream and red spotted silk dress was fresh, summery and striking. Her cream shoes were right and the straw hat finished off the outfit perfectly. Her lipstick and nail varnish were orange-red like the spots on the dress. She had thought about red shoes but decided they would look tarty.

She loved travelling: packing and unpacking her clothes, meeting new people, being pampered and cosseted and plied with champagne and food, and seeing new places. She was nervous about flying but crossing the Atlantic was the most glamorous voyage of all, for at the other end was America. She could hardly wait to get there. She had a film-goer's picture of what it was like: she saw herself in an art-deco apartment, all windows and mirrors, a uniformed maid helping her put on a white fur coat, and a long black car in the street outside with its engine running and a coloured chauffeur waiting to take her to a nightclub, where she would order a martini, very dry, and dance to a jazz band that had Bing Crosby as its singer. That was a fantasy, she knew, but she could hardly wait to discover the reality.

She felt ambivalent about leaving Britain just as the war was starting. It seemed a cowardly thing to do, yet she was thrilled to be going.

She knew a lot of Jewish people. Manchester had a big Jewish community; they had planted a thousand trees in Nazareth. Diana's Jewish friends watched the progress of events in Europe with horror and dread. It was not just the Jews, either: the Fascists hated the coloureds, and the gypsies, and the queers, and anyone else who disagreed with Fascism. Diana had an uncle who was queer and he had always been kind to her and treated her like a daughter.

She was too old to join up, but she probably ought to stay in Manchester and do voluntary work, winding bandages for the Red Cross . . .

That was a fantasy, even more unlikely than dancing to Bing Crosby. She was not the type to wind bandages. Austerity and uniforms did not suit her.

But none of that was truly important. The only thing that counted was that she was in love. She would go where Mark was. She would have followed him into the heart of a battlefield if necessary. They were going to get married and have children. He was going home, and she was going with him.

She would miss her twin nieces. She wondered how long it would be before she would see them. They might be grown up next time, wearing perfume and brassières instead of ankle socks and pigtails.

But she might have little girls of her own . . .

She was thrilled about travelling on the Pan American Clipper. She had read all about it in the *Manchester Guardian,* never dreaming that one day she would actually fly in it. To get to New York in little more than a day seemed like a miracle.

She had written Mervyn a note. It did not say any of the things she wanted to tell him, did not explain how he had slowly and inexorably lost her love through carelessness and indifference, did not even say that Mark was wonderful. *Dear Mervyn,* she had written, *I am leaving you. I feel you have become cold towards me, and I have fallen in love with someone else. By the time you read this we will be in America. I am sorry to hurt you but it is partly your fault.* She could not think of an appropriate way to sign off – she could not write 'yours' or 'with love' – so she just put, *Diana.*

At first she had intended to leave the note in the house on the kitchen table. Then she had become obsessed by the possibility that he would change his plans, and instead of staying at his club on Tuesday night he would go home, find the note, and make some kind of trouble for her and Mark before they were out of the country. So in the end she had mailed it to him at the factory where it would arrive today.

She looked at her wristwatch (a present from Mervyn, who liked her to be punctual). She knew his routine: he spent most of the morning on the factory floor, then towards midday he would go up to his office and look through the mail before going to lunch. She had marked the envelope 'Personal' so that his secretary would not open it. It would be lying on his desk in a pile of invoices, orders, letters and memos. He would be reading it about now. The thought made her guilty and sad, but also relieved that she was two hundred miles away.

'Our taxi's here,' Mark said.

She felt a little nervous. Across the Atlantic in a plane!

'Time to go,' he said.

She suppressed her anxiety. She put down her coffee cup, stood up, and gave him her brightest smile. 'Yes,' she said happily. 'Time to fly.'

Eddie had always been shy with girls.

He had graduated from Annapolis a virgin. When he was stationed at Pearl Harbor he had gone with prostitutes, and that experience had left him with a sense of self-disgust. After leaving the Navy he had been a loner, driving to a bar a few miles away any time he felt the need of companionship. Carol-Ann was a ground hostess working for the airline at Port Washington, the New York terminal for flying boats. She was a suntanned blonde with eyes of Pan American blue, and Eddie would never have dared to ask her for a date. But one day in the canteen a young radio operator gave him two tickets to *Life with Father* on Broadway, and when he said he did not have anyone to take, the radioman turned to the next table and asked Carol-Ann if she wanted to go.

'Ayuh,' she said, and Eddie realized she was from his part of the world.

He later learned that at that time she had been desperately lonely. She was a country girl, and the sophisticated ways of New Yorkers made her anxious and tense. She was a sensual person, but she did not know what to do when men took liberties, so in her embarrassment she rebuffed advances indignantly. Her nervousness got her the reputation of an ice queen and she was not often asked out.

But Eddie knew nothing of this at the time. He felt like a king with her on his arm. He took her to dinner, then back to her apartment in a taxi. On the doorstep he thanked her for a nice evening and screwed up his courage to kiss her cheek, whereupon she burst into tears and said he was the first decent man she had met in New York. Before he knew what he was saying he had asked her for another date.

He fell in love with her on that second date. They went to Coney Island on a hot Friday in July, and she wore white slacks and a sky-blue blouse. He realized, to his astonishment, that she was actually proud to be seen walking alongside him. They ate ice cream, rode a roller-coaster called the Cyclone, bought silly hats, held hands, and revealed trivial intimate secrets. When he took her home Eddie told her frankly that he had never been this happy in his entire life, and she astonished him again by saying she hadn't either.

Soon he was neglecting the farmhouse and spending all his leave in New York, sleeping on the couch of a surprised but encouraging fellow engineer. Carol-Ann took him to Bristol, New Hampshire, to meet her parents, two small, thin, middle-aged people, poor and hard-working. They reminded him of his own parents, but without the unforgiving religion. They could hardly believe they had produced a daughter so beautiful and Eddie understood how they felt, for he could hardly believe such a girl could have fallen in love with him.

He thought of how much he loved her as he stood in the grounds of the Langdown Lawn Hotel, staring at the bark of the oak tree. He was in a nightmare, one of those hellish dreams in which you start by feeling safe and happy but you think, in a fit of idle speculation, of the worst thing that could occur and suddenly it is actually happening, the worst thing in the world is actually, unstoppably, terrifyingly happening, and there is nothing you can do about it.

What made it even more terrible was that they had quarrelled just before he left home, and had parted without making it up.

She had been sitting on the couch, wearing a denim work shirt that belonged to him and not much else, her long sun-tanned legs stretched out in front, her fine fair hair lying across her shoulders like a shawl. She was reading a magazine. Her breasts were normally quite small but lately they had swollen. He felt an urge to touch them, and he thought, Why not? So he slid his hand inside the shirt and touched her nipple. She looked up at him and smiled lovingly, then went on with her reading.

He kissed the top of her head then sat down next to her. She had astonished him right from the start. They were both shy at first, but soon after they returned from their honeymoon holiday and started living together here in the old farmhouse, she had become wildly uninhibited.

First, she wanted to make love with the light on. Eddie felt awkward about it, but he consented, and he kind of liked it although he felt bashful. Then he noticed that she did not lock the door when she took a bath. After that he felt foolish about locking the door himself, so he did the same as her, and one day she just walked in with no clothes on and got right in the tub with him! Eddie had never felt so embarrassed in his life. No woman had seen him naked since he was about four years old. He got an enormous hard-on just watching Carol-Ann wash her underarms, and he covered his dick with a flannel until she laughed him out of it.

She started walking around the farmhouse in various states of undress. The way she was now, this was nothing, she was practically overdressed by her standards, you could only just see a little white triangle of cotton at the top of her legs where the shirt did not quite cover her panties. She was normally much worse. He would be making coffee in the kitchen and she would come in wearing nothing but her underwear and start toasting muffins; or he would be shaving and she would appear in her panties, with no brassière, and just brush her teeth like that; or she would come into the bedroom stark naked with his breakfast on a tray. He wondered if she was 'oversexed' – he had heard people use that term. But he also liked her to be this way. He liked it a lot. He had never dreamed he would have a beautiful wife who would walk around his house undressed. He felt so lucky.

Living with her for a year had changed him. He had gotten so uninhibited that he would walk naked from the bedroom to the bathroom; sometimes he did not even put on his pyjamas before getting into bed; once he even took her here in the living room, right on that couch.

He still wondered whether there was something psychologically abnormal about this kind of behaviour, but he had decided that it did not matter: he and Carol-Ann could do anything they liked. When he accepted that, he felt like a bird let out of a cage. It was incredible; it was wonderful; it was like being in heaven.

He sat beside her, saying nothing, just enjoying being with her and smelling the mild breeze coming in from the woods through the open windows. His bag was packed and in a few minutes he was leaving for Port Washington. Carol-Ann had left Pan American – she could not live in Maine and work in New York – and she had taken a job in a store in Bangor. Eddie wanted to talk to her about that before he left.

Carol-Ann looked up from *Life* magazine and said, 'What?'

'I didn't say anything.'

'But you're going to, aren't you?'

He grinned. 'How did you know?'

'Eddie, you know I can hear when your brain is working. What is it?'

He put his big, blunt hand on her belly and felt the slight swelling there. 'I want you to quit your job.'

'It's too early—'

'It's okay. We can afford it. And I want you to take real good care of yourself.'

'I'll take care of myself. I'll quit work when I need to.'

He felt hurt. 'I thought you'd be pleased. Why do you want to carry on?'

'Because we need the money and I have to have something to do.'

'I told you, we can afford it.'

'I'd get bored.'

'Most wives don't work.'

She raised her voice. 'Eddie, why are you trying to tie me down?'

He did not want to tie her down and the suggestion infuriated him. He said, 'Why are you so determined to go against me?'

'I'm not going against you! I just don't want to sit here like a lumper's helper!'

'Don't you have stuff to do?'

'What?'

'Knit baby clothes, make preserves, take naps—'

She was scornful. 'Oh, for heaven's sake—'

'What's wrong with that, for Christ's sake?' he said crossly.

'There'll be plenty of time for all that when the baby comes. I'd like to enjoy my last few weeks of freedom.'

Eddie felt humiliated but he was not sure how it had

happened. He wanted to get out of there. He looked at his watch. 'I've got a train to catch.'

Carol-Ann looked sad. 'Don't be angry,' she said in a conciliatory tone.

But he was angry. 'I guess I just don't understand you,' he said with irritation.

'I hate to be fenced in.'

'I was trying to be nice.' He stood up and went into the kitchen where his uniform jacket hung on a peg. He felt foolish and wrong-footed. He had set out to do something generous and she saw it as an imposition.

She brought his suitcase from the bedroom and handed it to him when he had his jacket on. She turned up her face and he kissed her briefly.

'Don't go out the door mad at me,' she said.

But he did.

And now he stood in a garden in a foreign country, thousands of miles from her, with a heart as heavy as lead, wondering if he would ever see his Carol-Ann again.

CHAPTER FIVE

For the first time in her life, Nancy Lenehan was putting on weight.

She stood in her suite at the Adelphi Hotel in Liverpool, beside a pile of luggage that was waiting to be taken on board the SS *Oriania*, and gazed, horrified, into the mirror.

She was neither beautiful nor plain, but she had regular features – a straight nose, straight dark hair and a neat chin – and she looked attractive when she dressed carefully, which was most of the time. Today she was wearing a featherweight flannel suit by Paquin, in cerise, with a grey silk blouse. The jacket was fashionably tight-waisted, and it was this that had revealed to her that she was gaining weight. When she fastened the buttons of the jacket, a slight but unmistakable crease appeared, and the lower buttons pulled against the buttonholes.

There was only one explanation for this. The waist of the jacket was smaller than the waist of Mrs Lenehan.

It was probably a result of having lunched and dined at all the best restaurants in Paris throughout August. She sighed. She would diet for the entire transatlantic crossing. When she reached New York she would have her figure back.

She had never had to diet before. The prospect did not trouble her: although she liked good food, she was not greedy. What really worried her was that she suspected it was a sign of age.

Today was her fortieth birthday.

She had always been slender, and she looked good in expensive tailored clothes. She had hated the draped, low-slung fashions of the twenties and rejoiced when waists came back into fashion. She spent a lot of time and money shopping and she enjoyed it. Sometimes she used the excuse that she had to look right because she was in the fashion business, but in truth she did it for pleasure.

Her father had started a shoe factory in Brockton, Massachusetts, outside Boston, in 1899, the year Nancy was born. He had high-class shoes sent over from London and made cheap copies; then he made a selling point out of his plagiarism. His advertisements showed a twenty-nine-dollar London shoe next to a ten-dollar Black's copy and asked, 'Can you tell the difference?' He worked hard and did well, and during the Great War he won the first of the military contracts that were still a staple of the business.

In the twenties he built up a chain of stores, mostly in New England, selling only his shoes. When the depression hit he reduced the number of styles from a thousand to fifty and introduced a standard price of six dollars sixty for every pair of shoes regardless of style.

His audacity paid off, and while everyone else was going broke, Black's profits increased.

He used to say that it cost as much to make bad shoes as good ones, and there was no reason why working people should be poorly shod. At a time when poor folk were buying shoes with cardboard soles that wore out in a few days, Black's boots were cheap and long-lasting. Pa was proud of this, and so was Nancy. For her, the good boots the family made justified the grand Back Bay house they lived in, the big Packard with the chauffeur, their parties and their pretty clothes and their servants. She was not like some of the rich kids, who took inherited wealth for granted.

She wished she could say the same for her brother.

Peter was thirty-eight. When Pa died, five years ago, he left Peter and Nancy equal shares in the company, forty per cent each. Pa's sister, Aunt Tilly, got ten per cent, and the remaining ten went to Danny Riley, his disreputable old lawyer.

Nancy had always assumed she would take over when Pa died. Pa had always favoured her over Peter. A woman running a company was unusual, but not unknown, especially in the clothing industry.

Pa had a deputy, Nat Ridgeway, an able lieutenant who made it clear that he thought he was the best man for the job of chairman of Black's Boots.

But Peter wanted it too, and he was the son. Nancy had always felt guilty about being Pa's favourite. Peter would be humiliated and bitterly disappointed if he did not inherit his father's mantle. Nancy did not have the heart to deal with such a crushing blow so she agreed that Peter should take over. Between them, she and her brother owned eighty per cent of the stock, so when they were in agreement they got their way.

Nat Ridgeway resigned and went to work for General Textiles in New York. He was a loss to the business, but in another way he was a loss to Nancy. Just before Pa died Nat and Nancy had started dating.

Nancy had not dated anyone since her husband Sean died – she had not wanted to – but Nat had picked his time perfectly, for after five years she was beginning to feel that her life was all work and no fun and she was ready for a little romance. They had enjoyed a few quiet dinners and a theatre visit or two, and she had kissed him goodnight, quite warmly. But that was as far as it had gone when the crisis hit, and when Nat left Black's the romance ended too, leaving Nancy feeling cheated.

Since then, he had done spectacularly well at General Textiles, and he was now president of the company. He had also got married, to a pretty blonde woman ten years younger than Nancy.

By contrast, Peter had done badly. The truth was that he was not up to the job. In the five years during which he had been in charge the business had gone steeply downhill. The stores were no longer making a profit, just breaking even. Peter had opened a swanky shoe store on Fifth Avenue in New York, selling expensive fashion shoes for ladies, which took all his time and attention – but it lost money.

Only the factory, which Nancy managed, was making

money. In the mid-thirties, as America came out of the depression, she had started making cheap open-toed sandals for women, and it had turned out to be an immensely popular line. She was convinced that in women's shoes the future lay in light, colourful products that were cheap enough to throw away.

She could sell double the number of shoes she was making, if she had the manufacturing capacity. But her profits were swallowed up by Peter's losses and there was nothing left for expansion.

Nancy knew what had to be done to save the business.

The chain of stores would have to be sold, perhaps to their managers, to raise cash. The money from the sale would be used to modernize the factory and switch to the conveyor-belt style of production, which was being introduced in all the more progressive shoe-manufacturing plants. Peter would have to hand over the reins to her, and confine himself to running his New York store, working within strict cost controls.

She was willing for him to retain the title of chairman and the prestige that went with it, and she would continue to subsidize his store from the factory's profits, within limits; but he would have to give up all real power.

She had put these proposals in a written report, for Peter's eyes only. He had promised to think about it. Nancy had told him, as gently as she could, that the decline of the company could not be allowed to continue, and that if he did not agree to her plan she would have to go over his head to the board – which would inevitably mean that he would be sacked and she would become chairman. She hoped fervently that he would see sense. If he were to provoke a crisis, it was sure to end with a humiliating defeat for him and a family split that might never be repaired.

So far he had not taken offence. He seemed calm and thoughtful, and remained friendly. They decided to go to Paris together. Peter bought fashion shoes for his store, and Nancy shopped for herself at the couturiers and kept an eye on Peter's expenditure. Nancy had loved Europe, Paris especially, and she had been looking forward to London. Then war was declared.

They decided to return to the States immediately – but so did everyone else, of course, and they had terrible trouble getting passage. In the end Nancy got tickets on a ship leaving from Liverpool. After a long journey from Paris by train and ferry they had arrived here yesterday, and they were due to embark today.

She was unnerved by England's war preparations. Yesterday afternoon a bellhop had come to her room and installed an elaborate light-proof screen over the window. All windows had to be completely blacked out every evening, so that the city would not be visible from the air at night. The window panes were criss-crossed with adhesive tape so that splinters of glass would not fly when the city was bombed. There were stacks of sandbags at the front of the hotel and an underground air-raid shelter at the back.

Her terrible fear was that America would get into the war and her sons Liam and Hugh would be conscripted. She remembered Pa saying, when Hitler first came to power, that the Nazis would stop Germany going Communist, and that was the last time she had thought about Hitler. She had too much to do to worry about Europe. She was not interested in international politics, the balance of power, or the rise of Fascism: such abstractions seemed foolish when set against the lives of her sons. The Poles, the Austrians, the Jews and the Slavs would have to take care of themselves. Her job was to take care of Liam and Hugh.

Not that they needed much taking care of. Nancy had married young and had her children right away, so the boys were grown up. Liam was married and living in Houston, and Hugh was in his final year at Yale. He was not studying as hard as he should, and she had been disturbed to learn that he had bought a fast sports car, but he was well past the age of listening to his mother's advice. So, as she could not keep them out of the army, there was not much to draw her home.

She knew that war would be good for business. There would be an economic boom in America, and people would have more money to buy shoes. Whether the USA got into the war or not, the military was bound to be expanded, and that meant increased orders on her government contracts. All in all, she guessed her sales would double and perhaps treble over the next two or three years – another reason for modernizing her factory.

However, all that paled into insignificance beside the glaring, awful possibility that her own sons would be conscripted, to fight and be wounded and perhaps to die in agony on a battlefield.

A porter came for her bags and interrupted her morbid thoughts. She asked the man whether Peter had yet dispatched his luggage. In a thick local accent she could hardly understand he told her that Peter had sent his bags to the ship last night.

She went along to his room to see whether he was ready to leave. When she knocked, the door was opened by a maid, who told her in the same guttural accent that he had left yesterday.

Nancy was puzzled. The two of them had checked in together yesterday evening. Nancy had decided to have dinner in her room and get an early night, and Peter had said he would do the same. If he had changed his mind, where had he gone? Where had he spent the night? And where was he now?

She went down to the lobby to phone, but she was not sure whom to call. Neither she nor Peter knew anybody in England. Liverpool was just across the water from Dublin: could Peter have gone to Ireland, to see the country where the Black family came from? It had been part of their original plan. But Peter would know he could not get back from there in time for the departure of the ship.

On impulse, she asked the operator for Aunt Tilly's number.

Calling America from Europe was a chancy business. There were not enough lines, and sometimes you could wait a long time. If you were lucky you might get through in a few minutes but the sound quality was generally bad and you had to shout.

It was a few minutes before 7 a.m. in Boston, but

Aunt Tilly would be up. Like many older people she slept little and woke early. She was very alert.

The lines were not busy at the moment – perhaps because it was too early for businessmen in the States to be at their desks – and after only five minutes the phone in the booth rang. Nancy picked it up to hear the familiar American ringing tone in her ear. She pictured Aunt Tilly in her silk dressing-gown and fur slippers, padding across the gleaming wood floor of her kitchen to the black telephone in the hall.

'Hello?'

'Aunt Tilly, this is Nancy.'

'My goodness, child, are you all right?'

'I'm fine. They've declared war but the shooting hasn't started yet, at least not in England. Have you heard from the boys?'

'They're both fine. I had a postcard from Liam in Palm Beach, he says Jacqueline is even more beautiful with a suntan. Hugh took me for a ride in his new car, which is very pretty.'

'Does he drive it very fast?'

'He seemed quite careful to me, and he refused a cocktail because he says people shouldn't drive powerful automobiles when they've been drinking.'

'That makes me feel better.'

'Happy birthday, dear! What are you doing in England?'

'I'm in Liverpool, about to take ship for New York, but I've lost Peter. I don't suppose you've heard from him, have you?'

'Why, my dear, of course I have. He's called a board

meeting for the day after tomorrow, first thing in the morning.'

Nancy was mystified. 'You mean Friday morning?'

'Yes, dear, Friday is the day after tomorrow,' Tilly said with a touch of pique. Her tone of voice implied, 'I'm not so old that I don't know what day of the week it is.'

Nancy was baffled. What was the point of calling a board meeting when neither she nor Peter would be there? The only other directors were Tilly and Danny Riley, and they would never decide anything on their own.

This had the marks of a plot. Was Peter up to something?

'What's on the agenda, Aunt?'

'I was just looking it over.' Aunt Tilly read aloud. 'To approve the sale of Black's Boots, Inc., to General Textiles, Inc., on the terms negotiated by the chairman.'

'Good God!' Nancy was so shocked that she felt faint. Peter was selling the company behind her back!

For a moment she was too stunned to speak. Then, with an effort, she said in a shaky voice, 'Would you mind reading that to me again, Aunt?'

Aunt Tilly repeated it.

Nancy suddenly felt cold. How had Peter managed to do this beneath her eyes? When had he negotiated the deal? He must have been working on it surreptitiously ever since she gave him her secret report. While pretending to consider her proposals he had in fact been plotting against her.

She had always known that Peter was weak, but she would never have suspected him of such shameful treachery.

'Are you there, Nancy?'

Nancy swallowed. 'Yes, I'm here. Just dumbstruck. Peter has kept this from me.'

'Really? That's not fair, is it?'

'He obviously wants it passed while I'm away . . . but he won't be at the meeting, either. We're taking ship today – we won't be home for five days.' And yet, she thought, Peter has disappeared . . .

'Isn't there an airplane now?'

'The Clipper!' Nancy remembered: it had been in all the papers. You could fly across the Atlantic in a day. Was that what Peter was doing?

'That's right, the Clipper,' said Tilly. 'Danny Riley says Peter's coming back on the Clipper and he'll be here in time for the board meeting.'

Nancy was finding it hard to take in the shameless way her brother had lied to her. He had travelled all the way to Liverpool with her, to make her think he was taking the ship. He must have left again, the moment they parted company in the hotel corridor, and driven overnight to Southampton in time for the plane. How could he have spent all that time with her, talking and eating together, discussing the forthcoming voyage, when all along he was scheming to do her down?

Aunt Tilly said, 'Why don't you come on the Clipper too?'

Was it too late? Peter must have planned this carefully.

He would have known she would make some enquiries when she discovered he was not going on the ship, and he would try to make sure that she was not able to catch up with him. But timing was not Peter's strength and he might have left a gap.

She hardly dared to hope.

'I'm going to try,' Nancy said with sudden determination. 'Goodbye.' She hung up.

She thought for a moment. Peter had left yesterday evening and must have travelled overnight. The Clipper must be scheduled to leave Southampton today and arrive in New York tomorrow, in time for Peter to get to Boston for the meeting on Friday. But what time did the Clipper take off? And could Nancy get to Southampton by then?

With her heart in her mouth, she went to the desk and asked the head porter what time the Pan American Clipper took off from Southampton.

'You've missed it, madam,' he said.

'Just check the time, please,' she said, trying to keep the note of impatience out of her voice.

He took out a timetable and opened it. 'Two o'clock.'

She checked her watch: it was just noon.

The porter said, 'You couldn't get to Southampton in time even if you had a private aeroplane standing by.'

'Are there any airplanes?' she persisted.

His face took on the tolerant expression of a hotel employee humouring a foolish foreigner. 'There's an airfield about ten miles from here. Generally you can find a pilot to take you anywhere, for a price. But you've got to get to the field, find the pilot, make the journey, land somewhere near Southampton, then get from that airfield to the docks. It can't be done in two hours, believe me.'

She turned away from him in frustration.

Getting mad was no use in business, she had learned long ago. When things went wrong you had to find a way to put them right. I can't get to Boston in time, she thought, so maybe I can stop the sale by remote control.

She returned to the phone booth. It was just after seven o'clock in Boston. Her lawyer, Patrick McBride, would be at home. She gave the operator his number.

Mac was the man her brother should have been. When Sean died he stepped in and took care of everything: the inquest, the funeral, the will, and Nancy's personal finances. He was marvellous with the boys, taking them to ball games, turning up to see them in school plays, and advising them on college and careers. At different times he had talked to each of them about the facts of life. When Pa died, Mac counselled Nancy against letting Peter become chairman; she went against his advice, and now events had proved that Mac had been right. She knew that he was more or less in love with her. It was not a dangerous attachment: Mac was a devout Catholic and faithful to his plain, dumpy, loyal wife. Nancy was very fond of him but he was not the kind of man she could ever fall in love with: he was a soft, round, mild-mannered type with a bald dome, and she was always attracted to strong-willed men with plenty of hair: men such as Nat Ridgeway.

While she waited for the connection, she had time

to reflect on the irony of her situation. Peter's co-conspirator against her was Nat Ridgeway, her father's one-time deputy and her old flame. Nat had left the company – and Nancy – because he could not be boss; and now, from his position as president of General Textiles, he was trying again to take control of Black's Boots.

She knew Nat had been in Paris for the collections, although she had not run into him. But Peter must have held meetings with him and closed the deal there, while pretending to be innocently buying shoes. Nancy had not suspected anything. When she thought how easily she had been deceived she felt furious with Peter and Nat – and most of all with herself.

The phone in the booth rang and she picked it up: she was lucky with connections today.

Mac answered with his mouth full of breakfast. 'Hmm?'

'Mac, it's Nancy.'

He swallowed rapidly. 'Thank God you called, I've been searching Europe for you. Peter is trying to—'

'I know, I just heard,' she interrupted. 'What are the terms of the deal?'

'One share in General Textiles, plus twenty-seven cents cash, for five shares in Black's.'

'Jesus, that's a giveaway!'

'On your profits it's not so low—'

'But our asset value is much higher!'

'Hey, I'm not fighting you,' he said mildly.

'Sorry, Mac, I'm just angry.'

'I understand.'

She could hear his children squabbling in the background. He had five, all girls. She could also hear a radio playing and a kettle whistling.

After a moment he went on, 'I agree that the offer is too low. It reflects the current profit level, yes, but it ignores asset value and future potential.'

'You can say that again.'

'There's something else, too.'

'Tell me.'

'Peter will be retained to run the Black's operation for five years following the takeover. But there's no job for you.'

Nancy closed her eyes. This was the cruellest blow of all. She felt sick. Lazy, dumb Peter, whom she had sheltered and covered for, would remain; she, who had kept the business afloat, would be thrown out. 'How could he do this to me?' she said. 'He's my brother!'

'I'm really sorry, Nan.'

'Thanks.'

'I never trusted Peter.'

'My father spent his life building up this business,' she cried. 'Peter can't be allowed to destroy it.'

'What do you want me to do?'

'Can we stop it?'

'If you could get here for the board meeting I believe you could persuade your aunt and Danny Riley to turn it down—'

'I can't get there, that's my problem. Can't you persuade them?'

'I might, but it would do no good – Peter outvotes them. They only have ten per cent each and he has forty.'

'Can't you vote my stock on my behalf?'

'I don't have your proxy.'

'Can I vote by phone?'

'Interesting idea . . . I think it would be up to the board, and Peter would use his majority to rule it out.'

There was a silence while they both racked their brains.

In the pause she remembered her manners, and said, 'How's the family?'

'Unwashed, undressed and unruly, right now. And Betty's pregnant.'

For a moment she forgot her troubles. 'No kidding!' She had thought they had stopped having children: the youngest was now five. 'After all this time!'

'I thought I'd found out what was causing it.'

Nancy laughed. 'Hey, congratulations!'

'Thanks, although Betty's a little . . . ambivalent about it.'

'Why? She's younger than I am.'

'But six is a lot of kids.'

'You can afford it.'

'Yes . . . Are you sure you can't make that plane?'

Nancy sighed. 'I'm in Liverpool. Southampton is two hundred miles away and the plane takes off in less than two hours. It's impossible.'

'Liverpool? That's not far from Ireland.'

'Spare me the travelogue—'

'But the Clipper touches down in Ireland.'

Nancy's heart skipped a beat. 'Are you sure?'

'I read it in the newspaper.'

This changed everything, she realized with a surge of hope. She might be able to make the plane after all! 'Where does it come down – Dublin?'

'No, some place on the west coast, I forget the name. But you might still make it.'

'I'll check it out and call you later. Bye.'

'Hey, Nancy?

'What?'

'Happy Birthday.'

She smiled at the wall. 'Mac . . . you're great.'

'Good luck.'

'Goodbye.' She hung up and went back to the desk. The head porter gave her a condescending smile. She resisted the temptation to put him in his place: that would make him even more unhelpful. 'I believe the Clipper touches down in Ireland,' she said, forcing herself to sound friendly.

'That's correct, madam. At Foynes, in the Shannon estuary.'

She wanted to say, 'So why didn't you tell me that before, you pompous little prick?' Instead she smiled and said, 'What time?'

He reached for his timetable. 'It's scheduled to land at three thirty and take off again at four thirty.'

'Can I get there by then?'

His tolerant smile vanished and he looked at her with more respect. 'I never thought of that,' he said. 'It's a two-hour flight in a small aeroplane. If you can find a pilot you can do it.'

Her tension went up a notch. This was beginning to look seriously possible. 'Get me a taxi to take me to that airfield right away, would you?'

He snapped his fingers at a bellhop. 'Taxi for the lady!' He turned back to Nancy. 'What about your trunks?' They were now stacked in the lobby. 'You won't get that lot in a small plane.'

'Send them to the ship, please.'

'Very good.'

'Bring my bill as quick as you can.'

'Right away.'

Nancy retrieved her small overnight case from the stack of luggage. In it she had her essential toiletries, make-up and a change of underwear. She opened a suitcase and found a clean blouse for tomorrow morning, in plain navy blue silk, and a nightdress and bathrobe. Over her arm she had a light-grey cashmere coat which she had intended to wear on deck if the wind was cold. She decided to keep it with her now: she might need it to keep warm in the plane.

She closed up her bags.

'Your bill, Mrs Lenehan.'

She scribbled a cheque and handed it over with a tip.

'Very kind of you, Mrs Lenehan. The taxi is waiting.'

She hurried outside and climbed into a cramped little British car. The porter put her overnight case on the seat beside her and gave instructions to the driver. Nancy added, 'And go as fast as you can!'

The car went infuriatingly slowly through the city

centre. She tapped the toe of her grey suede shoe impatiently. The delay was caused by men painting white lines down the middle of the road, on the kerbs and around roadside trees. She wondered irritably what their purpose was, then she figured out that the lines were to help motorists in the blackout.

The taxi picked up speed as it wound through the suburbs and headed into the country. Here she saw no preparations for war. The Germans would not bomb fields, unless by accident. She kept looking at her watch. It was already twelve thirty. If she found an aeroplane, and a pilot, and persuaded him to take her, and negotiated a fee, all without delay, she might take off by one o'clock. Two hours' flight, the porter had said. She would land at three. Then, of course, she would have to find her way from the airfield to Foynes. But that should not be too great a distance. She might well arrive with time to spare. Would there be a car to take her to the dockside? She tried to calm herself. There was no point in worrying that far ahead.

It occurred to her that the Clipper might be full: all the ships were.

She put the thought out of her mind.

She was about to ask her driver how much farther they had to go when, to her grateful relief, he abruptly turned off the road and steered through an open gate into a field. As the car bumped over the grass Nancy saw ahead of her a small hangar. All around it, small brightly coloured planes were tethered to the green turf, like a collection of butterflies on a velvet cloth.

There was no shortage of aircraft, she noted with satisfaction. But she needed a pilot too, and there seemed to be no one about.

The driver took her up to the big door of the hangar.

'Wait for me, please,' she said as she jumped out. She did not want to get stranded.

She hurried into the hangar. There were three planes inside but no people. She went out into the sunshine again. Surely the place could not be unattended, she thought anxiously. There had to be *someone* around, otherwise the door would be locked. She walked around the hangar to the back, and there at last she saw three men standing by a plane.

The aircraft itself was ravishing. It was painted canary yellow all over, with little yellow wheels that made Nancy think of toy cars. It was a biplane, its upper and lower wings joined by wires and struts, and it had a single engine in the nose. It sat there with its propeller in the air and its tail on the ground like a puppy begging to be taken for a walk.

It was being fuelled. A man in oily blue overalls and a cloth cap was standing on a stepladder pouring petrol from a can into a bulge on the wing over the front seat. On the ground was a tall, good-looking man of about Nancy's age wearing a flying helmet and a leather jacket. He was deep in conversation with a man in a tweed suit.

Nancy coughed and said, 'Excuse me.'

The two men glanced at her but the tall man continued speaking and they both looked away again.

It was not a good start.

Nancy said, 'I'm sorry to bother you. I want to charter a plane.'

The tall man interrupted his conversation to say, 'Can't help you.'

'It's an emergency,' Nancy said.

'I'm not a bloody taxi driver,' the man said, and turned away again.

Nancy was angered sufficiently to say, 'Why do you have to be so rude?'

That got his attention. He turned an interested, quizzical look at her, and she noticed that he had arched black eyebrows. 'I didn't intend to be rude,' he said mildly. 'But my plane isn't for hire, and nor am I.'

Desperately, she said, 'Please don't be offended, but if it's a matter of money, I'll pay a high price . . .'

He was offended: his expression froze and he turned away.

Nancy observed that there was a chalk-striped dark-grey suit under the leather jacket, and the man's black Oxford shoes were the genuine article, not inexpensive imitations such as Nancy made. He was obviously a wealthy businessman who flew his own plane for pleasure.

'Is there anybody else, then?' she said.

The mechanic looked up from the fuel tank and shook his head. 'Nobody about today,' he said.

The tall man said to his companion, 'I'm not in business to lose money. You tell Seward that what he's getting paid is the rate for the job.'

'The trouble is, he has a point, you know,' said the one in the tweed suit.

'I know that. Say we'll negotiate a higher rate for the next job.'

'That may not satisfy him.'

'In that case he can get his cards and bugger off.'

Nancy wanted to scream with frustration. Here was a perfectly good plane and a pilot, and nothing she said would make them take her where she needed to go. Close to tears, she said, 'I just *have* to get to Foynes!'

The tall man turned round again. 'Did you say Foynes?'

'Yes.'

'Why?'

At least she had succeeded in engaging him in conversation. 'I'm trying to catch up with the Pan American Clipper.'

'That's funny,' he said. 'So am I.'

Her hopes lifted again. 'Oh, my God,' she said. 'You're going to Foynes?'

'Aye.' He looked grim. 'I'm chasing my wife.'

It was an odd thing to say, she noticed, even though she was so wrought up: a man who would confess to that was either very weak or very self-assured. She looked at his plane. There appeared to be two cockpits, one behind the other. 'Are there two seats in your plane?' she asked with trepidation.

He looked her up and down. 'Aye,' he said. 'Two seats.'

'*Please* take me with you.'

He hesitated, then shrugged. 'Why not?'

She wanted to faint with relief. 'Oh, thank God,' she said. 'I'm so grateful.'

'Don't mention it.' He stuck out a big hand. 'Mervyn Lovesey. How do you do.'

She shook hands. 'Nancy Lenehan,' she replied. 'Am I pleased to meet you.'

Eddie needed to talk to someone.

It would have to be someone he could trust absolutely, someone who could keep it secret.

The only person he discussed this kind of thing with was Carol-Ann. She was his confidante. He would not even have discussed it with Pop when Pop was alive: he never liked to show weakness to his father. Was there anyone he could trust?

He considered Captain Baker. Marvin Baker was just the kind of pilot that passengers liked: good-looking, square-jawed, confident and assertive. Eddie respected him and liked him, too. But Baker's loyalty was to the plane and the safety of the passengers, and he was a stickler for the rules. He would insist on going straight to the police with this story. He was no use.

Anyone else?

Yes. There was Steve Appleby.

Steve was a lumberjack's son from Oregon, a tall boy with muscles as hard as wood, a Catholic from a dirt-poor family. They had been midshipmen together at Annapolis. They had become friends on their first day, in the vast white mess hall. While the other plebs were bitching about the chow, Eddie cleaned his plate.

Looking up, he saw that there was one other cadet poor enough to think this was great food: Steve. Their eyes had met and they understood one another perfectly.

They had been pals through the academy, then later they were both stationed at Pearl Harbor. When Steve married Nella, Eddie was best man, and last year Steve did the same service for Eddie. Steve was still in the Navy, stationed at the shipyard in Portsmouth, New Hampshire. They saw each other infrequently now but it did not matter, for theirs was a friendship that would survive long periods with no contact. They would not write letters unless they had something specific to say. When they both happened to be in New York they would have dinner or go to a ball game and would be as close as if they had parted company only the day before. Eddie would have trusted Steve with his soul.

Steve was also a great fixer. A weekend pass, a bottle of hooch, a pair of tickets for the big game – he could get them when no one else could.

Eddie decided to try to get in touch with him.

He felt a little better having made some kind of decision. He hurried back into the hotel.

He went to the little office and gave the number of the naval base to the hotel's proprietress, then he returned to his room. She would fetch him when the call came through.

He took off his overalls. He did not want to be in the tub when she came, so he scrubbed his hands and washed his face in the bedroom, then put on a clean white shirt and his uniform pants. The routine activity calmed him a little but he was feverishly impatient. He did not know what Steve would say but it would be a tremendous relief to share the problem.

He was knotting his tie when the proprietress knocked at the door, but he ran down the stairs and picked up the phone. He was connected with the switchboard operator at the base.

He said, 'Would you put me through to Steve Appleby, please?'

'Lieutenant Appleby cannot be reached by telephone at this time,' he said. Eddie's heart sank. She added, 'May I give him a message?'

Eddie was bitterly disappointed. He knew Steve would not have been able to wave a wand and rescue Carol-Ann, but at least they could have talked, and maybe some ideas would have come out of the discussion.

He said, 'Miss, this is an emergency. Where the hell is he?'

'May I ask who is calling, sir?'

'This is Eddie Deakin.'

She dropped her formal tone immediately. 'Oh, hi, Eddie! You were his best man, weren't you? I'm Laura Gross, we met.' She lowered her voice conspiratorially. 'Unofficially, Steve spent last night off the base.'

Eddie groaned inwardly. Steve was doing something he shouldn't – at just the wrong time. 'When do you expect him?'

'He should have been back before daybreak but he didn't show up.'

Worse yet – Steve was not just absent but possibly in trouble too.

The operator said, 'I could put you through to Nella, she's in the typing pool.'

'Okay, thanks.' He could not confide in Nella, of course, but he could find out a little more about where Steve might be. He tapped his foot restlessly while he waited for the connection. He could picture Nella: she was a warm-hearted, round-faced girl with long curly hair.

At last he heard her voice. 'Hello?'

'Nella, this is Eddie Deakin.'

'Hello, Eddie, where are you?'

'I'm calling from England. Nella, where's Steve?'

'Calling from England! My goodness! Steve is, uh, out of touch right now.' She sounded uneasy as she added, 'Is something wrong?'

'Ayuh. When do you think Steve will be back?'

'Some time this morning, maybe in an hour or so. Eddie, you sound really shook. What is it? Are you in some kind of trouble?'

'Maybe Steve could phone me here if he gets back in time.' He gave her the phone number of Langdown Lawn.

She repeated it. 'Eddie, won't you please tell me what's goin' on?'

'I can't. Just get him to call. I'll be here for another hour. After that I have to go to the plane – we fly back to New York today.'

'Whatever you say,' Nella said doubtfully. 'How's Carol-Ann?'

'I have to go now,' he said. 'Goodbye, Nella.' He hung up without waiting for her reply. He knew he was being discourteous but he was too upset to care. His insides felt tied in knots.

He did not know what to do next so he climbed the stairs and went to his room. He left the door ajar, so that he would hear the ring of the phone from the hall, and sat down on the edge of the single bed. He felt close to tears for the first time since he was a child. He buried his head in his hands and whispered, 'What am I going to do?'

He recalled the Lindbergh kidnapping. It had been in all the papers when he was at Annapolis, seven years ago. The child had been killed. 'Oh, God, keep Carol-Ann safe,' he prayed.

He did not often pray nowadays. Prayer had never done his parents any good. He believed in helping himself. He shook his head. This was no time to revert to religion. He had to think it out and do something.

The people who had kidnapped Carol-Ann wanted Eddie on the plane, that much was clear. Maybe that was a reason not to go. But if he stayed away he would never meet Tom Luther and find out what they wanted. He might frustrate their plans but he would lose any slight chance of gaining control of the situation.

He stood up and opened his small suitcase. He could not think of anything but Carol-Ann, but he automatically stowed his shaving kit, his pyjamas and his laundry. He brushed his hair absently and packed the brushes.

As he was sitting down again, the phone rang.

He was out of the room in two strides. He hurried down the stairs, but someone got to the phone before him. Crossing the hall, he heard the proprietress say, 'October the fourth? Just let me see whether we have a vacancy.'

Crestfallen, he turned back. He told himself there was nothing Steve could do anyway. Nobody could do anything. Someone had kidnapped Carol-Ann and Eddie was just going to have to do whatever they wanted, then he would get her back. No one could release him from the bind he was in.

With a heavy heart he recalled again that they had quarrelled the last time he saw her. He would never forgive himself for that. He wished with all his soul that he had bitten his tongue instead. What the hell had they been arguing about, anyway? He swore he would not fight with her ever again, if only he could have her back safe.

Why wouldn't that goddamn phone ring?

There was a tap on the door and Mickey came in, wearing his flight uniform and carrying his suitcase. 'Ready to go?' he said cheerfully.

Eddie felt panicky. 'It can't be time already!'

'Sure is!'

'Shit . . .'

'What's the matter, you like it so much here? You want to stay and fight the Germans?'

Eddie had to give Steve a few more minutes. 'You honk on ahead,' he said to Mickey. 'I'll catch you up.'

Mickey looked a little hurt that Eddie did not want to go with him. He shrugged, said, 'See you later,' and went out.

Where the hell was Steve Appleby?

He sat and stared at the wallpaper for the next fifteen minutes.

At last he picked up his case and went slowly down the stairs, staring at the phone as if it were a rattlesnake poised to strike. He stopped in the hall, waiting for it to ring.

Captain Baker came down and looked at Eddie in surprise. 'You're running late,' he said. 'You'd better come in the taxi with me.' The Captain had the privilege of a taxi to the hangar.

'I'm waiting for a telephone call,' Eddie said.

The ghost of a frown shadowed the Captain's brow. 'Well, you can't wait any longer. Let's go!'

Eddie did not move for a moment. Then he realized this was stupid. Steve was not going to call, and Eddie had to be on the plane if he was going to do anything. He forced himself to pick up his case and walk out through the door.

The taxi was waiting and they got in.

Eddie knew he had been almost insubordinate. He did not want to offend Baker, who was a good captain and had always treated Eddie decently. 'I'm sorry about that,' he said. 'I was expecting a call from the States.'

The Captain smiled forgivingly. 'Hell, you'll be there tomorrow!' he said cheerfully.

'Right,' Eddie said grimly.

He was on his own.

Part Two

Southampton to Foynes

CHAPTER SIX

As the train rolled south through the pine woods of Surrey towards Southampton, Margaret Oxenford's sister Elizabeth made a shocking announcement.

The Oxenford family were in a special carriage reserved for Pan American Clipper passengers. Margaret was standing at the end of the carriage, alone, staring out of the window. Her mood swung wildly between black despair and rising excitement. She was angry and miserable to be abandoning her country in its hour of need, but she could not help feeling thrilled at the prospect of flying to America.

Her sister Elizabeth detached herself from the family group and came up to her, looking solemn. After a moment's hesitation she said, 'I love you, Margaret.'

Margaret was touched. Over the last few years, since they had been old enough to understand the battle of ideas raging throughout the world, they had taken violently opposite points of view and because of that they had become estranged. But she had missed being close to her sister, and the estrangement made her sad. It would be wonderful if they could be real pals again. 'I love you, too,' she said, and she hugged Elizabeth hard.

After a moment Elizabeth said, 'I'm not coming to America.'

Margaret gasped with astonishment. 'How can you not?'

'I shall simply tell Mother and Father that I'm not going. I'm twenty-one – they can't force me.'

Margaret was not sure she was right about that, but she let it pass for the moment: she had too many other questions. 'Where will you go?'

'To Germany.'

'But, Elizabeth!' Margaret said, horrified. 'You'll get killed!'

Elizabeth looked defiant. 'It's not only socialists who are willing to die for a cause, you know.'

'But for Nazism!'

'It's not just for Fascism,' Elizabeth said, and there was an odd light in her eyes. 'It's for all the thoroughbred white people who are in danger of being swamped by niggers and half-breeds. It's for the human race.'

Margaret was revolted. It was bad enough to be losing her sister – but to lose her to such a wicked cause! However, Margaret did not want to go over the bitter old political argument now: she was more concerned about her sister's safety. She said, 'What will you live on?'

'I've got my own money.'

Margaret remembered that they both inherited money from their grandfather at the age of twenty-one. It was not much, but it might be enough to live on.

She thought of something else. 'But your luggage is checked through to New York.'

'Those cases are full of old tablecloths. I packed another set of bags and sent them ahead on Monday.'

Margaret was astonished. Elizabeth had arranged everything perfectly and carried out her scheme in total secrecy. Bitterly, Margaret reflected how impetuous and ill-thought-out her own escape attempt had been by comparison. While I was brooding and refusing to eat, she thought, Elizabeth was booking passage and sending her luggage on ahead. Of course, Elizabeth was the right side of twenty-one and Margaret the wrong, but that had not counted as much as careful planning and cool execution. Margaret felt ashamed that her sister, who was so stupid and wrong about politics, had behaved so much more intelligently.

Suddenly it struck her how she would miss Elizabeth. Although they were no longer great friends, Elizabeth was always around. Mostly they argued, quarrelled, and mocked one another's ideas, but Margaret would miss that, too. And they still supported one another in distress. Elizabeth always suffered bad period pains and Margaret would tuck her up in bed and bring her a cup of hot chocolate and *Picture Post* magazine. Elizabeth had been deeply sorry when Ian died, even though she disapproved of him, and she had been a comfort to Margaret. Tearfully, Margaret said, 'I shall miss you dreadfully.'

'Don't make a fuss,' Elizabeth said anxiously. 'I don't want them to know yet.'

Margaret composed herself. 'When will you tell them?'

'At the last minute. Can you act normally until then?'

'All right.' She forced a bright smile. 'I shall be as horrible as ever to you.'

'Oh, Margaret!' Elizabeth was on the point of tears. She swallowed and said, 'Go and talk to them while I calm down.'

Margaret squeezed her sister's hand, then returned to her seat.

Mother was leafing through *Vogue* magazine and reading occasional paragraphs to Father, oblivious of his complete lack of interest. 'Lace is being worn,' she quoted, adding, 'I haven't noticed, have you?' The fact that she got no reply did not discourage her in the least. 'White is glamour colour number one. Well, I don't like it. White makes me look kind of bilious.'

Father was wearing an unbearably smug expression. He was pleased with himself, Margaret knew, for reasserting his parental authority and crushing her rebellion. But he did not know that his elder daughter had planted a time-bomb.

Would Elizabeth have the pluck to go through with this? It was one thing to tell Margaret and quite another to tell Father. Elizabeth might lose her nerve at the last minute. Margaret herself had planned a confrontation with him but had ducked it in the end.

Even if Elizabeth went ahead and told Father it was not certain that she would escape. She might be twenty-one and have her own money but he was fearfully strong-willed and quite ruthless about getting his own way. If he could think of some means of stopping Elizabeth he would, Margaret felt sure. He might not mind her joining the Fascist side, in principle, but he would be furious that she was refusing to go along with his plans for the family.

Margaret had been in many such fights with Father. He had been furious when she learned to drive without his permission, and when he found out she had gone to hear a speech by Marie Stopes, the controversial pioneer of contraception, he had been apoplectic. But on those occasions she had succeeded only by going behind his back. She had never won in a direct conflict. He had refused to let her go on a camping holiday, at the age of sixteen, with her cousin Catherine and several of Catherine's friends, even though the whole thing was supervised by a vicar and his wife. Father had objected because there would be boys as well as girls. Their biggest battle had been over going to school. She had begged and pleaded, screamed and sobbed and sulked, and he had been stonily implacable. 'School is wasted on girls,' he had said. 'They only grow up and get married.'

But he could not go on bullying and bossing his children for ever, could he?

Margaret felt restless. She stood up and walked along the carriage; just for something to do. Most of the other Clipper passengers seemed to share her dual mood, half excited and half depressed. When they all joined the train at Waterloo station there had been a good deal of lively conversation and laughter. They had checked their baggage at Waterloo: there had been a fuss about Mother's steamer trunk, which exceeded the weight limit many times over, but she had blithely ignored everything the Pan American staff said and eventually the trunk had been accepted. A young man in uniform had taken their tickets and ushered them into their special carriage. Then, as they left London behind, the passengers had become quiet, as if privately saying goodbye to a country they might never see again.

There was a world-famous American film star among the passengers, which partly accounted for the undertone of excitement. Her name was Lulu Bell. Percy was sitting with her now, talking to her as if he had known her all his life. Margaret herself had wanted to speak to her, but she had not had the cheek just to go up and engage her in conversation. Percy was bolder.

In the flesh Lulu Bell looked older than on the screen. Margaret guessed she was in her late thirties, although she still played débutantes and newlyweds. All the same she was pretty. Small and lively, she made Margaret think of a little bird, a sparrow or a wren.

Margaret smiled at her, and Lulu said, 'Your kid brother has been keeping me entertained.'

'I hope he's being polite,' Margaret replied.

'Oh, sure. He's telling me all about your great-grandmother, Ruthie Fishbein.' Lulu's voice became solemn, as if she were speaking of tragic heroism. 'She must have been a *wonderful* woman.'

Margaret was embarrassed. It was wicked of Percy to tell lies to total strangers. What on earth had he said to this poor woman? Feeling flustered, she smiled vaguely – a trick she had learned from Mother – and passed on.

Percy had always been mischievous, but lately he

seemed to be getting bolder. He was growing taller, his voice was getting deeper, and his practical jokes were verging on dangerous. He was still afraid of Father, and would only go against parental authority if Margaret backed him up, but she had an idea that the day was coming when Percy would rebel openly. How would Father deal with that? Could he bully a boy as easily as he had bullied his girls? Margaret was not sure it would be quite the same.

At the far end of the carriage was a mysterious figure who seemed vaguely familiar to Margaret. A tall, intense-looking man with burning eyes, he stood out in this well-dressed, well-fed crowd because he was as thin as death and wore a shabby suit of thick, coarse cloth. His hair was cut painfully short like a prisoner's. He seemed worried and tense.

She looked at him now and he caught her eye. Suddenly she remembered him. They had never met but she had seen his photograph in the newspapers: he was Carl Hartmann, the German socialist and scientist. Deciding to be bold like her brother, Margaret sat down opposite him and introduced herself. A long-time opponent of Hitler, Hartmann had become a hero to young people such as Margaret for his bravery. Then he had disappeared about a year ago, and everyone had feared the worst. Margaret assumed he had escaped from Germany. He looked like a man who had been through hell.

'The whole world has been wondering what happened to you,' Margaret said to him.

He replied in heavily accented but correct English. 'I was placed under house arrest but permitted to continue with my scientific work.'

'And then?'

'I have escaped,' he said simply. He introduced the man beside him. 'Do you know my friend Baron Gabon?'

Margaret had heard of him. Philippe Gabon was a French banker who used his vast wealth to promote Jewish causes such as Zionism, which made him unpopular with the British government. He spent much of his time travelling the world trying to persuade countries to admit Jewish refugees from the Nazis. He was a small, rather plump man with a neat beard, wearing a stylish black suit with a dove-grey waistcoat and a silver tie. Margaret guessed he was paying for Hartmann's ticket. She shook his hand and returned her attention to Hartmann.

'Your escape hasn't been reported in the newspapers,' she said.

Baron Gabon said, 'We have tried to keep it quiet until Carl is safely out of Europe.'

That was ominous, Margaret thought. It sounded as if the Nazis might still be after him. 'What are you going to do in America?' she asked.

'I am going to Princeton, to work in the physics department there,' Hartmann replied. A bitter expression came over his face. 'I did not want to leave my country. But if I had stayed, my work might have contributed to a Nazi victory.'

Margaret did not know anything about his work, just

that he was a scientist. It was his politics that interested her. 'Your courage has been an inspiration to so many people,' she said. She was thinking of Ian, who had translated Hartmann's speeches, in the days when Hartmann had been allowed to make speeches.

Her praise seemed to make him uncomfortable. 'I wish I could have continued,' he said. 'I regret having given up.'

Baron Gabon interjected, 'You haven't given up, Carl. Don't accuse yourself. You did the only thing you could.'

Hartmann nodded, and Margaret could see that in his head he knew Gabon was right, but in his heart he felt he had let his country down. She would have liked to say something comforting but she did not know what. Her dilemma was resolved by the Pan American escort, who came by saying, 'Our luncheon is ready in the next car. Please take your seats.'

Margaret stood up and said, 'It's such an honour to know you. I hope we can talk some more.'

'I'm sure we will,' Hartmann said, and for the first time he smiled. 'We're going three thousand miles together.'

She moved into the restaurant car and sat down with her family. Mother and Father sat on one side of the table, and the three children were squeezed together on the other, Percy between Margaret and Elizabeth. Margaret looked sideways at Elizabeth. When would she drop her bombshell?

The waiter poured water and Father ordered a bottle of hock. Elizabeth was silent, looking out of the window.

Margaret waited in suspense. Mother sensed the tension and said, 'What's up with you girls?'

Margaret said nothing. Elizabeth said, 'I've got something important to tell you.'

The waiter came with cream of mushroom soup. Elizabeth paused while he served them. Mother asked for a salad.

When he had gone, Mother said, 'What is it, dear?'

Margaret held her breath.

Elizabeth said, 'I've decided not to go to America.'

'What the devil are you talking about?' Father said irritably. 'Of course you're going – we're on the way!'

'No, I shan't be flying with you,' Elizabeth persisted calmly. Margaret watched her closely. Elizabeth's voice was level but her long, rather plain face was white with tension and Margaret's heart went out to her.

Mother said, 'Don't be silly, Elizabeth, Father's bought you a ticket.'

Percy said, 'Perhaps we can get a refund.'

'Be quiet, foolish boy,' said Father.

Elizabeth said, 'If you try to force me, I shall refuse to go on board the aeroplane. I think you'll find that the airline will not permit you to carry me aboard kicking and screaming.'

How clever Elizabeth had been, Margaret thought. She had caught Father at a vulnerable moment. He could not take her aboard by force and he could not stay behind to deal with the problem because the authorities were about to arrest him as a Fascist.

But Father was not beaten yet. He now understood that she was serious. He put down his spoon. 'What on earth do you suppose you would do if you stayed behind?' he said scathingly. 'Join the army, as your feeble-minded sister proposed to do?'

Margaret flushed with anger at being called feeble-minded, but she bit her tongue and said nothing, waiting for Elizabeth to crush him.

Elizabeth said, 'I shall go to Germany.'

For a moment Father was shocked into silence.

Mother said, 'Darling, don't you think you're taking all this too far?'

Percy spoke in an accurate imitation of Father. 'This is what happens when girls are allowed to discuss politics,' he said pompously. 'I blame that Marie Stopes—'

'Shut up, Percy,' said Margaret, digging him in the ribs.

They were silent while the waiter cleared away their untouched soup. She's done it, Margaret thought. She actually had the guts to come out and say it. Now, will she get away with it?

Margaret could see that Father was already disconcerted. It had been easy for him to scorn Margaret for wanting to stay behind and fight against the Fascists but it was harder to deride Elizabeth because she was on his side.

However, moral doubt never troubled him for very long and when the waiter went away he said, 'I absolutely forbid it.' His tone was conclusive, as if that ended the discussion.

Margaret looked at Elizabeth. How would she respond? He wasn't even bothering to argue with her.

With surprising gentleness, Elizabeth said, 'I'm afraid you can't forbid it, Father dear. I'm twenty-one years old and I can do as I please.'

'Not while you're dependent on me,' he said.

'Then I may have to do without your support,' she said. 'I have a small income of my own.'

Father drank some hock very quickly and said, 'I shan't permit it and that's that.'

It sounded hollow. Margaret began to believe that Elizabeth might really get away with it. She did not know whether to feel delighted at the prospect of Elizabeth defeating Father, or revolted that she was going to join the Nazis.

They were served Dover sole. Only Percy ate. Elizabeth was pale with fright but there was a look of determination about her mouth. Margaret could not help admiring her fortitude, even though she despised her mission.

Percy said, 'If you're not coming to America, why did you get on the train?'

'I've booked passage on a ship from Southampton.'

'You can't get a ship to Germany from this country,' Father said triumphantly.

Margaret was appalled. Of course you couldn't. Had Elizabeth slipped up? Would her entire plan founder on this detail?

Elizabeth was unruffled. 'I'm taking a ship to Lisbon,' she said calmly. 'I've wired money to a bank there and I have a reservation at an hotel.'

'You deceitful child!' Father said furiously. His voice was loud and a man at the next table looked round.

Elizabeth went on as if he had not spoken. 'Once I'm there I'll be able to find a ship going to Germany.'

Mother said, 'And then?'

'I have friends in Berlin, Mother, you know that.'

Mother sighed. 'Yes, dear.' She looked very sad, and Margaret saw she had now accepted that Elizabeth would go.

Father said loudly, 'I have friends in Berlin, too.'

Several people at adjoining tables looked up, and Mother said, 'Hush, dear. We can all hear you just fine.'

Father went on more quietly, 'I have friends in Berlin who will send you packing the moment you arrive.'

Margaret's hand went to her mouth. Of course, Father could get the Germans to expel Elizabeth: in a Fascist country the government could do anything. Would Elizabeth's escape end with some wretched bureaucrat in a passport control booth shaking his head woodenly and refusing her an entry permit?

'They won't do that,' said Elizabeth.

'We shall see,' said Father, and to Margaret's ear he sounded unsure of himself.

'They'll welcome me, Father,' Elizabeth said, and the note of weariness in her voice somehow made her sound more convincing. 'They'll send out a press release to tell the world that I've escaped from England and joined their side, just the way the wretched British newspapers publicize the defection of prominent German Jews.'

Percy said, 'I hope they don't find out about Grandma Fishbein.'

Elizabeth was armoured against Father's attack but

Percy's cruel humour slipped under her guard. 'Shut up, you horrible boy!' she said, and she began to cry.

Once again the waiter took away their untouched plates. The next course was lamb cutlets with vegetables. The waiter poured wine. Mother took a sip, a rare sign that she was upset.

Father began to eat, attacking the meat with his knife and fork and chewing furiously. Margaret studied his angry face, and was surprised to detect a trace of bewilderment beneath the mask of rage. It was odd to see him shaken: his arrogance normally weathered every crisis. Studying his expression, she began to realize that his whole world was falling apart. This war was the end of his hopes: he had wanted the British people to embrace Fascism under his leadership, but instead they had declared war on Fascism and exiled him.

In truth, they had rejected him in the mid-thirties, but until now he had been able to turn a blind eye to that, and pretend to himself that one day they would come to him in their hour of need. That was why he was so awful, she supposed: he was living a lie. His crusading zeal had developed into obsessive mania, his confidence had degenerated into bluster and, having failed to become the dictator of Britain, he had been reduced to tyrannizing his children. But now he could no longer ignore the truth. He was leaving his country and might never be allowed to return.

On top of all that, at the moment when his political hopes were unmistakably turning to dust, his children were rebelling too. Percy was pretending to be Jewish,

Margaret had tried to run away and now even Elizabeth, his one remaining follower, was defying him.

Margaret had thought she would be grateful for any crack in his armour, but instead she felt uneasy. His unvarying despotism had been a constant in her life, and she was disconcerted by the thought that he might crumble. Like an oppressed nation faced with the prospect of revolution, she felt suddenly insecure.

She tried to eat but she could hardly swallow. Mother pushed a tomato around her plate for a while, then put her fork down. Suddenly she said, 'Is there a boy you like in Berlin, Elizabeth?'

'No,' Elizabeth said. Margaret believed her, but all the same Mother's question had been perceptive. Margaret knew that the appeal of Germany to Elizabeth was not purely ideological. There was something about the tall, blond soldiers, in their immaculate uniforms and gleaming jackboots, that thrilled Elizabeth at a deeper level. And whereas in London society Elizabeth was thought of as a rather plain, ordinary girl from an eccentric family, in Berlin she was something special: an English aristocrat, the daughter of a pioneering Fascist, a foreigner who admired German Nazism. Her defection at the outbreak of war would make her famous there: she would be lionized. She would probably fall in love with a young officer, or an up-and-coming Party official, and they would marry and have blond children who would grow up speaking German.

Mother said, 'What you're doing is so dangerous, dear. Father and I are only worried about your safety.'

Margaret wondered whether Father really was

concerned for Elizabeth's safety. Mother was, certainly, but Father was angry mainly at being disobeyed. Perhaps underneath his fury there was also a vestige of tenderness. He had not always been harsh: Margaret could remember moments of kindliness and even fun, in the old days. The thought made her sad.

Elizabeth said, 'I know it's dangerous, Mother, but my future is at stake in this war. I don't want to live in a world dominated by Jewish financiers and grubby little Communist trade unionists.'

'What absolute twaddle!' Margaret said, but no one was listening.

'Then come with us,' Mother said to Elizabeth. 'America is a good place.'

'Wall Street is run by Jews—'

'I do believe that's exaggerated,' Mother said firmly, avoiding Father's eye. 'There are too many Jews and other unsavoury types in American business, it's true, but they're far outnumbered by decent people. Remember that your grandfather owned a bank.'

Percy said, 'Incredible that we went from knife-grinding to banking in just two generations.' Nobody took any notice.

Mother went on, 'I agree with your views, dear, you know that, but believing in something doesn't mean you have to die for it. No cause is worth that.'

Margaret was shocked. Mother was implying that the Fascist cause was not worth dying for, which amounted almost to blasphemy in Father's eyes. She had never known Mother to go against him like this. Elizabeth was surprised, too, Margaret could see. They both looked at Father. He reddened slightly and grunted disapprovingly, but the outburst they were expecting did not come. And that was the most shocking thing of all.

Coffee was served and Margaret saw that they had reached the outskirts of Southampton. They would arrive at the station in a few minutes. Would Elizabeth really do it?

The train slowed down.

Elizabeth said to the waiter, 'I'm leaving the train at the main station. Would you please bring my suitcase from the other carriage? It's a red leather bag and the name is Lady Elizabeth Oxenford.'

'Certainly, m'Lady,' he said.

Red-brick suburban houses marched past the carriage windows like ranks of soldiers. Margaret was watching Father. He said nothing but his face was taut as a balloon with suppressed rage. Mother put a hand on his knee and said, 'Please don't make a scene, dear.' He did not reply.

The train pulled into the station.

Elizabeth was sitting by the window. She caught Margaret's eye. Margaret and Percy got up and let her out, then sat down again.

Father stood up.

The other passengers sensed the tension and looked at the little tableau: Elizabeth and Father facing one another in the aisle as the train came to a halt.

It struck Margaret once again that Elizabeth had chosen her moment well. It would be difficult for Father to use force in these circumstances: if he tried he might even be restrained by other passengers. Nevertheless she felt sick with fear.

Father's face was flushed and his eyes bulged. He was breathing hard through his nose. Elizabeth was shaking, but her mouth was set firm.

Father said, 'If you get off this train now, I never want to see you again.'

'Don't say that!' Margaret cried, but she was too late. It had been said, and he would never take it back.

Mother began to cry.

Elizabeth just said, 'Goodbye.'

Margaret stood up and threw her arms round her sister. 'Good luck!' she whispered.

'You, too,' Elizabeth said, hugging her back.

Elizabeth kissed Percy's cheek, then leaned awkwardly across the table and kissed Mother's face, which was wet with tears. Finally she looked at Father again and said in a trembling voice, 'Will you shake hands?'

His face was a mask of hate. He said, 'My daughter is dead.'

Mother gave a cry of distress.

The carriage was very quiet, as if everyone knew that a family drama was reaching its tragic conclusion.

Elizabeth turned and walked away.

Margaret wished she could pick her father up and shake him until his teeth rattled. His needless obstinacy made her livid. Why the hell couldn't he just give in for once? Elizabeth was an adult: she wasn't obliged to obey her parents for the rest of her life! Father had no right to banish her. In his rage he had split the family, pointlessly and vindictively. At that moment Margaret hated him. As he stood there, looking furious and belligerent, she wanted to tell him that he was mean and unjust and stupid but, as always with Father, she bit her lip and said nothing.

Elizabeth walked past the carriage window, carrying her red suitcase. She looked at them all, smiled tearfully, and gave a small, hesitant wave with her free hand. Mother began to sob quietly. Percy and Margaret waved back. Father looked away. Then Elizabeth passed out of sight.

Father sat down and Margaret followed suit.

A whistle blew and the train moved off.

They saw Elizabeth again, waiting in line at the exit. She glanced up as their carriage went by. This time there was no smile or wave: she just looked sad and grim.

The train picked up speed, and she was lost from view.

'Family life is a wonderful thing,' Percy said, and although he was being sarcastic, there was no humour in his voice, just bitterness.

Margaret wondered whether she would ever see her sister again.

Mother was dabbing at her eyes with a little linen handkerchief but she was unable to stop crying. It was rare for her to lose her composure. Margaret could not remember seeing her cry ever before. Percy looked shaken. Margaret was depressed by Elizabeth's foolish attachment to such an evil cause but she could not help also feeling a sense of exultation. Elizabeth had done it: she had defied Father and got away with it! She had stood up to him, defeated him, and escaped from him.

If Elizabeth could do it, so could Margaret.

She smelled the sea. The train entered the docks and ran along the waterfront, moving slowly past sheds, cranes and ocean liners. Despite her grief at parting with her sister, Margaret began to feel the thrill of anticipation.

The train stopped behind a building marked 'Imperial House'. It was an ultra-modern structure that looked a bit like a ship: its corners were rounded and the upper storey had a wide veranda like a deck, with a white rail all around.

With the other passengers, the Oxenfords retrieved their overnight bags and got off the train. While their checked baggage was being transferred from the train to the plane, they all went into Imperial House to complete the departure formalities.

Margaret felt dazed. The world around her was changing too rapidly. She had left her home, her country was at war, she had lost her sister, and she was about to fly to America. She wished she could stop the clock for a while and try to take it all in.

Father explained that Elizabeth would not be joining them, and a Pan American official said, 'That's all right – there's someone waiting here hoping to buy an unused ticket. I'll take care of it.'

Margaret noticed Professor Hartmann standing in a corner, smoking a cigarette, looking around him with nervous, wary glances. He seemed jumpy and impatient. People like my sister have made him like this, Margaret thought. Fascists have persecuted him and turned him into a nervous wreck. I don't blame him for being in a hurry to get out of Europe.

They could not see the plane from the waiting room, so Percy went off to find a better vantage point. He came back full of information. 'Take-off will be on schedule at two o'clock,' he said. Margaret felt a shiver of apprehension. He went on, 'It should take us an hour and a half to get to our first stop, which is Foynes. Ireland is on summer time, like Britain, so we should arrive there at half-past three. We wait there an hour while they refuel and finalize the flight plan, and take off again at half-past four.'

Margaret noticed that there were new faces here, people who had not been on the train. Some passengers must have come directly to Southampton this morning, or perhaps stayed overnight at a local hotel. As she thought this, a strikingly beautiful woman arrived in a taxi. She was a blonde in her thirties, and she wore a stunning dress, cream silk with red spots. She was accompanied by a rather ordinary, smiling man in a cashmere blazer. Everyone stared at them: they looked so happy and attractive.

A few minutes later the plane was ready for boarding.

They went out through the front doors of Imperial House directly on to the quay. The Clipper was moored there, rising and falling gently on the water, the sun gleaming off its silver sides.

It was *huge.*

Margaret had never seen a plane even half this size. It was as high as a house and as long as two tennis courts. A big American flag was painted on its whale-like snout. The wings were high, level with the very top of the fuselage. Four enormous engines were built into the wings, and the propellers looked about fifteen feet across.

How could such a thing *fly*?

'Is it very light?' she wondered aloud.

Percy heard her. 'Forty-one tons,' he said promptly.

It would be like taking to the air in a house.

They came to the edge of the quay. A gangplank led down to a floating dock. Mother trod gingerly, hanging on tight to the rail: she looked almost doddery, as if she had aged twenty years. Father had both their bags – Mother never carried anything, it was one of her foibles.

From the floating dock, a shorter gangplank took them on to what looked like a stubby secondary wing, half submerged in the water. 'Hydrostabilizer,' Percy said knowledgeably. 'Also known as a sea-wing. Prevents the plane from tipping sideways in the water.' The surface of the sea-wing was slightly curved: Margaret felt as if she might slip but she did not. Now she was in the shadow of the huge wing above her head. She would have liked to touch one of the vast propeller blades but she would not have been able to reach it.

There was a doorway in the fuselage just under the word AMERICAN in PAN AMERICAN AIRWAYS SYSTEM. Margaret ducked her head and stepped through the door.

There were three steps down to the floor of the plane.

Margaret found herself in a room about twelve feet square with a luxurious terracotta carpet, beige walls and blue chairs with a gay pattern of stars on the upholstery. There were dome lights in the ceiling and large square windows with venetian blinds. The walls and ceiling were straight, instead of curving with the fuselage: it was more like entering a house than boarding a plane.

Two doorways led from this room. Some passengers were directed towards the rear of the plane. Looking that way, Margaret could see that there was a series of lounges, all luxuriously carpeted and decorated in soft tans and greens. But the Oxenfords were seated forward. A small, rather plump steward in a white jacket introduced himself as Nicky and showed them into the next compartment.

This was a little smaller than the other room, and was decorated in a different colour scheme: turquoise carpet, pale green walls, and beige upholstery. To Margaret's right were two large three-seater divans, facing one another, with a small table between them under the window. To her left, on the other side of the aisle, was another pair of divans, these a little smaller, seating two.

Nicky directed them to the larger seats on the right. Father and Mother sat by the window, and Margaret and Percy next to the aisle, leaving two empty seats between them, and four empty seats on the other side of the aisle. Margaret wondered who would be sitting with them. The beautiful woman in the spotted dress would be interesting. So would Lulu Bell, especially if she wanted to talk about Grandma Fishbein! Best of all would be Carl Hartmann.

She could feel the plane moving up and down with

the slight rise and fall of the water. The movement was not much, just enough to remind her that she was at sea. The plane was like a magic carpet, she decided. It was impossible to grasp how mere engines could make it fly, much easier to believe that it would be borne through the air by the power of an ancient enchantment.

Percy stood up. 'I'm going to look around,' he said.

'Stay here,' Father said. 'You'll get in everyone's way if you start running around.'

Percy sat down promptly. Father had not lost all his authority.

Mother powdered her nose. She had stopped crying. She must be feeling better, Margaret decided.

She heard an American voice say, 'I'd really rather sit facing forward.' She looked up. Nicky the steward was showing a man to a seat on the other side of the compartment. Margaret could not tell who it was – he had his back to her. He had blond hair and wore a blue suit.

The steward said, 'No problem, Mr Vandenpost, take the opposite seat.'

The man turned around. Margaret looked at him with curiosity, and their eyes met.

She was astonished to recognize him.

He was not American and his name was not Mr Vandenpost.

His blue eyes flashed her a warning but he was too late.

'Good grief!' she blurted out. 'It's Harry Marks!'

CHAPTER SEVEN

Moments such as this brought out the best in Harry Marks.

Jumping bail, travelling on a stolen passport, using a false name, and pretending to be American, he had the incredibly bad luck to run into a girl who knew he was a thief, had heard him speak in different accents, and loudly called him by his real name.

For an instant he was possessed by blind panic.

A horrid vision of all he was running from appeared before his eyes: a trial, prison, and then the wretched life of a squaddie in the British Army.

Then he remembered that he was lucky, and he smiled.

The girl looked totally bewildered. He waited for her name to come back to him.

Margaret. Lady Margaret Oxenford.

She stared at him in amazement, too surprised to say anything, while he waited for inspiration.

'Harry Vandenpost is the name,' he said. 'But my memory is better than yours, I'll bet. You're Margaret Oxenford, aren't you? How are you?'

'I'm fine,' she said dazedly. She was more confused than he. She would let him take charge of the situation.

He put out his hand as if to shake and she extended her own, and in that moment inspiration came to him. Instead of shaking her hand, at the last moment he bent over it with an old-fashioned bow; and when his head was close to hers he said in a low voice, 'Pretend you never saw me in a police station and I'll do the same for you.'

He stood upright and looked into her eyes. They were an unusual shade of dark green, he noticed; quite beautiful.

For a moment she remained flustered. Then her face cleared, and she grinned broadly. She had cottoned on and was pleased and intrigued by the little conspiracy he was proposing. 'Of course, how silly of me, Harry Vandenpost,' she said.

Harry relaxed gratefully. Luckiest man in the world, he thought.

With a mischievous little frown Margaret added, 'By the way, where *did* we meet?'

Harry fielded that one easily. 'Was it at Pippa Matchingham's ball?'

'No, I didn't go.'

Harry knew very little about Margaret. Did she live in London right through the social 'season' or hide away in the countryside? Did she hunt, shoot, support charities, campaign for women's rights, paint watercolours, or carry out agricultural experiments on her father's farm? He decided to name one of the big events of the season. 'I'm sure we met at Ascot, then.'

'Yes, of course we did,' she said.

He allowed himself a little smile of satisfaction. He had turned her into a co-conspirator already.

She went on, 'But I don't think you've met my people. Mother, may I present Mr Vandenpost, from . . .'

'Pennsylvania,' Harry said rashly. He regretted it immediately. Where the hell was Pennsylvania? He had no idea.

'My mother, Lady Oxenford, my father, the Marquess. And this is my brother, Lord Isley.'

Harry had heard of them all, of course: they were a famous family. He shook hands all round with a hearty, over-friendly manner which the Oxenfords would think typically American.

Lord Oxenford looked like what he was: an overfed, bad-tempered old Fascist. He wore a brown tweed suit with a waistcoat that was about to pop its buttons and he had not taken off his brown trilby hat.

Harry spoke to Lady Oxenford. 'I'm thrilled to meet you, ma'am. I'm interested in antique jewellery, and I've heard you have one of the finest collections in the world.'

'Why, thank you,' she said. 'It is a particular interest of mine.'

He was shocked to hear her American accent. What he knew about her came from his careful reading of society magazines. He had thought she was British. But now he vaguely remembered some gossip about the Oxenfords. The Marquess, like many aristocrats with vast country estates, had almost gone bankrupt after the war because of the world slump in agricultural prices. Some had sold their estates and gone to live in Nice or Florence where their dwindling fortunes bought a higher standard of living. But Algernon Oxenford had married the heiress to an American bank and it was her money that had enabled him to continue to live in the style of his ancestors.

All of which simply meant that Harry's act was going to have to fool a genuine American. It had to be faultless, and he would have to keep it up for the next thirty hours.

He decided to be charming to her. He guessed she was not averse to compliments, especially from good-looking young men. He looked closely at the brooch pinned to the bosom of her burnt-orange travelling suit. It was made of emeralds, sapphires, rubies and diamonds in the form of a butterfly landing on a wild rose spray. It was extraordinarily realistic. He decided it was French from about 1880 and took a guess as to the maker. 'Is your brooch by Oscar Massin?'

'You're quite right.'

'It's very fine.'

'Thank you again.'

She was rather beautiful. He could understand why Oxenford had married her, but it was harder to see why she had fallen for him. Perhaps he had been more attractive twenty-five years ago.

'I think I know the Philadelphia Vandenposts,' she said.

Harry thought, Blimey, I hope not. However, she sounded rather vague.

'My family are the Glencarrys of Stamford, Connecticut,' she added.

'Indeed!' said Harry, pretending to be impressed. He was still thinking about Philadelphia. Had he said he came from Philadelphia, or Pennsylvania? He could not remember. Maybe they were the same place. They seemed to go together. Philadelphia, Pennsylvania. Stamford, Connecticut. He remembered that when you asked Americans where they came from they always gave two answers. Houston, Texas; San Francisco, California. Yeah.

The boy said, 'My name's Percy.'

'Harry,' said Harry, glad to be back on familiar ground. Percy's was a courtesy title, for the heir to use until his father died, whereupon he would become the Marquess of Oxenford. Most of these people were ludicrously proud of their stupid titles. Harry had once been introduced to a snot-nosed three-year-old as Baron Portrail. However, Percy seemed all right. He was courteously letting Harry know that he did not want to be addressed formally.

Harry sat down. He was facing forward, so Margaret was next to him across the narrow aisle, and he would be able to talk to her without the others hearing. The plane was as quiet as a church. Everyone was rather awestruck.

He tried to relax. It was going to be a tense trip. Margaret knew his true identity, and that created a big new risk. Even though she had accepted his subterfuge, she could change her mind, or let something slip by accident. Harry could not afford to arouse misgivings.

He could get through US Immigration if no searching questions were asked, but if something happened to make them suspicious, and they decided to check up on him, they would quickly find out that he was using a stolen passport and it would be all over.

Another passenger was brought to the seat opposite Harry. He was quite tall, with a bowler hat and a dark grey suit which had once been all right but was now past its best. Something about him struck Harry, who watched the man taking off his overcoat and settling in his seat. He had stout, well-worn black shoes, heavy-weight wool socks, and a wine-coloured waistcoat under his double-breasted jacket. His dark blue tie looked as if it had been tied in the same place every day for ten years.

If I didn't know the price of a ticket on this flying palace, Harry thought, I'd swear blind that man was a copper.

It was not too late to stand up and get off the plane.

No one would stop him. He could simply walk away and disappear.

But he had paid ninety pounds!

Besides, it might be weeks before he could get another transatlantic passage and while he was waiting he might be re-arrested.

He thought again about going on the run in England, and once again dismissed the idea. It would be difficult, in wartime, with every busybody on the look-out for foreign spies; but, more importantly, life as a fugitive would be unbearable – living in cheap boarding-houses, avoiding policemen, always on the move.

The man opposite him, if he were a policeman, was certainly not after Harry, of course – otherwise he would not be sitting down and making himself comfortable for the flight. Harry could not imagine what the man was doing, but for the moment he put that out of his mind and concentrated on his own predicament. Margaret was the danger factor. What could he do to protect himself?

She had entered into his subterfuge in a spirit of fun. As things stood he could not rely on her to keep it up. But he could improve his chances by getting close to her. If he could win her affection, she might begin to feel a sense of loyalty to him, and then she would take his charade more seriously and be careful not to betray him.

Getting to know Margaret Oxenford would not be an unpleasant duty. He studied her out of the corner of his eye. She had the same pale autumnal colouring as her mother: red hair, cream skin with a few freckles, and those fascinating dark green eyes. He could not tell what her figure was like, but she had slender calves and narrow feet. She wore a rather plain camel-coloured lightweight coat over a red-brown dress. Although her clothes looked expensive she did not have her mother's sense of style: that might come as she grew older and more confident. She wore no interesting jewellery, just a plain single strand of pearls around her neck. She had neat, regular features and a determined chin. She was not his usual type – he always picked girls with a weakness, because they were so much easier to romance. Margaret was too good-looking to be a pushover. However, she seemed to like him and that was a start. He made up his mind to win her heart.

The steward, Nicky, came into the compartment. He was a small, plump, effeminate man in his middle twenties, and Harry thought he was probably a queer. A lot of waiters were like that, he had noticed. Nicky handed out a typewritten sheet with the names of the passengers and crew on today's flight.

Harry studied it with interest. He knew of Baron Philippe Gabon, the wealthy Zionist. The next name, Professor Carl Hartmann, also rang a bell. He had not heard of Princess Lavinia Bazarov, but her name suggested a Russian who had fled from the Communists and her presence on this plane presumably meant she had got at least part of her wealth out of the country. He had most certainly heard of Lulu Bell, the film star. Only a week ago he had taken Rebecca Maugham-Flint to see her in *A Spy in Paris* at the Gaumont in Shaftesbury Avenue. She had played a plucky girl, as usual. Harry was very curious to meet her.

Percy, who sat facing the rear and could see into the next compartment, said, 'They've closed the door.'

Harry began to feel nervous again.

For the first time he noticed that the plane was rising and falling gently on the water.

There was a rumble, like the gunfire of a distant battle. Harry anxiously looked out of the window. As he watched, the noise increased, and a propeller began to turn. The engines were being started. He heard the third and the fourth give voice. Although the noise was muffled by heavy sound-proofing, the vibration of the mighty motors could be felt and Harry's apprehension increased.

On the floating dock a seaman cast off the flying boat's moorings. Harry had a foolish feeling of inevitable doom as the ropes tying him to the land were carelessly dropped into the sea.

He was embarrassed about being afraid and did not want anyone else to know how he felt, so he took out a newspaper, opened it, and sat back with his legs crossed.

Margaret touched his knee. She did not need to raise her voice to be heard: the soundproofing was amazing. 'I'm scared, too,' she said.

Harry was mortified. He thought he had succeeded in appearing calm.

The plane moved. He grabbed the arm of his chair, holding on tight; then he forced himself to let go. Of course she could tell he was scared. He was probably as white as the newspaper he was pretending to read.

She was sitting with her knees pressed close together and her hands clasped tightly in her lap. She seemed apprehensive and excited at the same time, as if she were about to take a roller-coaster ride. Her flushed cheeks, wide eyes and slightly open mouth made her look sexy. Harry wondered again what her body was like under that coat.

He looked at the others. The man opposite him was calmly fastening his safety belt. Margaret's parents were gazing out of the windows. Lady Oxenford appeared unperturbed, but Lord Oxenford kept clearing his throat noisily, a sure sign of tension. Young Percy was so thrilled he could hardly sit still, but he did not seem in the least frightened.

Harry stared at his paper but he could not read a word, so he lowered it and looked out of the window instead. The mighty aircraft was taxiing majestically out into Southampton Water. He could see the ocean liners in a row along the dockside. They were already some distance away and there were several smaller craft between him and the land. Can't get off now, he thought.

The water became choppy as the aircraft moved into the middle of the estuary. Harry was not normally seasick but now he felt distinctly uncomfortable as the Clipper began to ride the waves. The compartment looked like a room in a house but the motion reminded him that he was sailing in a boat, a fragile craft of thin aluminium.

The plane reached the middle of the estuary, slowed, and began to swing round. It rocked with the breeze, and Harry realized it was turning into the wind for take-off. Then it seemed to pause, hesitating, pitching a little with the wind and rolling with the slight swell, as if it were a monstrous animal sniffing the air with its enormous snout. The suspense was almost too much: it took an effort of will for Harry to restrain himself from leaping out of his seat and yelling to be let off.

Suddenly there was a terrific roar, like a fearsome storm breaking out, as the four huge engines were pushed to full power. Harry let out a cry of shock but it was drowned. The aircraft seemed to settle a little in the water, as if it were sinking under the strain, but a moment later it surged forward.

It picked up speed rapidly, like a fast boat, except that no boat this big could accelerate so quickly. White water sped past the windows. The Clipper still pitched and rolled with the movement of the sea. Harry wanted to close his eyes but he was afraid to. He felt panicky. I'm going to die, he thought hysterically.

The Clipper went faster and faster. Harry had never travelled at such a pace across water: no speedboat could reach this velocity. They were doing fifty, sixty, seventy miles an hour. Spray flew past the window, hazing his view. We're going to sink, explode, or crash, Harry thought.

There was a new vibration, like being in a car driving over ruts. What was it? Harry felt sure that something was terribly wrong, and the plane was about to break up. It occurred to him that it had begun to rise and the vibration was caused by its bumping across the waves like a speedboat. Was that normal?

Suddenly the water seemed to exert less drag. Peering through the spray, Harry saw that the surface of the estuary appeared to have tilted, and he realized that the plane's nose must be up, although he had not felt the change. He was terrified and wanted to throw up. He swallowed hard.

The vibration changed. Instead of bumping across ruts they seemed to be jumping from wave to wave, like a stone skimming the surface. The engines screamed and the propellers thrashed the air. It might be impossible, Harry thought; maybe such a huge machine could not take to the air after all; perhaps it could only ride the waves like an overweight dolphin. Then, suddenly, he sensed that the plane had been set free. It surged forward and up, and he felt the restraining water fall away underneath him. The view from the window cleared as the spray was left behind, and he saw the water receding below as the plane went up. Gorblimey, we're flying, he thought; this huge great palace is actually bloody flying!

Now that he was in the air his fear dropped away and was replaced by a tremendous feeling of exhilaration. It was as if he were personally responsible for the fact that the plane had succeeded in taking off. He wanted to cheer. Looking around, he saw that everyone else was smiling with relief. Becoming conscious of other people again, he discovered he was wet with sweat. He took out a white linen handkerchief, surreptitiously wiped his face and quickly stuffed it back into his pocket.

The plane continued to rise. Harry saw the south coast of England disappear beneath the stubby lower sea-wings, then he looked ahead and saw the Isle of Wight. After a while the plane levelled out and the roar of the engines was suddenly reduced to a low hum.

Nicky the steward reappeared in his white jacket and black tie. He did not have to raise his voice, now that the engines had been throttled back. He said, 'Would you care for a cocktail, Mr Vandenpost?'

That's exactly what I would care for, Harry thought. 'Large Scotch,' he said immediately. Then he remembered he was supposed to be American. 'On the rocks,' he added in the correct accent.

Nicky took orders from the Oxenfords and then disappeared through the forward doorway.

Harry drummed his fingers restlessly on the arm of the seat. The carpet, the soundproofing, the soft seats and the soothing colours made him feel as if he was in a padded cell, comfortable but trapped. After a moment he unbuckled his safety belt and got up.

He went forward, the way the steward had gone, and stepped through the doorway. On his left was the galley, a tiny kitchen gleaming with stainless steel, where the steward was making the drinks. On his right was a door marked 'Men's Retiring Room' which he assumed was the carsey. I must remember to call it the john, he thought. Next to the john was a staircase spiralling up, presumably to the flight deck. Beyond was another passenger compartment, decorated in different colours, and occupied by uniformed flight crew. For a moment Harry wondered what they were doing there, then he realized that on a flight lasting almost thirty hours crew members would have to take rests and be replaced.

He walked back along the plane, passing the galley and going through his compartment and the larger compartment by which they had boarded. Beyond that, towards the rear of the plane, were three more passenger compartments, decorated in alternating colour schemes, turquoise carpet and pale green walls or terracotta carpet with beige walls. There were steps up between the compartments, for the hull of the plane was curved, and the floor rose towards the rear. As he passed through he gave several friendly nods in the vague direction of the other passengers, as a wealthy and self-confident young American might do.

The fourth compartment had two small couches on one side, and on the other the Ladies' Powder Room – another fancy name for a carsey, no doubt. Beside the door to the ladies' room, a ladder on the wall led up to a trapdoor in the ceiling. The aisle, which ran the length of the plane, ended at a door. This must be the famous honeymoon suite that had caused so much press comment. Harry tried the door: it was locked.

Strolling back the length of the plane, he took another look at his fellow passengers.

He guessed that the man in smart French clothes was Baron Gabon. With him was a nervous fellow with no socks on. That was very peculiar. Perhaps he was Professor Hartmann. He wore a really terrible suit and looked half-starved.

Harry recognized Lulu Bell but was shocked to find that she looked about forty: he had imagined she was the age she appeared in her films, which was about nineteen. She was wearing a lot of good quality modern jewellery: rectangular earrings, big bracelets and a rock crystal brooch, probably by Boucheron.

He saw again the beautiful blonde he had noticed in the coffee lounge of the South-Western Hotel. She had taken off her straw hat. She had blue eyes and clear skin. She was laughing at something her companion was saying. She was obviously in love with him, even though he was not strikingly good-looking. But women like a man who makes them laugh, Harry thought.

The old duck with the Fabergé pendant in rose diamonds was presumably the Princess Lavinia. She wore a frozen expression of distaste, like a Baptist in a nightclub.

The larger compartment through which they had boarded had been empty during take-off but now, Harry observed, it was in use as a communal lounge. Four or five people had moved into it, including the tall man who had been seated opposite Harry. Some of the men were playing cards, and it crossed Harry's mind that a professional gambler might make a lot of money on a trip such as this.

He returned to his seat and the steward brought him his Scotch. 'The plane seems half empty,' Harry said.

Nicky shook his head. 'We're full up.'

Harry looked around. 'But there are four spare seats in this compartment, and all the others are the same.'

'Sure, this compartment seats ten on a daytime flight. But it only sleeps six. You'll see why when we make up the bunks after dinner. Meanwhile, enjoy the space.'

Harry sipped his drink. The steward was perfectly polite and efficient but not as obsequious as, say, a waiter in a London hotel. Harry wondered whether American waiters had a different attitude. He hoped so. On his expeditions into the strange world of London's high society, he had always found it a bit degrading to be bowed and scraped to and called 'sir' every time he turned round.

It was time to further his friendship with Margaret Oxenford, who was sipping a glass of champagne and leafing through a magazine. He had flirted with dozens of girls of her age and social station, and he went into his routine automatically. 'Do you live in London?'

'We've got a house in Eaton Square, but we spend most of our time in the country,' she said. 'Our place is in Berkshire. Father also has a shooting lodge in Scotland.' Her tone was rather too matter-of-fact, as if she found the question boring and wanted to dispose of it as quickly as possible.

'Do you hunt?' Harry said. This was a standard conversational ploy: most rich people did, and they loved to talk about it.

'Not much,' she said. 'We shoot more.'

'Do *you* shoot?' he asked in surprise: it was not considered a ladylike pursuit.

'When they let me.'

'I suppose you have lots of admirers.'

She turned to face him and lowered her voice. 'Why are you asking me all these stupid questions?'

Harry was floored. He hardly knew what to say. He had asked dozens of girls the same questions and none of them had reacted this way. 'Are they stupid?' he fumbled.

'You don't care where I live or whether I hunt.'

'But that's what people talk about in high society.'

'But you're not in high society,' she said bluntly.

'Stone the crows!' he exclaimed in his natural accent. 'You don't beat about the bush, do you?'

She laughed. 'That's better.'

'I can't keep changing my accent, I'll get confused.'

'All right. I'll put up with your American accent if you promise not to make silly small talk.'

'Thanks, honey,' he said, reverting to the role of Harry Vandenpost. She's no pushover, he was thinking. She was a girl who knew her own mind, all right. But that made her a lot more interesting.

'You're very good at it,' she was saying. 'I would never have guessed you were faking it. I suppose it's part of your *modus operandi*.'

They always baffled him when they spoke Latin. 'I guess it is,' he said without having the faintest idea what she meant. He would have to change the subject. He wondered what was the way to her heart. It was clear that he could not flirt with her the way he had with all the others. Perhaps she was the psychic type, interested in seances and necromancy. 'Do you believe in ghosts?' he tried.

That drew another sharp response. 'What do you take me for?' she said crossly. 'And why do you have to change the subject?'

He would have laughed it off with any other girl, but for some reason Margaret got to him. 'Because I don't speak Latin,' he snapped.

'What on earth are you talking about?'

'I don't understand words like *modus andy*.'

She looked mystified and irritated for a moment, then her face cleared and she repeated the phrase. '*Modus operandi*.'

'I never stayed at school long enough to learn that stuff,' he said.

The effect on her was quite startling. She flushed with shame and said, 'I'm most dreadfully sorry. How rude of me.'

He was surprised by the turnaround. A lot of them seemed to feel it was their duty to stuff their education down a man's throat. He was glad that Margaret had better manners than most of her kind. He smiled at her and said, 'All forgiven.'

She surprised him yet again by saying, 'I know how it feels, because I've never had a proper education either.'

'With all your money?' he said incredulously.

She nodded. 'We never went to school, you see.'

Harry was amazed. For respectable working-class Londoners it was shameful not to send your children to school, almost as bad as having the police round or being turned out by the bailiffs. Most children had to take a day off when their boots were at the mender's, for they did not have a spare pair, and mothers were embarrassed enough about that. 'But children have to go to school – it's the law!' said Harry.

'We had these stupid governesses. That's why I can't go to university – no qualifications.' She looked sad. 'I think I should have liked university.'

'It's unbelievable. I thought rich people could do anything they liked.'

'Not with my father.'

'What about the kid?' Harry nodded at Percy.

'Oh, he's at Eton, of course,' she said bitterly. 'It's different for boys.'

Harry considered. 'Does that mean,' he said diffidently, 'that you don't agree with your father in other things – politics, for instance?'

'I certainly don't,' she said fiercely. 'I'm a socialist.'

This, Harry thought, could be the key to her. 'I used to belong to the Communist Party,' he said. It was true: he had joined when he was sixteen and left after three weeks. He waited for her reaction before deciding how much to tell her.

She immediately became animated. 'Why did you leave?'

The truth was that political meetings bored him stiff, but it might be a mistake to say so. 'It's hard to put into words, exactly,' he prevaricated.

He should have known that would not wash with her. 'You must know why you left,' she said impatiently.

'I guess it was too much like Sunday School.'

She laughed at that. 'I know just what you mean.'

'Anyway, I reckon I've done more than the Commies in the way of returning wealth to the workers who produced it.'

'How is that?'

'Well, I liberate cash from Mayfair and take it to Battersea.'

'You mean you only rob the rich?'

'There's no point in robbing the poor, they haven't got any money.'

She laughed again. 'But surely you don't give away your ill-gotten gains, like Robin Hood?'

He considered what to tell her. Would she believe him if he pretended he robbed the rich to give to the poor? Although she was intelligent, she was also naïve –

but, he decided, not that naïve. 'I'm not a charity,' he said with a shrug. 'But I do help people sometimes.'

'This is amazing,' she said. Her eyes sparkled with interest and animation, and she looked quite ravishing. 'I suppose I knew there were people like you, but it's just extraordinary to actually meet you and talk to you.'

Don't overdo it, girl, Harry thought. He was nervous of women who became too enthusiastic about him: they were liable to feel outraged when they found out he was human. 'I'm not that special,' he said. 'I just come from a world you've never seen.'

She gave him a look that said she thought he *was* special.

This had gone far enough, he decided. It was time to change the subject. 'You're embarrassing me,' he said bashfully.

'I'm sorry,' she said quickly. She thought for a moment then added, 'Why are you going to America?'

'To get away from Rebecca Maugham-Flint.'

She laughed. 'No, seriously.'

She was like a terrier when she got hold of something, he thought: she wouldn't let go. She was impossible to control, which made her dangerous. 'I had to leave to stay out of jail,' he said.

'What will you do when you get there?'

'I thought I might join the Canadian Air Force. I'd like to learn to fly.'

'How exciting.'

'What about you? Why are you going to America?'

'We're running away,' she said disgustedly.

'What do you mean?'

'You know that my father is a Fascist?'

Harry nodded. 'I've read about him in the papers.'

'Well, he thinks the Nazis are wonderful and he doesn't want to fight against them. Besides, the government would put him in jail if he stayed.'

'So you're going to live in America?'

'My mother's family come from Connecticut.'

'And how long will you be there?'

'My parents are going to stay at least for the duration of the war. They may never come back.'

'But you don't want to go?'

'Certainly not,' she said forcefully. 'I want to stay and fight. Fascism is the most frightful wickedness and this war is dreadfully important, and I want to do my bit.' She started to talk about the Spanish Civil War but Harry was only half listening. He had been struck by a thought so shocking that his heart was beating faster and he had to make an effort to keep a normal expression on his face.

When people flee a country at the outbreak of war, they do not leave their valuables behind.

It was quite simple. Peasants would drive their livestock before them as they ran from invading armies. Jews fled from the Nazis with gold coins sewn inside their coats. After 1917, Russian aristocrats such as Princess Lavinia arrived in all the capitals of Europe clutching their Fabergé eggs.

Lord Oxenford must have considered the possibility that he would never return. Moreover, the government had brought in exchange controls to prevent the British upper classes from transferring all their money abroad.

The Oxenfords knew they might never again see what they left behind. It was certain they had brought whatever assets they could carry.

It was a little risky, of course, carrying a fortune in jewellery in your luggage. But what would be less risky? Mailing it? Sending it by courier? Leaving it behind, possibly to be confiscated by a vengeful government, looted by an invading army, or even 'liberated' in a post-war revolution?

No. The Oxenfords would have their jewellery with them.

In particular, they would be carrying the Delhi Suite.

The very thought of it took his breath away.

The Delhi Suite was the centrepiece of Lady Oxenford's famous collection of antique jewellery. Made of rubies and diamonds in gold settings, it consisted of a necklace with matching earrings and a bracelet. The rubies were Burmese, the most precious kind, and huge: they had been brought to England in the eighteenth century by the general Robert Clive, known as Clive of India, and set by the Crown jewellers.

The Delhi Suite was said to be worth a quarter of a million pounds – more money than a man could ever spend.

And it was almost certainly on this plane.

No professional thief would steal while travelling on a ship or plane: the list of suspects was too short. Furthermore, Harry was impersonating an American, travelling on a false passport, jumping bail and sitting opposite a policeman. It would be madness to try to get his hands on the suite, and he felt shaky just at the thought of the risks involved.

On the other hand, he would never have another chance like this. And suddenly he needed those jewels the way a drowning man gasps for air.

He would not be able to sell the suite for a quarter of a million, of course. But he would get about a tenth of its value, say twenty-five thousand pounds, which was more than a hundred thousand dollars.

In either currency it was enough for him to live on for the rest of his life.

The thought of that much money made his mouth water – but the jewellery itself was irresistible. Harry had seen pictures of it. The graduated stones of the necklace were perfectly matched; the diamonds set off the rubies like teardrops on a baby's cheek; and the smaller pieces, the earrings and the bracelet, were perfectly proportioned. The whole ensemble, on the neck, ears and wrist of a beautiful woman, would be utterly ravishing.

Harry knew he would never again be this close to such a masterpiece. Never.

He had to steal it.

The risks were appalling – but then, he had always been lucky.

'I don't believe you're listening to me,' Margaret said.

Harry grinned. 'I'm sorry. Something you said sent me into a daydream.'

'I know,' she said. 'From the look on your face, you were dreaming about someone you love.'

CHAPTER EIGHT

NANCY LENEHAN waited in a fever of impatience while Mervyn Lovesey's pretty yellow aeroplane was readied for take-off. He was giving last-minute instructions to the man in the tweed suit, who seemed to be the foreman of a factory he owned. Nancy gathered that he had union trouble and a strike was threatened.

When he had finished he turned to Nancy and said, 'I employ seventeen toolmakers and every one of them's a ruddy individualist.'

'What do you make?' she asked.

'Fans,' he replied. He pointed at the plane. 'Aircraft propellers, screws for ships, that kind of thing. Anything that has complex curves. But the engineering is the easy part. It's the human factor that gives me grief.' He smiled condescendingly and added, 'Still, you're not interested in industrial problems.'

'But I am,' she said. 'I run a factory too.'

He was taken aback. 'What kind?'

'I make five thousand seven hundred pairs of shoes a day.'

He was impressed, but he also seemed to feel he had been trumped, for he said, 'Good for you,' in a tone that mixed mockery with admiration. Nancy guessed that his business was much smaller than hers.

'Maybe I ought to say I *used* to make shoes,' she said, and the taste of bile was in her mouth as she admitted it. 'My brother is trying to sell the business out from under my feet. That', she added with an anxious look at the plane, 'is why I have to catch the Clipper.'

'You will,' he said confidently. 'My Tiger Moth will get us there with an hour to spare.'

She hoped with all her heart that he was right.

The mechanic jumped down from the plane. 'All set, Mr Lovesey.'

Lovesey looked at Nancy. 'Fetch her a helmet,' he said to the mechanic. 'She can't fly in that bloody silly little hat.'

Nancy was taken aback by the sudden reversion to his previous offhand manner. Clearly, he was happy enough to talk to her while there was nothing else to do but as soon as something important cropped up he lost interest. She was not used to such a casual attitude from men. Although not the seductive type, she was attractive enough to catch a man's eye and she carried a certain authority. Men patronized her often enough, but they rarely treated her with Lovesey's insouciance. However, she was not going to protest. She would put up with a lot worse than rudeness for the chance of catching up with her treacherous brother.

She was mightily curious about his marriage. 'I'm chasing my wife,' he had said, a surprisingly candid admission. She could see why a woman would run away from him. He was terribly good-looking, but he was also self-absorbed and insensitive. That was why it was so odd that he was running after his wife. He seemed the type who would be too proud. Nancy would have guessed he would say, 'Let her go to hell.' Perhaps she had misjudged him.

She wondered what the wife was like. Would she be pretty? Sexy? Selfish and spoilt? A frightened mouse? Nancy would find out soon – if they could catch up with the Clipper.

The mechanic brought her a helmet and she put it on. Lovesey climbed aboard, shouting over his shoulder, 'Give her a leg up, will you?'

The mechanic, more courteous than his master, helped her put on her coat, saying, 'It's chilly up there, even when the sun shines.' Then he hoisted her up and she clambered into the back seat. He passed her overnight case to her and she stowed it under her feet.

As the engine turned over she realized, with a shiver of nervousness, that she was about to take to the air with a total stranger.

For all she knew, Mervyn Lovesey might be a completely incompetent pilot, inadequately trained, with a poorly maintained plane. He could even be a white slaver, intent on selling her into a Turkish brothel. No, she was too old for that. But she had no reason to trust him. All she knew was that he was an Englishman with an aeroplane.

Nancy had flown three times before but always in larger planes with enclosed cabins. She had never experienced an old-fashioned biplane. It was like taking off in an open-top car. They sped down the runway with the roar of the engine in their ears and the wind buffeting their helmets.

The passenger aircraft Nancy had flown in seemed to ease gently into the air, but this went up with a jump, like a racehorse taking a fence. Then Lovesey banked so steeply that Nancy held on tight, terrified she would fall out despite her safety belt. Did he even have a pilot's licence?

He straightened up and the little plane climbed rapidly. Its flight seemed more comprehensible, less miraculous, than that of a big passenger aircraft. She could see the wings and breathe the wind and hear the howl of the little engine, and she could *feel* how it stayed aloft, feel the propeller pumping air and the wind lifting the broad fabric wings, the way you could feel a kite riding the wind when you held its string. There was no such sensation in an enclosed plane.

However, being in touch with the little plane's struggle to fly also gave her an uneasy sensation in the pit of her stomach. The wings were only flimsy things of wood and canvas; the propeller could get stuck, or break, or fall off; the helpful wind might change faithlessly and turn against them; there might be fog, or lightning, or hailstorms.

But all that seemed unlikely as the plane rose into the sunshine and turned its nose bravely towards Ireland. Nancy felt as if she were riding on the back of a big yellow dragonfly. It was scary but exhilarating, like a fairground ride.

They soon left the coast of England behind. She allowed herself a small moment of triumph as they headed west over the water. Peter would be boarding the Clipper soon and, as he did so, would congratulate himself on having outwitted his clever older sister. But his jubilation would be premature, she thought with angry satisfaction. He had not got the best of her yet. He would get a tremendous shock when he saw her arrive in Foynes. She could hardly wait to see the look on his face.

She still had a fight ahead, of course, even after she had caught up with Peter. She would not defeat him just by appearing at the board meeting. She would have to convince Aunt Tilly and Danny Riley that they would do better to hold on to their shares and stick with her.

She wanted to expose Peter's vicious behaviour to them all, so that they would know how he had lied to his sister and plotted against her; she wanted to crush him and mortify him by showing them all what a snake he was. But a moment's reflection told her that was not the smart thing to do. If she let her fury and resentment show, they would think she was opposing the merger for purely emotional reasons. She had to talk coolly and calmly about the prospects for the future, and act as if her disagreement with Peter was merely a business matter. They all knew she was a better manager than her brother.

Anyway, her argument made simple sense. The price they were being offered for their shares was based on Black's profits, which were low because of Peter's bad management. Nancy guessed they could make more by closing down the company and selling off all the shops.

But best of all would be to restructure the company according to her plan and make it profitable again.

There was another reason for waiting: the war. War was good for business in general and especially for companies such as Black's that supplied to the military. The US might not get into the war but there was sure to be a precautionary build-up. So profits were set to rise anyway. No doubt that was why Nat Ridgeway wanted to buy the company.

She brooded over the situation as they crossed the Irish Sea, blocking out her speech in her head. She rehearsed key lines and phrases, speaking them out loud, confident that the wind would whip the words away before they could reach the helmeted ears of Mervyn Lovesey a yard in front of her.

She became so absorbed in her speech that she hardly noticed the first time the engine faltered.

'The war in Europe will double this company's value in twelve months,' she was saying. 'If the US gets into the war, the price will double again—'

The second time it happened Nancy snapped out of her reverie. The continuous high roar altered momentarily, like the sound of a tap with air trapped in the pipe. It recovered to normal, then changed again and settled into a different note, a ragged, altogether feebler sound that unnerved her.

The plane began to lose height.

'What's going on?' she yelled at the top of her voice, but there was no response. Either he could not hear her or he was too busy to reply.

The engine note changed again, mounting higher, as if he had stepped on the gas, and the plane levelled out.

Nancy was agitated. What was happening? Was the problem serious or not? She wished she could just see his face, but it remained resolutely turned forward.

The engine sound was no longer constant. Sometimes it seemed to recover to its previous full-throated roar; then it would quaver again and become uneven. Scared, Nancy peered forward, trying to discern some change in the spin of the propeller, but she could see none. However, each time the engine stuttered the plane lost a little height.

She could not stand the tension any longer. She unbuckled her safety belt, leaned forward, and tapped Lovesey's shoulder. He turned his head to one side and she shouted in his ear, 'What's wrong?'

'Don't know!' he yelled back.

She was too frightened to accept that. 'What's happening?' she persisted.

'Engine's missing on one cylinder, I think.'

'Well, how many cylinders has it got?'

'Four.'

The plane suddenly lurched lower. Nancy hastily sat back and buckled up. She was a car driver and had a notion that a car could keep going with one cylinder missing. However, her Cadillac had twelve. Could a plane fly on three out of four cylinders? The uncertainty was torture.

They were losing height steadily now. Nancy guessed the plane could fly on three cylinders, but not for long.

How soon would they fall into the sea? She gazed into the distance and, to her relief, saw land ahead. Unable to restrain herself, she undid her belt and spoke to Lovesey again. 'Can we reach the land?'

'Don't know!' he shouted.

'You don't know anything!' she yelled. Fear turned her shout into a scream. She forced herself to be calm again. 'What's your best estimate?'

'Shut your mouth and let me concentrate!'

She sat back again. I may die now, she thought, and once again she fought down the panic and made herself think calmly. It's lucky I raised my boys before this happened, she told herself. It will be hard for them, especially after losing their father in a car crash. But they're men, big and strong, and they'll never lack for money. They'll be okay.

I wish I'd had another lover. It's been . . . how long? Ten years! No wonder I'm getting used to it. I might as well be a nun. I should have gone to bed with Nat Ridgeway: he would have been nice.

She had had a couple of dates with a new man, just before leaving for Europe, an unmarried accountant of about her own age, but she did not wish she had gone to bed with him. He was kind but weak, like too many of the men she met. They saw her as strong and they wanted her to take care of them. But I want someone to take care of me! she thought.

If I survive this I'm going to make damn sure I have one more lover before I die.

Peter would win now. That was a damn shame. The business was all that was left of their father and now it would be absorbed and disappear into the amorphous mass of General Textiles. Pa had worked hard all his life to build that company and Peter had destroyed it in five idle, selfish years.

Sometimes she still missed her father. He had been such a clever man. When there was a problem, whether it was a major business crisis such as the depression or a little family matter like one of the boys doing poorly at school, Pa would come up with a positive, hopeful way of dealing with it. He had been very good with mechanical things, and the people who manufactured the big machines used in shoemaking would often consult him before finalizing a design. Nancy understood the production process perfectly well, but her expertise was in predicting what styles the market wanted, and since she took over the factory they had made more profit from women's shoes than men's. She never felt overshadowed by her father, the way Peter did; she just missed him.

Suddenly the thought that she would die seemed ridiculous and unreal. It would be like the curtain coming down before the play ended, when the leading actor was in the middle of a speech: that was simply not how things happened. For a while she felt irrationally cheerful, confident that she would live.

The plane continued to lose height, but the coast of Ireland came rapidly nearer. Soon she could see emerald fields and brown bogs. This is where the Black family originated, she thought with a little thrill.

Immediately in front of her, Mervyn Lovesey's head and shoulders began to move, as if he was struggling with the controls. Nancy's mood switched again, and she started to pray. She had been raised Catholic but she had not gone to mass since Sean was killed; in fact, the last time she had been inside a church had been his funeral. She did not really know whether she was a believer or not, but now she prayed hard, figuring that she had nothing to lose, anyway. She said the Our Father, then she asked God to save her so that she could be around for Hugh at least until he got married and settled down; and so that she might see her grandchildren; and because she wanted to turn the business around and continue to employ all those men and women and make good shoes for ordinary people; and because she wanted a little happiness for herself. Her life, she felt suddenly, had been all work for too long.

She could see the white tops of the waves now. The blur of the approaching coastline resolved into surf, beach, cliff and green field. She wondered, with a shiver of fear, whether she would be able to swim to shore if the plane came down in the water. She thought of herself as a strong swimmer but stroking happily up and down a pool was very different from surviving in the turbulent sea. The water would be bone-chillingly cold. What was the word used when people died of cold? Exposure. 'Mrs Lenehan's plane came down in the Irish Sea and she died of exposure', the Boston *Globe* would say. She shivered inside her cashmere coat.

If the plane crashed she probably would not live to feel the temperature of the water. She wondered how fast it was travelling. It cruised at about ninety miles per hour, Lovesey had told her, but it was losing speed now. Say it was down to fifty. Sean had crashed at fifty and he had died. No, there was no point in speculating how far she could swim.

The shore came nearer. Perhaps her prayers had been answered, she thought. Perhaps the plane would make landfall after all. There had been no further deterioration in the engine sound: it went on at the same high, ragged roar, with an angry tone, like the vengeful buzzing of a wounded wasp. Now she began to worry about where they would land if they did make it. Could a plane come down on a sandy beach? What about a pebble beach? A plane could land in a field, if it were not too rough, but what about a peat bog?

She would know only too soon.

The coast was now about a quarter of a mile away. She could see that the shoreline was rocky and the surf heavy. The beach looked awfully uneven, she saw with a sinking heart: it was littered with jagged boulders. There was a low cliff rising to a stretch of moorland with a few grazing sheep. She studied the moorland. It looked smooth, with no hedges and few trees. Perhaps the plane could land there. She did not know whether to hope for that or try to prepare herself for death.

The yellow plane struggled bravely on, still losing height. The salty smell of the sea reached Nancy's nose. It would surely be better to come down on the water, she thought fearfully, than to try to land on that beach. Those sharp stones would tear the flimsy little plane to pieces – and her, too.

She hoped she would die quickly.

When the shore was a hundred yards away she saw that the plane was not going to hit the beach: it was still too high. Lovesey was obviously aiming at the clifftop pasture. But would he get there? They now seemed almost on a level with the cliff top, and they were still losing height. They were going to smash into the cliff. She wanted to close her eyes but she did not dare. Instead she stared hypnotically at the cliff rushing at her.

The engine howled like a sick animal. The wind blew sea spray into Nancy's face. The sheep on the cliff were scattering in all directions as the plane zoomed at them. Nancy gripped the rim of the cockpit so hard her hands hurt. She seemed to be flying straight at the very lip of the cliff. It came at her in a rush. We're going to hit it, she thought; this is the end. Then a gust of wind lifted the plane a fraction, and she thought they were clear. But it dropped again. The cliff edge was going to knock the little yellow wheels off their struts, she thought. Then, with the cliff a split second away, she closed her eyes and screamed.

For a moment nothing happened.

Then there was a bump, and Nancy was thrown forward hard against her seat belt. For an instant she thought she was going to die. Then she felt the plane rise again. She stopped screaming and opened her eyes.

They were in the air still, just two or three feet above the clifftop grass. The plane bumped down again, and this time it stayed down. Nancy was shaken mercilessly as it juddered over the uneven ground. She saw that they were headed for a patch of bramble and they could yet crash. Then Lovesey did something and the plane turned, avoiding the hazard. The shaking eased; they were slowing down. Nancy could hardly believe she was still alive. The plane came unsteadily to a halt.

Relief shook her like a fit. She could not stop trembling. For a moment she let herself shudder. Then she felt hysteria coming on and took a grip on herself. 'It's over,' she said aloud. 'It's over, it's over, I'm all right.'

In front of her, Lovesey got up and climbed out of his seat with a toolbox in his hand. Without looking at her, he jumped down and walked round to the front of the aircraft where he opened the hood and peered in at the engine.

He might have asked me if I'm all right, Nancy thought.

In an odd way, Lovesey's rudeness calmed her. She looked around. The sheep had returned to their grazing as if nothing had happened. Now that the engine was silent, she could hear the waves exploding on the beach. The sun was shining, but she could feel a cold, damp wind on her cheek.

She sat still for a moment, then, when she was sure her legs would hold her, she stood up and clambered out of the aircraft. She stood on Irish soil for the first time in her life and felt moved almost to tears. This is where we came from, she thought, all those years ago. Oppressed by the British, persecuted by the Protestants, starved by potato blight, we crowded into wooden ships and sailed away from our homeland to a new world.

And a very Irish way this is to come back, she thought with a grin. I almost died landing here.

That was enough sentiment. She was alive, so could she still catch the Clipper? She looked at her wrist-watch. It was two-fifteen. The Clipper had just taken off from Southampton. She could get to Foynes in time, if this plane could be made to fly, and if she could summon up the nerve to get back into it.

She walked around to the front of the plane. Lovesey was using a big spanner to loosen a nut. Nancy said, 'Can you fix it?'

He did not look up. 'Don't know.'

'What's the problem?'

'Don't know.'

Clearly he had reverted to his taciturn mood. Exasperated, Nancy said, 'I thought you were supposed to be an engineer.'

That stung him. He looked at her and said, 'I studied mathematics and physics. My speciality is wind resistance of complex curves. I'm not a bloody motor mechanic!'

'Then maybe we should fetch a motor mechanic.'

'You won't find one in bloody Ireland. This country is still in the Stone Age.'

'Only because the people have been trodden down by the brutal British for so many centuries!'

He withdrew his head from the engine and stood upright. 'How the hell did we get on to politics?'

'You haven't even asked me if I'm all right.'

'I can see you're all right.'

'You nearly killed me!'

'I saved your life.'

The man was impossible.

She looked around the horizon. About a quarter of a mile away was a line of hedge or wall that might border a road, and a little farther she could see several low thatched roofs in a cluster. Maybe she could get a car and drive to Foynes. 'Where are we?' she said. 'And don't tell me you don't know!'

He grinned. It was the second or third time he had surprised her by not being as bad-tempered as he seemed. 'I think we're a few miles outside Dublin.'

She decided she was not going to stand there and watch him fiddle with the engine. 'I'm going to get help.'

He looked at her feet. 'You won't get far in those shoes.'

I'll show him something, she thought angrily. She lifted her skirt and quickly unfastened her stockings. He stared at her, shocked, and blushed crimson. She rolled her stockings down and took them off along with her shoes. She enjoyed discomposing him. Tucking her shoes into the pockets of her coat, she said, 'I shan't be long,' and walked off barefoot.

When her back was turned and she was a few yards away she permitted herself a broad grin. He had been completely nonplussed. It served him right for being so goddamn condescending.

The pleasure of having bested him soon wore off. Her feet rapidly became wet, cold and filthy dirty. The cottages were farther away than she had thought. She did not even know what she was going to do when she got there. She guessed she would try to get a ride into Dublin. Lovesey was probably right about the scarcity of motor mechanics in Ireland.

It took her twenty minutes to reach the first house. Behind it she found a small woman in clogs digging in a vegetable garden. Nancy called out, 'Hello.'

The woman looked up and gave a cry of fright.

Nancy said, 'There's something wrong with my airplane.'

The woman stared at her as if she had come from outer space.

Nancy realized that she must be a somewhat unusual sight, in a cashmere coat and bare feet. Indeed, a creature from outer space would be hardly less surprising, to a peasant woman digging her garden, than a woman in an aeroplane. The woman reached out a tentative hand and touched Nancy's coat. Nancy was embarrassed: the woman was treating her like a goddess.

'I'm Irish,' Nancy said, in an effort to make herself seem more human.

The woman smiled and shook her head, as if to say, 'You can't fool me.'

'I need a ride to Dublin,' Nancy said.

That made sense to the woman, and she spoke at last. 'Oh, yes, you do!' she said. Clearly she felt that apparitions such as Nancy belonged in the big city.

Nancy was relieved to hear her use English: she had

been afraid the woman might speak only Gaelic. 'How far is it?'

'You could get there in an hour and a half, if you had a decent pony,' the woman said in a musical lilt.

That was no good. In two hours the Clipper was due to take off from Foynes, on the other side of the country. 'Does anyone around here have an automobile?'

'No '

'Damn.'

'But the smith has a motorcycle.' She pronounced it 'motor sickle'.

'That'll do!' In Dublin she might get a car to take her to Foynes. She was not sure how far Foynes was, or how long it would take to get there, but she felt she had to try. 'Where's the smith?'

'I'll take you.' The woman stuck her spade in the ground.

Nancy followed her round the house. The road was just a mud track, Nancy saw with a sinking heart: a motorcycle could not go much faster than a pony on such a surface.

Another snag occurred to her as they walked through the hamlet. A motorcycle would take only one passenger. She had been planning to go back to the downed plane and pick up Lovesey, if she could get a car. But only one of them could be taken on a bike – unless the owner would sell it, in which case Lovesey could drive and Nancy could ride. Then, she thought excitedly, they could drive all the way to Foynes.

They walked to the last house and approached a lean-to workshop at the side. Nancy's high hopes were dashed instantly: the motorcycle was in pieces all over the earth floor and the blacksmith was working on it. 'Oh, hell,' Nancy said.

The woman spoke to the smith in Gaelic. He looked at Nancy with a trace of amusement. He was very young, with the Irish black hair and blue eyes, and he had a bushy moustache. He nodded, then said to Nancy, 'Where's your aeroplane?'

'About half a mile away.'

'Maybe I should take a look.'

'Do you know anything about planes?' she said sceptically.

He shrugged. 'Engines are engines.'

If he could take a motorcycle to pieces he might be able to fix an aero-engine.

The smith went on, 'However, it sounds to me as if I might be too late.'

Nancy frowned, then she heard what he had noticed: the sound of an airplane. Could it be the Tiger Moth? She ran outside and looked up into the sky. Sure enough, the little yellow plane was flying low over the hamlet.

Lovesey had fixed it – and he had taken off without waiting for her!

She gazed up unbelievingly. How could he do this to her? He even had her overnight case!

The plane swooped low over the hamlet, as if to mock her. She shook her fist at it. Lovesey waved to her and then climbed away.

She watched the plane recede. The smith and the peasant woman were standing beside her. 'He's leaving without you,' the smith said.

'He's a heartless fiend.'

'Is it your husband?'

'Certainly not!'

'Just as well, I suppose.'

Nancy felt sick. Two men had betrayed her today. Was there something wrong with her? she wondered.

She thought she might as well give up. She could not catch the Clipper now. Peter would sell the company to Nat Ridgeway and that would be the end of it.

The plane banked and turned. Lovesey was setting course for Foynes, she presumed. He would catch up with his runaway wife. Nancy hoped she would refuse to go back to him.

Unexpectedly, the plane kept on turning. When it was pointing towards the hamlet it straightened up. What was he doing now?

It came in along the line of the mud road, losing height. Why was he coming back? As the plane approached, Nancy began to wonder whether he was going to land. Was the engine faltering again?

The little plane touched down on the mud road and bounced along towards the three people outside the blacksmith's house.

Nancy almost fainted with relief. He had come back for her!

The plane juddered to a halt. Mervyn shouted something she could not make out. 'What?' she yelled.

Impatiently, he beckoned to her. She ran up to the

plane. He leaned towards her and shouted, 'What are you waiting for? Get in!'

She looked at her watch. It was a quarter to three. They could still make it to Foynes in time. Her spirits bounded with optimism again. I'm not finished yet! she thought.

The young blacksmith came up with a twinkle in his eye and shouted, 'Let me help you up.' He made a step with his linked hands. She put her muddy bare foot on it and he boosted her up. She scrambled into her seat.

The plane pulled away immediately.

A few seconds later they were in the air.

CHAPTER NINE

MERVYN LOVESEY'S wife was very happy.

Diana had been frightened when the Clipper took off, but now she felt nothing but elation.

She had not flown before. Mervyn had never invited her to go up in his little plane, even though she had spent days painting it a lovely bright yellow for him. She discovered that, once you got over the nervousness, it was a terrific thrill to be this high in the air in something like a first-class hotel with wings, looking down on England's pastures and cornfields, roads and railways, houses and churches and factories. She felt free. She was free. She had left Mervyn and run away with Mark.

Last night, at the South-Western Hotel in Southampton, they had registered as Mr and Mrs Alder and had spent their first whole night together. They had made love, then gone to sleep, then woken up in the morning and made love again. It seemed such a luxury, after three months of short afternoons and snatched kisses.

Flying the Clipper was like living in a movie. The décor was opulent, the people were elegant, the two stewards were quietly efficient, everything happened on cue as if it were scripted, and there were famous faces everywhere. There was Baron Gabon, the wealthy Zionist, always in intense discussion with his haggard companion. The Marquess of Oxenford, the famous Fascist, was on board with his beautiful wife. Princess Lavinia Bazarov, one of the pillars of Paris society, was in Diana's compartment in the window seat of Diana's divan.

Opposite the princess, in the other window seat on this side, was the movie star Lulu Bell. Diana had seen her in lots of films: *My Cousin Jake, Torment, The Secret Life, Helen of Troy* and many others had come to the Paramount Cinema in Oxford Street, Manchester. But the biggest surprise was that Mark knew her. As they were settling into their seats, a strident American voice had called out, 'Mark! Mark Alder! Is that really you?' and Diana had turned round to see a small blonde woman like a canary swooping on him.

It turned out they had worked together on a radio show in Chicago years ago, before Lulu was a big star. Mark had introduced Diana, and Lulu had been very sweet, saying how beautiful Diana was and how lucky Mark had been to find her. But naturally she was more interested in Mark, and the two of them had been chatting ever since take-off, reminiscing about the old days when they were young and short of money and lived in flophouses and stayed up all night drinking bootleg liquor.

Diana was surprised that Lulu was so short. In her films she seemed taller. Also younger. And in real life you could see that her hair was not naturally blonde, as

Diana's was, but dyed. However, she did have the chirpy, pushy personality she displayed in most of the movies. She was the centre of attention even now. Although she was talking to Mark, everyone was looking at her: Princess Lavinia in the corner, Diana opposite Mark, and the two men on the other side of the aisle.

She was telling a story about a radio broadcast during which one of the actors had left, thinking his part was over, when in fact he had one line to speak right at the end. 'So I said my line, which was: "Who ate the Easter cake?" And everybody looked around – but George had disappeared! And there was a *long* silence.' She paused for dramatic effect. Diana smiled. What on earth *did* people do when things went wrong during radio shows? She listened to the radio a lot but she could not remember anything like this happening. Lulu resumed. 'So I said my line again: "Who ate the Easter cake?" Then I went like this.' She lowered her chin and spoke in an astonishingly convincing gruff male voice. '"I think it must have been the cat."'

Everyone laughed.

'And that was the end of the show,' she finished.

Diana remembered a broadcast during which an announcer had been so shocked at something that he said, 'Jesus H. Christ!' in astonishment. 'I heard an announcer swear once,' she said.

She was about to tell the story, but Mark said, 'Oh, that happens all the time,' and turned back to Lulu, saying, 'Remember when Max Gifford said Babe Ruth had clean balls, and then couldn't stop laughing?'

Both Mark and Lulu giggled helplessly over that and

Diana smiled, but she was beginning to feel left out. She reflected that she was rather spoilt: for three months, while Mark had been alone in a strange town, she had had his undivided attention. Obviously that could not go on for ever. She would have to get used to sharing him with other people from now on. However, she did not have to play the part of audience. She turned to Princess Lavinia, sitting on her right, and said, 'Do you listen to the wireless, Princess?'

The old Russian woman looked down her thin, beaked nose and replied, 'I find it slightly vulgar.'

Diana had met sniffy old ladies before, and they did not intimidate her. 'How surprising,' she said. 'Only last night we tuned in to some Beethoven quintets.'

'German music is so mechanical,' the Princess returned.

There would be no pleasing her, Diana decided. She had once belonged to the most idle and privileged class the world had ever seen and she wanted everyone to know it, so she pretended that everything she was offered was not as good as what she had once been used to. She was going to be a bore.

The steward assigned to the rear half of the aircraft, whose name was Davy, arrived to take orders for cocktails. He was a small, neat, charming young man with fair hair, and he walked the carpeted aisle with a bouncy step. Diana asked for a dry martini. She did not know what it was, but she remembered from the movies that it was a chic drink in America.

She studied the two men on the other side of the compartment. They were both looking out of the windows. Nearest her was a handsome young man in a rather flashy suit. He was broad-shouldered, like an athlete, and wore several rings. His dark colouring led Diana to wonder whether he was South American. Opposite him was a man who looked rather out of place. His suit was too big and his shirt collar was worn. He did not look as if he could afford the price of a Clipper ticket. He was also as bald as a light bulb. The two men did not speak or look at one another but Diana was sure they were together.

She wondered what Mervyn was doing right now. He had almost certainly read her note. He might be crying, she thought guiltily. No, that was not like him. He was more likely to be raging. But who would he rage at? His poor employees, perhaps. She wished her note had been kinder, or at least more enlightening, but she had been too distraught to do better. He would probably phone her sister Thea, she guessed. He would think Thea might know where she had gone. Well, Thea didn't. She would be shocked. What would she tell the twins? The thought upset Diana.

Davy came back with their drinks. Mark raised his glass to Lulu, and then to Diana – almost as an afterthought, she reflected sourly. She tasted her martini and nearly spat it out. 'Ugh!' she said. 'It tastes like neat gin!'

Everyone laughed at her. 'It is mostly gin, honey,' said Mark. 'Haven't you had a martini before?'

Diana felt humiliated. She had not known what she was ordering, like a schoolgirl in a bar. All these cosmopolitan people now thought she was an ignorant provincial.

Davy said, 'Let me bring you something else, ma'am.'

'A glass of champagne, then,' she said sulkily.

'Right away.'

Diana spoke crossly to Mark. 'I haven't had a martini before. I just thought I'd try it. There's nothing wrong with that, is there?'

'Of course not, honey,' he said, and patted her knee.

Princess Lavinia said, 'This brandy is disgusting, young man. Bring me some tea instead.'

'Right away, Your Highness.'

Diana decided to go to the ladies' room. She stood up, said 'Excuse me,' and went out through the arched doorway that led rearwards.

She passed through another passenger compartment just like the one she had left, then found herself at the back of the plane. On one side was a small compartment with just two people in it, and on the other side a door marked 'Ladies' Powder Room'. She went in.

The powder room cheered her up. It really was very pretty. There was a neat dressing-table with two stools upholstered in turquoise leather, and the walls were covered with beige fabric. Diana sat down to repair her make-up. Mark called it rewriting her face. Paper tissues and cold cream were laid out neatly in front of her.

But when she looked at herself she saw an unhappy woman. Lulu Bell had come like a cloud blocking the sun. She had taken Mark's attention away and made him treat Diana like a slight inconvenience. Of course,

Lulu was nearer to Mark's age: he was thirty-nine and she had to be past forty. Diana was only thirty-four. Did Mark know how old Lulu was? Men could be stupid about things like that.

The real trouble was that Lulu and Mark had so much in common: both in show business, both American, both veterans of the early days of radio. Diana had not done anything like that. If you wanted to be harsh, you could say that she had not done anything except be a socialite in a provincial city.

Would it always be this way with Mark? She was going to his country. From now on he would know everything, but all would be unfamiliar to her. They would be mixing with his friends, for she had none in America. How many more times would she be laughed at for not knowing what everyone else knew, like the fact that a dry martini tasted of nothing but cold gin?

She wondered how much she would miss the comfortable, predictable world she had left behind, the world of charity balls and Masonic dinners at Manchester hotels where she knew all the people and all the drinks and all the menus, too. It was dull, but it was safe.

She shook her head, making her hair fluff out prettily. She was not going to think like that. I was bored to distraction in that world, she thought; I longed for adventure and excitement; and now that I've got it, I'm going to enjoy it.

She decided to make a determined effort to win back Mark's attention. What could she do? She did not want to confront him directly and tell him she resented his behaviour. That seemed weak. Maybe a taste of his own medicine would do the trick. She could talk to someone else the way he was talking to Lulu. That might make him sit up and take notice. Who would it be? The handsome boy across the aisle would do just fine. He was younger than Mark, and bigger. That ought to make Mark jealous as hell.

She dabbed perfume behind her ears and between her breasts, then left the powder room. She swung her hips a little more than was necessary as she walked along the plane, and she took pleasure in the lustful stares of the men and the admiring or envious looks of the women. I'm the most beautiful woman on the plane and Lulu Bell knows it, she thought.

When she reached her compartment she did not take her seat, but turned to the left-hand side and looked out of the window over the shoulder of the young man in the striped suit. He gave her a good-to-see-you smile.

She smiled back and said, 'Isn't this wonderful?'

'Ain't it just?' he said; but she noticed he threw a wary glance at the man opposite, as if he expected a reprimand. It was almost as if the other man was his chaperon.

Diana said, 'Are you two together?'

The bald man answered curtly. 'You could say we're associates.' Then he seemed to remember his manners, and held out his hand, saying, 'Ollis Field.'

'Diana Lovesey.' She shook his hand reluctantly. He had dirty fingernails. She turned back to the younger man.

'Frank Gordon,' he said.

Both men were American, but all resemblance ended there. Frank Gordon was smartly dressed, with a pin through his collar and a silk handkerchief in his breast pocket. He smelled of cologne and his curly hair was lightly oiled. 'What part is this, that we're flying over – is this still England?' he asked.

Diana leaned over him and looked out of the window, letting him smell her perfume. 'I think that must be Devon,' she said, although she really did not know.

'What part are you from?' he said.

She sat down beside him. 'Manchester,' she said. She glanced over at Mark, caught his startled look, and returned her attention to Frank. 'That's in the north-west.'

Opposite, Ollis Field lit a cigarette with a disapproving air. Diana crossed her legs.

Frank said, 'My family come from Italy.'

The Italian government was Fascist. Diana said candidly, 'Do you think Italy will enter the war?'

Frank shook his head. 'Italian people don't want war.'

'I don't suppose anybody wants war.'

'So why does it happen?'

She found him difficult to make out. He obviously had money but he seemed uneducated. Most men were eager to explain things to her, to show off their knowledge, whether or not she wanted it. This one had no such impulse. She looked over at his companion and said, 'What do you think, Mr Field?'

'No opinion,' he said grumpily.

She turned back to the younger man. 'Perhaps war is the only way Fascist leaders can keep their people under control.'

She looked at Mark again, and was disappointed to see that once again he was deep in conversation with Lulu, and they were giggling together like schoolchildren. She felt let down. What was the matter with him? Mervyn would have been ready to punch Frank's nose by now.

She looked back at Frank. The words on her lips were, 'Tell me all about yourself,' but suddenly she could not face the boredom of listening to his reply and she said nothing. At that point Davy brought her champagne and a plate of caviar on toast. She took the opportunity to return to her seat, feeling despondent.

She listened resentfully to Mark and Lulu for a while, then her thoughts drifted away. She was silly to get upset about Lulu. Mark was committed to her, Diana. He was just enjoying talking about old times. There was no point in Diana's worrying about America: the decision had been taken, the die was cast, Mervyn had read her note. It was stupid to start having second thoughts on account of a forty-five-year-old bottle-blonde such as Lulu. She would soon learn American ways, their drinks, their radio shows and their manners. Before long she would have more friends than Mark: she was like that, she attracted people to her.

She began to look forward to the long flight across the Atlantic. She had thought, when she read about the Clipper in the *Manchester Guardian*, that it sounded like the most romantic journey in the world. From Ireland to Newfoundland was almost two thousand miles, and it took for ever, something like seventeen hours. There was time to have dinner, and go to bed, and sleep all night and get up again, before the plane landed. The idea of wearing the nightclothes that she had worn with Mervyn had seemed wrong but she had not had time to shop for the trip. Fortunately she had a beautiful *café-au-lait* silk robe and salmon-pink pyjamas which she had never worn. There were no double beds, not even in the honeymoon suite – Mark had checked – but his bunk would be over hers. It was thrilling, and at the same time frightening, to think of going to bed high over the ocean and flying on, hour after hour, hundreds of miles from land. She wondered if she would be able to sleep. The engines would work just as well whether she was awake or not, but all the same she would worry that they might stop while she slept.

Glancing out of the window she saw that they were now over water. It must be the Irish Sea. People said a flying boat could not come down in the open sea because of the waves, but it seemed to Diana that it surely had a better chance than a land plane.

They flew into clouds and she could see nothing. After a while the plane began to shake. Passengers looked at one another and smiled nervously, and the steward went around asking everyone to fasten their safety belts. Diana felt anxious with no land in sight. Princess Lavinia was gripping the arm of her seat hard, but Mark and Lulu carried on talking as if nothing was happening. Frank Gordon and Ollis Field appeared calm but both lit cigarettes and drew hard on them.

Just as Mark was saying, 'What the hell happened to Muriel Fairfield?' there was a thud and the plane seemed to fall. Diana felt as if her stomach came up into her throat. In another compartment, a passenger screamed. But then the aircraft righted itself, almost as if it had landed.

Lulu answered, 'Muriel married a millionaire.'

'No kidding!' said Mark. 'But she was so ugly.'

Diana said, 'Mark, I'm scared!'

He turned to her. 'It was only an air pocket, honey. It's normal.'

'But it felt as if we were going to crash!'

'We won't. It happens all the time.'

He turned back to Lulu. For a moment Lulu gazed at Diana, expecting her to say something but Diana looked away, furious with Mark.

Mark went on, 'How did Muriel get a millionaire?'

Lulu paused. 'I don't know, but now they live in Hollywood and he puts money into movies.'

'Unbelievable!'

Unbelievable was right, Diana thought. As soon as she could get Mark on his own she was going to give him a piece of her mind.

His lack of sympathy made her feel more scared. By nightfall they would be over the Atlantic Ocean, rather than the Irish Sea. How would she feel then? She imagined the Atlantic as a vast, featureless blank, cold and deadly for thousands of miles. The only things you ever saw, according to the *Manchester Guardian*, were icebergs. If there had been some islands to relieve the seascape Diana might have felt less jittery. It was the complete blankness of the picture that was so frightening: nothing but the plane and the moon and the heaving sea. In a funny way it was like her anxiety about going to America: in her head she knew it was not dangerous, but the scenery was strange and there was not one single familiar landmark.

She was getting jumpy. She tried to think of other things. She was looking forward to the seven-course dinner, for she enjoyed long, elegant meals. Climbing into bunk beds would be childishly thrilling, like going to sleep in a tent in the garden. And the dizzying towers of New York were waiting for her on the other side. But the excitement of a journey into the unknown had now turned to fear. She drained her glass and ordered more champagne, but it failed to calm her. She longed for the feel of firm ground under her feet again. She shivered, thinking how cold the sea must be. Nothing she did could take her mind off her fear. If she had been alone, she would have hidden her face in her hands and shut her eyes tight. She stared malevolently at Mark and Lulu, who were chatting cheerfully, oblivious to her torment. She was even tempted to make a scene, to burst into tears or have hysterics, but she swallowed hard and stayed calm. Soon the plane would come down at Foynes and she could get off and walk around on dry land.

But then she would have to board again for the long transatlantic flight.

Somehow she could not bear that idea.

I can hardly get through an hour like this, she thought. How can I do it all night? It will kill me.

But what else can I do?

Of course, no one was going to force her to get back on the plane at Foynes.

And if no one forced her, she did not think she could do it.

But what would I do?

I know what I'd do.

I would telephone Mervyn.

She could hardly believe that her bright dream should collapse like this; but she knew it was going to happen.

Mark was being eaten alive in front of her eyes by an older woman with dyed hair and too much make-up, and Diana was going to telephone Mervyn and say, 'I'm sorry, I made a mistake, I want to come home.'

She knew he would forgive her. Feeling so sure of his reaction made her a little ashamed. She had wounded him, but he would still take her in his arms and be happy that she had returned.

But I don't want that, she thought miserably. I want to go to America and marry Mark and live in California. I love him.

No, that was a foolish dream. She was Mrs Mervyn Lovesey of Manchester, sister of Thea and Auntie Diana to the twins, the not-very-dangerous rebel of Manchester society. She would never live in a house with palm trees in the garden and a swimming pool. She was married to a loyal, grumpy man who was more interested in his business than in her. Most of the women she knew were in exactly the same situation, so it must be normal. They were all disappointed, but they were better off than the one or two who had married wastrels and drunks, so they commiserated with each other, agreed that it could be worse, and spent their husband's hard-earned money in department stores and hairdressing salons. But they never went to California.

The plane plunged into emptiness again, then righted itself as before. Diana had to concentrate hard not to throw up. But for some reason she was no longer scared. She knew what the future held. She felt safe.

She just wanted to cry.

CHAPTER TEN

FLIGHT ENGINEER Eddie Deakin thought of the Clipper as a giant soap bubble, beautiful and fragile, which he must carry carefully across the sea, while the people inside made merry, oblivious of how thin was the film between them and the howling night.

The journey was more hazardous than they knew, for the technology of the aircraft was new and the night sky over the Atlantic was uncharted territory, full of unexpected dangers. Nevertheless, Eddie always felt, proudly, that the skill of the Captain, the dedication of the crew and the reliability of American engineering would take them safely home.

On this journey, however, he was sick with fear.

There was a Tom Luther on the passenger list. Eddie had kept looking out of the flight deck windows as the passengers boarded, wondering which of them was responsible for kidnapping Carol-Ann, but of course he could not tell – they were just the usual crowd of well-dressed, well-fed tycoons and movie stars and aristocrats.

For a while, preparing for take-off, he had been able to turn his mind away from tormenting thoughts of Carol-Ann and concentrate on the task in hand:

checking his instruments, priming the four massive radial engines, warming them up, adjusting the fuel mixture and the cowl flaps, and governing engine speeds during taxiing. But once the plane reached its cruising altitude there was less for him to do. He had to synchronize engine speeds, regulate the engine temperature, and adjust the fuel mixture; then his job consisted mainly of monitoring the engines to check that they were performing smoothly. And his mind started wandering again.

He had a desperate, irrational need to know what Carol-Ann was wearing. He would feel just a little less bad if he could picture her in her sheepskin coat, buttoned and belted, and wet-weather boots, not because she might be cold – it was only September – but so that the shape of her body would be disguised. However, it was more likely she would have on the lavender-coloured sleeveless dress he loved so much, which showed off her lush figure. She was going to be locked up with a bunch of brutes for the next twenty-four hours and the thought of what might happen if they started drinking was agony to him.

What the hell did they want from him?

He hoped the rest of the crew would not notice the state he was in. Fortunately they were all concentrating on their own tasks and they were not crammed together as closely as in most aircraft. The flight deck of the Boeing B-314 was very large. The spacious cockpit was only part of it. Captain Baker and co-pilot Johnny Dott sat on raised seats side by side at their controls, with a gap between them leading to a trapdoor which gave access to the bow compartment in the nose of the plane. Heavy curtains could be drawn behind the pilots at night, so that the light from the rest of the cabin would not diminish their night vision.

That section alone was bigger than most flight decks, but the rest of the Clipper's flight cabin was even more generous. Most of the port side, on the left as you faced forward, was taken up by the seven-foot-long chart table, at which navigator Jack Ashford now stood, bending over his maps. Aft of that was a small conference table, at which the Captain could sit when he was not actually flying the plane. Beside the table was an oval hatch leading to the crawlway insidc the wing, a special feature of the Clipper, from which the engines could be reached during flight so that Eddie could do simple maintenance or repairs, such as fixing an oil leak, without the plane having to come down.

On the starboard, right-hand side, immediately behind the co-pilot's seat was the staircase leading down to the passenger deck. Then came the radio operator's station, where Ben Thompson sat facing forward. Behind Ben sat Eddie. He faced sideways, looking at a wall of dials and a bank of levers. A little to his right was the oval hatch leading to the starboard wing crawlway. At the back of the flight deck, a doorway led to the cargo holds.

The whole thing was twenty-one feet long and nine feet wide, with full headroom throughout. Carpeted, soundproofed, and decorated with soft green wall fabric and brown leather seats, it was the most unbelievably luxurious flight deck ever made: when Eddie first saw it he thought it was some kind of joke.

Now, however, he saw only the bent backs and concentrated frowns of his crew-mates, and judged, with relief, that they had not noticed that he was beside himself with fear.

Desperate to understand why this nightmare was happening to him, he wanted to give the unknown Mr Luther an early opportunity to present himself. After take-off he hunted around for an excuse to pass through the passenger cabin. He could not think of a good reason, so he made do with a bad one. He stood up, mumbled to the navigator, 'Just going to check the rudder trim control cables,' and went quickly down the stairs. If anyone should ask him why he took it into his head to perform that check at that moment he would just say, 'Hunch.'

He walked slowly through the passenger cabin. Nicky and Davy were serving cocktails and snacks. The passengers were relaxing and conversing in several languages. There was already a card game in progress in the main lounge. Eddie saw some familiar faces but he was too distracted to figure out who the famous people were. He made eye contact with several passengers, hoping that one would reveal himself to be Tom Luther, but no one spoke to him.

He reached the back of the plane and climbed a wall-mounted ladder beside the door to the ladies' powder room. This led to a hatch in the ceiling which gave access to the empty space in the tail. He could have reached the same place by remaining on the upper deck and going back through the baggage holds.

He checked the rudder control cables in a perfunctory way then closed the hatch and descended the ladder. A boy of fourteen or fifteen was standing there watching him with lively curiosity. Eddie forced himself to smile. Encouraged, the boy said, 'Can I see the flight deck?'

'Sure you can,' Eddie said automatically. He did not want to be bothered right now, but on this of all planes the crew had to be charming to the passengers, and anyway the distraction might take his mind off Carol-Ann briefly.

'Super, thanks!'

'Honk back to your seat for a minute and I'll pick you up.'

A puzzled look passed briefly over the boy's face, then he nodded and hurried away. 'Honk back' was a New England expression, Eddie remembered: it was not familiar to New Yorkers, let alone Europeans.

Eddie walked even more slowly back along the aisle, waiting for someone to approach him, but no one did and he had to assume the man would wait for a more discreet opportunity. He could have asked the stewards where Mr Luther was seated, but they would naturally wonder why he wanted to know, and he was reluctant to arouse their curiosity.

The boy was in No. 2 compartment, near the front, with his family. Eddie said, 'Okay, kid, come on up,' and smiled at the parents. They nodded rather frostily at him. A girl with long red hair – the boy's sister, maybe – gave him a grateful smile and his heart missed a beat: she was beautiful when she smiled.

'What's your name?' he asked the boy as they went up the spiral staircase.

'Percy Oxenford.'

'I'm Eddie Deakin, the flight engineer.'

They reached the top of the stairs. 'Most flight decks ain't as nice as this,' Eddie said, forcing himself to be cheerful.

'What are they like usually?'

'Bare and cold and noisy. And they have sharp projections that stick into you every time you turn around.'

'What does an engineer do?'

'I take care of the engines – keep them drivin' all the way to America.'

'What are all those levers and dials for?'

'Let's see . . . These levers here control the propeller speed, the engine temperature and the fuel mixture. There's one complete set for each of the four engines.' This was all a bit vague, he realized, and the boy was quite bright. He made an effort to be more informative. 'Here, sit in my chair,' he said. Percy sat down eagerly. 'Look at this dial. It shows that the temperature of number two engine, at its head, is two hundred and five degrees Centigrade. That's a little too close to the maximum permissible, which is two hundred and thirty-two degrees while cruising. So we'll cool it down.'

'How do you do that?'

'Take that lever in your hand and pull it down a

fraction . . . that's just enough. Now you've opened the cowl flap an inch more to let in extra cold air, and in a few moments you'll see that temperature drop. Have you studied much physics?'

'I go to an old-fashioned school,' Percy said. 'We do a lot of Latin and Greek but they're not very keen on science.'

It seemed to Eddie that Latin and Greek were not going to help Britain win the war, but he kept the thought to himself.

Percy asked, 'What do the rest of them do?'

'Well, now, the most important person is the navigator: that's Jack Ashford, standing at the chart table.' Jack, a dark-haired, blue-chinned man with regular features, looked up and gave a friendly smile. Eddie went on, 'He has to figure out where we are, which can be difficult in the middle of the Atlantic. He has an observation dome, back there between the cargo holds, and he takes sightings on the stars with his sextant.'

Jack said, 'Actually, it's a bubble octant.'

'What's that?'

Jack showed Percy the instrument. 'The bubble is just to tell you when the octant is level. You identify a star then look at it through the mirror, and adjust the angle of the mirror until the star appears to be on the horizon. You read off the angle of the mirror here, and look it up in the book of tables, and that gives you your position on the earth's surface.'

'It sounds simple,' Percy said.

'It is in theory,' Jack said with a laugh. 'One of the

problems on this route is that we can be flying through cloud for the whole journey, so I never get to see a star.'

'But surely, if you know where you started and you keep heading in the same direction, you can't go wrong.'

'That's called dead reckoning. But you *can* go wrong, because the wind blows you sideways.'

'Can't you guess how much?'

'We can do better than guess. There's a little trap-door in the wing, and I drop a flare in the water and watch it carefully as we fly away from it. If it stays in line with the tail of the plane we're not drifting, but if it seems to move to one side or the other, that shows me our drift.'

'It sounds a bit rough-and-ready.'

Jack laughed again. 'It is. If I'm unlucky, and I don't get a look at the stars all the way across the ocean, and I make a wrong estimate of our drift, we can end up a hundred miles or more off course.'

'And then what happens?'

'We find out about it as soon as we come within range of a beacon, or a radio station, and we set about correcting our course.'

Eddie watched as curiosity and understanding showed on the boyish, intelligent face. One day, he thought, I'll explain things to my own child. That made him think of Carol-Ann, and the reminder hurt like a pain in his heart. If only the faceless Mr Luther would make himself known Eddie would feel better. When he knew what was wanted of him he would at least understand why this awful thing was happening.

Percy said, 'May I see inside the wing?'

'Sure.' Eddie opened the hatch to the starboard wing. The roar of the huge engines immediately sounded much louder, and there was a smell of hot oil. Inside the wing was a low passage with a crawlway like a narrow plank. Behind each of the two engines was a mechanic's station with room for a man to stand upright, just about. Pan American's interior decorators had not got into this space, and it was a utilitarian world of struts and rivets, cables and pipes. 'That's what most flight decks are like,' Eddie shouted.

'May I go inside?'

Eddie shook his head and closed the door. 'No passengers beyond this point, I'm sorry.'

Jack said, 'I'll show you my observation dome.' He took Percy through the door at the back of the flight deck, and Eddie checked the dials he had been ignoring for the past few minutes. All was well.

The radioman, Ben Thompson, sang out the conditions at Foynes. 'Westerly wind, twenty-two knots, choppy sea.'

A moment later, on Eddie's board, the light over the word 'Cruising' winked out and the light over 'Landing' came on. He scanned his temperature dials and reported, 'Engines okay for landing.' The check was necessary because the high-compression motors could be damaged by too abrupt throttling back.

Eddie opened the door to the rear of the plane.

There was a narrow passage with cargo holds either side, and a dome, above the passage, reached by a ladder. Percy was standing on the ladder looking through the octant. Beyond the cargo holds was a space which was supposed to be for crew beds, but it had never been furnished: off-duty crew used No. 1 compartment. At the back of that area was a hatch leading to the tail space where the control cables ran. Eddie called, 'Landing, Jack.'

Jack said, 'Time to get back to your seat, young man.'

Eddie had a feeling that Percy was too good to be true. Although the boy did as he was told, there was a mischievous glint in his eye. However, for the moment he was on his best behaviour and he went obediently forward to the staircase and down to the passenger deck.

The engine note changed and the plane began to lose height. The crew went automatically into the smoothly co-ordinated landing routine. Eddie wished he could tell the others what was happening to him. He felt desperately lonely. These were his friends and colleagues; they trusted one another; they had flown the Atlantic together; he wanted to explain his plight and ask their advice. But it was too risky.

He stood up for a moment to look out of the window. He could see a small town which he guessed was Limerick. Outside the town, on the north bank of the Shannon estuary, a large new airport was being constructed, for land planes and seaplanes. Until it was finished the flying boats were coming down on the south side of the estuary, in the lee of a small island, off the village of Foynes.

Their course was north-west, so Captain Baker had to turn the plane through forty-five degrees to land into the westerly wind. A launch from the village would be patrolling the landing zone to check for large floating debris that might damage the aircraft. The refuelling boat would be standing by, loaded with fifty-gallon drums, and there would be a crowd of sightseers on the shore, come to watch the miracle of a ship that could fly.

Ben Thompson was talking into his radio microphone. At any distance greater than a few miles he had to use Morse code, but now he was close enough for voice radio. Eddie could not distinguish the words but he could tell from the calm, relaxed tone of voice that all was well.

They lost height steadily. Eddie watched his dials vigilantly, making occasional adjustments. One of his most important tasks was to synchronize engine speeds, a job that became more demanding when the pilot made frequent throttle changes.

Landing in a calm sea could be almost imperceptible. In ideal conditions the hull of the Clipper went into the water like a spoon into cream. Eddie, concentrating on his instrument panel, often was not aware that the plane had touched down until it had been in the water for several seconds. However, today the sea was choppy – which was as bad as it got in any of the places where the Clipper came down on this route.

The lowest point of the hull, which was called the

step, touched first, and there was a light thud-thud-thud as it clipped the tops of the waves. That lasted only a second or two, then the huge aircraft eased down another few inches and cleaved the surface. Eddie found it much smoother than coming down in a land plane, when there was always a perceptible bump, and sometimes several. Very little spray reached the windows of the flight deck, which was on the upper level. The pilot throttled right down and the aircraft slowed immediately. The plane was a boat again.

Eddie looked out of the windows again as they taxied to their mooring. On one side was the island, low and bare: he saw a small white house and a few sheep. On the other side was the mainland. He could see a sizeable concrete jetty with a large fishing-boat tied up to its side, several big oil storage tanks, and a straggle of grey houses. This was Foynes.

Unlike Southampton, Foynes did not have a purpose-built jetty for flying boats, so the Clipper would moor in the estuary and the people would be landed by launch. Mooring was the engineer's responsibility.

Eddie went forward, knelt between the two pilots' seats and opened the hatch leading to the bow compartment. He descended the ladder into the empty space. Stepping into the nose of the plane, he opened a hatch and stuck out his head. The air was fresh and salty, and he took a deep breath.

A launch came alongside. One of the hands waved to Eddie. The man was holding a rope attached to a buoy. He threw the rope into the water.

There was a collapsible capstan on the nose of the

flying boat. Eddie lifted it and locked it into position, then he took a boat-hook from inside and used it to pick up the rope that was floating in the water. He attached the rope to the capstan, and the aircraft was moored. Looking up to the windscreen behind him, he gave Captain Baker the thumbs-up sign.

Another launch was already coming alongside to take the passengers and crew off the plane.

Eddie closed the hatch and returned to the flight deck. Captain Baker and Ben, the radioman, were still at their stations, but the co-pilot, Johnny, was leaning on the chart table chatting to Jack. Eddie sat at his station and closed down the engines. When everything was shipshape he put on his black uniform jacket and white cap. The crew went down the stairs, passed through No. 2 passenger compartment, went into the lounge and stepped out on to the sea-wing. From there they boarded the launch. Eddie's deputy, Mickey Finn, remained behind to supervise the refuelling.

The sun was shining but there was a cool, salty breeze. Eddie surveyed the passengers on the launch, wondering yet again which one was Tom Luther. He recognized a woman's face, and realized with a faint shock that he had seen her making love to a French count in a movie called *A Spy in Paris*: she was the film star Lulu Bell. She was chatting animatedly to a guy in a blazer. Could he be Tom Luther? With them was a beautiful woman in a spotted dress who looked miserable. There were several other familiar faces but most of the passengers were anonymous men in suits and hats and rich women in furs.

If Luther did not make his move soon, Eddie would seek him out and to hell with discretion, he decided. He could not stand the waiting.

The launch puttered away from the Clipper towards the land. Eddie stared across the water, thinking of his wife. He kept picturing the scene as the men burst into the house. Carol-Ann might have been eating eggs, or making coffee, or getting dressed for work. What if she had been in the bathtub? Eddie loved to look at her in the tub. She would pin up her hair, showing her long neck, and lie in the water languidly sponging her suntanned limbs. She liked him to sit on the edge and talk to her. Until he met her, he had thought this kind of thing only happened in erotic daydreams. But now the picture was blighted by three coarse men in fedoras who burst in and grabbed her—

The thought of her fear and shock as they seized her maddened Eddie almost beyond endurance. He felt his head spinning and he had to concentrate to stay upright in the launch. It was his utter helplessness that made the predicament so agonizing. She was in desperate trouble and there was nothing he could do, nothing. He found he was clenching his fists spasmodically, and forced himself to stop.

The launch reached the shore and tied up to a floating pontoon connected by a gangway to the dock. The crew helped the passengers disembark then followed them up the gangway. They were directed to the customs shed.

The formalities were brief. The passengers drifted into the little village. Across the road from the harbour was a former inn which had been almost entirely taken over by airline personnel, and the crew headed for that.

Eddie was the last to leave, and as he came out of the customs shed he was approached by a passenger who said, 'Are you the engineer?'

Eddie tensed. The passenger was a man of about thirty-five, shorter than he but stocky and muscular. He wore a pale grey suit, a tie with a stickpin and a grey felt hat. Eddie said, 'Yes, I'm Eddie Deakin.'

'My name is Tom Luther.'

A red haze blurred Eddie's vision and his rage boiled over in an instant. He grabbed Luther by the lapels, swung him around, and banged him against the wall of the customs shed. 'What have you done to Carol-Ann?' he spat. Luther was taken completely by surprise: he had expected a frightened, compliant victim. Eddie shook him until his teeth rattled. 'You Christless son of a whore, where is my wife?'

Luther recovered quickly from the shock. The stunned look left his face. He broke Eddie's hold with a swift, powerful move and threw a punch. Eddie dodged it and hit him in the stomach twice. Luther expelled air like a cushion and doubled up. He was strong but out of condition. Eddie grabbed him by the throat and started to squeeze.

Luther stared at him out of terrified eyes.

After a moment Eddie realized he was killing the man.

He eased his grip, then let go completely. Luther slumped against the wall, gasping for air, his hand on his bruised neck.

The Irish customs officer looked out of the shed. He must have heard the thump as Eddie threw Luther against the wall. 'What happened?'

Luther stood upright with an effort. 'I stumbled, but I'm okay,' he managed.

The customs man bent down and picked up Luther's hat. He gave a curious look as he handed it over but he said no more and went back inside.

Eddie looked around. No one else had observed the scuffle. The passengers and crew had disappeared round the other side of the little railway station.

Luther put his hat on. In a hoarse voice he said, 'If you mess this up we'll both be killed as well as your damn wife, you imbecile.'

The reference to Carol-Ann maddened Eddie all over again and he drew back his fist to hit Luther, but Luther raised a protective arm and said, 'Calm down, will you? You won't get her back that way. Don't you understand that you need me?'

Eddie understood that perfectly well: he had simply lost his reason for a few moments. He took a step back and studied the man. Luther was well spoken and expensively dressed. He had a bristly blond moustache and pale eyes full of hate. Eddie had no regrets about punching him. He had needed to hit something and Luther was an appropriate target. Now he said, 'What do you want from me, you pile of shit?'

Luther put his hand inside his suit jacket. It crossed Eddie's mind that there might be a gun in there, but Luther took out a postcard and handed it over.

Eddie looked at it. It was a picture of Bangor, Maine. 'What the hell does this mean?'

Luther said, 'Turn over.'

On the other side was written: '44.70N, 67.00W'.

'What are these numbers – map co-ordinates?' Eddie asked.

'Yes. That's where you have to bring the plane down.'

Eddie stared at him. 'Bring the plane down?' he repeated stupidly.

'Yes.'

'That's what you want from me – that's what this is all about?'

'Bring the plane down right there.'

'But why?'

'Because you want your pretty wife back.'

'Where is this location?'

'Off the coast of Maine.'

People often assumed a seaplane could splash down anywhere, but in fact it needed very calm waters. For safety, Pan American would not allow a touchdown in waves more than three feet high. If the plane came down in a heavy sea it would break up. Eddie said, 'You can't land a flying boat in the open sea—'

'We know that. This is a sheltered place.'

'That doesn't mean—'

'Just check it out. You can come down there. I made sure of it.'

He sounded so confident that Eddie sensed he really had made sure. But there were other snags. 'How am I supposed to bring the plane down? I'm not the Captain.'

'I've looked into this very carefully. The Captain could bring the plane down in theory, but what excuse would he have? You're the engineer, you can make something go wrong.'

'You want me to crash the plane?'

'You'd better not – I'm going to be on board. Just have something go wrong so the Captain is forced to make an unscheduled splashdown.' He touched the postcard with a manicured finger. 'Right there.'

The engineer *could* create a problem that would force the plane down, no doubt about that; but an emergency was difficult to control and Eddie could not immediately see how to arrange an unscheduled splashdown at such a precise location. 'It just ain't that easy—'

'I know it's not easy, Deakin. But I know it can be done. I checked.'

Who had he checked with? Who was he? 'Who the hell are you, anyway?'

'Don't ask.'

Eddie had started out threatening this man but somehow the tables had turned and now he felt intimidated. Luther was part of a ruthless team that had planned this carefully. They had picked out Eddie to be their tool; they had kidnapped Carol-Ann; they had him in their power.

He put the postcard in the pocket of his uniform jacket and turned away.

'So you'll do it?' Luther said anxiously.

Eddie turned back and gave him a cold stare. He held Luther's eyes for a long moment, then walked away without speaking.

He was acting tough but in truth he was floored. Why were they doing this? At one point he had speculated that the Germans wanted to steal a Boeing B-314 to copy it, but that far-fetched theory was now washed out completely, for the Germans would want to steal the plane in Europe, not Maine.

The fact that they were so precise about the location at which they wanted the Clipper to come down was a clue. It suggested there would be a boat waiting there. But what for? Did Luther want to smuggle something or somebody into the United States – a suitcase full of opium, a bazooka, a Communist agitator or a Nazi spy? The person or thing would have to be pretty damned important to be worth all this trouble.

At least he knew why they had picked on him. If you wanted to bring the Clipper down, the engineer was your man. The navigator could not do it, nor could the radio operator, and a pilot would need the co-operation of his co-pilot; but an engineer, all on his own, could stop the engines.

Luther must have got a list of Clipper engineers out of Pan American. That would not be too difficult: someone could have broken into the offices one night, or just bribed a secretary. Why Eddie? For some reason Luther decided on this particular flight and got hold of the roster. Then he asked himself how to make Eddie Deakin co-operate and came up with the answer: kidnap his wife.

It would break Eddie's heart to help these gangsters. He hated crooks. Too greedy to live like regular people and too lazy to earn a buck, they cheated and stole from hard-working citizens and lived high on the hog. While others broke their backs ploughing and reaping, or worked eighteen hours a day to build up a business, or dug for coal under the ground, or sweated all day in a steelworks, the gangsters went around in fancy suits and big cars and did nothing but bully people and beat them up and scare them to death. The electric chair was too good for them.

His father had felt the same. He remembered what Pop had said about bullies at school: 'Those guys are mean, all right, but they ain't smart.' Tom Luther was mean, but was he smart? 'It's tough to fight those guys, but it ain't so hard to fool 'em,' Pop had said. But Tom Luther would not be easy to fool. He had thought up an elaborate plan and so far it seemed to be working perfectly.

Eddie would have done almost anything for a chance to fool Luther. But Luther had Carol-Ann. Anything Eddie did to foul up Luther's scheme might lead them to hurt her. He could not fight them *or* fool them: he just had to try to do what they wanted. Seething with frustration, he left the harbour and crossed the single road that led through the village of Foynes.

The air terminal was a former inn with a central yard. Since the village had become an important flying-boat airport, the building had been almost entirely taken over by Pan American, although there was still a bar, called Mrs Walsh's pub, in a small room with its own street door. Eddie went upstairs to the Operations Room, where Captain Marvin Baker and First Officer Johnny Dott were in conference with the Pan American station chief. Here, amid the coffee cups and ashtrays and the piles of radio messages and weather reports, they would take the final decision whether to make the long transatlantic crossing.

The crucial factor was the strength of the wind. The westward trip was a constant battle against the prevailing wind. Pilots would change altitude constantly in a search for the most favourable conditions, a game known as 'hunting the wind'. The lightest winds were generally found at lower altitudes, but below a certain point the plane would be in danger of colliding with a ship or, more likely, an iceberg. Strong winds required more fuel and sometimes the forecast winds were so strong that the Clipper simply could not carry enough to last the two thousand miles to Newfoundland. Then the flight would have to be postponed and the passengers taken to a hotel to wait until the weather improved.

But if that should happen today, what would become of Carol-Ann?

Eddie took a preliminary glance at the weather reports. The winds were strong and there was a storm in mid-Atlantic. He knew that the plane was full. Therefore there would have to be a careful calculation before the flight could get the go-ahead. The thought ratcheted up his anxiety: he could not bear to be stuck in Ireland while Carol-Ann was in the hands of those bastards on the other side of the ocean. Would they feed her? Did she have somewhere to lie down? Was she warm enough, wherever they were holding her?

He went to the Atlantic chart on the wall and checked the map reference Luther had given him. The spot had been quite well chosen. It was close to the Canadian border, a mile or two off shore, in a channel between the coast and a large island, in the Bay of Fundy. Someone who knew a little about flying boats would think it an ideal place to come down. It was not ideal – the ports used by the Clippers were even more sheltered – but it would be calmer than the open sea and the Clipper would probably be able to splash down there without great risk. Eddie was somewhat relieved: at least that part of the scheme might be made to work. He realized he had a big investment in the success of Luther's plan. The thought left a sour taste in his mouth.

He was still worried about just how he would bring the plane down. He could fake engine trouble, but the Clipper could fly on three engines and there was an assistant engineer, Mickey Finn, who could not be fooled for very long. He racked his brains but did not come up with a solution.

Plotting to do this to Captain Baker and the others made him feel like the worst kind of heel. He was betraying people who trusted him. But he had no choice.

Now an even greater hazard occurred to him. Tom Luther might not keep his promise. Why should he? He was a crook! Eddie might bring the plane down and still not get Carol-Ann back.

The navigator, Jack, came in with some more

weather reports, and shot a peculiar look at Eddie. Eddie realized that no one had spoken to him since he came into the room. They seemed to be tiptoeing around him: had they noticed how preoccupied he was? He had to make more effort to behave normally. 'Try not to get lost this trip, Jack,' he said, repeating an old joke. He was not much of an actor, and the gag seemed forced to him, but they laughed and the atmosphere eased.

Captain Baker looked at the fresh weather reports and said, 'This storm is getting worse.'

Jack nodded. 'It's going to be what Eddie would call a honker.'

They always ribbed him about his New England dialect. He managed to grin, and said, 'Or a baster.'

Baker said, 'I'm going to fly around it.'

Together, Baker and Johnny Dott produced a flight plan to Botwood, in Newfoundland, skirting the edge of the storm and avoiding the worst of the head winds. When they had finished, Eddie sat down with the weather forecasts and began his calculations.

For each sector of the trip he had predictions of the wind direction and force at one thousand feet, four thousand, eight thousand and twelve thousand. Knowing the cruising air-speed of the plane and the wind force, Eddie could calculate the ground speed. That gave him a flight time for each sector at the most favourable altitude. Then he would use printed tables to find the fuel consumption over that time with the current payload of the Clipper. He would plot the fuel requirement stage by stage, on a graph which the crew called the Howgozit Curve, work out the total and add a safety margin.

When he completed his calculations he saw to his consternation that the amount of fuel required to get them to Newfoundland was more than the Clipper could carry.

For a moment he did nothing.

The shortfall was terribly small: just a few pounds of payload too much, a few gallons of gas too little. And Carol-Ann was waiting somewhere, scared to death.

He should now tell Captain Baker that take-off would have to be postponed until the weather improved, unless he was willing to fly through the heart of the storm.

But the gap was so small.

Could he lie?

There was a safety margin built in, anyhow. If things went badly the plane could fly through the storm instead of going around it.

He hated the thought of deceiving his captain. He had always been aware that the lives of the passengers depended on him, and he was proud of his meticulous accuracy.

On the other hand, his decision was not irrevocable. Every hour during the trip he had to compare actual fuel consumption with the projection on the Howgozit Curve. If they burned more than anticipated they simply had to turn back.

He might be found out, and that would be the end of his career, but what did that matter when the lives of his wife and his unborn baby were at stake?

He worked through the calculation again, but this time, when checking the tables, he made two deliberate errors, taking fuel consumption for the lower payload in the next column of figures. Now the result came inside the safety margin.

Still he hesitated. Lying did not come easily to him, even in this appalling predicament.

Finally Captain Baker got impatient and looked over Eddie's shoulder, saying, 'Snap it up, Ed – do we go or stay?'

Eddie showed him the doctored result on the pad and kept his eyes down, not wanting to look Baker in the eye. He cleared his throat nervously, then did his best to speak in a firm, confident voice.

He said: 'It's close, Captain – but we go.'

Part Three

Foynes to mid-Atlantic

CHAPTER ELEVEN

DIANA LOVESEY stepped on to the dock at Foynes and felt pathetically grateful for the feeling of solid ground under her feet.

She was sad but calm. She had made her decision: she was not going to get back on the Clipper, she was not going to fly to America and she was not going to marry Mark Alder.

Her knees seemed wobbly, and for a moment she was afraid she might fall, but the sensation passed and she walked along the dock to the customs shed.

She put her arm through Mark's. She would tell him as soon as they were alone. It would break his heart, she thought with a stab of grief: he loved her very much. But it was too late to think of that now.

Most of the passengers had disembarked. The exceptions were the odd couple sitting near Diana, handsome Frank Gordon and bald Ollis Field, who had stayed on board. Lulu Bell had not stopped chatting to Mark. Diana ignored her. She no longer felt angry with Lulu. The woman was intrusive and overbearing, but she had enabled Diana to see her true situation.

They passed through customs and left the dock. They found themselves at the western end of a one-street village. A herd of cows was being driven through it and they had to wait for them to pass.

Diana heard Princess Lavinia say loudly, 'Why have I been brought to this *farm*?'

Davy, the little steward, replied in a soothing voice, 'I'll take you into the terminal building, Your Highness.' He pointed across the road to a large building like an old inn with ivy growing up the walls. 'There's a very comfortable bar, called Mrs Walsh's pub, where they sell excellent Irish whiskey.'

When the cows had gone, several of the passengers followed Davy to Mrs Walsh's pub. Diana said to Mark, 'Let's walk through the village.' She wanted to get him on his own as soon as possible. He smiled and agreed. However, some other passengers had the same idea, Lulu among them, and it was a small crowd that strolled along the main street of Foynes.

There was a railway station, a post office and a church, then two rows of grey stone houses with slate roofs. Some of the houses had shop fronts. There were several pony carts parked along the street but only one motorized truck. The villagers, dressed in tweeds and homespun, stared at the visitors in silk and furs, and Diana felt as if she was in a procession. Foynes had not yet got used to being a stopover for the world's wealthy and privileged élite.

She was hoping that the party would split up, but they stayed together in a knot, like explorers afraid of getting lost. She began to feel trapped. Time was passing. They went by another bar, and she suddenly said to Mark, 'Let's go in there.'

Lulu immediately said, 'What a great idea – there's nothing to see in Foynes.'

Diana had had quite enough of Lulu. 'I'd really like to talk to Mark alone,' she said crossly.

Mark was embarrassed. 'Honey!' he protested.

'Don't worry!' Lulu said immediately. 'We'll walk on and leave you lovers alone. There'll be another bar, if I know anything at all about Ireland!' Her tone was gay, but her eyes were cold.

Mark said, 'I'm sorry, Lulu—'

'Don't be!' she said brightly.

Diana did not like Mark apologizing for her. She turned on her heel and went into the building, leaving him to follow at his leisure.

The place was dim and cool. There was a high bar, with bottles and barrels racked behind it. In front were a few wooden tables and chairs on a plank floor. Two old men sitting in the corner stared up at Diana. She was wearing an orange-red silk coat over her spotted dress. She felt like a princess in a pawnshop.

A small woman in an apron appeared behind the bar. Diana said, 'May I have a brandy, please?' She wanted some Dutch courage. She sat down at a small table.

Mark came in – probably having apologized some more to Lulu, Diana thought sourly. He sat beside her and said, 'What was all that about?'

'I've had enough of Lulu,' Diana said.

'Why did you have to be so rude?'

'I wasn't rude. I simply said I wanted to talk to you alone.'

'Couldn't you have found a more tactful way of saying so?'

'I think she's probably oblivious to hints.'

He looked annoyed and defensive. 'Well, you're wrong. She's actually a sensitive person, although she seems brash.'

'It doesn't matter, anyway.'

'How can it not matter? You've just offended one of my oldest friends!'

The barmaid brought Diana's brandy. She drank some quickly to steel her nerve. Mark ordered a glass of Guinness. Diana said, 'It doesn't matter because I've changed my mind about this whole thing, and I'm not coming to America with you.'

He went pale. 'You can't mean that.'

'I've been thinking. I don't want to go. I'm going back to Mervyn – if he'll have me.' But she felt sure he would.

'You don't love him. You told me that. And I know it's true.'

'What do you know? You've never been married.' He looked hurt and she softened. She put her hand on his knee. 'You're right, I don't love Mervyn the way I love you.' She felt ashamed of herself, and took her hand away. 'But it's no good.'

'I've been paying too much attention to Lulu,' Mark said penitently. 'I'm sorry, honey. I apologize. I guess I got wrapped up in her because it's so long since I last saw her. I've been ignoring you. This is our big adventure, and I forgot that for an hour. Please forgive me.'

He was sweet when he felt he had been wrong: he had a sorrowful expression that looked boyish. Diana forced herself to remember how she had been feeling an hour ago. 'It's not just Lulu,' she said. 'I think I've been foolhardy.'

The barmaid brought Mark's drink but he did not touch it.

Diana went on, 'I've left everything I know – home, husband, friends and country. I'm on a flight across the Atlantic which is dangerous in itself. And I'm going to a strange country where I have no friends, no money, nothing.'

Mark looked distraught. 'Oh, God, I see what I've done. I abandoned you just when you were feeling vulnerable. Baby, I feel such a horse's ass. I promise I'll never do that again.'

Perhaps he would keep such a promise, and perhaps he would not. He was loving, but he was also easy-going. It was not in him to stick to a plan. He was sincere now, but would he remember his vow next time he ran into an old friend? It was his playful attitude to life that had attracted Diana in the first place and now, ironically, she saw that that very attitude made him unreliable. One thing you could say for Mervyn was that he was reliable: good or bad, his habits never changed.

'I don't feel I can rely on you,' she said.

He looked angry. 'When have I ever let you down?'

She could not think of an instance. 'You will, though,' she said.

'Anyway, you *want* to leave all these things behind.

You're unhappy with your husband, your country's at war, and you're bored with your home and your friends – you told me that.'

'Bored, but not frightened.'

'There's nothing to be frightened of. America is like England. People speak the same language, go to the same movies, listen to the same jazz bands. You're going to love it. I'll take care of you, I promise.'

She wished she could believe him.

'And there's another thing,' he went on. 'Children.'

That shaft went home. She did so long to have a baby, and Mervyn was adamant that he would not. Mark would be such a good father, loving and happy and tender. Now she felt confused, and her determination weakened. Maybe she *should* give up everything, after all. What was home and security to her if she could not have a family?

But what if Mark were to abandon her half-way to California? Suppose another Lulu turned up in Reno, just after the divorce, and Mark went off with her? Diana would be stranded with no husband, no children, no money and no home.

She wished now that she had been slower to say yes to him. Instead of throwing her arms around him and agreeing to everything right away, she should have discussed the future carefully and thought of all the snags. She should have asked for some kind of security, even just the price of a ticket home, in case things went wrong. But that might have offended him, and anyway it was going to take more than a ticket to get across the Atlantic once the war started in earnest.

I don't know what I should have done, she thought miserably, but it's too late for regrets. I've made my decision and I won't be talked out of it.

Mark took her hands in his own, and she was too sad to withdraw them. 'You changed your mind once, now change it back,' he said persuasively. 'Come with me, and be my wife, and we'll have children together. We'll live in a house right on the beach, and take our toddlers paddling in the waves. They'll be blond and suntanned, and grow up playing tennis and surfing and riding bicycles. How many kids would you like? Two? Three? Six?'

But her moment of weakness had passed. 'It's no good, Mark,' she said wistfully. 'I'm going back home.'

She could see from his eyes that now he believed her. They looked at one another sadly. For a while neither of them spoke.

Then Mervyn walked in.

Diana could not believe her eyes. She stared at him as if he were a ghost. He could not be here, it was impossible!

'So there you are,' he said in his familiar baritone voice.

Diana was swamped by contrary emotions. She was appalled, thrilled, frightened, relieved, embarrassed and ashamed. She realized her husband was looking at her holding hands with another man. She snatched her hands out of Mark's grasp.

Mark said, 'What is it? What's the matter?'

Mervyn came up to their table and stood with his hands on his hips, staring at them.

Mark said, 'Who the hell is this jerk?'

'Mervyn,' Diana said weakly.

'Christ Jesus!'

Diana said, 'Mervyn . . . how did you get here?'

'Flew,' he said with his customary terseness.

She noticed he was wearing a leather jacket and carrying a helmet. 'But – but how did you know where to find us?'

'Your letter said you were flying to America and there's only one way to do that,' he said with a note of triumph.

She could see that he was pleased with himself for having worked out where she was and intercepted her, somewhat against the odds. She had never imagined he could catch them up in his own plane: it simply had not occurred to her. She found herself weak with gratitude to him for caring enough to chase after her this way.

He sat down opposite them. 'Bring me a large Irish whiskey,' he called to the barmaid.

Mark picked up his beer glass and sipped nervously. Diana looked at him. At first he had seemed intimidated by Mervyn but now he had realized Mervyn was not going to start a fist fight he just looked uneasy. He moved his chair back from the table an inch, as if to distance himself from Diana. Perhaps he, too, felt ashamed at being caught holding hands.

Diana sipped some brandy to give her strength. Mervyn was watching her anxiously. His expression of bewilderment and hurt made her want to throw herself into his arms. He had come all this way without knowing what sort of reception he would get. She reached out and touched his arm reassuringly.

To her surprise, he looked uncomfortable and threw a worried glance at Mark, as if he felt disconcerted at being touched by his wife in front of her lover. His whiskey came and he drank it quickly. Mark looked wounded, and moved his chair closer to the table again.

Diana felt flustered. She had never been in a situation like this. They both loved her. She had been to bed with both of them – and they both knew it. It was unbearably embarrassing. She wanted to comfort them both, but she was afraid to. Feeling defensive she leaned back, putting more space between herself and them. 'Mervyn,' she said, 'I didn't want to hurt you.'

He looked hard at her. 'I believe you,' he said evenly.

'Do you . . . can you understand what happened?'

'I can grasp the broad outlines, simple soul though I am,' he said sarcastically. 'You've run off with your fancy man.' He looked at Mark and leaned towards him aggressively. 'An American, I gather; the weedy type that'll let you have your own way.'

Mark leaned back and said nothing, but stared intently at Mervyn. Mark was not a confronter. He did not look offended, just intrigued. Mervyn had been a major figure in Mark's life although they had never met. All these months Mark must have been consumed with curiosity about the man Diana slept with every night. Now he was finding out and he was fascinated. Mervyn, by contrast, was not the least interested in Mark.

Diana watched the two men. They could hardly have

been more different. Mervyn was tall, aggressive, bitter, nervy; Mark was small, neat, alert, open-minded. The thought occurred to her that Mark would probably use this scene in a comedy script one day.

Her eyes were heavy with tears. She took out a handkerchief and blew her nose. 'I know I've been imprudent,' she said.

'Imprudent!' Mervyn snapped, mocking the inadequacy of the word. 'You've been bloody daft.'

Diana winced. His scorn always cut her to the quick but on this occasion she deserved it.

The barmaid and the two men in the corner were following the conversation with unabashed interest. Mervyn waved to the barmaid and called out, 'Could I have a plate of ham sandwiches, love?'

'With pleasure,' she said politely. Barmaids always liked Mervyn.

Diana said, 'I just . . . I've been so miserable lately. I was only looking for a little happiness.'

'Looking for happiness! In America – where you've no friends, no relations, no home . . . Where's your sense?'

She was grateful to him for coming, but she wished he would be kinder. She felt Mark's hand on her shoulder. 'Don't listen to him,' he said quietly. 'Why shouldn't you be happy? There's nothing wrong with that.'

She looked fearfully at Mervyn, afraid of offending him further. He might yet reject her. How humiliating it would be if he should spurn her in front of Mark (and, she thought in the back of her mind, while the horrible Lulu Bell was on the scene). He was capable of it: that was the kind of thing he did. She wished now that he had not followed her. It meant he would have to make a spot decision. Given more time, she could have soothed his wounded pride. This was too rushed. She picked up her glass and put it to her lips, then set it down untasted. 'I don't want this,' she said.

Mark said, 'I expect you'd like a cup of tea.'

That was just what she wanted. 'Yes, I'd love it.'

He went to the bar and ordered it.

Mervyn would never have done that: to his way of thinking, tea was got by women. He gave Mark a look of contempt. 'Is that what's wrong with me?' he asked her angrily. 'I don't fetch your tea, is that it? You want me to be housemaid as well as breadwinner?' His sandwiches came but he did not eat any.

Diana did not know how to answer him. 'There's no need for a row,' she said softly.

'No need for a row? When is there need for one, then, if not now? You run off with this little pillock, without saying goodbye, leaving me a silly bloody note . . .' He took a piece of paper out of his jacket pocket and Diana recognized her letter. She blushed scarlet, feeling humiliated. She had shed tears over that note: how could he wave it about in a bar? She moved back from him, feeling resentful.

The tea came and Mark picked up the pot. He looked at Mervyn and said, 'Would you like a cup of tea poured by a little pillock?' The two Irishmen in the corner burst out laughing, but Mervyn glared stonily and said nothing.

Diana began to feel angry with him. 'I may be bloody daft, Mervyn, but I've got a right to be happy.'

He pointed an accusing finger at her. 'You made a vow when you married me and you've no right to leave.'

She felt mad with frustration: he was so completely unyielding, it was like explaining something to a block of wood. Why couldn't he be reasonable? Why did he have to be so damn certain he was always right and everyone else was wrong?

Suddenly she recognized this feeling. She had had it about once a week for five years. During the last few hours, in her panic on the plane, she had forgotten how awful he could be and how unhappy he could make her. Now it all came back like the horror of a remembered nightmare.

Mark said, 'She can do what she likes, Mervyn. You can't make her do a single thing. She's a grown-up. If she wants to go home with you, she will; and if she wants to come to America and marry me, she'll do that.'

Mervyn banged his fist on the table. 'She can't marry you, she's already married to me!'

'She can divorce you.'

'On what grounds?'

'You don't need grounds in Nevada.'

Mervyn turned his angry eyes on Diana. 'You're not going to Nevada. You're coming back to Manchester with me.'

She looked at Mark. He smiled gently at her. 'You don't have to obey anyone,' he said. 'Do what *you* want.'

Mervyn said, 'Get your coat on.'

In his blundering way, Mervyn had given Diana back her sense of proportion. She now saw her fear of the flight and her anxieties about living in America as minor worries by comparison with the all-important question: who did she want to live with? She loved Mark and Mark loved her, and all other considerations were marginal. A tremendous sense of relief came over her as she made her decision and announced it to the two men who loved her. She took a deep breath. 'I'm sorry, Mervyn,' she said. 'I'm going with Mark.'

CHAPTER TWELVE

NANCY LENEHAN enjoyed a minute of jubilation as she looked down from Mervyn Lovesey's Tiger Moth and saw the Pan American Clipper floating majestically on the calm water of the Shannon estuary.

The odds had been against her but she had caught up with her brother and foiled at least part of his plan. You've got to get up very early in the morning to outsmart Nancy Lenehan, she thought, in a rare moment of self-congratulation.

Peter was going to have the shock of his life when he saw her.

As the little yellow plane circled and Mervyn searched for a place to land, Nancy began to feel tense about the forthcoming confrontation with her brother. She still found it hard to believe that he had deceived and betrayed her with such complete ruthlessness. How could he? As children they had been bathed together. She had put Band-Aids on his knees, told him how babies were made and always given him a chew of her gum. She had kept his secrets and told him her own. After they grew up she had nursed his ego, never letting him be embarrassed because she was so much smarter even though she was a girl.

All their lives she had taken care of him. And when Pa died she had allowed Peter to become chairman of the company. That had cost her dearly. Not only had she suppressed her own ambition to make way for him: at the same time she had stifled a budding romance; for Nat Ridgeway, Pa's deputy, had resigned when Peter took charge. Whether anything would have come of that romance, she would never know, for Ridgeway had since married.

Her friend and lawyer, 'Mac' McBride, had advised her not to let Peter be chairman, but she had gone against his counsel, and her own best interests, because she knew how wounded Peter would be that people thought he was not fit to fill his father's shoes. When she remembered all she had done for him, and then thought of how he had tried to cheat her and lie to her, she wanted to weep with resentment and rage.

She was desperately impatient to find him, stand in front of him and look into his eyes. She wanted to know how he would act and what he would say to her.

She was also eager to join battle. Her catching up with Peter was only the first step. She had to get on the plane. That might be straightforward but if it was full she would have to try to buy someone else's seat, or use her charm on the Captain, or even bribe her way on board. Then, when she got to Boston, she had to persuade the minority shareholders, her aunt Tilly and her father's old lawyer Danny Riley, that they should refuse to sell their holdings to Nat Ridgeway. She felt she could do that, but Peter would not give up without a fight, and Nat Ridgeway was a formidable opponent.

Mervyn brought down the plane on a farm track at the edge of the little village. In an uncharacteristic display of good manners, he helped Nancy climb down to the ground. As she set foot on Irish soil for the second time she thought of her father, who although he had talked constantly of the old country never actually went there. She felt that was sad. He would have been pleased to know that his children had made it to Ireland. But it would have broken his heart to know how the company that had been his life had been run down by his son. Better that he was not here to see that.

Mervyn roped the plane down. Nancy was relieved to leave it behind. Pretty though it was, it had almost killed her. She still shivered every time she remembered flying towards that cliff. She did not intend to get into a small plane again for the rest of her life.

They walked briskly into the village, following a horse-drawn wagon loaded with potatoes. Nancy could tell that Mervyn, too, was feeling a mixture of triumph and apprehension. Like her, he had been deceived and betrayed and had refused to take it lying down; and like her he got great satisfaction from defying the expectations of those who had plotted against him. But for both of them the real challenge was still ahead.

A single street led through Foynes. Half-way along it they met a group of well-dressed people who could only be Clipper passengers: they looked as if they had wandered on to the wrong set at a film studio. Mervyn approached them and said, 'I'm looking for

Mrs Diana Lovesey – I believe she's a passenger on the Clipper.'

'She sure is!' said one of the women, and Nancy recognized the movie star Lulu Bell. There was a note in her voice that suggested she did not like Mrs Lovesey. Once again Nancy wondered what Mervyn's wife was like. Lulu Bell went on, 'Mrs Lovesey and her . . . companion? . . . went into a bar just along the street here.'

Nancy said, 'Could you direct me to the ticket office?'

'If I ever get cast as a tour guide, I won't need to rehearse!' said Lulu, and the passengers with her laughed. 'The airline building is at the far end of the street, past the railroad station, opposite the harbour.'

Nancy thanked her and walked on. Mervyn had already started and she had to run to catch up with him. However, he stopped suddenly when he caught sight of two men strolling up the street, deep in conversation. Nancy looked curiously at the men, wondering why they had stopped Mervyn in his tracks. One was a silver-haired swell in a black suit with a dove-grey waistcoat, obviously a passenger from the Clipper. The other was a scarecrow of a man, tall and bony with hair so short he almost looked bald and the expression of someone who has just woken up from a nightmare. Mervyn went up to the scarecrow and said, 'You're Professor Hartmann, aren't you?'

The man's reaction was quite shocking. He jumped back a pace and held up his hands defensively, as if he thought he was about to be attacked.

His companion said, 'It's all right, Carl.'

Mervyn said, 'I'd be honoured to shake your hand, sir.'

Hartmann dropped his arms, although he still looked wary. He shook hands.

Nancy was surprised at Mervyn's behaviour. She would have said that Mervyn Lovesey thought nobody in the world was his superior, yet here he was acting like a schoolboy asking a baseball star for his autograph.

Mervyn said, 'I'm glad to see you got out. We feared the worst, you know, when you disappeared. By the way, my name is Mervyn Lovesey.'

Hartmann said, 'This is my friend Baron Gabon, who helped me to escape.'

Mervyn shook hands with Gabon, then said, 'I won't intrude any more. *Bon voyage*, gentlemen.'

Hartmann must be something very special, Nancy thought, to have distracted Mervyn, even for a few moments, from his single-minded pursuit of his wife. As they walked on through the village she said, 'So who's he?'

'Professor Carl Hartmann, the greatest physicist in the world,' Mervyn replied. 'He's been working on splitting the atom. He got into trouble with the Nazis for his political views and everyone thought he was dead.'

'How do you know about him?'

'I did physics at university. I thought of becoming a research scientist, but I haven't the patience for it. I still keep up with developments, though. It so happens there have been some amazing discoveries in the field over the last ten years.'

'Such as?'

'There's an Austrian woman – another refugee from the Nazis, by the way – called Lise Meitner, working in Copenhagen, who managed to break the uranium atom into two smaller atoms, barium and krypton.'

'I thought atoms were indivisible.'

'So did we all until recently. That's what's so amazing. It makes a very big bang when it happens, which is why the military are so interested. If they can control the process they'll be able to make the most destructive bomb ever known.'

Nancy looked back over her shoulder at the frightened, shabby man with the burning gaze. The most destructive bomb ever known, she said to herself, and she shivered. 'I'm surprised they let him walk around unguarded,' she said.

'I'm not sure he is unguarded,' Mervyn said. 'Look at that chap.'

Following the direction of Mervyn's nod, Nancy looked across the street. Another Clipper passenger was idling along on his own: a tall, hefty man in a bowler hat and a grey suit with a wine-red waistcoat. 'Do you think that's his bodyguard?' she said.

Mervyn shrugged. 'The man looks like a copper to me. Hartmann may not know it but I'd say he's got a guardian angel in size twelve boots.'

Nancy had not thought Mervyn was that observant.

'I think this must be the bar,' Mervyn said, switching from the cosmic to the mundane without pausing for breath. He stopped at the door.

'Good luck,' Nancy said. She meant it. In a funny way she had grown to like him, despite his infuriating ways.

He smiled. 'Thanks. Good luck to you, too.'

He went inside and Nancy continued along the street.

At the far end, across the road from the harbour, was an ivy-grown building larger than anything else in the village. Inside, Nancy found a makeshift office and a good-looking young man in a Pan American uniform. He looked at her with a twinkle in his eye, even though he had to be fifteen years her junior.

'I want to buy a ticket to New York,' she told him.

He was surprised and intrigued. 'Is that so! We don't generally sell tickets here – in fact, we don't have any.'

That did not sound like a serious problem. She smiled at him: a smile always helped in overcoming trivial bureaucratic obstacles. 'Well, a ticket is only a piece of paper,' she said. 'If I give you the fare, I guess you'll let me on the plane, won't you?'

He grinned. She figured he would oblige her if he could. 'I guess so,' he said. 'But the plane is full.'

'Hell!' she muttered. She felt crushed. Had she gone through all this for nothing? But she was not yet ready to give up, not by a long way. 'There must be *something*,' she said. 'I don't need a bed. I'll sleep in a seat. Even a crew seat would do.'

'You can't take a crew seat. The only thing vacant is the honeymoon suite.'

'Can I take that?' she said hopefully.

'Why, I don't even know what price to charge—'

'But you could find out, couldn't you?'

'I guess it has to cost at least as much as two regular fares, and that would make it seven hundred and fifty bucks one way, but it could be more.'

She didn't care if it cost seven thousand dollars. 'I'll give you a blank cheque,' she said.

'Boy, you really want to ride this airplane, don't you?'

'I have to be in New York tomorrow. It's . . . very important.' She could not find words to express how important it was.

'Let's go ask the Captain,' the boy said. 'This way please, ma'am.'

Nancy followed him, wondering whether she had been wasting her efforts on someone who did not have the authority to make a decision.

He led her to an upstairs office. Six or seven of the Clipper's crew were there in their shirtsleeves, smoking and drinking coffee while they studied charts and weather reports. The young man introduced her to Captain Marvin Baker. When the handsome Captain shook her hand she had the oddest feeling that he was going to take her pulse, and she realized it was because he had a doctor's bedside manner.

The young fellow said, 'Mrs Lenehan needs to get to New York real bad, Captain, and she's willing to pay for the honeymoon suite. Can we take her?'

Nancy waited anxiously for the reply, but the Captain

asked another question. 'Is your husband with you, Mrs Lenehan?'

She fluttered her eyelashes, always a useful move when you were hoping to persuade a man to do something. 'I'm a widow, Captain.'

'I'm sorry. Do you have any baggage?'

'Just this overnight case.'

'We'll be glad to take you to New York, Mrs Lenehan,' he said.

'Thank God,' Nancy said fervently. 'I can't tell you how important it is to me.' For a moment her knees felt weak. She sat in the nearest chair. She was embarrassed about feeling so emotional. To cover up, she rummaged in her handbag and took out her cheque book. With a shaky hand she signed a blank cheque and gave it to the young man.

Now it was time to confront Peter.

'I saw some passengers in the village,' she said. 'Where would the rest of them be?'

'Most are in Mrs Walsh's pub,' the young man said. 'It's a bar in this building. The entrance is around the side.'

She stood up. The shaky spell had passed. 'I'm much obliged to you,' she said.

'Glad to be able to help.'

Nancy went out.

As she closed the door she heard a buzz of comment break out and she knew they were making ribald remarks about an attractive widow who could afford to sign blank cheques.

She went outside. It was a mild afternoon with weak

sunlight and the air was pleasantly damp with the salty taste of the sea. Now she had to look for her faithless brother.

She went around to the side of the building and entered the bar.

It was the kind of place into which she would never normally go: small, dark, roughly furnished, very masculine. Clearly it was originally intended to serve beer to fishermen and farmers, but now it was full of millionaires drinking cocktails. The atmosphere was stuffy and the noise level was high in several languages: there was something of a party atmosphere among the passengers. Was it her imagination, or was there a faintly hysterical note in the laughter? Did the jollification mask anxiety about the long flight over the ocean?

She scanned the faces and spotted Peter.

He did not notice her.

She stared at him for a moment, anger boiling up inside her. She felt her cheeks flush with rage. She had a powerful urge to slap his face. But she suppressed her fury. She would not show him how upset she was. It was always smarter to play it cool.

He was sitting in a corner, and Nat Ridgeway was with him. That was another shock. Nancy had known Nat was in Paris for the collections, but it had not occurred to her that he might fly back with Peter. She wished he were not here. The presence of an old flame just complicated matters. She would just have to forget that she had once kissed him. She put the thought out of her mind.

She pushed through the crowd and went up to their

table. Nat was the first to look up. His face showed shock and guilt, which gave her some satisfaction. Noticing his expression, Peter looked up.

Nancy met his eye.

He went pale and started up out of his chair. 'Good Christ!' he exclaimed. He looked scared to death.

'Why are you so frightened, Peter?' Nancy said contemptuously.

He swallowed hard and sank back into his seat.

Nancy continued, 'You actually paid for a ticket on the SS *Oriana*, knowing you weren't going to use it. You came to Liverpool with me and checked into the Adelphi Hotel, even though you weren't going to stay there. And all because you were afraid to tell me you were taking the Clipper!'

He stared back at her, white-faced and silent.

She had not planned to make a speech but the words just came. 'You slunk out of the hotel yesterday and rushed all the way to Southampton, hoping I wouldn't find out!' She leaned on the table and he shrank away from her. 'What are you so scared of? I'm not going to *bite* you!' As she said the word *bite* he flinched, as if she might really do it.

She had not troubled to lower her voice. The people nearby had gone quiet. Peter looked around with an embarrassed expression. Nancy said, 'I'm not surprised you feel foolish. After all I've done for you! All these years I've protected you, covered up for your stupid mistakes, and let you go on being chairman of the company even though you couldn't organize a church bazaar! After all that, you tried to steal the business from me! How could you do it? Doesn't it make you feel like a *worm*?'

He flushed crimson. 'You've never protected me, you've always looked after yourself,' he protested. 'You always wanted to be boss – but you didn't get the job! I got it, and you've been scheming to take it away from me ever since.'

This was so unjust that Nancy did not know whether to laugh, cry, or spit in his face. 'You idiot, I've been scheming ever since to let you *keep* the chairmanship.'

He pulled some papers from his pocket with a flourish. 'Like this?'

Nancy recognized her report. 'You bet like that,' she said. 'That plan is the only way for you to keep your job.'

'While you take control! I saw through it right away.' He looked defiant. 'That's why I came up with my own plan.'

'Which hasn't worked,' Nancy said triumphantly. 'I've got a seat on the plane and I'm coming back for the board meeting.'

For the first time she turned to Nat Ridgeway and spoke to him. 'I guess you still can't take control of Black's Boots, Nat.'

Peter said, 'Don't be so sure.'

She looked at him. He was petulantly aggressive. Surely he could not have something up his sleeve? He was not that smart. She said, 'You and I own forty per cent each, Peter. Aunt Tilly and Danny Riley hold the balance. They've always followed my lead. They know me and they know you. I make money and you lose it, and they understand that, even if they're polite to you for Pa's sake. They'll vote the way I ask them to.'

'Riley will vote with me,' Peter said obstinately.

There was something in his mulishness that worried her. 'Why would he vote with you when you've practically run the company into the ground?' she said scornfully, but she was not as confident as she made herself sound.

He sensed her anxiety. 'I've got you scared now, haven't I?' he sneered.

Unfortunately he was right. She was beginning to feel worried. He did not look as crushed as he should. She had to find out whether there was anything behind this bluster. 'I guess you're just talking through your hat,' she jeered.

'No, I'm not.'

If she kept taunting him he would feel compelled to prove her wrong, she knew. 'You always pretend to have something up your sleeve but it generally amounts to nothing at all.'

'Riley has promised.'

'And Riley is as trustworthy as a rattlesnake,' she said dismissively.

Peter was stung. 'Not if he gets . . . an incentive.'

So that was it: Danny Riley had been bribed. That bothered Nancy. Danny was nothing if not corruptible. What had Peter offered him? She had to know, so that she could either spoil the bribe or offer more. She said, 'Well, if your plan hinges on Danny Riley's reliability, I guess I don't have anything to worry about!' and she laughed derisively.

'It hinges on Riley's *greed*,' Peter said.

She turned to Nat. 'If I were you I'd be very sceptical about all this.'

'Nat knows it's true.' Peter was smug.

Nat clearly would have preferred to remain silent, but when they both stared at him he gave a reluctant nod of assent.

Peter said, 'He's giving Riley a big chunk of General Textiles work.'

That was a blow, and Nancy's breath caught in her throat. There was nothing Riley would have liked better than to get a foot in the door of a major corporation such as General Textiles. To a small New York law firm it was the opportunity of a lifetime. For a bribe like that Riley would sell his mother.

Peter's shares plus Riley's came to fifty per cent. Nancy's plus Aunt Tilly's also amounted to fifty per cent. With the votes divided equally, the issue would be decided by the casting vote of the chairman – Peter.

Peter could see he had trumped Nancy, and he allowed himself a smile of victory.

Nancy was not yet willing to concede defeat. She pulled out a chair and sat down. She turned her attention to Nat Ridgeway. She had sensed his disapproval all the way through the argument and wondered if he knew that Peter had been working behind her back. She decided to put it to him. 'I suppose you knew Peter was lying to me about this?'

He stared at her, tight-lipped, but she could do that, too, and she simply waited, looking expectant. Finally she outstared him, and he said, 'I didn't ask. Your family quarrels are none of my concern. I'm not a social worker, I'm a businessman.'

But there was a time, she thought, when you held my hand in restaurants and kissed me goodnight; and once you caressed my breasts. She asked, 'Are you an honest businessman?'

'You know I am,' he said stiffly.

'In that case, you won't approve of dishonest methods being used on your behalf.'

He thought for a moment, then said, 'This a takeover, not a tea-party.'

He was going to say more but she jumped in. 'If you're willing to gain by my brother's dishonesty, you're dishonest yourself. You've changed since you worked for my father.' She turned back to Peter before Nat could reply. 'Don't you realize you could get twice the price for your shares if you let me implement my plan for a couple of years?'

'I don't like your plan.'

'Even without restructuring, the company is going to be worth more because of the war. We've always supplied soldiers' boots – think of the extra business if the US gets into the war!'

'The US won't get into this war.'

'Even so, the war in Europe will be good for business.' She looked at Nat. 'You know that, don't you? That's why you want to buy us out.'

Nat said nothing.

She turned back to Peter. 'But we'd do better to wait. Listen to me. Have I ever been wrong about this sort of thing? Have you ever lost money by following my advice? Have you ever made money by disregarding it?'

'You just don't understand, do you?' Peter said.

Now she could not imagine what was coming. 'What don't I understand?'

'Why I'm merging the company, why I'm doing this.'

'All right, why?'

He stared at her in silence, and she saw the answer in his eyes.

He hated her.

She was shocked rigid. She felt as if she had run headlong into an invisible brick wall. She wanted to disbelieve it, but the grotesque expression of malevolence on his distorted face could not be ignored. There had always been tension between them, natural sibling rivalry, but this, this was awful, weird, pathological. She had never suspected this. Her little brother Peter hated her.

This is what it must be like, she thought, when the man you have been married to for twenty years tells you he's having an affair with his secretary and he doesn't love you any more.

She felt dizzy, as if she had banged her head. It was going to take a while to adjust to this.

Peter was not merely being foolish, or mean, or spiteful. He was actually doing himself harm in order to ruin his sister. That was pure hatred.

He had to be at least a little bit crazy.

She needed to think. She decided to leave this hot, smoky bar and get some air. She stood up and left them without saying goodbye.

As soon as she stepped outside she felt a little better. There was a cool breeze blowing in off the estuary. She crossed the road and walked along the dockside, listening to the seagulls cry.

The Clipper was out in mid-channel. It was bigger than she had imagined: the men refuelling it looked tiny. She found its huge engines and enormous propellers reassuring. She would not feel nervous on this plane, she thought; not after surviving a trip across the Irish Sea in a single-engined Tiger Moth.

But what would she do when she got home? Peter would never be talked out of his plan. There were too many years of hidden anger behind his behaviour. She felt sorry for him in a way: he had been so unhappy all this time. But she was not going to give in to him. There might still be a way to save her birthright.

Danny Riley was the weak link. A man who could be bribed by one side could be bribed by the other. Perhaps Nancy could think of something else to offer him, something that would tempt him to change sides. But that would be tough. Peter's bribe, a chunk of General Textiles' law business, was hard to top.

Maybe she could threaten him. That would be cheaper, too. But how? She could take away some family and personal business from his firm, but that would not amount to much, nothing compared to the new business he would get from General Textiles. What Danny would like best would be straight cash, of course, but her fortune was mostly tied up in Black's Boots. She could lay her hands on a few thousand dollars without much trouble, but Danny would want more, maybe a hundred grand. She could not get hold of that much cash in time.

While she was deep in thought, her name was called. She turned around to see the young Pan American employee waving at her. 'There's a telephone call for you,' he shouted. 'A Mr McBride from Boston.'

She felt suddenly hopeful. Maybe Mac could think of a way out of this. He knew Danny Riley. Both men were like her father, second-generation Irish who spent all their time with other Irishmen and were suspicious of Protestants even if they were Irish. Mac was honest and Danny was not, but otherwise they were alike. Pa had been honest, but he had been willing to turn a blind eye to a little sharp practice, especially if it would help a buddy from the old country.

Pa had saved Danny from ruin once, she recalled as she hurried back along the dock. It was just a few years ago, not long before Pa died. Danny had been losing a big and important case, and in desperation he had approached the judge at their golf club and tried to bribe him. The judge had not been bribable and he had told Danny to retire or be disbarred. Pa had intervened with the judge and persuaded him that it was a momentary lapse. Nancy knew all about it: Pa had confided in her a lot towards the end of his life.

That was Danny: slippery, unreliable, rather foolish, easily swayed. Surely she could win him back to her own side.

But she only had two days.

She went into the building and the young man showed her the phone. She put the earpiece to her ear and picked up the stand. It was good to hear the familiar, affectionate voice of Mac. 'So you caught up with the Clipper,' he said jubilantly. 'Attagirl!'

'I'll be at the board meeting – but the bad news is that Peter says he's got Danny's vote tied up.'

'Do you believe him?'

'Yes. General Textiles is giving Danny a chunk of corporate business.'

Mac's voice became despondent. 'Are you sure it's true?'

'Nat Ridgeway is here with him.'

'That snake!'

Mac had never liked Nat and had hated him when he started dating Nancy. Even though Mac was happily married he was jealous of anyone who showed a romantic interest in Nancy.

'I pity General Textiles, having Danny do their law work,' Mac added.

'I guess they'll give him the low-grade stuff. Mac, is it legal for them to offer him this incentive?'

'Probably not, but the violation would be hard to prove.'

'Then I'm in trouble.'

'I guess so. I'm sorry, Nancy.'

'Thanks, old friend. You warned me not to let Peter be the boss.'

'I sure did.'

That was enough crying over spilt milk, Nancy decided. She adopted a brisker tone. 'Listen, if we were relying on Danny, we'd be worried, right?'

'You bet we would—'

'Worried that he'd change sides, worried that the opposition would make him a better offer. So what do we think his price is?'

'Hmm.' There was silence on the line for a few moments, then Mac said, 'Nothing springs to mind.'

Nancy was thinking about Danny trying to bribe a judge. 'Do you remember that time Pa got Danny out of a hole? It was the Jersey Rubber case.'

'I sure do. No details on the phone, okay?'

'Yes. Can we use that case somehow?'

'I don't see how.'

'To threaten him?'

'With exposure, you mean?'

'Yes.'

'Do we have proof?'

'Not unless there's something in Pa's old papers.'

'You have all those papers, Nancy.'

There were several cartons of Pa's personal records in the cellar of Nancy's house in Boston. 'I've never looked through them.'

'And there's no time for that now.'

'But we could pretend,' she said thoughtfully.

'I'm not following you.'

'I'm just thinking aloud. Bear with me for a minute. We could pretend to Danny that there is something, or might be something, in Pa's old papers, something that would bring that whole business out into the open.'

'I don't see how that—'

'No, listen to me, Mac, this is an idea.' Nancy's voice

rose with excitement as she began to see possibilities. 'Suppose the Bar Association, or whoever it is, decided to open an inquiry into the Jersey Rubber case.'

'Why would they do that?'

'Someone could tell them it was fishy.'

'All right, what then?'

Nancy began to feel she might have the makings of a workable plan. 'Suppose they heard that there was crucial evidence among Pa's stuff.'

'They would ask you if they could examine the papers.'

'Would it be up to me whether I let them?'

'In a simple Bar inquiry, yes. If there was a criminal inquiry you could be subpoenaed, and then of course you'd have no choice.'

A scheme was forming in Nancy's mind faster than she could explain it aloud. She hardly dared to hope that it might work. 'Listen, I want you to call Danny,' she said urgently. 'Ask him the following question—'

'Let me pick up a pencil. Okay, go ahead.'

'Ask him this. If there were a Bar inquiry into the Jersey Rubber case, would he want me to hand over Pa's papers?'

Mac was puzzled. 'You think he'll say no.'

'I think he'll panic, Mac! He'll be scared to death. He doesn't know what's there – notes, diaries, letters, could be anything.'

'I'm beginning to see how this could work,' Mac said, and Nancy could hear the hope creeping into his voice. 'Danny would think you have something he wants . . .'

'He'll ask me to protect him, as Pa did. He'll ask me to refuse the Bar permission to look at the papers. And I'll agree – on condition he votes with me against the merger with General Textiles.'

'Wait a minute. Don't open the champagne yet. Danny may be venal but he's not stupid. Won't he suspect that we've cooked this whole thing up to pressure him?'

'Of course he will,' Nancy said. 'But he won't be sure. And he won't have long to think about it.'

'Yeah. And right now it's our only chance.'

'Want to give it a try?'

'Okay.'

Nancy was feeling much better: full of hope and the will to win. 'Call me at our next stop.'

'Where's that?'

'Botwood, Newfoundland. We should be there in seventeen hours.'

'Do they have phones there?'

'They must, if there's an airport. You should book the call in advance.'

'Okay. Enjoy the flight.'

'Bye, Mac.'

She put the earpiece on the hook. Her spirits were high. There was no telling whether Danny would fall for it but she felt immensely cheered just to have a ploy.

It was twenty past four, time to board the plane. She left the room and passed through another office in which Mervyn Lovesey was speaking on another telephone. He put out his hand to stop her as she went by. Through the window she could see the passengers on the dockside boarding the launch, but she paused for a moment. He said into the phone, 'I can't be bothered with that now. Give the buggers the rate they're asking for and get on with the job.'

She was surprised. She recalled that there had been some kind of industrial dispute at his factory. It sounded as if he was giving in, which did not seem characteristic of him.

The person he was talking to seemed to be surprised too, for after a moment Mervyn said, 'Yes, I do bloody well mean it, I'm too busy to argue with toolmakers. Goodbye!' He hung up the earpiece. 'I've been looking for you,' he said to Nancy.

'Were you successful?' she asked him. 'Did you persuade your wife to come back?'

'No. But I didn't put it to her right.'

'That's too bad. Is she out there now?'

He looked through the window. 'That's her in the red coat.'

Nancy saw a blonde woman in her early thirties. 'Mervyn, she's beautiful!' she said. Somehow she had imagined Mervyn's wife as a tougher, less cute type, Bette Davis rather than Lana Turner. 'I can see why you don't want to lose her.' The woman was holding on to the arm of a man in a blue blazer, presumably the boyfriend. He was not nearly as handsome as Mervyn. He was a little below average height and his hair was beginning to recede. But he had a pleasant, easy-going look about him. Nancy could see instantly that the woman had gone for Mervyn's opposite. She felt sympathy for Mervyn. 'I'm sorry, Mervyn,' she said.

'I haven't given up,' Mervyn said. 'I'm coming to New York.'

Nancy smiled. This was more like Mervyn. 'Why not?' she said. 'She looks like the kind of woman a man might chase all the way across the Atlantic.'

'The thing is, it's up to you,' he said. 'The plane is full.'

'Of course. So how can you come? Why is it up to me?'

'You own the only remaining seat. You've taken the honeymoon suite. It seats two. I'm asking you to sell me the spare seat.'

She laughed. 'Mervyn, I can't share a honeymoon suite with a man. I'm a respectable widow, not a chorus girl!'

'You owe me a favour,' he said insistently.

'I owe you a favour, not my reputation!'

His handsome face took on an obstinate expression. 'You didn't think about your reputation when you wanted to fly across the Irish Sea with me.'

'That didn't involve our spending the night together!' She wished she could help him: there was something touching about his determination to get his beautiful wife back. 'I'm sorry, I really am,' she said. 'But I can't be involved in a public scandal at my age.'

'Listen. I've enquired about this honeymoon suite, and it's not that much different from the rest of the plane. There's two separate bunk beds. If we leave the door open at night we'll be in exactly the same situation as two total strangers who happen to be allocated adjoining bunks.'

'But think what people would say!'

'Who are you worried about? You've no husband to get offended, and your parents aren't alive. Who cares what you do?'

He could be extremely blunt when he wanted something, she thought. 'I've got two sons in their early twenties,' she protested.

'They'll think it's a lark, I bet.'

They probably would, she thought ruefully. 'I'm also worried about the whole of Boston society. Something like this would be sure to get around.'

'Look. You were desperate when you came to me on that airfield. You were in trouble and I saved your bacon. Now I'm desperate – you can see that, can't you?'

'Yes, I can.'

'I'm in trouble and I'm appealing to you. This is my last chance to save my marriage. You can do it. I saved you and you can save me. All it will cost you is a whiff of scandal. That never killed anybody. Please, Nancy.'

She thought about that 'whiff' of scandal. Did it really matter if a widow was faintly indiscreet on her fortieth birthday? It would not kill her, as he said, and it probably would not even damage her reputation. The matrons of Beacon Hill would think her 'fast', but people of her own age would probably admire her nerve. It's not as if I'm supposed to be a virgin, she thought.

She looked at his hurt, stubborn face and her heart went out to him. To hell with Boston society, she thought; this is a man in pain. He helped me when I needed it. Without him I wouldn't be here. He's right. I owe him.

'Will you help me, Nancy?' he begged. 'Please?'

Nancy took a deep breath. 'Hell, yes,' she said.

CHAPTER THIRTEEN

Harry Marks's last sight of Europe was a white lighthouse, standing proud on the north bank of the mouth of the Shannon, while the Atlantic Ocean angrily lashed the foot of the cliff below. A few minutes later there was no land in sight: whichever way he looked he saw nothing but the endless sea.

When I get to America I'm going to be rich, he thought.

Being this close to the famous Delhi Suite was so tantalizing as to be almost sexy. Somewhere on this plane, no more than a few yards from where he sat, was a fortune in jewellery. His fingers itched to touch it.

A million dollars in gems would be worth at least a hundred thousand from a fence. I could buy a nice flat and a car, he thought, or maybe a house in the country with a tennis court. Or perhaps I should invest it and live on the interest. I'd be a toff with a private income!

But first he had to get hold of the stuff.

Lady Oxenford was not wearing the jewellery, therefore it had to be in one of two places: the cabin baggage, right here in the compartment, or the checked baggage in the hold. If it were mine I'd keep it really close, Harry thought. I'd have it in my cabin bag. I'd be scared to let it out of my sight. But there was no telling how her mind worked.

He would check her cabin bag first. He could see it, under her seat, an expensive burgundy leather case with brass corners. He wondered how he might get inside it. Perhaps there would be a chance during the night when everyone was asleep.

He would find a way. It would be risky: thieving was a dangerous game. But somehow he always got away with it, even when things went wrong. Look at me, he thought; yesterday I was caught red-handed, with stolen cufflinks in my trousers pocket; I spent last night in jail and now here I am going to New York on the Pan American Clipper. Lucky? It's not the word!

He had once heard a joke about a man who jumped out of a tenth-floor window, and falling past the fifth floor was heard to say, 'So far, so good.' But that was not him.

The steward, Nicky, brought the dinner menu and offered him a cocktail. He did not need a drink but he ordered a glass of champagne just because it seemed like the right thing to do. This is the life, Harry boy, he said to himself. His elation at being on the world's most luxurious plane vied with his anxiety about flying across the ocean, but as the champagne took effect, elation won out.

He was surprised to see that the menu was in English. Did the Americans not know that posh menus were supposed to be in French? Perhaps they were just too sensible to print menus in a foreign language. Harry had a feeling he was going to like America.

The dining room seated only fourteen so dinner would be served in three sittings, the steward explained. 'Would you like to dine at six, seven thirty, or nine o'clock, Mr Vandenpost?'

This might be his chance, Harry realized. If the Oxenfords ate earlier or later than he, he might be left alone in the compartment. But which sitting would they choose? Harry mentally cursed the steward for starting with him. A British steward would automatically have spoken to the titled people first, but this democratic American was probably going by seat numbers. He would have to guess which the Oxenfords would choose. 'Let me see,' he said to gain time. Rich people ate their meals late, in his experience. A labourer might have breakfast at seven, dinner at noon and tea at five, but a lord would breakfast at nine, have lunch at two and dine at eight thirty. The Oxenfords would eat late so Harry picked the first sitting. 'I'm kinda hungry,' he said. 'I'll eat at six.'

The steward turned to the Oxenfords, and Harry held his breath.

Lord Oxenford said, 'Nine o'clock, I think.'

Harry suppressed a smile of satisfaction.

But Lady Oxenford said, 'That's too long for Percy to wait – let's make it earlier.'

All right, Harry thought uneasily, but not too early, for heaven's sake.

Lord Oxenford said, 'Seven thirty, then.'

Harry felt a little glow of pleasure. He was one step nearer the Delhi Suite.

Now the steward turned to the passenger opposite

Harry, the guy in the wine-red waistcoat who looked like a policeman. His name was Clive Membury, he had told them. Say seven thirty, Harry thought, and leave me alone in the compartment. But to his disappointment Membury was not hungry, and chose nine o'clock.

What a nuisance, Harry thought. Now Membury would be here while the Oxenfords were eating. Maybe he would step out for a few minutes: he was a restless type, always up and down. But if he would not go of his own accord Harry would have to find a way to get rid of him. That would have been easy if they had not been on a plane: Harry would have told him he was wanted in another room, or there was a telephone call for him, or there was a naked woman in the street outside. Here it might be harder.

The steward said, 'Mr Vandenpost, the engineer and the navigator will join you at your table, if that's agreeable.'

'Sure is,' Harry said. He would enjoy talking to some of the crew.

Lord Oxenford ordered another whisky. There was a man that had a thirst, as the Irish would say. His wife was pale and quiet. She had a book in her lap but she never turned a page. She looked depressed.

Young Percy went forward to talk to the off-duty crew, and Margaret came and sat next to Harry. He caught a breath of her scent and identified it as Tosca. She had taken off her coat, and he was able to see that she had her mother's figure: she was quite tall, with square shoulders and a deep bust, and long legs. Her clothes, good quality but plain, did not do her justice: Harry could imagine her in a long evening dress with a plunging neckline, her red hair up and her long white neck graced by drop earrings in carved emeralds by Louis Cartier in his Indian period . . . She would be stunning. Obviously that was not how she saw herself. She was embarrassed about being a wealthy aristocrat so she dressed like a vicar's wife.

She was a formidable girl and Harry was a little intimidated by her, but he could also see her vulnerable side, and he found that endearing. He thought: Never mind endearing, Harry boy – just remember that she's a danger to you and you need to cultivate her.

He asked her if she had flown before. 'Only to Paris with Mother,' she said.

Only to Paris with Mother, he thought wonderingly. His mother would never see Paris or fly in a plane. 'What was it like?' he asked. 'To be so privileged?'

'I hated those trips to Paris,' she said. 'I had to have tea with boring English people when I wanted to go to smoky restaurants that had Negro bands.'

'My ma used to take me to Margate,' Harry said. 'I used to paddle in the sea, and we had ice cream and fish and chips.'

As the words came out he remembered that he was supposed to lie about this, and he felt panicky. He should be mumbling something vague about boarding school and a remote country house, as he normally did when forced to talk about his childhood to upper-class girls. But Margaret knew his secret, and no one else could hear what he was saying above the hum of the

Clipper's engines. All the same, as he found himself spilling out the truth he felt as if he had jumped out of the plane and was waiting for his parachute to open.

'We never went to the seaside,' Margaret said wistfully. 'Only the common people went paddling in the sea. My sister and I used to envy the poor children. They could do anything they liked.'

Harry was amused. Here was further proof that he had been born lucky: the wealthy children, driving in big black cars, wearing coats with velvet collars and eating meat every day, had envied him his barefoot freedom and his fish and chips.

'I remember the smells,' she went on. 'The smell outside a pie shop door at lunchtime, the smell of the oiled machinery as you go past a fairground, the cosy smell of beer and tobacco that comes out when a pub door opens on a winter evening. People always seemed to be having such fun in those places. I've never been in a pub.'

'You haven't missed much,' said Harry, who did not like pubs. 'The food is better at the Ritz.'

'We each prefer the other's way of life,' she mused.

'But I've tried both,' Harry pointed out. 'I *know* which is best.'

She looked thoughtful for a minute, then asked, 'What are you going to do with your life?'

It was a peculiar question. 'Enjoy myself,' Harry said.

'No, but really.'

'What do you mean, "really"?'

'Everyone wants to enjoy themselves. What will you *do*?'

'What I do now.' Impulsively, Harry decided to tell her something he had never revealed before. 'Did you ever read *The Amateur Cracksman*, by Hornung?' She shook her head. 'It's about a gentleman thief called Raffles, who smokes Turkish cigarettes and wears beautiful clothes and gets invited to people's houses and steals their jewellery. I want to be like him.'

'Oh, come on, don't be silly,' she said brusquely.

He was a little hurt. She could be brutally direct when she thought you were talking nonsense. But this was not nonsense, this was his dream. Now that he had opened his heart to her, he felt the need to convince her that he was telling the truth. 'It's not silly,' he snapped.

'But you can't be a thief all your life,' she said. 'You'll end up growing old in jail. Even Robin Hood got married and settled down eventually. What would you *really* like?'

Harry normally answered this question with a shopping list: a flat, a car, girls, parties, Savile Row suits and fine jewels. But he knew she would pour scorn on that. He resented her attitude; but all the same it was true that his ambitions were not quite so materialistic. He very much wanted her to believe in his dreams. 'I'd like to live in a big country house with ivy growing up the walls,' he said.

He stopped. Suddenly he felt emotional. He was embarrassed, but for some reason he wanted very badly to tell her this. 'A house in the country with a tennis court and stables, and rhododendrons all up the drive,' he went on. He could see it in his mind, and it seemed like the safest, most comfortable place in the world. 'I'd walk around the grounds in brown boots and a tweed suit, talking to the gardeners and the stable boys, and they'd all think I was a real gent. I'd have all my money in rock-solid investments and never spend half the income. I'd give garden parties in the summer, with strawberries and cream. And five daughters all as pretty as their mother.'

'Five!' she laughed. 'You'd better marry someone strong!' But she became serious immediately. 'It's a lovely dream,' she said. 'I hope it comes true.'

He felt very close to her, as if he could ask her anything. 'What about you?' he said. 'Have you got a dream?'

'I want to be in the war,' she said. 'I'm going to join the ATS.'

It still seemed funny to talk about women joining the army, but of course it was common now. 'What would you do?'

'Drive. They need women to be dispatch riders and ambulance drivers.'

'It will be dangerous.'

'I know. I don't care. I just want to be in the fight. This is our last chance to stop Fascism.' Her jaw was set firm and there was a reckless look in her eye, and Harry thought she was terribly brave.

He said, 'You seem very determined.'

'I had a . . . friend who was killed by the Fascists in Spain, and I want to finish the work he began.' She looked sad.

On impulse, Harry asked, 'Did you love him?'

She nodded.

He could see that she was close to tears. He touched her arm in sympathy. 'Do you still love him?'

'I always will, a little bit.' Her voice dropped to a whisper. 'His name was Ian.'

Harry felt a lump in his throat. He wanted to take her in his arms and comfort her, and he would have done so had it not been for her red-faced father sitting on the far side of the compartment drinking whisky and reading *The Times.* He had to be content with giving her hand a quick, discreet squeeze. She smiled gratefully, seeming to understand.

The steward said, 'Dinner is served, Mr Vandenpost.'

Harry was surprised that it was six o'clock already. He was sorry to break off his conversation with Margaret.

She read his mind. 'We've got lots more time to talk,' she said. 'We're going to be together for the next twenty-four hours.'

'Right.' He smiled. He touched her hand again. 'See you later,' he murmured.

He had started out befriending her in order to manipulate her, he remembered. He had ended up telling her all his secrets. She had a way of overturning his plans that was kind of worrying. Worst of all was that he liked it.

He went into the next compartment. He was a little startled to see that it had been completely transformed, from a lounge into a dining room. There were three tables each for four people, plus two smaller serving-tables. It was set out like a good restaurant, with linen tablecloths and napkins, and bone china crockery, white with the blue Pan American symbol. He noticed that the walls in this area were papered with a design showing a map of the world and the same winged Pan American symbol.

The steward showed him to a seat opposite a short, thickset man in a pale grey suit that Harry rather envied. His tie was fixed with a pin that had a large, genuine pearl. Harry introduced himself, and the man stuck out a hand and said, 'Tom Luther.' Harry saw that his cufflinks matched the tiepin. Here was a man who spent money on jewellery.

Harry sat down and unfolded his napkin. Luther had an American accent with something else at the bottom of it, some European intonation. 'Where are you from, Tom?' Harry said, probing.

'Providence, Rhode Island. You?'

'Philadelphia.' Harry wished to hell he knew where Philadelphia was. 'But I've lived all over. My father was in insurance.'

Luther nodded politely, not much interested. That suited Harry. He did not want to be questioned about his background: it was too easy to slip up.

The two crew members arrived and introduced themselves. Eddie Deakin, the engineer, was a broad-shouldered, sandy-haired type with a pleasant face: Harry got the impression he would have liked to undo his tie and take off his uniform jacket. Jack Ashford, the navigator, was dark-haired and blue-chinned, a regular, precise man who looked as if he had been born in a uniform.

As soon as they sat down, Harry sensed hostility

between Eddie the engineer and Luther the passenger. That was interesting.

The dinner started with shrimp cocktail. The two crew members drank Coke. Harry had a glass of hock and Tom Luther ordered a martini.

Harry was still thinking about Margaret Oxenford and the boyfriend killed in Spain. He looked out of the window, wondering how much she still felt for the boy. A year was a long time, especially at her age.

Jack Ashford followed his look and said, 'We're lucky with the weather, so far.'

Harry noticed that the sky was clear and the sun was shining on the wings. 'What's it usually like?' he said.

'Sometimes it rains all the way from Ireland to Newfoundland,' Jack said. 'We get hail, snow, ice, thunder and lightning.'

Harry remembered something he had read. 'Isn't ice dangerous?'

'We plan our route to avoid freezing conditions. But in any event the plane is fitted with rubber de-icing boots.'

'Boots?'

'Just rubber covers that fit over the wings and tail where they tend to ice up.'

'So what's the forecast for the rest of the trip?'

Jack hesitated momentarily, and Harry saw that he wished he had not mentioned the weather. 'There's a storm in the Atlantic,' he said.

'Bad?'

'In the centre it's bad, but we'll only touch the skirt of it, I expect.' He sounded only half convinced.

Tom Luther asked, 'What's it like in a storm?' He was smiling, showing his teeth, but Harry saw fear in his pale blue eyes.

'It gets a little bumpy,' Jack said.

He did not elaborate, but the engineer, Eddie, spoke up. Looking directly at Tom Luther, he said, 'It's kind of like trying to ride an unbroken horse.'

Luther blanched. Jack frowned at Eddie, plainly disapproving of his tactlessness.

The next course was turtle soup. Both stewards were serving now, Nicky and Davy. Nicky was fat and Davy was small. In Harry's estimation they were both homosexual – or 'musical', as the Noël Coward set would say. Harry liked their informal efficiency.

The engineer seemed preoccupied. Harry studied him covertly. He did not look the sulky type: he had an open, good-natured face. In an attempt to draw him out, Harry said, 'Who's flying the plane while you're eating dinner, Eddie?'

'The assistant engineer, Mickey Finn, is doing my job,' Eddie said. He spoke pleasantly enough, although he did not smile. 'We carry a crew of nine, not counting the two stewards. All except the Captain work alternate four-hour shifts. Jack and I have been on duty since we took off from Southampton at two o'clock, so we stood down at six, a few minutes ago.'

'What about the Captain?' Tom Luther said worriedly. 'Does he take pills to stay awake?'

'He naps when he can,' Eddie said. 'He'll probably take a long break when we pass the point of no return.'

'So we'll be flying through the sky and the Captain

will be asleep?' Luther said, and his voice was a little too loud.

'Sure,' said Eddie with a grin.

Luther was looking terrified. Harry tried to steer the conversation into calmer waters. 'What's the point of no return?'

'We monitor our fuel reserves constantly. When we don't have enough fuel to get back to Foynes, we've passed the point of no return.' Eddie spoke brusquely, and Harry now had no doubt the engineer was trying to scare Tom Luther.

The navigator broke in, trying to be reassuring. 'Right now we have enough fuel to reach our destination or return home.'

Luther said, 'But what if you don't have enough to get there or get back?'

Eddie leaned across the table and grinned humourlessly at Luther. 'Trust me, Mr Luther,' he said.

'It would never happen,' the navigator said hastily. 'We'd turn back for Foynes before we reached that point. And for extra safety, we make the calculations based on three engines instead of four, just in case something should go wrong with one engine.'

Jack was trying to restore Luther's confidence, but of course talk of engines going wrong only made the man more frightened. He tried to drink some soup but his hand was shaking and he spilled it on his tie.

Eddie sank back into silence, apparently satisfied. Jack tried to make small talk, and Harry did his best to help out, but there was an awkward atmosphere. Harry wondered what the hell was going on between Eddie and Luther.

The dining room filled up rapidly. The beautiful woman in the spotted dress came to sit at the next table with her blue-blazered escort. Harry had found out that their names were Diana Lovesey and Mark Alder. Margaret should dress like Mrs Lovesey, Harry thought: she could look even better. However, Mrs Lovesey did not look happy – in fact she looked as miserable as sin.

The service was fast and the food was good. The main course was *filet mignon* with asparagus hollandaise and mashed potatoes. The steak was about twice as big as would have been served in an English restaurant. Harry did not eat it all and he refused another glass of wine. He wanted to be alert. He was going to steal the Delhi Suite. The thought thrilled him but also made him apprehensive. It would be the biggest job of his career, and it could be the last, if he so chose. It could buy him that ivy-grown country house with a tennis court.

After the steak they served a salad, which surprised Harry. Salad was not often served in fancy restaurants in London, and certainly not as a separate course following the main dish.

Peach melba, coffee and *petits fours* came in rapid succession. Eddie the engineer seemed to realize he was being unsociable and made an effort to converse. 'May I ask what's the purpose of your trip, Mr Vandenpost?'

'I guess I want to stay out of the way of Hitler,' Harry said. 'At least until America gets into the war.'

'You think that will happen?' Eddie asked sceptically.

'It did last time.'

Tom Luther said, 'We have no quarrel with the Nazis. They're against Communism and so are we.'

Jack nodded in agreement.

Harry was taken aback. In England everyone thought America would come into the war. But around this table there was no such assumption. Perhaps the British were kidding themselves, he thought pessimistically. Maybe there was no help to be had from America. That would be bad news for Ma, back in London.

Eddie said, 'I think we may have to fight the Nazis.' There was an angry note in his voice. 'They're like gangsters,' he said, looking directly at Luther. 'In the end, people of that type just have to be exterminated, like rats.'

Jack stood up abruptly, looking worried. 'If we're through, Eddie, we'd better get a little rest,' he said firmly.

Eddie looked startled at this sudden demand, but after a moment he nodded assent and the two crew members took their leave.

Harry said, 'That engineer was kind of rude.'

'Was he?' said Luther. 'I didn't notice.'

You bloody liar, Harry thought. He practically called you a gangster!

Luther ordered a brandy. Harry wondered if he really was a gangster. The ones Harry knew in London were much more showy, with multiple rings and fur coats and two-tone shoes. Luther looked more like a self-made millionaire businessman, a meat packer or shipbuilder, something industrial. On impulse Harry asked him, 'What do you do for a living, Tom?'

'I'm a businessman in Rhode Island.'

It was not an encouraging reply, and a few moments later Harry stood up, gave a polite nod and left.

When he re-entered his compartment, Lord Oxenford said abruptly, 'Dinner any good?'

Harry had enjoyed it thoroughly, but upper-class people were never too enthusiastic about food. 'Not bad,' he said neutrally. 'And there's a drinkable hock.'

Oxenford grunted and went back to his newspaper. There's no one as rude as a rude lord, Harry thought.

Margaret smiled and looked pleased to see him. 'What was it like, really?' she said in a conspiratorial murmur.

'Delicious,' he replied, and they both laughed.

Margaret looked different when she laughed. In repose she was pale and unremarkable, but now her cheeks turned pink and she opened her mouth, showing two rows of even teeth, and tossed her hair; and she let out a throaty chuckle that Harry found sexy. He wanted to reach across the narrow aisle and touch her. He was about to do so when he caught the eye of Clive Membury, sitting opposite him, and for some reason that made him resist the impulse.

'There's a storm over the Atlantic,' he told her.

'Does that mean we'll have a rough ride?'

'Yes. They'll try to fly around the edge of it, but all the same it's going to be bumpy.'

It was hard to talk to her because the stewards were constantly passing along the aisle between them, carrying food to the dining room and returning with trays of dirty crockery. Harry was impressed that just two men were able to do the cooking and serving for so many diners.

He picked up a copy of *Life* magazine that Margaret had discarded and began to leaf through it while he waited impatiently for the Oxenfords to go to dinner. He had not brought any books or magazines: he was not much of a reader. He liked to see what was in the newspaper, but for entertainment he preferred the radio and the cinema.

At last the Oxenfords were called for dinner, and Harry was left alone with Clive Membury. The man had sat in the main lounge, playing cards, on the first leg of the trip, but now that the lounge had become the dining room he had settled in his seat. Perhaps he'll go to the carsey, Harry thought; and perhaps I'd better start calling it the john before I get caught out.

He wondered again whether Membury was a policeman, and if so what he was doing on the Pan American Clipper. If he was following a suspect, the crime would have to be a major one for the British police force to fork out for a Clipper ticket. But perhaps he was one of those people who save up for years and years to take some dream trip, a cruise down the Nile or a ride on the Orient Express. He might be an aircraft fanatic who just wanted to make the great transatlantic flight. If so I hope he's enjoying it, Harry thought. Ninety quid is a hell of a lot of money for a copper.

Patience was not Harry's strong point, and when after half an hour Membury had not moved, he decided to take matters into his own hands. 'Have you seen the flight deck, Mr Membury?' he asked.

'No—'

'Apparently it's really something. They say it's as big as the entire interior of a Douglas DC-3, and that's a pretty big airplane.'

'Goodness.' Membury was only politely interested. He was not an aircraft enthusiast, then.

'We ought to go look at it.' Harry stopped Nicky, who was going by with a tureen of turtle soup. 'Can passengers visit the flight deck?'

'Yes, sir, and welcome!'

'Is now a good time?'

'It's a very good time, Mr Vandenpost. We're not landing or taking off, the crew aren't changing watches, and the weather is calm. You couldn't pick a better moment.'

Harry had been hoping he would say that. He stood up and looked expectantly at Membury. 'Shall we?'

Membury looked as if he was about to refuse. He was not the type to be easily bullied. On the other hand, it might seem churlish to refuse to go and see the flight deck; and perhaps Membury would not want to seem disagreeable. After a moment's hesitation, he got to his feet, saying, 'By all means.'

Harry led him forward, past the kitchen and the men's room, and turned right, mounting the twisting staircase. At the top he emerged on to the flight deck. Membury was right behind him.

Harry looked around. It was nothing like his picture of the cockpit of an aeroplane. Clean, quiet and comfortable, it looked more like an office in a modern building. Harry's dinner companions, the navigator and the engineer, were not present, of course, as they were off duty; this was the alternative shift. However, the Captain was here, sitting behind a small table at the rear of the cabin. He looked up, smiled pleasantly, and said, 'Good evening, gentlemen. Would you like to look around?'

'Sure would,' said Harry. 'But I got to get my camera. Is it okay to take a picture?'

'You bet.'

'I'll be right back.'

He hurried down the stairs, pleased with himself but tense too. He had got Membury out of the way for a while, but his search would have to be very quick.

He returned to the compartment. One steward was in the galley and the other in the dining room. He would have liked to wait until both were busy serving at tables, so that he could feel confident they would not pass through the compartment for a few minutes, but he did not have time. He would just have to take a chance on being interrupted.

He pulled Lady Oxenford's bag out from under her seat. It was too big and heavy for a cabin bag, but she probably did not carry it herself. He put it on the seat and opened it. It was not locked: that was a bad sign – even she was not likely to be so innocent as to leave priceless jewellery in an unlocked case.

All the same he rummaged through it quickly, watching out of the corner of his eye in case anyone should walk in. There was scent and make-up, a silver brush-and-comb set, a chestnut-coloured dressing-gown, a nightdress, dainty slippers, peach-coloured silk underwear, stockings, a sponge bag containing a toothbrush and the usual toiletries, and a book of Blake's poems – but no jewels.

Harry cursed silently. He had felt this was the likeliest place it would be. Now he began to doubt his whole theory.

The search had taken about twenty seconds.

He closed the case quickly and put it back under the seat.

He wondered whether she had asked her husband to carry the jewels.

He looked at the bag under Lord Oxenford's seat. The stewards were still busy. He decided to push his luck.

He pulled out Oxenford's bag. It was like a carpet-bag, but leather. It was fastened with a zip at the top and the zip had a little padlock. Harry carried a penknife with him for moments such as this. He used the knife to snap the padlock, then unzipped the bag.

As he was rifling through the contents, the little steward, Davy, came through, carrying a tray of drinks from the galley. Harry looked up at him and smiled; Davy looked at the bag. Harry held his breath and kept his frozen smile. The steward passed on into the dining room. He had naturally assumed the bag was Harry's own.

Harry breathed again. He was a master at disarming suspicion, but every time he did it he was scared to death.

Oxenford's bag contained the masculine equivalent of what his wife was carrying: shaving tackle, hair oil, striped pyjamas, flannel underwear and a biography of Napoleon. Harry zipped it up and replaced the padlock. Oxenford would find it broken and wonder how it had happened. If he was suspicious he would check to see whether anything was missing. Finding everything in place, he would imagine the lock had been faulty.

Harry put the bag back in its place.

He had got away with it, but he was no nearer the Delhi Suite.

It was unlikely the children were carrying the jewels but, recklessly, he decided to go through their luggage.

If Lord Oxenford had decided to be sly and put his wife's jewellery in his children's luggage, he would be more likely to pick Percy, who would be thrilled by the conspiracy, than Margaret, who was disposed to defy her father.

Harry picked up Percy's canvas hold-all and put it on the seat just where he had placed Oxenford's bag, hoping that if Davy the steward passed through again he would think it was the same bag.

Percy's things were so neatly packed that Harry was sure a servant had done it. No normal fourteen-year-old boy would fold his pyjamas and wrap them in tissue paper. His sponge bag contained a new toothbrush and a fresh tube of toothpaste. There was a pocket chess set, a small bundle of comics, and a packet of chocolate biscuits – put there, Harry imagined, by a fond cook or housemaid. Harry looked inside the chess set, riffled through the comics and broke open the biscuit packet, but he found no jewels.

As he was replacing the bag, a passenger walked through on the way to the men's room. Harry ignored him.

He could not believe Lady Oxenford had left the Delhi Suite behind, in a country that might be invaded and conquered within a few weeks. But she was not wearing it, or carrying it, as far as he could tell. If it was not in Margaret's bag, it had to be in the checked baggage. That would be tough to get at. Could you get into the hold while the plane was in the air? The alternative might be to follow the Oxenfords to their hotel in New York . . .

The Captain and Clive Membury would be wondering how he could take so long to fetch his camera.

He picked up Margaret's bag. It looked like a birthday present: a small, round-cornered case made of soft cream leather with beautiful brass fittings. When he opened it he smelled her perfume, Tosca. He found a cotton nightdress with a pattern of small flowers, and tried to picture her in it. It was too girlish for her. Her underwear was plain white cotton. He wondered whether she was a virgin. There was a small framed photograph of a boy about twenty-one, a handsome fellow with longish dark hair and black eyebrows, wearing a college gown and a mortar-board hat: the boy who died in Spain, presumably. Had she slept with him? Harry rather thought she might have, despite her schoolgirl underpants. She was reading a novel by D. H. Lawrence. I bet her mother doesn't know about that, Harry thought. There was a little stack of linen handkerchiefs embroidered 'M.O.'. They smelled of Tosca.

The jewels were not here. Damn it to hell.

Harry decided to take one of the scented handkerchiefs as a souvenir; and just as he picked it up, Davy the steward passed through carrying a tray stacked high with soup bowls.

He glanced at Harry and then stopped, frowning. Margaret's bag looked quite different from Lord Oxenford's, of course. It was plain that Harry could not be the owner of both bags; therefore he had to be looking in other people's.

Davy stared at him for a moment, obviously suspicious but also frightened of accusing a passenger. Eventually he stammered, 'Sir, is that your case?'

Harry showed him the little handkerchief. 'Would I blow my nose in this?' He closed the case and replaced it.

Davy still looked worried. Harry said, 'She asked me to fetch it. The things we do . . .'

Davy's expression changed and he looked embarrassed. 'I'm sorry, sir, but I hope you understand—'

'I'm happy you're on your toes,' Harry said. 'Keep up the good work.' He patted Davy's shoulder. Now he had to give the damn handkerchief to Margaret in order to lend credence to his story. He stepped into the dining room.

She was at a table with her parents and her brother. He held out the handkerchief to her, saying, 'You dropped this.'

She was surprised. 'Did I? Thank you!'

'You bet.' He got out fast. Would Davy check his story by asking her whether she had told Harry to fetch her a clean handkerchief? He doubted it.

He went back through his compartment, passed the galley where Davy was stacking the dirty dishes, and climbed the spiral staircase. How the hell was he going to get into the baggage hold? He did not even know where it was: he had not watched the luggage being loaded. But there had to be a way.

Captain Baker was explaining to Clive Membury how they navigated across the featureless ocean. 'Most of the time we're out of range of the radio beacons, so the stars provide our best guide – when we can see them.'

Membury looked up at Harry. 'No camera?' he said sharply.

Definitely a copper, Harry thought. 'I forgot to load it with film,' he said. 'Dumb, huh?' He looked around. 'How can you see the stars from in here?'

'Oh, the navigator just steps outside for a moment,' the Captain said straight-faced. Then he grinned. 'Just kidding. There's an observatory. I'll show you.' He opened a door at the rear end of the flight deck and stepped through. Harry followed and found himself in a narrow passage. The Captain pointed up. 'This is the observation dome.' Harry looked up without much interest: his mind was still on Lady Oxenford's jewellery. There was a glazed bubble in the roof, and a folding ladder hung on a hook to one side. 'He just climbs up there with his octant any time there's a break in the cloud. This is also the baggage loading hatch.'

Harry was suddenly attentive. 'The baggage comes in through the roof?' he said.

'Sure. Right here.'

'And then where is it stowed?'

The Captain pointed to the two doors either side of the narrow passage. 'In the baggage holds.'

Harry could hardly believe his luck. 'So all the bags are right here, behind those doors?'

'Yes, sir.'

Harry tried one of the doors. It was not locked. He looked inside. There were the suitcases and trunks of the passengers, carefully stacked and roped to the struts so they would not move in flight.

Somewhere in there was the Delhi Suite, and a life of luxury for Harry Marks.

Clive Membury was looking over Harry's shoulder. 'Fascinating,' he murmured.

'You can say that again,' said Harry.

CHAPTER FOURTEEN

MARGARET WAS in high spirits. She kept forgetting that she did not want to go to America. She could hardly believe she had made friends with a real thief! Ordinarily, if someone had said to her, 'I'm a thief,' she would not have believed him; but in Harry's case she knew it was true because she had met him in a police station and seen him accused.

She had always been fascinated by people who lived outside the ordered social world: criminals, Bohemians, anarchists, prostitutes and tramps. They seemed so free. Of course, they might not be free to order champagne or fly to New York or send their children to university – she was not so naïve as to overlook the restrictions of being an outcast. But people such as Harry never had to do anything just because they were ordered to, and that seemed wonderful to her. She dreamed of being a guerrilla fighter, living in the hills, wearing trousers and carrying a rifle, stealing food and sleeping under the stars and never having her clothes ironed.

She never met people like that; or if she met them she did not recognize them for what they were – had she not sat on a doorstep in 'the most notorious street in London' without realizing she would be taken for a prostitute? How long ago that seemed, although it was only last night.

Getting to know Harry was the most interesting thing that had happened to her for ages. He represented everything she had ever longed for. He could do anything he liked! This morning he had decided to go to America and this afternoon he was on his way. If he wanted to dance all night and sleep all day he just did. He ate and drank what he liked, when he felt like it, at the Ritz or in a pub or on board the Pan American Clipper. He could join the Communist Party and then leave it without explaining himself to anyone. When he needed money he just took some from people who had more than they deserved. He was a complete free spirit!

She longed to know more about him, and resented the time she had to waste having dinner without him.

There were three tables of four in the dining room. Baron Gabon and Carl Hartmann were at the next table to the Oxenfords. Father had thrown a dirty look at them when they came in, presumably because they were Jewish. Sharing their table were Ollis Field and Frank Gordon. Frank Gordon was a boy a bit older than Harry, a handsome devil, though with something of a brutal look to his mouth, and Ollis Field was a washed-out-looking older man, completely bald. These two had attracted some comment by remaining on board the plane when everyone else had disembarked at Foynes.

At the third table were Lulu Bell and Princess Lavinia, who was loudly complaining that there was too much salt in the sauce on the shrimp cocktail. With them were two people who had joined the plane at Foynes, Mr Lovesey and Mrs Lenehan. Percy said the new people were sharing the honeymoon suite although they were not married. Margaret was surprised that Pan American allowed that. Perhaps they were bending the rules because so many people were desperate to get to America.

Percy sat down to dinner wearing a black Jewish skull-cap. Margaret giggled. Where on earth had he got that? Father snatched it off his head, growling furiously, 'Foolish boy!'

Mother's face had the glazed look it had shown ever since she stopped crying over Elizabeth. She said vaguely, 'It seems awfully early to be dining.'

'It's half-past seven,' Father said.

'Why isn't it getting dark?'

Percy answered, 'It is, back in England. But we're three hundred miles off the Irish coast. We're chasing the sun.'

'But it will get dark eventually.'

'About nine o'clock, I should think,' Percy said.

'Good,' Mother said.

'Do you realize that if we went fast enough, we would keep up with the sun and it would never get dark?' said Percy.

Father said condescendingly, 'I don't think there's any chance men will ever build planes that fast.'

The steward, Nicky, brought their first course. 'Not for me, thank you,' Percy said. 'Shrimps aren't kosher.'

The steward shot him a startled look but said nothing. Father went red.

Margaret hastily changed the subject. 'When do we reach the next stop, Percy?' He always knew such things.

'Journey time to Botwood is sixteen and a half hours,' he said. 'We should arrive at nine a.m. British Summer Time.'

'But what will the time be there?'

'Newfoundland Standard Time is three and a half hours behind Greenwich Mean Time.'

'Three and a *half*?' Margaret was surprised. 'I didn't know there were places that took odd half-hours.'

Percy went on, 'And Botwood is on Daylight Saving, like Britain, so the local time when we land will be five thirty in the morning.'

'I shan't be able to wake up,' Mother said tiredly.

'Yes, you will,' Percy said impatiently. 'You'll *feel* as if it's nine o'clock.'

Mother murmured, 'Boys are so good at technical things.'

She irritated Margaret when she pretended to be stupid. She believed it was not feminine to understand technicalities. 'Men don't like girls to be too clever, dear,' she had said to Margaret, more than once. Margaret no longer argued with her but she did not believe it. Only stupid men felt that way, in her opinion. Clever men liked clever girls.

She became conscious of slightly raised voices at the next table. Baron Gabon and Carl Hartmann were arguing, while their dinner companions looked on in bemused silence. Margaret had noticed that Gabon and Hartmann had been deep in discussion every time she looked at them. Perhaps it was not surprising: if you were talking to one of the greatest brains in the world you wouldn't make small talk. She heard the word 'Palestine'. They must be discussing Zionism. She shot a nervous glance at Father. He too had heard, and was looking bad-tempered. Before he could say anything Margaret said, 'We're going to fly through a storm. It could get bumpy.'

'How do you know?' Percy said. There was a jealous note in his voice: he was the expert on flight details, not Margaret.

'Harry told me.'

'And how would *he* know?'

'He dined with the engineer and the navigator.'

'I'm not scared,' Percy said, in a tone which suggested that he was.

It had not occurred to Margaret to worry about the storm. It might be uncomfortable, but surely there was no real danger?

Father drained his glass and asked the steward irritably for more wine. Was he frightened of the storm? He was drinking even more than usual, she had observed. His face was flushed and his pale eyes seemed to stare. Was he nervous? Perhaps he was still upset over Elizabeth.

Mother said, 'Margaret, you should talk more to that quiet Mr Membury.'

Margaret was surprised. 'Why? He seems to want to be left alone.'

'I expect he's just shy.'

It was not like Mother to take pity on shy people,

especially if they were, like Mr Membury, unmistakably middle-class. 'Out with it, Mother,' said Margaret. 'What do you mean?'

'I just don't want you to spend the entire flight talking to Mr Vandenpost.'

That was exactly what Margaret *was* going to do. 'Why on earth shouldn't I?' she said.

'Well, he's your age, you know, and you don't want to give him ideas.'

'I might rather like to give him ideas. He's frightfully good-looking.'

'No, dear,' she said firmly. 'There's something about him that isn't quite *quite*.' She meant he was not upper class. Like many foreigners who married into the aristocracy, Mother was even more snobbish than the English.

So she had not been completely taken in by Harry's impersonation of a wealthy young American. Her social antennae were infallible. 'But you said you knew the Philadelphia Vandenposts,' Margaret said.

'I do, but now that I think about it I'm sure he's not from that family.'

'I may cultivate him just to punish you for being such a snob, Mother.'

'It's not snobbery, dear, it's breeding. Snobbery is vulgar.'

Margaret gave up. The armour of Mother's superiority was impenetrable. It was useless to reason with her. But Margaret had no intention of obeying her. Harry was far too interesting.

Percy said, 'I wonder what Mr Membury is? I like his

red waistcoat. He doesn't look like a regular transatlantic traveller.'

Mother remarked, 'I expect he's some kind of functionary.'

That was just what he looked like, Margaret thought. Mother had the sharpest eye for that sort of thing.

Father said, 'He probably works for the airline.'

'More like a civil servant, I should say,' Mother said.

The stewards brought the main course. Mother refused the *filet mignon.* 'I never eat cooked food,' she told Nicky. 'Just bring me some celery and caviar.'

From the next table Margaret heard Baron Gabon say, 'We must have a land of our own – there's no other solution!'

Carl Hartmann replied, 'But you've admitted that it will have to be a militarized state—'

'For defence against hostile neighbours!'

'And you concede that it will have to discriminate against Arabs in favour of Jews – but militarism and racism combined make Fascism, which is what you're supposed to be fighting against!'

'Hush, not so loud,' Gabon said, and they lowered their voices.

In normal circumstances Margaret would have been interested in the argument: she had discussed it with Ian. Socialists were divided about Palestine: some said it was an opportunity to create an ideal state; others that it belonged to the people who lived there and could not be 'given' to the Jews any more than Ireland, or Hong Kong, or Texas. The fact that so many socialists were Jewish only complicated the issue.

However, now she just wished Gabon and Hartmann would calm down so that Father would not hear.

Unfortunately it was not to be. They were arguing about something close to their hearts. Hartmann raised his voice again and said, 'I don't want to live in a racist state!'

Father said loudly, 'I didn't know we were travelling with a pack of Jews.'

'Oy, vey,' said Percy.

Margaret looked at her father in dismay. There had been a time when his political philosophy had made a kind of sense. When millions of able-bodied men were unemployed and starving, it had seemed courageous to say that both capitalism and socialism had failed and that democracy did the ordinary man no good. There had been something appealing about the idea of an all-powerful State directing industry under the leadership of a benevolent dictator. But those high ideals and bold policies had now degenerated into this mindless bigotry. She had thought of Father when she found a copy of *Hamlet* in the library at home and read the line, 'O, what a noble mind is here o'erthrown!'

She did not think the two men had heard Father's crass remark, for he had his back to them and they were absorbed in the debate. To get Father off the subject she said brightly, 'What time should we all go to bed?'

Percy said, 'I'd like to go early.' That was unusual, but of course he was looking forward to the novelty of sleeping on a plane.

Mother said, 'We'll go at the usual time.'

'But in what time zone?' Percy said. 'Shall I go at ten thirty British Summer Time, or ten thirty Newfoundland Daylight Saving Time?'

'America is racist!' Baron Gabon exclaimed. 'So is France – England – the Soviet Union – all racist states!'

Father exclaimed, 'For God's sake!'

Margaret said, 'Half-past nine would suit me fine.'

Percy noticed the rhyme. 'I'll be more dead than alive by ten-oh-five,' he countered.

It was a game they had played as children. Mother joined in. 'You won't see me again after quarter to ten.'

'Show me your tattoo at a quarter to.'

'I'll be the last at twenty past.'

'Your turn, Father,' said Percy.

There was a moment of silence. Father had played the game with them, in the old days, before he became bitter and disappointed. For an instant his face softened, and Margaret thought he would join in.

Then Carl Hartmann said, 'So why set up yet another racist state?'

That did it. Father turned round, red-faced and spluttering. Before anybody could do anything to stop him he burst out, 'You Jewboys had better keep your voices down.'

Hartmann and Gabon stared at him in astonishment.

Margaret felt her face flush bright red. Father had spoken loudly enough for everyone to hear, and the room had gone completely quiet. She wanted the floor to open up and swallow her. She was mortified that people should look at her and know she was the daughter of the coarse, drunken fool sitting opposite her. She caught the eye of Nicky, and saw by his face that he felt sorry for her; and that made her feel worse.

Baron Gabon turned pale. For a moment it seemed that he would say something in return, but then he changed his mind and looked away. Hartmann gave a twisted grin, and the thought flashed through Margaret's mind that to him, coming from Nazi Germany, this sort of thing probably seemed mild.

Father had not finished. 'This is a first class compartment,' he added.

Margaret was watching Baron Gabon. In an attempt to ignore Father, he picked up his spoon, but his hand was shaking and he spilled soup on his dove-grey waistcoat. He gave up and put the spoon down.

This visible sign of his distress touched Margaret's heart. She felt fiercely angry with her father. She turned to him and for once she had the courage to tell him what she thought. She said furiously, 'You have just grossly insulted two of the most distinguished men in Europe!'

He said, 'Two of the most distinguished *Jews* in Europe.'

Percy said, 'Remember Granny Fishbein.'

Father rounded on him. Wagging a finger he said, 'You're to stop that nonsense, do you hear me?'

'I need to go to the lavatory,' Percy said, getting up. 'I feel sick.' He left the room.

Margaret realized that both Percy and she had stood up to Father, and he had not been able to do anything about it. That had to be some kind of milestone.

Father lowered his voice and spoke to Margaret.

'Remember that these are the people who have driven us out of our home!' he hissed. Then he raised his voice again. 'If they want to travel with us they ought to learn manners.'

'That's enough!' said a new voice.

Margaret looked across the room. The speaker was Mervyn Lovesey, the man who had got on at Foynes. He was standing up. The stewards, Nicky and Davy, stood frozen still, looking scared. Lovesey came across the dining room and leaned on the Oxenfords' table, looking dangerous. He was a tall, authoritative man in his forties with thick greying hair, black eyebrows and chiselled features. He wore an expensive suit but spoke with a Lancashire accent. 'I'll thank you to keep those views to yourself,' he said in a quietly threatening tone.

Father said, 'None of your damn business—'

'But it is,' said Lovesey.

Margaret saw Nicky leave hastily, and guessed he was going to summon help from the flight deck.

Lovesey went on, 'You wouldn't know anything about this, but Professor Hartmann is the leading physicist in the world.'

'I don't care what he is—'

'No, you wouldn't. But I do. And I find your opinions as offensive as a bad smell.'

'I shall say what I please,' Father said, and he made to get up.

Lovesey held him down with a strong hand on his shoulder. 'We're at war with people like you.'

Father said weakly, 'Clear off, will you?'

'I'll clear off if you'll shut up.'

'I shall call the Captain—'

'No need,' said a new voice, and Captain Baker appeared, looking calmly authoritative in his uniform cap. 'I'm here. Mr Lovesey, may I ask you to return to your seat? I'd be much obliged to you.'

'Aye, I'll sit down,' said Lovesey. 'But I'll not listen in silence while the most eminent scientist in Europe is told to keep his voice down and called a Jewboy by this drunken oaf.'

'Please, Mr Lovesey.'

Lovesey returned to his seat.

The Captain turned to Father. 'Lord Oxenford, perhaps you were misheard. I'm sure you would not call another passenger the word mentioned by Mr Lovesey.'

Margaret prayed that Father would accept this way out, but to her dismay he became more belligerent. 'I called him a Jewboy because that's what he is!' he blustered.

'Father, stop it!' she cried.

The Captain said to Father, 'I must ask you not to use such terms while you're on board my aircraft.'

Father was scornful. 'Is he ashamed of being a Jewboy?'

Margaret could see that Captain Baker was getting angry. 'This is an American airplane, sir, and we have American standards of behaviour. I insist that you stop insulting other passengers, and I warn you that I am empowered to have you arrested and confined to prison by the local police at our next port of call. You should be aware that in such cases, rare though they are, the airline always presses charges.'

Father was shaken by the threat of imprisonment. For a moment he was silenced. Margaret felt deeply humiliated. Although she had tried to stop her father, and protested against his behaviour, nevertheless she felt ashamed. His oafishness reflected on her: she was his daughter. She buried her face in her hands. She could not take any more.

She heard Father say, 'I shall return to my compartment.' She looked up. He was getting to his feet. He turned to Mother. 'My dear?'

Mother stood up, Father holding her chair. Margaret felt that all eyes were on her.

Harry suddenly appeared out of nowhere. He rested his hands lightly on the back of Margaret's chair. 'Lady Margaret,' he said with a little bow. She stood up, and he drew back the chair. She felt deeply grateful for this gesture of support.

Mother walked away from the table, her face expressionless, her head held high. Father followed her.

Harry gave Margaret his arm. It was only a little thing, but it meant a great deal to her. Although she was blushing furiously, she felt able to walk out of the room with dignity.

A buzz of conversation broke out behind her as she passed into the compartment.

Harry handed her to her seat.

'That was so gracious of you,' she said with feeling. 'I don't know how to thank you.'

'I could hear the row from in here,' he said quietly. 'I knew you'd be feeling bad.'

'I've never been so humiliated,' she said abjectly.

But Father had not yet finished. 'They'll be sorry one day, the damn fools!' he said. Mother sat in her corner and stared blankly at him. 'They're going to lose this war, you mark my words.'

Margaret said, 'No more, Father, please.' Fortunately only Harry was present to hear the tirade continue: Mr Membury had disappeared.

Father ignored her. 'The German army will sweep across England like a tidal wave!' he said. 'And then what do you think will happen? Hitler will install a Fascist government, of course.' Suddenly there was an odd light in his eye. My God, he looks crazy, Margaret thought; my father is going insane. He lowered his voice, and his face took on a crafty expression. 'An *English* Fascist government, of course. And he will need an English Fascist to lead it!'

'Oh, my God,' said Margaret. She saw what he was thinking and it made her despair.

Father thought Hitler was going to make him dictator of Britain.

He thought Britain would be conquered, and Hitler would call him back from exile to be the leader of a puppet government.

'And when there's a Fascist Prime Minister in London – *then* they'll dance to a different tune!' Father said triumphantly, as if he had won some argument.

Harry was staring at Father in astonishment. 'Do you imagine . . . do you expect Hitler to ask *you* . . .?'

'Who knows?' Father said. 'It would have to be someone who bore no taint of the defeated administration. If called upon . . . my duty to my country . . . fresh start, no recriminations . . .'

Harry looked too shocked to say anything.

Margaret was in despair. She had to get away from Father. She could not take any more. She shuddered when she recalled the ignominious upshot of her last attempt to run away, but she should not let one failure discourage her. She had to try again.

It would be different this time. She would learn by Elizabeth's example. She would think carefully and plan ahead. She would make sure she had money, friends and a place to sleep. This time she would make it work.

Percy emerged from the men's room, having missed most of the drama. However, he appeared to have been in a drama of his own: his face was flushed and he looked excited. 'Guess what!' he said to the compartment in general. 'I just saw Mr Membury in the washroom – he had his jacket undone and he was tucking his shirt into his trousers – and he's got a shoulder holster under his jacket – and there's a gun in it!'

CHAPTER FIFTEEN

THE CLIPPER was approaching the point of no return.

Eddie Deakin, distracted, nervy, unrested, went back on duty at 10 p.m., British time. By this hour the sun had raced ahead, leaving the aircraft in darkness. The weather had changed too. Rain lashed the windows, cloud obscured the stars, and inconstant winds buffeted the mighty plane disrespectfully, shaking up the passengers.

The weather was generally worse at low altitudes, but despite this Captain Baker was flying close to sea level. He was 'hunting the wind', searching for the altitude at which the westerly head wind was least strong.

Eddie was worried because he knew the plane was low on fuel. He sat down at his station and began to calculate the distance the plane could travel on what remained in the tanks. Because the weather was a little worse than forecast, the engines must have burned more fuel than anticipated. If there was not sufficient left to carry the plane to Newfoundland, it would have to turn back before it reached the point of no return.

And then what would happen to Carol-Ann?

Tom Luther was nothing if not a careful planner and he must have considered the possibility that the Clipper would be delayed. He had to have some way of contacting his cronies to confirm or alter the time of the rendezvous.

But if the plane turned back, Carol-Ann would remain in the hands of the kidnappers for at least another twenty-four hours.

Eddie had sat in the forward compartment, fidgeting restlessly and looking out of the window at nothing at all, for most of his off-duty shift. He had not even tried to sleep, knowing it would be hopeless. Images of Carol-Ann had tormented him constantly: Carol-Ann in tears, or tied up, or bruised; Carol-Ann frightened, pleading, hysterical, desperate. Every five minutes he wanted to put his fist through the fuselage, and he had fought constantly against the impulse to run up the stairs and ask his replacement, Mickey Finn, about the fuel consumption.

It was because he was so distracted that he had allowed himself to needle Tom Luther in the dining room. His behaviour had been very dumb. A piece of real bad luck had put them at the same table. Afterwards, the navigator, Jack Ashford, had lectured Eddie, and he saw how stupid he had been. Now Jack knew something was going on between Eddie and Luther. Eddie had refused to enlighten Jack further, and Jack had accepted that – for now. Eddie had mentally vowed to be more careful. If Captain Baker should even suspect that his engineer was being blackmailed he would abort the flight, and then Eddie would be powerless to help Carol-Ann. Now he had that to worry about as well.

Eddie's attitude to Tom Luther had been forgotten, during the second dinner sitting, in the excitement of the near-fight between Mervyn Lovesey and Lord Oxenford. Eddie had not witnessed it – he had been in the forward compartment, worrying – but the stewards had told him all about it soon afterwards. Oxenford seemed to Eddie to be a brute who needed to be brought down a peg or two, and that was what Captain Baker had done. Eddie felt sorry for the boy, Percy, being raised by such a father.

The third sitting would be coming to an end in a few minutes, and then things would start to go quiet on the passenger deck. The older ones would go to bed. The majority would sit for a couple of hours, riding the bumps, too excited or nervous to feel sleepy; then, one by one, they would succumb to nature's timetable and retire to bed. A few diehards would start a card game in the main lounge, and they would continue drinking, but it would be the quiet, steady kind of all-night drinking that rarely led to trouble.

Eddie anxiously plotted the plane's fuel consumption on the Howgozit Curve. The red line which showed actual consumption was consistently above the pencil line of his forecast. That was almost inevitable, since he had faked his forecast. But the difference was greater than he had expected because of the weather.

He got more worried as he worked out the plane's effective range with the remaining fuel. When he made the calculation on the basis of three engines – which he was obliged to do by the safety rules – he found that there was not enough fuel to take them to Newfoundland.

He should have told the Captain immediately, but he did not.

The shortfall was very small: with four engines there would be enough fuel. Furthermore, the situation might change in the next couple of hours. The winds might be lighter than forecast so that the plane used less fuel than anticipated, and there would be more left for the rest of the journey. And finally, if the worst came to the worst, they could change their route and fly through the heart of the storm, thereby shortening the distance. The passengers would just have to suffer the bumps.

On his left the radio operator, Ben Thompson, was transcribing a Morse code message, his bald head bent over his console. Hoping it would be a forecast of better weather, Eddie stood behind him and read over his shoulder.

The message astonished and mystified him.

It was from the FBI, addressed to someone called Ollis Field. It read:

> THE BUREAU HAS RECEIVED INFORMATION THAT ASSOCIATES OF KNOWN CRIMINALS MAY BE ON YOUR FLIGHT. TAKE EXTRA PRECAUTIONS WITH THE PRISONER.

What did it mean? And did it have something to do with the kidnapping of Carol-Ann? For a moment Eddie's head spun with the possibilities.

Ben tore the page off his pad and said, 'Captain! You'd better take a look at this.'

Jack Ashford glanced up from his chart table, alerted by the urgent note in the radioman's voice. Eddie took the message from Ben, showed it to Jack for a moment, then passed it to Captain Baker, who was eating steak and mashed potatoes from a tray at the conference table at the rear of the cabin.

The Captain's face darkened as he read. 'I don't like the look of this,' he said. 'Ollis Field must be an FBI agent.'

'Is he a passenger?' Eddie asked.

'Yes. I thought there was something strange about him. Drab character, not a typical Clipper passenger. He stayed on board during the stopover at Foynes.'

Eddie had not noticed him, but the navigator had. 'I think I know who you mean,' said Jack, scratching his blue chin. 'Bald guy. There's a younger fellow with him, kind of flashily dressed. They seem like an odd couple.'

The Captain said, 'The kid must be the prisoner. I think his name is Frank Gordon.'

Eddie's mind was working fast. 'That's why they stayed on board at Foynes: the FBI man doesn't want to give his prisoner a chance to escape.'

The Captain nodded grimly. 'Gordon must have been extradited from Britain – and you don't get extradition orders for shoplifters. The guy must be a dangerous criminal. And they put him on my plane without telling me!'

The radio operator said, 'I wonder what he did.'

'Frank Gordon,' Jack mused. 'It rings a bell. Wait a minute – I bet he's Frankie Gordino!'

Eddie remembered reading about Gordino in the newspapers. He was an enforcer for a New England gang. The particular crime he was wanted for involved a Boston nightclub owner who refused to pay protection money. Gordino had bust into the club, shot the owner in the stomach, raped the man's girlfriend, then torched the club. The guy died but the girl escaped the fire and identified Gordino from pictures.

'We'll soon find out if it's him,' said Baker. 'Eddie, do me a favour, go and ask this Ollis Field to come up here.'

'Sure thing.' Eddie put on his cap and uniform jacket and went down the stairs, turning this new development over in his mind. He was sure there was some connection between Frankie Gordino and the people who had Carol-Ann, and he tried frantically to figure it out, without success.

He looked into the galley, where a steward was filling a coffee jug from the massive fifty-gallon urn. 'Davy,' he said. 'Where's Mr Ollis Field?'

'Compartment number four, port side, facing the rear,' the steward said.

Eddie walked along the aisle, keeping his balance on the unsteady floor with a practised gait. He noticed the Oxenford family looking subdued in No. 2 compartment. In the dining room the last sitting was just about finished, the after-dinner coffee spilling into the saucers as the gathering storm buffeted the plane. He went through No. 3 then up a step to No. 4.

In the rear-facing seat on the port side was a bald man of about forty, looking sleepy, smoking a cigarette and staring through the window at the darkness outside. This was not Eddie's picture of an FBI agent: he could not see this man with a gun in his hand bursting into a room full of bootleggers.

Opposite Field was a younger man, much better dressed, with the build of a retired athlete who is putting on weight. That would have to be Gordino. He had the puffy, sulky face of a spoilt child. Would he shoot a man in the stomach? Eddie wondered. Yes, I think he would.

Eddie spoke to the older man. 'Mr Field?'

'Yes.'

'The Captain would like a word, if you can spare him a moment.'

A slight frown crossed Field's face, followed by a look of resignation. He had guessed that his secret was out, and he was irritated, but his look implied that in the long run it was all the same to him. 'Of course,' he said. He crushed out his cigarette in the wall-mounted ashtray, unfastened his seat belt, and stood up.

'Follow me, please,' Eddie said.

On the way back, passing through No. 3 compartment, Eddie saw Tom Luther, and their eyes met. In that instant Eddie had a flash of inspiration.

Tom Luther's mission was to rescue Frankie Gordino.

He was so struck by the explanation that he stopped, and Ollis Field bumped into his back.

Luther stared at him with a panicky look in his eyes,

obviously afraid Eddie was going to do something that would give the game away.

'Pardon me,' Eddie said to Field, and he walked on.

Everything was becoming clear. Frankie Gordino had been forced to flee the States, but the FBI had tracked him down in Britain and got him extradited. They had decided to fly him back, and somehow his partners in crime had found out about it. They were going to try to get Gordino off the plane before it reached the United States.

That was where Eddie came in. He would bring the Clipper down in the sea off the Maine coast. There would be a fast boat waiting. Gordino would be taken off the Clipper and would speed away in the boat. A few minutes later he would go ashore at some sheltered inlet, possibly on the Canadian side of the border. A car would be waiting to whisk him into hiding. He would have escaped justice – thanks to Eddie Deakin.

As he led Field up the spiral staircase to the flight deck, Eddie felt relieved that at last he understood what was going on, and horrified that in order to save his wife he had to help a murderer go free.

'Captain, this is Mr Field,' he said.

Captain Baker had put on his uniform jacket and was seated behind the conference table with the radio message in his hand. His dinner tray had been taken away. His cap covered his blond hair, and gave him an air of authority. He looked up at Field but did not ask him to sit down. 'I've received a message for you – from the FBI,' he said.

Field held out his hand for the paper, but Baker did not give it to him.

'Are you an agent of the FBI?' the Captain asked.

'Yes.'

'And are you on Bureau business right now?'

'Yes, I am.'

'What is that business, Mr Field?'

'I don't think you need to know that, Captain. Please give me the message. You did say it was addressed to me, not to you.'

'I'm the Captain of this vessel, and it's my judgement that I do need to know what business you're on. Don't argue with me, Mr Field, just do as I say.'

Eddie studied Field. He was a pale, tired man with a bald head and watery blue eyes. He was tall and had once been powerfully built, but he was now round-shouldered and slack-looking. Eddie guessed him to be arrogant rather than brave and this was confirmed when Field immediately caved in under pressure from the Captain.

'I'm escorting an extradited prisoner back to the United States for trial,' he said. 'His name is Frank Gordon.'

'Also known as Frankie Gordino?'

'That's right.'

'I want you to know, mister, that I object to your bringing a dangerous criminal on board my airplane without telling me.'

'If you know the man's real name, you probably also know what he does for a living. He works for Raymond Patriarca, who is responsible for armed robberies, extortion, loansharking, illegal gambling and prostitution from Rhode Island to Maine. Ray Patriarca has been declared Public Enemy Number One by the Providence Board of Public Safety. Gordino is what we call an enforcer: he terrorizes, tortures and murders people on Patriarca's orders. We couldn't warn you about him for security reasons.'

'Your security is shit, Field.' Baker was really angry: Eddie had never known him to swear at a passenger. 'The Patriarca gang knows all about it.' He handed over the radio message.

Field read it and turned grey. 'How the *hell* did they find out?' he muttered.

'I have to ask which passengers are the "associates of known criminals",' said the Captain. 'Do you recognize anyone on board?'

'Of course not,' Field said irritably. 'If I had, I would have alerted the Bureau already.'

'If we can identify the people I'll put them off the plane at the next stop.'

Eddie thought, I know who they are – Tom Luther and me.

Field said, 'Radio the agency with a complete list of passengers and crew. They'll run a check on every name.'

A shiver of anxiety ran through Eddie. Was there any risk that Tom Luther would be exposed by this check? That could ruin everything. Was he a known criminal? Was Tom Luther his real name? If he was using a false name he needed a forged passport too – but that might not be a problem if he was in league with big-time racketeers. Surely he would have taken that precaution? Everything else he had done had been well organized.

Captain Baker bristled. 'I don't think we need to worry about the crew.'

Field shrugged. 'Please yourself. The Bureau will get the names from Pan American in a minute.'

Field was a tactless man, Eddie reflected. Did FBI agents get advice on how to be unpleasant from J. Edgar Hoover?

The Captain picked up the passenger manifest and crew list from his table and handed it to the radio operator. 'Send that right away, Ben,' he said. He paused, then added, 'Include the crew.'

Ben Thompson sat at his console and began to tap out the message in Morse.

'One more thing,' the Captain said to Field. 'I'll have to relieve you of your weapon.'

That was smart, Eddie thought. It had not even occurred to him that Field might be armed – but he had to be, if he was escorting a dangerous criminal.

Field said, 'I object—'

'Passengers are not allowed to carry firearms. There are no exceptions to this rule. Hand over your gun.'

'If I refuse?'

'Mr Deakin and Mr Ashford will take it from you anyway.'

Eddie was surprised by this announcement, but he played the part and moved threateningly closer to Field. Jack did the same.

Baker continued, 'And if you oblige me to use force,

I will have you put off the plane at our next stop, and I will not permit you to re-board.'

Eddie was impressed at how the Captain maintained his superiority despite the fact that his antagonist was armed. This was not how it happened in the movies, where the man with the gun was able to boss everyone else around.

What would Field do? The FBI would not approve of his giving up his gun, but on the other hand it would surely be worse to get thrown off the plane.

Field said, 'I'm escorting a dangerous prisoner – I need to be armed.'

Eddie saw something out of the corner of his eye. The door at the rear of the cabin, that led to the observation dome and the cargo holds, was ajar, and behind it something moved.

Captain Baker said, 'Take his gun, Eddie.'

Eddie reached inside Field's jacket. The man did not move. Eddie found the shoulder holster, unbuttoned the flap and withdrew the gun. Field looked ahead stonily.

Then Eddie stepped to the rear of the cabin and threw open the door.

Young Percy Oxenford stood there.

Eddie was relieved. He had half imagined that some of Gordino's gang would be waiting there with machine-guns.

Captain Baker stared at Percy and said, 'Where did you come from?'

'There's a ladder next to the ladies' powder room,' Percy said. 'It leads up into the tail of the plane.' That was where Eddie had inspected the rudder trim control cables. 'You can crawl along from there. It comes out by the baggage holds.'

Eddie was still holding Ollis Field's gun. He put it in the navigator's chart drawer.

Captain Baker said to Percy, 'Go back to your seat, please, young man, and don't leave the passenger cabin at any time during the remainder of the flight.' Percy turned to go back the way he had come. 'Not that way,' Baker snapped. 'Down the stairs.'

Looking a little scared, Percy hurried through the cabin and scuttled off down the stairs.

'How long had he been there, Eddie?' said the Captain.

'I don't know. I guess he probably heard the whole thing.'

'There goes our hope of keeping this from the passengers.' For a moment Baker looked weary, and Eddie had a flash of insight into the weight of responsibility the Captain carried. Then Baker became brisk again. 'You may return to your seat, Mr Field. Thank you for your co-operation.' Ollis Field turned around and left without speaking. 'Let's get back to work, men,' the Captain finished.

The crew returned to their stations. Eddie checked his dials automatically, although his mind was in turmoil. He observed that the fuel tanks in the wings, which fed the engines, were getting low, and he proceeded to transfer fuel from the main tanks, which were located in the hydrostabilizers or sea-wings. But his thoughts were on Frankie Gordino. Gordino had shot a man and raped a woman and burned down a nightclub, but he had been caught and would be punished for his horrible crimes – except that Eddie Deakin was going to save him. Thanks to Eddie, that girl would see her rapist get away scot-free.

Worse still, Gordino would almost certainly kill again. He was probably no good for anything else. So a day would come when Eddie would read in the papers of some ghastly crime – it might be a revenge murder, the victim tortured and mutilated before being finished off, or perhaps a building torched with women and children burned to death inside, or a girl held down and raped by three different men – and the police would link it with Ray Patriarca's gang, and Eddie would think, Was that Gordino? Am I responsible for that? Did those people suffer and die because I helped Gordino escape?

How many murders would he have on his conscience if he went ahead with this?

But he had no choice. Carol-Ann was in the hands of Ray Patriarca. Every time he thought of it he felt cold sweat dampen his temples. He had to protect her, and the only way he could do that was to co-operate with Tom Luther.

He looked at his watch: it was midnight.

Jack Ashford gave him the plane's current position, as best he could estimate it: he had not yet been able to shoot a star. Ben Thompson produced the latest weather forecasts: the storm was a bad one. Eddie read off a new set of figures from the fuel tanks and began to update his calculations. Perhaps this would resolve his dilemma:

if they did not have enough fuel to reach Newfoundland they would have to turn back, and that would be the end of it. But the thought was no consolation to him. He was no fatalist: he had to *do* something.

Captain Baker sang out, 'How goes it, Eddie?'

'Not quite done,' he replied.

'Look sharp – we must be close to the point of no return.'

Eddie felt a bead of sweat drip down his cheek. He wiped it away with a quick, surreptitious movement.

He finished the arithmetic.

The remaining fuel was not enough.

For a moment he said nothing.

He bent over his scratch pad and his tables, pretending he had not yet finished. The situation was worse than it had been at the start of his shift. Now there was not enough fuel to finish the journey, on the route the Captain had chosen, even on four engines: the safety margin had disappeared. The only way they could make it was to shorten the journey by flying through the storm instead of skirting it; and even then, if they should lose an engine they would be finished.

All these passengers would die, and I would too; and then what would happen to Carol-Ann?

'Come on, Eddie,' said the Captain. 'What's it to be? On to Botwood or back to Foynes?'

Eddie gritted his teeth. He could not bear the thought of leaving Carol-Ann with the kidnappers for another day. He would rather risk everything.

'Are you prepared to change course, and fly through the storm?' he said.

'Do we have to?'

'Either that, or turn back.' Eddie held his breath.

'Damn,' said the Captain. They all hated turning back halfway across the Atlantic: it was such a let-down.

Eddie waited for the Captain's decision.

'Heck with it,' said Captain Baker. 'We'll fly through the storm.'

Part Four

Mid-Atlantic to Botwood

CHAPTER SIXTEEN

DIANA LOVESEY was furious with her husband, Mervyn, for boarding the Clipper at Foynes. She was, first of all, painfully embarrassed by his pursuit of her, and afraid people would think the whole situation highly comical. More importantly, she did not want the opportunity to change her mind which he was giving her. She had made her decision, but Mervyn had refused to accept it as final, and somehow that cast doubt on her determination. Now she would have to make the decision again and again, as he would keep asking her to reconsider. Finally, he had completely spoiled her pleasure in the flight. It was supposed to be the trip of a lifetime, a romantic journey with her lover. But the exhilarating sense of freedom she had felt as they took off from Southampton had gone for good. She got no pleasure from the flight, the luxurious plane, the elegant company or the gourmet food. She was afraid to touch Mark, to kiss his cheek or stroke his arm or hold his hand, in case Mervyn should happen to pass through the compartment at that moment and see what she was doing. She was not sure where Mervyn was sitting, but she expected to see him at every moment.

Mark was completely flattened by this development. After Diana turned Mervyn down at Foynes, Mark had been elated, affectionate and optimistic, talking about California and making jokes and kissing her at every opportunity, quite his usual self. Then he had watched in horror as his rival had stepped on board the plane. Now he was like a punctured balloon. He sat silently beside her, leafing disconsolately through magazines without reading a word. She could understand his feeling depressed. Once already she had changed her mind about running away with him: with Mervyn on board, how could he be sure she would not change it again?

To make matters worse, the weather had become stormy, and the plane bumped like a car crossing a field. Every now and again a passenger would pass through the compartment on the way to the bathroom, looking green. People said it was forecast to get worse. Diana was glad now that she had been feeling too upset to eat much at dinner.

She wished she knew where Mervyn was sitting. Perhaps if she did she would stop expecting him to materialize at any moment. She decided to go to the ladies' room and look for him on the way.

She was in No. 4 compartment. She took a quick look into No. 3, the next one forward, but Mervyn was not there. Turning back, she walked aft, holding on to anything she could grab as the plane bucked and swayed. She passed through No. 5 and established that he was not there either. That was the last big compartment. Most of No. 6 was taken up by the ladies' powder room, on the starboard side, leaving room for only two people on the port side. These seats were occupied by two businessmen. They were not very attractive seats, Diana thought: fancy paying all that money and then sitting outside the ladies' toilet for the whole flight! Beyond No. 6 there was nothing but the honeymoon suite. Mervyn must be seated farther forward, then, in No. 1 or 2, unless he was in the main lounge, playing cards.

She went into the powder room. There were two stools in front of the mirror, one already occupied by a woman Diana had not yet spoken to. As Diana closed the door behind her, the plane plunged again and she almost lost her balance. She staggered in and fell into the vacant seat.

'Are you all right?' the other woman said.

'Yes, thanks. I hate it when the plane does this.'

'So do I. But someone said it's going to get worse. There's a big storm ahead.'

The turbulence eased, and Diana opened her handbag and started to brush her hair.

'You're Mrs Lovesey, aren't you?' the woman said.

'Yes. Call me Diana.'

'I'm Nancy Lenehan.' The woman hesitated, looking awkward, then went on, 'I got on the plane at Foynes. I came over from Liverpool with your . . . with Mr Lovesey.'

'Oh!' Diana felt her face go pink. 'I didn't know he had a companion.'

'He helped me out of a jam. I needed to catch the plane, but I was stuck in Liverpool with no way of getting to Southampton in time, so I just drove out to the airfield and begged a ride.'

'I'm glad for you,' Diana said. 'But it's frightfully embarrassing for me.'

'I don't see why *you* should be embarrassed. It must be nice to have two men desperately in love with you. I don't even have one.'

Diana looked at her in the mirror. She was attractive rather than beautiful, with regular features and dark hair, and she wore a very smart red suit with a grey silk blouse. She had a brisk, confident air. Mervyn *would* give you a lift, Diana thought; you're just his type. 'Was he polite to you?' she asked.

'Not very,' Nancy said with a rueful smile.

'I'm sorry. His manners aren't his strong point.' Diana took out her lipstick.

'I was just grateful for the ride.' Nancy blew her nose delicately on a tissue. Diana noticed that she wore a wedding ring. 'He is a little abrupt,' Nancy went on. 'But I think he's a nice man. I had dinner with him, too. He makes me laugh. And he's terribly handsome.'

'He is a nice man,' Diana found herself saying. 'But he's as arrogant as a duchess and he's got no patience at all. I drive him up the wall because I hesitate and change my mind and don't always say what I mean.'

Nancy ran a comb through her hair. It was thick and dark, and Diana wondered whether she dyed it to conceal grey streaks. Nancy said, 'He seems willing to go a long way to get you back.'

'That's just pride,' Diana said. 'It's because another man has taken me away. Mervyn's competitive. If I'd left him and gone to live at my sister's house he wouldn't have cared tuppence.'

Nancy laughed. 'It sounds as if he has no chance of getting you back.'

'None whatsoever.' Suddenly Diana did not want to talk to Nancy Lenehan any longer. She felt unaccountably hostile. She put away her make-up and her comb and stood up. She smiled to cover her sudden feeling of dislike, saying, 'Let's see if I can cakewalk back to my seat.'

'Good luck!'

As she left the powder room, Lulu Bell and Princess Lavinia came in, carrying their overnight cases. When she got back to the compartment, Davy the steward was converting their seat into a double bunk. Diana was intrigued to see how an ordinary-looking divan seat could be made into two beds. She sat down and watched.

First he took off all the cushions and pulled the armrests out of their slots. Reaching over the seat frame, he pulled down two flaps in the wall at chest level to reveal hooks. Bending over the seat, he unfastened a strap and lifted out a flat frame. He hung this from the wall hooks to form the base of the upper bunk. The outward side slotted into a hole in the side wall. Diana was just thinking that it did not look very strong when Davy picked up two stout-looking struts and attached them to both upper and lower frames to form bedposts. Now the structure looked more sturdy.

He replaced the seat cushions on the lower bed and used the back cushions as a mattress for the upper one.

He took pale blue sheets and blankets from under the seat and made up the beds with fast, practised movements.

The bunks looked comfortable but rather public. However, Davy broke out a dark blue curtain, complete with hooks and hung it from a moulding on the ceiling which Diana had thought was merely decorative. He attached the curtain to the bunk frames with press-studs, making a tight fit. He left a triangular opening, like the entrance to a tent, for the sleeper to climb inside. Finally he unfolded a little stepladder and placed it convenient to the upper bunk.

He turned to Diana and Mark with a faintly pleased look, as if he had performed a magic trick. 'Just let me know when you're ready and I'll make up your side,' he said.

'Doesn't it get stuffy in there?' Diana asked him.

'Each bunk has its own ventilator,' he replied. 'If you look just above your head you can see yours.' Diana looked up and saw a grille with an open/closed lever. 'You've also got your own window, electric light, clothes hanger and shelf; and if you need anything else, press this button to call me.'

While he had been working, the two passengers on the port side, handsome Frank Gordon and bald Ollis Field, had picked up their overnight bags and trooped off to the men's room; now Davy began to make up the bunk on that side. The arrangement was slightly different over there. The aisle was not in the centre of the plane, but nearer to the port side, so on that side there was only one pair of bunks, placed lengthwise rather than across the width of the plane.

Princess Lavinia returned in a floor-length navy blue *peignoir* trimmed with blue lace, and a matching turban. Her face was a mask of frozen dignity: obviously she found it painfully uncomfortable to appear in public in her nightclothes. She looked at the bunk in horror. 'I shall *die* of claustrophobia,' she moaned. No one took any notice. She stepped out of little silk slippers and climbed into the lower bunk. Without saying goodnight, she pulled the curtain shut and fastened it tight.

A moment later Lulu Bell appeared in a rather flimsy pink chiffon ensemble that did little to conceal her charms. She had been stiffly polite with Diana and Mark since Foynes, but now she seemed to have suddenly forgotten her pique. She sat down beside them on the divan and said, 'You'll never guess what I just heard about our companions!' She jerked a thumb at the seats vacated by Field and Gordon.

Mark looked nervously at Diana and said, 'What did you hear, Lulu?'

'Mr Field is an FBI man!'

That was not so startling, Diana thought. An FBI agent was only a policeman.

Lulu went on, 'And what's more, Frank Gordon is a prisoner!'

Mark asked sceptically, 'Who told you this?'

'Everyone's talking about it in the ladies' room.'

'That doesn't make it true, Lulu.'

'I knew you wouldn't believe me!' she said. 'That kid overheard a row between Field and the Captain of the plane. The Captain was mad as hell because the FBI didn't warn Pan American that they had a dangerous prisoner on board. There was a real set-to and in the end the crew took away Mr Field's gun!'

Diana recalled thinking that Field seemed like Gordon's chaperon. 'What do they say Frank did?'

'He's a mobster. He shot a guy and raped a girl and torched a nightclub.'

Diana found that hard to believe. She had talked to the man herself! He was not very refined, it was true, but he was handsome and nicely dressed, and he had flirted with her politely. She could see him as a confidence trickster or a tax dodger, and she could imagine his being involved in illegal gambling, say; but it did not seem possible that he had deliberately killed people. Lulu was an excitable person who would believe anything.

Mark said, 'It's kinda hard to credit.'

'I give up,' Lulu said with a deprecating wave of her hand. 'You guys have no sense of adventure.' She stood up. 'I'm going to bed. If he starts raping people, wake me up.' She climbed the little step-ladder and crawled into the top bunk. She pulled the curtains, then looked out again and spoke to Diana. 'Honey, I understand why you got ticked off at me back there in Ireland. I been thinking about it, and I figure I asked for what I got. I was kind of all over Mark. Dumb, I know. I'm ready to forget it as soon as you are. Goodnight.'

It was close enough to an apology, and Diana did

not have the heart to reject it. 'Goodnight, Lulu,' she said.

Lulu closed the curtain.

Mark said, 'It was my fault as much as hers. I'm sorry, baby.'

By way of reply, Diana kissed him.

Suddenly she felt comfortable and at ease with him again. Her whole body relaxed and she slumped back on the seat, still kissing him. She was conscious that her right breast was pressing up against his chest. It was nice to be getting physical with him again. The tip of his tongue touched her lips and she parted them a fraction to let him in. He began to breathe harder. This was going a bit too far, Diana thought. She opened her eyes – and saw Mervyn.

He was passing through the compartment, going forward, and he might not have noticed her, but he turned and glanced over his shoulder and froze, almost in mid-stride. His face paled with shock.

Diana knew him so well that she could read his mind. Although he had been told that she was in love with Mark, he was too downright stubborn to accept it, so it came as a blow to him to see her actually kissing someone else, almost as bad as if he had had no warning.

His brow darkened and his black eyebrows contracted in an angry frown. For a split second Diana thought he was going to start a fight. Then he turned away and walked on.

Mark said, 'What's the matter?' He had not seen Mervyn – he had been too busy kissing Diana.

She decided not to tell him. 'Someone might see,' she murmured.

Reluctantly he drew away from her.

She was relieved for a moment, then she began to feel angry. Mervyn had no right to follow her across the world and frown at her every time she kissed Mark. Marriage was not slavery: she had left him, and he had to accept that. Mark lit a cigarette. Diana felt the need to confront Mervyn. She wanted to tell him to get out of her life.

She stood up. 'I'm going to see what's happening in the lounge,' she said. 'You stay there and smoke.' She left without waiting for a reply.

She had established that Mervyn was not seated to the rear, so she went forward. The turbulence had eased enough for her to walk without holding on. Mervyn was not in No. 3 compartment. In the main lounge the card-players were settling down to a long game, their seat belts fastened, clouds of smoke around them and bottles of whisky on the tables. She went into No. 2. The Oxenford family took up one side of that compartment. Everyone on the plane knew that Lord Oxenford had insulted Carl Hartmann, the scientist, and that Mervyn Lovesey had sprung to his defence. Mervyn had his good points: she had never denied that.

Next she came to the kitchen. Nicky, the fat steward, was washing dishes at a tremendous pace while his colleague was making beds farther back. The men's room door was opposite the kitchen. After that was the staircase to the flight deck, and beyond that, in the nose of the plane, No. 1 compartment. She assumed

Mervyn had to be there, but in fact it was occupied by off-duty flight crew.

She went up the stairs to the flight cabin. It was as luxurious as the passenger deck, she noticed. However, the crew all looked terrifically busy, and one of them said to her, 'We'd love to show you around at another time, ma'am, but while we're flying through this bad weather we have to ask you to remain seated and fasten your safety belt.'

Mervyn had to be in the men's room, then, she thought as she went down the stairs. She still had not found out where he was sitting.

When she reached the foot of the staircase she bumped into Mark. She gave a guilty start. 'What are you doing?' she said.

'I was wondering that about you,' he said, and there was something unpleasant in his tone of voice.

'I was just looking around.'

'Looking for Mervyn?' he said accusingly.

'Mark, why are you angry with me?'

'Because you're sneaking off to see him.'

Nicky interrupted them. 'Folks, would you return to your seats, please? We're getting a smooth ride for the moment but it's not going to last.'

They made their way back to their compartment. Diana felt foolish. She had been following Mervyn and Mark had been following her. It seemed silly.

They sat down. Before they could continue their conversation, Ollis Field and Frank Gordon followed them in. Frank wore a yellow silk dressing-gown with a dragon on the back, Field a grubby old woollen one.

Frank took off his dressing-gown to reveal red pyjamas with white piping. He stepped out of his carpet-slippers and climbed the little ladder to the top bunk.

Then, to Diana's horror, Field took a pair of gleaming silvery handcuffs from the pocket of his brown robe. He said something to Frank in a low voice. Diana could not hear the reply, but she could tell that Frank was protesting. However, Field insisted, and in the end Frank offered one wrist. Field clapped one cuff on him and attached the other to the frame of the bunk. Then he drew the curtain on Frank and fastened the press-studs.

It was true, then; Frank *was* a prisoner.

Mark said, 'Well, shit.'

Diana whispered, 'I still don't believe he's a *murderer.*'

'I hope not!' Mark said. 'We would have been safer paying fifty bucks and travelling steerage in a tramp steamer!'

'I wish he hadn't put the handcuffs on. I don't know how that boy can sleep chained to his bed. He won't even be able to roll over!'

'You're soft-hearted,' Mark said, giving her a hug. 'The man is probably a rapist and you're feeling sorry for him because he might not be able to sleep.'

She put her head on his shoulder. He stroked her hair. He had been mad at her a couple of minutes ago but that seemed to have passed. 'Mark,' she said. 'Do you think two people can get into one of these bunks?'

'Are you frightened, honey?'

'No.'

He gave her a puzzled look, then he understood and

grinned. I guess you could get two in – though not side by side . . .'

'Not side by side?'

'It looks too narrow.'

'Well . . .' She lowered her voice. 'One of us will have to get on top.'

He murmured into her ear, 'Would you like to get on top?'

She giggled. 'I think I might.'

'I'll have to consider that,' he said thickly. 'What do you weigh?'

'Eight stone and two breasts.'

'Shall we get changed?'

She took off her hat and put it down on the seat beside her. Mark pulled their cases from under the seat. His was a well-used cordovan Gladstone bag, hers a small hard-sided tan leather case with her initials in gold lettering.

Diana stood up.

'Be quick,' Mark said. He kissed her.

She gave him a swift hug, and as he pressed against her she felt his erection. 'Goodness,' she said. In a whisper she added, 'Can you keep it like that until you get back?'

'I don't think so. Not unless I pee out the window.' She laughed. He added, 'But I'll show you a quick way to make it hard again.'

'I can't wait,' she whispered.

Mark picked up his case and went out, going forward towards the men's room. As he left the compartment he passed Mervyn coming the other way. They looked at one another like cats across a fence, but they did not speak.

Diana was startled to see Mervyn dressed in a coarse flannel nightshirt with broad brown stripes. 'What on *earth* have you got on?' she said incredulously.

'Go on, laugh,' he said. 'It was all I could find in Foynes. The local shop has never heard of silk pyjamas – they didn't know whether I was queer or just daft.'

'Well, your friend Mrs Lenehan won't fancy you in that get-up.' Now why did I say that? Diana wondered.

'I don't suppose she'd fancy me in anything,' Mervyn said crossly, and he passed on out of the compartment.

The steward came in. Diana said, 'Oh, Davy, would you make up our beds now, please?'

'Right away, ma'am.'

'Thank you.' She picked up her case and went out.

As she passed through No. 5 compartment it occurred to her to wonder where Mervyn was sleeping. None of these bunks was made up yet, nor any in No. 6, and yet he had disappeared. It dawned on Diana that he must be in the honeymoon suite. An instant later she realized that she had not seen Mrs Lenehan seated anywhere when she walked the length of the plane a few moments earlier. She stood outside the ladies' room, with her bag in her hand, frozen still with surprise. It was outrageous. Mervyn and Mrs Lenehan must be sharing the honeymoon suite!

Surely the airline would not allow it. Perhaps Mrs Lenehan had already gone to bed, and was out of sight in a curtained bunk in a forward compartment.

Diana had to know.

She stepped to the door of the honeymoon suite and hesitated.

Then she turned the handle and opened the door.

The suite was about the same size as a regular compartment, and had a terracotta carpet, beige walls and the blue upholstery with the pattern of stars that was also in the main lounge. At the rear of the room was a pair of bunks. On one side was a couch and a coffee table, and on the other a stool, a dressing-table and a mirror. There were two windows on each side.

Mervyn stood in the middle of the room, startled by her sudden appearance. Mrs Lenehan was not present, but her grey cashmere coat was draped over the couch.

Diana slammed the door behind her and said, 'How could you do this to me?'

'Do what?'

It was a good question, she thought in the back of her mind. What was she so angry about? 'Everyone will know that you're spending the night with her!'

'I had no choice,' he protested. 'There were no other seats left.'

'Don't you know how people will laugh at us? It's bad enough your following me like this!'

'Why would I care? Everyone laughs at a chap whose wife runs off with another fellow.'

'But this is making it worse! You should have accepted the situation and made the best of it.'

'You ought to know me better than that.'

'I do – that's why I tried to prevent you following me.'

He shrugged. 'Well, you failed. You're not clever enough to outwit me.'

'And you're not clever enough to know when to give in gracefully!'

'I've never pretended to be graceful.'

'And what kind of tramp is she? She's married – I saw her ring!'

'She's a widow. Anyway, what right have you got to be so damn superior? You're married, and you're spending the night with your fancy man.'

'At least we'll be in separate bunks in a public compartment, not tucked away in a cosy little bridal suite,' she said, suppressing a guilty pang as she recalled how she had planned to share a bunk with Mark.

'But I'm not having an affair with Mrs Lenehan,' he said in an exasperated tone. 'Whereas you've been dropping your drawers for that playboy all bloody summer, haven't you?'

'Don't be so vulgar,' she hissed, but she felt somehow he was right. That was exactly what she had been doing: whipping her panties off as quick as she could every time she got near Mark. He was right.

'If it's vulgar to say it, it must be worse to do it,' he said.

'At least I was discreet – I didn't flaunt it and humiliate you.'

'I'm not so sure about that. I'll probably find I was the only person in Manchester who didn't know what you were up to. Adulterers are never as discreet as they think.'

'Don't call me that!' she protested. It made her feel ashamed.

'Why not? It's what you are.'

'It sounds vile,' she said, looking away.

'Be thankful we don't stone adulteresses like they did in the Bible.'

'It's a horrible word.'

'You should be ashamed of the deed, not the word.'

'You're so bloody righteous,' she said wearily. 'You've never done anything wrong, have you?'

'I've always done right by you!' he said angrily.

She became thoroughly exasperated with him. 'Two wives have run away from you but you've always been the innocent party. Will it ever occur to you to wonder where *you* might be going wrong?'

That got to him. He grabbed her, holding her arms above the elbow, and shook her. 'I gave you everything you wanted!'

'But you don't care how I feel about things,' she shouted. 'You never did. That's why I left you.' She put her hands on his chest to push him away – and at that moment the door opened and Mark came in.

He stood there in his pyjamas, staring at the two of them, and said, 'What the hell is this, Diana? Are you planning to spend the night in the honeymoon suite?'

She pushed Mervyn away and he let her go. 'No, I'm not,' she said to Mark. 'This is Mrs Lenehan's accommodation – Mervyn's sharing it.'

Mark laughed scornfully. 'That's rich!' he said. 'I have to put this in a script some time!'

'It's not funny!' she protested.

'But it is!' he said. 'This guy comes chasing his wife like a lunatic, then what does he do, he shacks up with a girl he meets on the way!'

Diana resented his attitude and found herself unwillingly defending Mervyn. 'They're not shacked up,' she said impatiently. 'These were the only seats left.'

'You should be glad,' Mark said. 'If he falls for her maybe he'll stop chasing you.'

'Can't you see I'm upset?'

'Sure, but I don't understand why,' he said. 'You don't love Mervyn any more. Sometimes you talk as if you hate him. You've left him. So why do you care who he sleeps with?'

'I don't know, but I do! I feel humiliated!'

Mark was too cross to be sympathetic. 'A few hours ago you decided to go back to Mervyn. Then he annoyed you and you changed your mind. Now you're mad at him for sleeping with someone else.'

'I'm not sleeping with her,' Mervyn put in.

Mark ignored him. 'Are you sure you're not still in love with Mervyn?' he said angrily to Diana.

'That's a horrible thing to say to me!'

'I know, but is it true?'

'No, it isn't true, and I hate you for thinking it might be.' She was in tears now.

'Then prove it to me. Forget about him and where he sleeps.'

'I was never any good at tests!' she shouted. 'Stop being so bloody logical! This is not the Debating Society!'

'No, it's not!' said a new voice. The three of them turned around and saw Nancy Lenehan in the door, looking very attractive in a bright blue silk robe. 'In fact,' she said, 'I believe this is my suite. What the hell is going on?'

CHAPTER SEVENTEEN

MARGARET OXENFORD was angry and ashamed. She felt sure the other passengers were staring at her, thinking about the dreadful scene in the dining room, and assuming that she shared her father's horrible attitudes. She was afraid to look anyone in the eye.

Harry Marks had rescued the shreds of her dignity. It had been clever of him, and so gracious, to step in and hold her chair like that, then offer her his arm as she walked out: a small gesture, almost silly, but for her it had made a world of difference.

Still, it was only a vestige of her self-respect that she had retained, and she boiled with resentment towards Father for putting her in such a shameful position.

There was a cold silence in the compartment for two hours after dinner. When the weather started to get rough, Mother and Father retired to change into their nightclothes. Then Percy surprised Margaret by saying, 'Let's apologize.'

Her first thought was that this would involve further embarrassment and humiliation. 'I don't think I've got the courage,' she said.

'We'll just go up to Baron Gabon and Professor Hartmann and say we're sorry Father was so rude.'

The idea of somehow mitigating her father's offence was very tempting. It would make her feel a lot better. 'Father would be furious, of course,' she said.

'He doesn't have to know. But I don't care if he is angry. I think he's going round the bend. I'm not even afraid of him any more.'

Margaret wondered whether that was true. As a small boy Percy had often said he was not afraid when in fact he was terrified. But he was not a small boy any more.

She was actually a little worried by the thought that Percy might no longer be under Father's control. Only Father could restrain Percy. With no rein on his mischief, what might he do?

'Come on,' Percy said. 'Let's do it now. They're in number three compartment – I checked.'

Still Margaret hesitated. She cringed at the thought of walking up to the men Father had insulted so. It could cause them more pain. They might prefer to forget the whole thing as quickly as possible. But they might also be wondering how many other passengers secretly agreed with Father. Surely it was more important to make a stand against racial prejudice?

Margaret decided to do it. She had often been faint-hearted and she had usually regretted it. She stood up, steadying herself by holding on to the arm of her seat, for the plane was bucking every few moments. 'All right,' she said. 'Let's apologize.'

She was trembling a little with apprehension but her shakiness was masked by the unsteadiness of the plane.

She led the way through the main lounge into No. 3 compartment.

Gabon and Hartmann were on the port side, facing each other. Hartmann was absorbed in reading, his long thin body in a curve, his close-cropped head bent, his arched nose pointing at a page of mathematical calculations. Gabon was doing nothing, apparently bored, and he saw them first. When Margaret stopped beside him and held on to the back of his seat for support, he stiffened and looked hostile.

Margaret said quickly, 'We've come to apologize.'

'I'm surprised you are so bold,' Gabon said. He spoke English perfectly, with only the trace of a French accent.

It was not the reaction Margaret had hoped for, but she ploughed on regardless. 'I'm most dreadfully sorry about what happened, and my brother feels the same way. I admire Professor Hartmann so much, I told him earlier.'

Hartmann had looked up from his book, and now he nodded agreement. But Gabon was still angry. 'It's too easy for people like you to be sorry,' he said. Margaret stared at the floor and wished she had not come. 'Germany is full of polite, wealthy people who are "most dreadfully sorry" for what is happening there,' Gabon went on. 'But what do they do? What do *you* do?'

Margaret felt her face flush crimson. She did not know what to do or say.

'Hush, Philippe,' Hartmann said softly. 'Can't you

see that they're young?' He looked at Margaret. 'I accept your apology, and thank you.'

'Oh dear,' she said. 'Have I made everything worse?'

'Not at all,' Hartmann said. 'You have made it a little better, and I'm grateful to you. My friend the Baron is terribly upset, but he will see it my way eventually, I think.'

'We'd better go,' Margaret said wretchedly.

Hartmann nodded.

She turned away.

Percy said, 'I'm terribly sorry.' He followed her out.

They staggered back to their compartment. Davy was making up the bunks. Harry had disappeared, presumably to the men's room. Margaret decided to get ready for bed. She picked up her overnight case and made her way to the ladies' room to change. Mother was just coming out, looking stunning in her chestnut-coloured dressing-gown. 'Goodnight, dear,' she said. Margaret passed her without speaking.

In the crowded ladies' room she changed quickly into her cotton nightdress and towelling bathrobe. Her nightclothes seemed dowdy among the brightly coloured silks and cashmeres of the other women, but she hardly cared. Apologizing had brought her no relief in the end because Baron Gabon's remarks had rung true. It *was* too easy to say sorry and do nothing about the problem.

When she returned to her compartment, Father and Mother were in bed behind closed curtains, and a muffled snore came from Father's bunk. Her own bed was not ready, so she had to sit in the lounge.

She knew very well that there was only one way out of her predicament. She *had* to leave her parents and live on her own. She was now more determined than ever to do so; but she was no nearer to solving the practical problems of money, work and accommodation.

Mrs Lenehan, the attractive woman who had joined the plane at Foynes, came and sat beside her, wearing a bright blue robe over a black négligé. 'I came to ask for a brandy, but the stewards seem so busy,' she said. She did not seem very disappointed. She waved a hand to indicate all the passengers. 'This is like a pyjama party, or a midnight feast in the dormitory – everyone wandering around *en déshabille*. Don't you agree?'

Margaret had never been to a pyjama party or slept in a dormitory, so she just said, 'It's very strange. It makes us all seem like one family.'

Mrs Lenehan fastened her seat belt: she was in a mood to chat. 'It's not possible to be formal when you're in your nightclothes, I guess. Even Frankie Gordino looked cute in his red p.j.s, didn't he?'

At first Margaret was not sure who she meant; then she remembered that Percy had overheard an angry exchange between the Captain and an FBI agent. 'Is that the prisoner?'

'Yes.'

'Aren't you afraid of him?'

'I guess not. He won't do me any harm.'

'But people are saying he's a murderer, and worse than that.'

'There will always be crime in the slums. Take

Gordino away and somebody else will do the killing. I'd leave him there. Gambling and prostitution have been going on since God was a boy, and if there has to be crime it might as well be organized.'

This was a rather shocking speech. Perhaps something about the atmosphere of the plane led people to be unusually candid. Margaret also guessed that Mrs Lenehan would not have talked like this in mixed company: women were always more down-to-earth when there were no men around. Whatever the reason, Margaret was fascinated. 'Wouldn't it be better for crime to be *dis*organized?' she said.

'Certainly not. Organized, it's contained. The gangs each have their own territory and they stay there. They don't rub people out on Fifth Avenue and they don't demand protection money from the Harvard Club, so why bother them?'

Margaret could not let this pass. 'What about the poor people who waste their money gambling? What about the wretched girls who ruin their health?'

'It's not that I don't care about them,' Mrs Lenehan said. Margaret looked carefully at her face, wondering whether she was sincere. 'Listen,' she went on. 'I make shoes.' Margaret must have looked surprised, for Mrs Lenehan added, 'That's what I do for a living, I own a shoe factory. My men's shoes are cheap, and they last for five or ten years. If you want to you can buy even cheaper shoes, but they're no good – they have cardboard soles that last about ten days. And, believe it or not, some people buy the cardboard ones! Now, I figure I've done my duty by making good shoes. If people are dumb enough to buy bad shoes there's nothing I can do about it. And if people are dumb enough to spend their money gambling when they can't afford to buy a steak for supper, that's not my problem either.'

'Have you ever been poor yourself?' Margaret asked.

Mrs Lenehan laughed. 'Smart question. No, I haven't, so maybe I shouldn't shoot off my mouth. My grandfather made boots by hand and my father opened the factory that I now run. I don't know anything about life in the slums. Do you?'

'Not much, but I think there are reasons why people gamble and steal and sell their bodies. They aren't just stupid. They're victims of a cruel system.'

'I suppose you're some kind of Communist.' Mrs Lenehan said this without hostility.

'Socialist,' Margaret said.

'That's good,' she said surprisingly. 'You may change your mind later – everyone's notions alter as they get older – but if you don't have ideals to start with, what is there to improve? I'm not cynical. I think we should learn from experience but hold on to our ideals. Why am I preaching at you like this? Maybe because today is my fortieth birthday.'

'Many happy returns.' Margaret normally resented people who said she would change her mind when she was older: it was a condescending thing to say, and often said when they had lost an argument but would not admit it. However, Mrs Lenehan was different. 'What are your ideals?' Margaret asked her.

'I just want to make good shoes.' She gave a self-deprecating smile. 'Not much of an ideal, I guess, but it's important to me. I have a nice life. I live in a beautiful home, my sons have everything they need, I spend a fortune on clothes. Why do I have all this? Because I make good shoes. If I made cardboard shoes I'd feel like a thief. I'd be as bad as Frankie.'

'A rather socialist point of view,' Margaret said with a smile.

'I just adopted my father's ideals, really,' Mrs Lenehan said reflectively. 'Where do your ideals come from? Not your father, I know.'

Margaret blushed. 'You heard about the scene at dinner.'

'I was there.'

'I've got to get away from my parents.'

'What's keeping you?'

'I'm only nineteen.'

Mrs Lenehan was mildly scornful. 'So what? People run away from home at ten!'

'I did try,' Margaret said. 'I got into trouble and the police picked me up.'

'You give in pretty easy.'

Margaret wanted Mrs Lenehan to understand that it was not from lack of courage that she had failed. 'I've no money and no skills. I've never had a proper education. I don't know how I'd make a living.'

'Honey, you're on your way to America. Most people arrived there with a lot less than you, and some of them are millionaires now. You can read and write English, you're personable, intelligent, pretty . . . You could get a job easily. I'd hire you.'

Margaret's heart seemed to turn over. She had been beginning to feel resentful of Mrs Lenehan's unsympathetic attitude. Now she realized she was being given an opportunity. 'Would you?' she said. 'Would you hire me?'

'Sure.'

'As what?'

Mrs Lenehan thought for a moment. 'I'd put you in the sales office – licking stamps, going for coffee, answering the phone, being nice to customers. If you made yourself useful you'd soon be promoted to assistant sales manager.'

'What does that involve?'

'It means doing the same things for more money.'

To Margaret it seemed like an impossible dream. 'Oh, my goodness, a real job in a real office,' she said longingly.

Mrs Lenehan laughed. 'Most people think of it as drudgery!'

'To me it would be such an adventure.'

'At first, maybe.'

'Do you really mean it?' Margaret said solemnly. 'If I come to your office in a week's time, will you give me a job?'

Mrs Lenehan looked startled. 'My God, you're deadly serious, aren't you?' she said. 'I kind of thought we were talking theoretically.'

Margaret's heart sank. 'Then you won't give me a job?' she said plaintively. 'All this was just talk?'

'I'd like to hire you, but there's a snag. In a week's time I may not have a job myself.'

Margaret wanted to cry. 'What do you mean?'

'My brother is trying to take the company away from me.'

'How can he do that?'

'It's complicated, and he may not succeed. I'm fighting him off, but I can't be sure how it will end.'

Margaret could hardly believe that this chance had been snatched away from her after only a few moments. 'You must win!' she said fiercely.

Before Mrs Lenehan could reply, Harry appeared, looking like a sunrise in red pyjamas and a sky-blue robe. The sight of him made Margaret feel calmer. He sat down and Margaret introduced him. 'Mrs Lenehan came to get a brandy but the stewards are busy,' she added.

Harry looked surprised. 'They may be busy, but they can still serve drinks.' He stood up and put his head into the next compartment. 'Davy, just bring a cognac for Mrs Lenehan right away, would you please?'

Margaret heard the steward say, 'Sure thing, Mr Vandenpost!' Harry had a way of getting people to do what he wanted.

He sat down again. 'I couldn't help noticing your earrings, Mrs Lenehan,' he said. 'They're absolutely beautiful.'

'Thank you,' she said with a smile. She seemed pleased by the compliment.

Margaret looked more closely. Each earring was a single large pearl inside a latticework of gold wire and diamond chips. They were quietly elegant. She wished she had on some exquisite jewellery to excite Harry's interest.

'Did you get them in the States?' Harry asked.

'Yes, they're from Paul Flato.'

Harry nodded. 'But I think they were designed by Fulco di Verdura.'

'I wouldn't know,' Mrs Lenehan said. 'Jewellery is an unusual interest for a young man,' she added perceptively.

Margaret wanted to say, 'He's mainly interested in stealing it, so watch out!' But she was impressed by his expertise. He always noticed the finest pieces, and often knew who had designed them.

Davy brought Mrs Lenehan's brandy. He seemed able to walk without staggering, despite the tossing of the plane.

She took it and stood up. 'I'm going to get some sleep.'

'Good luck,' Margaret said, thinking of Mrs Lenehan's battle with her brother. If she won it she would hire Margaret, she had promised.

'Thanks. Goodnight.'

As Mrs Lenehan staggered off towards the rear of the plane, Harry said a little jealously, 'What were you talking about?'

Margaret hesitated to tell him about Nancy offering her a job. She was thrilled about it, but there was a snag, so she could not ask Harry to rejoice with her. She decided to hug it to herself a little longer. 'We started off talking about Frankie Gordino,' she said. 'Nancy believes that people like him should be left alone. All they do is organize things like gambling and . . . prostitution . . . which do no harm except to people who choose to take part in them.' She felt herself blush faintly: she had never spoken the word 'prostitution' aloud before.

Harry looked thoughtful. 'Not all prostitutes are volunteers,' he said after a minute. 'Some are forced into it. You've heard of white slavery.'

'Is that what it means?' Margaret had seen the phrase in newspapers, but had vaguely imagined that girls were kidnapped and sent off to be chambermaids in Istanbul. How silly she had been.

Harry said, 'There's not as much of it as the papers make out. There's only one white slaver in London – his name's Benny the Malt, he's from Malta.'

Margaret was riveted. To think all this was going on under her nose! 'It might have happened to me!'

'It could have, that night you ran away from home,' Harry said. 'That's just the kind of situation Benny can work with. A young girl on her own, with no money and nowhere to sleep. He'd have given you a nice dinner and offered you a job with a dance troupe leaving for Paris in the morning, and you'd think he was your salvation. The dance troupe would turn out to be a strip show, but you wouldn't find that out until you were stuck in Paris with no money and no way of getting home, so you'd stand in the back row and wiggle as best you could.' Margaret put herself in that situation and realized that she would probably do exactly that. 'Then one night they'd ask you to "be nice" to a drunk stockbroker from the audience, and if you refused they'd hold you down for him.' Margaret closed her eyes, revolted and scared to think what might have happened to her. 'Next day you might walk out, but where would you go? You might have a few francs, but it wouldn't be enough to get you home. And you'd start thinking about what you were going to tell your family when you arrived. The truth? Never. So you'd drift back to your lodgings with the other girls, who at least would be friendly and understanding. And then you'd start to think that if you've done it once you can do it again, and the next stockbroker would be a little easier. Before you know it you're looking forward to the tips the clients leave on the nightstand in the morning.'

Margaret shuddered. 'That's the most horrible thing I've ever heard.'

'It's why I don't think Frankie Gordino should be left alone.'

They were both quiet for a minute or two, then Harry said meditatively, 'I wonder what the connection is between Frankie Gordino and Clive Membury.'

'Is there one?'

'Well, Percy says Membury's got a gun. I'd already guessed he might be a copper.'

'Really? How?'

'That red waistcoat. A copper would think it was just the thing to make him look like a playboy.'

'Perhaps he's helping to guard Frankie Gordino.'

Harry looked dubious. 'Why? Gordino's an American villain on his way to an American jail. He's out of British territory and in the custody of the FBI. I can't think why Scotland Yard would send someone to help guard him, especially given the cost of a Clipper ticket.'

Margaret lowered her voice. 'Could he be following you?'

'To America?' Harry said sceptically. 'On the Clipper? With a gun? For a pair of cufflinks?'

'Can you think of another explanation?'

'No.'

'Anyway, perhaps all the fuss about Gordino will take people's minds off my father's appalling behaviour at dinner.'

'Why do you think he let rip like that?' Harry said curiously.

'I don't know. He wasn't always like this. I remember him being quite reasonable when I was younger.'

'I've run into a few Fascists,' Harry said. 'They're normally frightened people.'

'Is that so?' Margaret found the idea surprising and rather implausible. 'They seem so aggressive.'

'I know. But inside they're terrified. That's why they like marching up and down and wearing uniforms – they feel safe when they're part of a gang. That's why they don't like democracy – too uncertain. They feel happier in a dictatorship where you know what's going to happen next and the government can't be turned out all of a sudden.'

This made a lot of sense to Margaret and she nodded thoughtfully. 'I remember, even before he got so bitter, he would get unreasonably angry about Communists, or Zionists, or trade unions, or Fenians, or fifth columnists – there was always someone about to bring the country to its knees. Come to think of it, it was never very likely that Zionists would bring England to its knees, was it?'

Harry smiled. 'Fascists are always angry, too. They're often people who are disappointed in life for some reason.'

'That applies to Father as well. When my grandfather died and Father inherited the estate, he found it was bankrupt. He was broke until he married Mother. Then he stood for Parliament and never got in. Now he's been thrown out of his country.' She suddenly felt she understood her father better. Harry was surprisingly perceptive. 'Where did you learn all this?' she said. 'You're not much older than I am.'

He shrugged. 'Battersea is a very political place. Biggest Communist Party branch in London, I believe.'

Understanding her father's emotions better, she felt a little less ashamed of what had happened. There was still no excuse for him, of course, but all the same it was comforting to think of him as a disappointed and frightened man rather than a deranged and vindictive one. How clever Harry Marks was. She wished she could have his help in escaping from her family. She wondered whether he would still want to see her after they got to America. 'Do you know where you're going to live now?' she said.

'I suppose I'll get lodgings in New York,' he said. 'I've got some money and I can soon find more.'

He made it sound so easy. Probably it *was* easier for men. A woman needed protection. 'Nancy Lenehan offered me a job,' she said impulsively. 'But she may not be able to keep her promise because her brother is trying to take the company away from her.'

He looked at her then looked away again with an uncharacteristically diffident expression on his face, as if he were a little unsure of himself for once. 'You know, if you want, I wouldn't mind, I mean, giving you a hand.'

It was what she had been hoping to hear. 'Would you, really?' she said.

He seemed to think there was not much he could do. 'I could help you look for a room.'

The relief was tremendous. 'That would be wonderful,' she said. 'I've never looked for lodgings, I don't know where to begin.'

'You look in the paper,' he said.

'What paper?'

'The newspaper.'

'Newspapers tell you about lodgings?'

'They have advertisements.'

'They don't advertise lodgings in *The Times*.' It was the only newspaper Father took.

'The evening papers are best.'

She felt foolish, not knowing such a simple thing. 'I really need a friend to help me.'

'I guess I can protect you from the American equivalent of Benny the Malt, at least.'

'I feel so happy,' Margaret said. 'First Mrs Lenehan, then you. I know I can make a life for myself if I have friends. I'm so grateful to you, I don't know what to say.'

Davy came into the main lounge. Margaret realized the plane had been flying smoothly for the past five or ten minutes. Davy said, 'Look out of the port windows, everyone. You'll see something in a few seconds.'

Margaret looked out. Harry unfastened his belt and came closer to look over her shoulder. The plane tilted to port. After a moment Margaret saw that they were flying low over a big passenger liner, all lit up like Piccadilly Circus. Someone said, 'They must have put the lights on for us: they normally sail without lights since war was declared – they're afraid of submarines.' Margaret was very conscious of Harry's closeness to her, and she did not mind in the least. The crew of the Clipper must have talked by radio with the crew of the ship, for the ship's passengers had all come out on deck and stood there looking up at the plane and waving. They were so close that Margaret could see their clothes: the men wore white dinner jackets and the women long gowns. The ship was moving fast, its pointed bows knifing effortlessly through the huge waves, and the plane passed it quite slowly. It was a special moment: Margaret felt enchanted. She glanced at Harry and they smiled at one another, sharing the magic. He rested his right hand on her waist, on the side shielded by his body where no one could see it. His touch was feather-light yet she felt it like a burn. It made her hot and confused but she did not want him to take his hand away. After a while the ship receded, and its lights were dimmed, then extinguished altogether. The Clipper passengers returned to their seats and Harry moved back.

More people drifted off to bed and now only the card-players were left in the main lounge with Margaret and Harry. Margaret was bashful and did not know what to do with herself. She felt so awkward that she found herself saying, 'It's getting late. We'd better go to bed.' Why did I say that? she thought. I don't *want* to go to bed!

Harry looked disappointed. 'I guess I'll make a move in a minute.'

Margaret stood up. 'Thank you so much for your offer of help,' she said.

'Not at all,' he said.

Why are we being so formal? Margaret wondered. I don't want to say goodnight like this. 'Sleep well,' she said.

'You too.'

She turned away, then back. 'You do mean it, about helping me, don't you? You won't let me down?'

His face softened and he gave her a look which was almost loving. 'I won't let you down, Margaret, I promise.'

Suddenly she felt terribly fond of him. On impulse, without thinking about it, she bent down and kissed him. It was a fleeting brush of her lips on his but she felt desire like an electric shock when they touched. She straightened up immediately, startled by what she had done and the way she felt. For an instant they stared into one another's eyes. Then she stepped into the next compartment.

She felt weak-kneed. Looking around, she saw that Mr Membury had taken the top bunk on the port side, leaving the lower one free for Harry. Percy had also taken a top bunk. She got into the one below Percy's and fastened the curtain.

I kissed him, she thought, and it was nice.

She slid under the covers and turned off the little light. It was just like being in a tent and she felt quite cosy. She could see out of the window but there was nothing to look at: just clouds and rain. All the same it was exciting. It reminded her of times when she and Elizabeth had been allowed to pitch a tent in the grounds and sleep out on warm summer nights when they were little girls. She had always felt she would never go to sleep, it was so exciting; but the next thing she knew it would be light, and Cook would be tapping on the canvas and handing in a tray of tea and toast.

She wondered where Elizabeth was now.

Just as she was thinking that, there was a soft tap on her curtain.

At first she thought she had imagined it because she was thinking of Cook. Then it came again, a sound like a fingernail, tap, tap, tap. She hesitated, then lifted herself, leaning on her elbow, and pulled the sheet up around her throat.

Tap, tap, tap.

She opened the curtain a fraction and saw Harry.

'What is it?' she hissed, although she thought she knew.

'I want to kiss you again,' he whispered.

She was both pleased and horrified. 'Don't be silly!'

'Please.'

'Go away.'

'No one will see.'

It was an outrageous request, but she was sorely tempted. She remembered the electric tingle of the first kiss and wanted another. Almost involuntarily, she opened the curtain a little more. He put his head through and gave her a pleading look. It was irresistible. She kissed his mouth. He smelled of toothpaste. She intended a quick kiss like the last one, but he had other ideas. He nibbled her lower lip. She found it exciting. She instinctively opened her mouth a fraction, and she felt his tongue brush her lips drily. Ian had never done that. It was a weird sensation, but nice. Feeling depraved, she put out her own tongue to meet his. He began to breathe heavily. Suddenly Percy moved in the bunk over her head, reminding her of where she was. She felt panicked: how could she do this? She was publicly kissing a man she hardly knew! If Father should see there would be hell to pay! She broke away, panting. Harry pushed his head in farther, wanting to kiss her again, but she shoved him away.

'Let me in,' he said.

'Don't be ridiculous!' she hissed.

'Please.'

This was impossible. She was not even tempted: she was scared. 'No, no, no,' she said.

He looked crestfallen.

She softened. 'You're the nicest man I've met for a long time, perhaps ever, but you're not that nice,' she said. 'Go to bed.'

Harry realized she meant it. He gave a rueful half-smile. He seemed about to speak, but Margaret closed the curtain before he could.

She listened intently and thought she heard a soft footfall as he went away.

She turned off the light and lay back, breathing hard. Oh, my God, she thought, that was dreamy. She smiled in the dark, reliving the kiss. She had really wanted to go farther. She caressed herself gently as she thought about it.

Her mind went back to her first lover, Monica, a cousin who had come to stay the summer Margaret was thirteen. Monica was sixteen, blonde and pretty, and seemed to know everything, and Margaret adored her from the beginning.

She lived in France, and perhaps because of that, or perhaps just because her parents were more easy-going than Margaret's, Monica naturally walked around naked in the bedrooms and bathroom of the children's wing. Margaret had never seen a grown-up naked, and she had been fascinated by Monica's big breasts and the bush of honey-coloured hair between her legs: she herself had only a small bust and a little downy hair, at that age.

But Monica had seduced Elizabeth first – ugly, bossy Elizabeth, who had spots on her chin! Margaret had heard them murmuring and kissing in the night, and she had been by turns mystified, angry, jealous and finally envious. She saw that Monica became very fond of Elizabeth. She felt hurt and excluded by the little glances that went between them and the apparently accidental touch of hands as they walked in the woods or sat at tea.

Then, one day when Elizabeth went to London with Mother for some reason, Margaret came on Monica in the bath. She was lying in the hot water with her eyes closed, touching herself between the legs. She heard Margaret, and blinked, but she did not stop, and Margaret watched, scared but fascinated, while she masturbated to a climax.

That night Monica came to Margaret's bed instead of Elizabeth's; but Elizabeth threw a tantrum and threatened to tell all, so in the end they shared her, like wife and mistress in a jealous triangle. Margaret felt guilty and deceitful all summer, but the intense affection and the new-found physical delight was too wonderful to give up, and it ended only when Monica went back to France in September.

After Monica, going to bed with Ian had been a rude shock. He had been awkward and clumsy and Margaret discovered that a young man such as he knew next to nothing about women's bodies, so naturally he could not give her pleasure as Monica had. She soon got over the initial disappointment, however, and Ian loved her so desperately that his passion made up for his inexperience.

Thinking of Ian made her want to cry, as always. She wished with all her heart that she had made love to him more willingly and oftener. She had been very resistant at first, although she longed for it as badly as he did, and he had pleaded with her for months before finally she gave in. After the first time, although she wanted to do it again, she had made difficulties. She had been unwilling to make love in her bedroom in case someone should find the door locked and wonder why; she had been frightened of doing it in the open air, even though she knew lots of hiding-places in the woods around their home; and she had been uncomfortable about using his friends' flats for fear she would get a bad reputation. Behind it all had been the terror of what Father would do if ever he found out.

Torn apart by conflicting desire and anxiety, she had always made love furtively, hurriedly and guiltily, and they had managed it only three times before he went to Spain. Of course, she had blithely imagined that they had all the time in the world ahead of them. Then he had been killed, and with the news came the dreadful realization that she would never touch his body again; and she had cried so hard that she thought her heart would burst. She had thought they would spend the rest of their lives learning how to make one another happy, but she never saw him again.

Now she wished she had given herself to him freely, right from the start, and made love recklessly at every opportunity. Her fears seemed so trivial now that he was buried on a dusty hillside in Catalonia.

Suddenly it occurred to her that she might be making the same mistake again, right now.

She wanted Harry Marks. Her body ached for him. He was the only man who had made her feel this way since Ian. But she had turned him down. Why? Because she was afraid. Because she was on a plane, and the bunks were small, and someone might hear, and her father was close by, and she was terrified of being caught.

Was she being foolishly faint-hearted again?

What if the plane should crash? They were on a pioneering transatlantic flight. Right now they were half-way between Europe and America, hundreds of miles from land in any direction: if something should go wrong they would all die in minutes. And her last thought would be regret that she had never made love to Harry Marks.

The plane was not going to crash, but even so this might be her last chance. She had no idea what was going to happen when they got to America. She planned to join the armed forces as soon as she possibly could, and Harry had spoken about becoming a pilot in the Canadian Air Force. He might die fighting, like Ian. What did her reputation matter, who could worry about parental anger, when life could be so short? She almost wished she had let Harry in.

Would he try again? She thought not. She had given him a very firm no. Any boy who ignored that kind of rejection would have to be a complete pest. Harry had been persistent, flatteringly so, but he was not mulish. He would not ask her again tonight.

What a fool I am, she thought. He might be here now: all I had to say was yes. She hugged herself, imagining that Harry was hugging her, and in her mind she put out a tentative hand and stroked his naked hip. There would be curly blond hair on his thighs, she thought.

She decided to get up and go to the ladies' room.

Perhaps Harry would get up at the same time, by lucky chance; or he might call the steward for a drink, or something. She put her arms into her dressing-gown, unfastened her curtains and sat up. Harry's bunk was tightly curtained. She slid her feet into her slippers and stood up.

Almost everyone had gone to bed now. She peeped into the galley: it was empty. Of course, the stewards needed sleep too. They were probably dozing in No. 1 compartment with the off-duty crew. Going in the opposite direction, she passed through the lounge and saw the diehards, all men, still playing poker. There was a whisky bottle on the table and they were helping themselves. She continued towards the back, weaving from side to side as the plane lurched. The floor rose towards the tail, and there were steps between the compartments. Two or three people sat up reading, with the curtains drawn back, but most bunks were closed and silent.

The ladies' powder room was empty. Margaret sat in front of the mirror and looked at herself. It struck her as odd that a man should find this woman desirable. Her face was rather ordinary, her skin very pale, her eyes an odd shade of green. Her hair was her only good feature, she sometimes thought: it was long and straight, and the colour was a glowing bronze. Men often noticed her hair.

What would Harry have thought of her body, if she had let him in? He might be revolted by big breasts: they might make him think of motherhood or cows' udders or something. She had heard that men liked small, neat breasts, the same shape as the little glasses champagne was served in at parties. You couldn't get one of mine into a champagne glass, she thought ruefully.

She would have liked to be petite, like the models in *Vogue* magazine, but instead she looked like a Spanish dancer. Whenever she put on a ball-gown she had to wear a corset underneath it otherwise her bust wobbled uncontrollably. But Ian had loved her body. He said model girls looked like dolls. 'You're a real woman,' he had said one afternoon, in a snatched moment in the old nursery wing, kissing her neck and stroking both her breasts at the same time with his hands under her cashmere sweater. She had liked her breasts then.

The plane entered a bad patch of turbulence, and she had to hold on to the edge of the dressing-table to avoid being thrown off the stool. Before I die, she thought morbidly, I'd like to have my breasts stroked again.

When the plane steadied she went back to her compartment. All the bunks were still tightly buttoned up. She stood there for a moment, willing Harry to open his curtain, but he did not. She looked along the aisle, up and down the length of the plane. No one stirred.

All her life she had been faint-hearted.

But she had never wanted anything this much.

She shook Harry's curtain.

For a moment nothing happened. She had no plan: she did not know what she was going to do or say.

There was no sound from inside. She shook the curtain again.

A moment later Harry looked out.

They stared at one another in silence: he startled, she tongue-tied.

Then she heard a sound behind her.

Looking over her shoulder, she saw movement behind her father's curtain. A hand grasped it from inside. He was about to get up and go to the bathroom.

Without another thought, Margaret pushed Harry back on to his bed and clambered in with him.

As she closed the curtain behind her she saw Father emerge from his bunk. By a miracle, he did not see her, thank God!

She knelt at the foot of the bunk and looked at Harry. He was sitting at the other end with his knees under his chin, staring at her in the dim light that filtered through the curtain. He looked like a child who had seen Santa Claus come down the chimney: he could hardly believe his good fortune. He opened his mouth to speak, and Margaret silenced him with a finger on his lips.

Suddenly she realized she had left her slippers behind when she jumped in.

They were embroidered with her initials, so anyone could tell whose they were; and they were lying on the floor beside Harry's, just like shoes outside a hotel bedroom, so that everyone would know she was sleeping with him.

Only a couple of seconds had passed. She peeped out. Father was climbing down the step-ladder from his bunk, and his back was to her. She reached out between the curtains. If he should turn around now she was finished. She scrabbled for the slippers and found them. She picked them up just as Father put his bare feet on the airline carpet. She whipped them inside and closed the curtain a split second before he turned his head.

She should have been scared, but instead she felt thrilled.

She did not have a clear idea of what she wanted to happen now. She just knew she wanted to be with Harry. The prospect of spending the night lying in her own bunk wishing he were there had become intolerable. But she was not going to give herself to him. She would like to – very much – but there were all sorts of practical problems, not the least of which was Mr Membury, fast asleep a few inches above them.

In the next moment she realized that, unlike her, Harry knew exactly what he wanted.

He leaned forward, put his hand behind her head, pulled her to him and kissed her lips.

After a momentary hesitation she abandoned all thought of resistance and gave herself up to the sensation.

She had been thinking about it for so long that she felt as if she had already been making love to him for hours. But this was real: there was a strong hand on her neck, a real mouth kissing hers, a real person mingling his breath with her own. It was a slow, tender kiss, gentle and tentative, and she was aware of every small detail: his fingers moving in her hair, the roughness of his shaved chin, his warm breath on her soft cheek, his moving mouth, his teeth nibbling her lips, and finally his exploring tongue pressing between her lips and seeking her own. Yielding to an irresistible impulse, she opened her mouth wide.

After a moment they broke apart, panting. Harry's gaze dropped to her bosom. Looking down, she saw that her dressing-gown had fallen open and her nipples were pressing against the cotton of her nightdress. Harry gazed as if hypnotized. Moving in slow motion, he reached out with one hand and lightly brushed her left breast with his fingers, stroking the sensitive tip through the fine fabric, causing her to gasp with pleasure.

Suddenly clothing seemed intolerable. She shrugged off her dressing-gown quickly. She grasped the hem of her nightdress, then hesitated. A warning voice in the back of her mind said, 'After this, there's no turning back,' and she thought, Good! and pulled her nightdress over her head and knelt in front of him naked.

She felt vulnerable and shy, but somehow the anxiety heightened her excitement. Harry's eyes roamed over her body and she saw in his face both adoration and desire. Twisting in the cramped space, he got on his knees and leaned forward, bringing his head down to her bosom. She felt a moment of uncertainty: what was he going to do? His lips brushed the tops of her breasts, first one then the other. She felt his hand beneath her left breast, first stroking, then weighing, then squeezing softly. His lips tracked down until they came to her nipple. He nibbled gently. Her nipple was so taut it felt as if it would burst. Then he began to suck, and she groaned with delight.

After a while she wanted him to do the same to the other one, but she was too shy to ask. However, perhaps he sensed her desire, for he did what she wanted a moment later. She stroked the bristly hair at the back of his head, then, yielding to an impulse, she pressed his head to her breast. He sucked harder in response.

She wanted to explore his body. When he paused, she pushed him away and undid the buttons of his pyjama jacket. Both of them were breathing like sprinters but neither spoke for fear of being heard. He shrugged out of his jacket. There was no hair on his chest. She wanted him to be completely naked, as she was. She found the drawstring of his pyjama trousers and, feeling wanton, pulled it undone.

He looked hesitant and a little startled, giving Margaret the uneasy feeling that she might be bolder than other girls in his experience; but she felt she had to continue what she had begun. She pushed him back until he was lying down with his head on the pillow, then grasped the waistband of his trousers and tugged. He raised his hips.

There was a thatch of dark-blond hair at the base of his belly. She drew the red cotton down farther, and then gasped as his penis sprang free, sticking up like a flagpole. She stared at it, fascinated. The skin was stretched taut over the veins and the end was swollen like a blue tulip. He lay still, sensing that this was what she wanted; but her looking at it seemed to inflame him, and she heard his breathing become hoarse. She felt impelled, by curiosity and some other emotion, to touch it. Her hand was drawn forward irresistibly. He gave a low groan as he saw what she was about to do. She hesitated at the last instant. Her pale hand wavered next to the dark penis. He made a sound like a whimper. Then, with a sigh, she grasped it, her slender fingers wrapping around the thick shaft. The skin was hot to her touch, and soft, but when she squeezed slightly – making him gasp – she found it was hard as a bone underneath. She glanced at him. His face was flushed with desire and he was breathing hard through his mouth. She longed to please him. Shifting her grip, she began to rub his penis in a motion she had learned from Ian: gripping firmly to push down, then easing her grasp for the upward stroke.

The effect took her by surprise. He moaned, closed his eyes tight, and pressed his knees together; and then, as she pressed down a second time, he jerked convulsively, his face screwed up in a grimace, and white semen spurted from the end of his penis. Astonished and mesmerized, Margaret continued the action, and with each downstroke more came out. She herself was possessed by lust: her breasts felt heavy, her throat was dry, and she could feel moisture trickling down the inside of her thigh. At last, at the fifth or sixth stroke, it ended. His thighs relaxed, his face became smooth, and his head slumped sideways on the pillow.

Margaret lay down beside him.

He looked ashamed. 'I'm sorry,' he whispered.

'Don't be sorry,' she replied. 'It was amazing. I've never done that. I feel wonderful.'

He was surprised. 'Did you enjoy it?'

She was too abashed to say yes aloud, so she just nodded.

He said, 'But I didn't. I mean, you didn't . . .'

She said nothing. There was something he could do for her, but she was afraid to ask.

He rolled on to his side so that they faced one another in the narrow bunk. He said, 'In a few minutes, maybe . . .'

I can't wait a few minutes, she thought. Why shouldn't I ask him to do for me what I did for him? She found his hand and squeezed it. Still she could not say what she wanted. She closed her eyes, then drew his hand to her groin. Her mouth was next to his ear, and she whispered, 'Be gentle.'

He got the idea. His hand moved, exploring. She was wet, dripping wet. His fingers slid easily between her lips. She put her arms around his neck and hugged him hard. His finger moved inside her. She wanted to say 'Not there, higher!' and as if reading her thoughts he drew his finger out and slid it up to the most sensitive place. She was instantly transfixed. Her body was racked with spasms of pleasure. She shuddered convulsively, and to stop herself crying out she sank her teeth into the flesh of Harry's upper arm and bit. He froze, but she rubbed herself against his hand and the sensations continued unabated.

When at last the pleasure eased, Harry moved his finger again, and she was abruptly shaken by another climax as intense as the first.

Then finally the spot became too sensitive, and she pushed his hand away.

After a moment Harry eased away from her and rubbed his arm where she had bitten him.

Breathlessly, she panted, 'I'm sorry – did it hurt?'

'Yes, it bloody did,' he whispered, and they both began to giggle. Trying not to laugh aloud made it worse, and for a minute or two they were both helpless with suppressed laughter.

When they calmed down he said, 'Your body is wonderful – wonderful.'

'So is yours,' she said fervently.

He did not believe her. 'No, I mean it,' he said.

'So do I!' She would never forget his swollen penis standing up from the thatch of golden hair. She ran her hand over his stomach, searching for it, and found it lying across his thigh like a hose pipe, neither stiff nor shrivelled. The skin was silky. She felt she would like to kiss it, and was shocked by her own depravity.

Instead she kissed his arm where she had bitten him. Even in the near-dark she could see the marks her teeth had made. He was going to have a bad bruise. 'I'm sorry,' she whispered, too low for him to hear. She felt quite sad that she had damaged his perfect flesh after his body had given her such joy. She kissed the bruise again.

They were limp with exhaustion and pleasure, and they both drifted into a light doze. Margaret seemed to hear the drone of the engines all through her sleep, as if she were dreaming of planes. Once she heard footsteps pass through the compartment and return a few minutes later, but she was too contented to be curious about what they meant.

For a while the motion of the plane was smooth, and she fell into a real sleep.

She woke with a shock. Was it daytime? Had everyone got up? Would they all see her climbing out of Harry's bunk? Her heart raced.

'What is it?' he whispered.

'What's the time?'

'It's the middle of the night.'

He was right. There was no movement outside, the cabin lights were dim, and there was no sign of daylight at the window. She could sneak out in safety. 'I must go back to my own bunk, right now, before we're discovered,' she said frantically. She began looking for her slippers and could not find them.

Harry put a hand on her shoulder. 'Calm down,' he whispered. 'We've got hours.'

'But I'm worried that Father—' She stopped herself. Why was she so worried? She took a deep breath and looked at Harry. When their eyes met in the semi-darkness, she remembered what had happened before they went to sleep, and she could tell he was thinking the same thing. They smiled at one another, a knowing, intimate, lovers' smile.

Suddenly she was not so worried. She did not need to go yet. She wanted to stay here, so she would. There was plenty of time.

Harry moved against her, and she felt his stiffening penis. 'Don't go yet,' he said.

She sighed happily. 'All right, not yet,' she said, and she began to kiss him.

CHAPTER EIGHTEEN

Eddie Deakin had himself under rigid control, but he was a boiling kettle with the lid jammed on, a volcano waiting to blow. He sweated constantly, his guts ached, and he could hardly sit still. He was managing to do his job, but only just.

He was due to go off duty at 2 a.m., British time. As the end of his shift approached he faked one more set of fuel figures. Earlier he had understated the plane's consumption to give the impression that there was just enough fuel to complete the journey, so that the Captain would not turn back. Now he overstated, to compensate, so that when his replacement, Mickey Finn, came on duty and read the fuel gauges there would be no discrepancy. The Howgozit Curve would show fuel consumption fluctuating wildly, and Mickey would wonder why; but Eddie would explain it as due to the stormy weather. Anyway, Mickey was the least of his worries. His deep anxiety, the one that held his heart in the cold grip of fear, was that the plane would run out of fuel before it reached Newfoundland.

It did not have the regulation minimum. The regulations left a safety margin, of course; but safety margins were there for a reason. This flight no longer had an extra reserve of fuel for emergencies such as engine failure. If something went wrong it would plunge into the stormy Atlantic Ocean. It could not splash down safely in mid-ocean: it would sink within a few minutes. There would be no survivors.

Mickey came up to the flight cabin a few minutes before two, looking fresh and young and eager. 'We're running very low,' Eddie said right away. 'I've told the Captain.'

Mickey nodded noncommittally and picked up the flashlight. His first duty on taking over was to make a visual inspection of all four engines.

Eddie left him to it and went down to the passenger deck. The first officer, Johnny Dott, the navigator, Jack Ashford, and the radio operator, Ben Thompson, followed him down the stairs as their replacements arrived. Jack went to the galley to make a sandwich. The thought of food nauseated Eddie: he got a cup of coffee and went to sit in No. 1 compartment.

When he was not working he had nothing to take his mind off the thought of Carol-Ann in the hands of her kidnappers.

It was just after 9 p.m. in Maine now. It would be dark. Carol-Ann would be weary and dispirited at best. She tended to fall asleep much earlier since she got pregnant. Would they give her somewhere to lie down? She would not sleep tonight, but perhaps she could rest her body. Eddie just hoped that the thought of bedtime did not put ideas into the heads of the hoodlums who were guarding her . . .

Before his coffee was cold the storm hit in earnest.

The ride had been bumpy for several hours, but now it became really rough. It was like being on a ship in a storm. The huge aircraft was like a boat on the waves, rising slowly then dropping fast, hitting the trough with a thump and then climbing again, rolling and tossing from side to side as the winds caught it. Eddie sat on a bunk and braced himself with his feet on the corner-post. The passengers began to wake up, ring for stewards, and rush to the bathroom. The two stewards, Nicky and Davy, who had been dozing in No. 1 compartment with the off-duty crew, buttoned their collars and put on their jackets, then hurried off to answer the bells.

After a while Eddie went to the galley for more coffee. As he got there, the door of the men's room opened and Tom Luther came out, looking pale and sweaty. Eddie stared at him contemptuously. He felt an urge to take the man by the throat, but he fought it down.

'Is this normal?' Luther said in a scared voice.

Eddie felt not a shred of sympathy. 'No, this is not normal,' he replied. 'We ought to fly around the storm, but we don't have enough fuel.'

'Why not?'

'We're running out.'

Luther was scared. 'But you told us you would turn back before the point of no return!'

Eddie was more worried than Luther, but he took grim satisfaction in the other man's distress. 'We should have turned back, but I faked the figures. I have a special reason for wanting to complete this flight on schedule, remember?'

'You crazy bastard!' Luther said despairingly. 'Are you trying to kill us all?'

'I'd rather take the chance of killing you than leave my wife with your friends.'

'But if we all die that won't help your wife!'

'I know.' Eddie was taking a dreadful risk, but he could not bear the thought of leaving Carol-Ann with the kidnappers for another day. 'Maybe I am crazy,' he said to Luther.

Luther looked ill. 'But this plane can land on the sea, right?'

'Wrong. We can only splash down on calm water. If we went down in mid-Atlantic in a storm like this, the plane would break up in seconds.'

'Oh, God,' Luther moaned. 'I should never have got on this plane.'

'You should never have messed with my wife, you bastard,' Eddie said through his teeth.

The plane lurched crazily, and Luther turned and staggered back into the bathroom.

Eddie stepped through No. 2 compartment and into the lounge. The card-players were strapped into their seats and hanging on tight. Glasses, cards and a bottle rolled around the carpet as the aircraft swayed and shook. Eddie looked along the aisle. After the initial panic the passengers were calming down. Most had returned to their bunks and strapped themselves in, realizing that was the best way to ride the bumps. They lay with their curtains open, some looking cheerfully resigned to the discomfort, others clearly scared to death. Everything that was not tied down had fallen to the floor and the carpet was a litter of books, spectacles, dressing-gowns, false teeth, change, cufflinks and all the other things people kept beside their beds at night. The rich and the glamorous of the world suddenly looked very human, and Eddie suffered an agonizing stab of conscience. Were all these people going to die because of him?

He returned to his seat and strapped himself in. There was nothing he could do now about the fuel consumption, and the only way he could help Carol-Ann was make sure the emergency splashdown went according to plan.

As the plane shuddered on through the night, he tried to suppress his seething anger and run over his scenario.

He would be on duty when they took off from Shediac, the last port before New York. He would immediately begin to jettison fuel. The gauges would show this, of course. Mickey Finn might notice the loss, if he should come up to the flight deck for any reason; but by that time, twenty-four hours after leaving Southampton, off-duty crew were not interested in anything but sleep. And it was not likely that any other crew member would look at the fuel gauges, especially on the short leg of the flight when fuel consumption was no longer critical. He loathed the thought of deceiving his colleagues, and for a moment his rage boiled up again. He balled his fists, but there was nothing to hit. He tried to concentrate on his plan.

As the plane approached the place where Luther wanted to splash down, Eddie would jettison more fuel, judging it finely so that they would almost have run out when they reached the right area. At that point he would tell the Captain that they were out of fuel and had to come down.

He would have to monitor their route carefully. They did not follow exactly the same course every time: navigation was not that precise. But Luther had selected his rendezvous cleverly. It was clearly the best place within a wide radius for a flying boat to splash down, so that even if they were some miles off course, the Captain was sure to head there in an emergency.

If there was time, the Captain would ask – angrily – how come Eddie had not noticed the dramatic loss of fuel before it became critical. Eddie would have to answer that all the gauges must have got stuck, a wildly unlikely notion. He ground his teeth as he thought of it. His colleagues relied on him to perform the crucial task of monitoring the aircraft's fuel consumption. They trusted him with their lives. They would know he had let them down.

A fast launch would be waiting in the area and would approach the Clipper. The Captain would think they had come to help. He might invite them aboard, but failing that Eddie would open the door to them. Then the gangsters would overpower the FBI man, Ollis Field, and rescue Frankie Gordino.

They would have to be quick. The radio operator would have sent out a Mayday before the plane touched water, and the Clipper was big enough to be seen from some distance, so other vessels would approach before too long. There was even a chance the Coast Guard might be quick enough to interfere with the rescue. That could ruin it for Luther's gang, Eddie thought; and for a moment he felt hopeful – then he remembered that he wanted Luther to succeed, not fail.

He just could not get into the habit of hoping that the criminals would get what they wanted. He racked his brains constantly for some way of foiling Luther's plan, but everything he came up with had the same snag: Carol-Ann. If Luther did not get Gordino, Eddie would not get Carol-Ann.

He had tried to think of some way to ensure that Gordino would get caught twenty-four hours later, when Carol-Ann was safe; but it was impossible. Gordino would be far away by then. The only alternative was to persuade Luther to surrender Carol-Ann earlier, and he had more sense than to agree to that. The trouble was, Eddie had nothing with which to threaten Luther. Luther had Carol-Ann, and Eddie had . . .

Well, he thought suddenly, I've got Gordino.

Wait a minute.

They've got Carol-Ann, and I can't get her back without co-operating with them. But Gordino is on this plane, and they can't get him back unless they co-operate with me. Maybe they don't hold all the cards.

He wondered whether there was a way for him to take charge, seize the initiative.

He stared blindly at the opposite wall, holding on tight, lost in thought.

There was a way.

Why should they get Gordino first? An exchange of hostages should be simultaneous.

He fought down surging hope and forced himself to think coolly.

How would the exchange work? They would have to bring Carol-Ann to the Clipper on the launch that would take Gordino away.

Why not? *Why the hell not?*

He wondered frantically whether it could be arranged in time. He had calculated that she was being held no more than sixty or seventy miles from their home, which in turn was about seventy miles from the location of the emergency splashdown. At worst, then, she was four hours' drive away. Was that too much?

Suppose Tom Luther agreed. His first chance to call his men would come at the next stop, Botwood, where the Clipper was due at 9 a.m. British time. After that the plane went on to Shediac. The unscheduled splashdown would take place an hour out of Shediac, at about 4 p.m. British time, seven hours later. The gang could get Carol-Ann there with a couple of hours to spare.

Eddie could hardly contain his excitement as he contemplated the prospect of getting Carol-Ann back earlier. It also occurred to him that it might give him a chance, albeit slender, of doing something to spoil Luther's rescue. And that might redeem him in the eyes of the rest of the crew. They might forgive his treachery to them if they saw him catch a bunch of murdering gangsters.

Once again he told himself not to raise his hopes. All this was only an idea. Luther probably would not buy the deal. Eddie could threaten not to bring the plane down unless they met his terms; but they might see that as an empty threat. They would reckon that Eddie would do anything to save his wife, and they would be right. They were only trying to save a buddy. Eddie was more desperate, and that made him weaker, he thought; and he plunged once more into despair.

But still he would be presenting Luther with a problem, creating a doubt and a worry in the man's mind. Luther might not believe Eddie's threat, but how could he be sure? It would take guts to call Eddie's bluff, and Luther was not a brave man, at least not right now.

Anyway, he thought, what do I have to lose?

He would give it a try.

He got up from his bunk.

He thought he probably should plan the whole conversation carefully, preparing his answers to Luther's objections; but he was already screwed up to screaming pitch and he could not sit still and think any longer. He had to do it or go mad.

Holding on to anything he could grab, he picked his way along the rocking, swaying plane to the main lounge.

Luther was one of the passengers who had not gone to bed. He was in a corner of the lounge, drinking whisky, but not joining in the card game. The colour had returned to his face and he appeared to have got over his nausea. He was reading a British magazine, *The Illustrated London News.* Eddie tapped him on the shoulder. He looked up, startled and a little frightened.

When he saw Eddie his face turned hostile. Eddie said, 'The Captain would like a word with you, Mr Luther.'

Luther looked anxious. He sat still for a moment. Eddie beckoned him with a peremptory jerk of the head. Luther put down his magazine, unfastened his seat belt and stood up.

Eddie led him out of the lounge and through No. 2 compartment, but instead of going up to the flight deck he opened the door of the men's room and held it for Luther.

There was a faint smell of vomit. Unfortunately they were not alone: a passenger in pyjamas was washing his hands. Eddie pointed to the lavatory and Luther went inside while Eddie combed his hair and waited. After a few moments the passenger left. Eddie tapped on the lavatory door and Luther came out. 'What the hell is going on?' he asked.

'Shut your mouth and listen up,' Eddie said. He had not planned to be aggressive but Luther just made him mad. 'I know what you're here for, I've figured out your plan, and I'm making a change. When I bring this plane down, Carol-Ann has to be on the boat waiting.'

Luther was scornful. 'You can't make demands.'

Eddie had not expected him to cave in immediately. Now he had to bluff. 'Okay,' he said with as much conviction as he could muster. 'The deal is off.'

Luther looked a little worried, but he said, 'You're full of shit. You want your little wife back. You'll bring down this plane.'

It was the truth, but Eddie shook his head. 'I don't trust you,' he said. 'Why should I? I could do everything you want and you could double-cross me. I'm not going to take that chance. I want a new deal.'

Luther's confidence was not yet shaken. 'No new deal.'

'Okay.' It was time for Eddie to play his trump card. 'Okay, so you go to jail.'

Luther laughed nervously. 'What are you talking about?'

Eddie felt a little more confident: Luther was weakening. 'I'll tell the Captain the whole thing. You'll be taken off the plane at the next stop. The police will be waiting for you. You'll go to jail – in Canada, where your hoodlum friends won't be able to spring you. You'll be charged with kidnapping, piracy – hell, Luther, you may never come out.'

At last Luther was rattled. 'Everything's set up,' he protested. 'It's too late to change the plan.'

'No, it's not,' Eddie said. 'You can call your people from the next stop and tell them what to do. They'll have seven hours to get Carol-Ann on that launch. There's time.'

Luther suddenly caved in. 'Okay, I'll do it.'

Eddie did not believe him: the switch had been too quick. His instinct told him Luther had decided to double-cross him. 'Tell them they have to call me at the last stop, Shediac, and confirm that they've made the arrangements.'

A look of anger passed briefly across Luther's face, and Eddie knew his suspicion had been correct.

Eddie went on, 'And when the launch meets the Clipper, I have to *see* Carol-Ann, on the deck of the boat, before I open the doors, you understand? If I don't see her I'll give the alarm. Ollis Field will grab you before you can open the door, and the Coast Guard will be here before your goons can break in. So you make sure this is done exactly right or you're all dead.'

Luther got his nerve back suddenly. 'You won't do any of this,' he sneered. 'You wouldn't risk your wife's life.'

Eddie tried to foster doubt. 'Are you sure, Luther?'

It was not enough. Luther shook his head decisively. 'You ain't that crazy.'

Eddie knew he had to convince Luther right away. This was the moment of crisis. The word 'crazy' gave him the inspiration he needed. 'I'll show you how crazy I am,' he said. He pushed Luther up against the wall next to the big square window. For a moment the man was too surprised to resist. 'I'll show you just how goddamn crazy I am.' He kicked Luther's legs away with a sudden movement, and the man fell heavily to the floor. At that moment he *felt* crazy. 'You see this window, shitheel?' Eddie took hold of the venetian blind and ripped it from its fastenings. 'I'm crazy enough to throw you out this fucking window, that's how crazy I am.' He jumped up on to the washstand and kicked at the window pane. He was wearing stout boots but the window was made of strong Plexiglass, three-sixteenths of an inch thick. He kicked again, harder, and this time it cracked. One more kick broke it. Shattered glass flew into the room. The plane was travelling at 125 miles per hour, and the icy wind and freezing rain blew in like a hurricane.

Luther was scrambling to his feet, terrified. Eddie jumped back on to the floor and stopped him getting away. Catching the man off balance, he pushed him up against the wall. Rage gave him the strength to overpower Luther, although they were much the same weight. He took Luther by the lapels and shoved the man's head out of the window.

Luther screamed.

The noise of the wind was so loud that the scream was almost inaudible.

Eddie pulled him back in and shouted in his ear, 'I'll throw you out, I swear to God!' He pushed Luther's head out again and lifted him off the floor.

If Luther had not panicked he might have broken free, but he had lost control and was helpless. He screamed again, and Eddie could just make out the words, 'I'll do it, I'll do it, let me go, let me go!'

Eddie felt a powerful urge to push him all the way out; then he realized he was in danger of losing control too. He did not want to kill Luther, he reminded himself; just scare him half to death. He had achieved that already. It was enough.

He lowered Luther to the floor and relaxed his grip.

Luther ran for the door.

Eddie let him go.

I do a pretty good crazy act, Eddie thought, but he knew he had not really been acting.

He leaned against the washstand, catching his breath. The mad rage left him as quickly as it had come. He felt calm, but shocked by his own violence, almost as if someone else had done it.

A moment later a passenger came in.

It was the man who had joined the flight at Foynes, Mervyn Lovesey, a tall guy in a striped nightshirt that looked pretty funny. He was a down-to-earth Englishman of about forty. He looked at the damage and said, 'By heck, what happened here?'

Eddie swallowed. 'A broken window,' he said.

Lovesey gave him a satiric look. 'That much I worked out for myself.'

'It sometimes happens in a storm,' Eddie said. 'These violent winds carry lumps of ice or even stones.'

Lovesey was sceptical. 'Well! I've been flying my own plane for ten years and I never heard that.'

Eddie was right, of course. Windows did sometimes break on trips, but it usually happened when the plane was in harbour, not in mid-Atlantic. For such eventualities they carried aluminium window covers called deadlights, which happened to be stowed right here in the men's room. Eddie opened the locker and pulled one out. 'That's why we carry these,' he said.

Lovesey was convinced at last. 'Fancy that,' he remarked. He went into the cubicle.

Stowed with the deadlights was the screwdriver which was the only tool required to install them. Eddie decided that it would minimize the fuss if he did the job himself. In a few seconds he took off the window frame, unscrewed the remainder of the broken pane, screwed the deadlight in its place, and replaced the frame.

'Very impressive,' said Mervyn Lovesey, coming out of the toilet. Eddie had a feeling he was not completely reassured, all the same. However, he was not likely to do anything about it.

Eddie went out and found Davy making a milk drink in the galley. 'The window's broken in the john,' he told him.

'I'll fix it as soon as I've given the Princess her cocoa.'

'I've installed the deadlight.'

'Gee, thanks, Eddie.'

'But you need to sweep up the glass as soon as you can.'

'Okay.'

Eddie would have liked to offer to sweep up himself, because he had made the mess. That was how his mother had trained him. However, he was in danger of appearing suspiciously over-helpful, and betraying his guilty conscience. So, feeling bad, he left Davy to it.

He had achieved something, anyway. He had scared Luther badly. He now thought Luther would go along with the new plan and have Carol-Ann brought to the rendezvous in the launch. At least he had reason to hope.

His mind returned to his other worry; the plane's fuel reserve. Although it was not yet time for him to go back on duty, he went up to the flight deck to speak to Mickey Finn.

'The curve is all over the place!' Mickey said excitably as soon as Eddie arrived.

But have we got enough? Eddie wondered. However, he maintained a superficial calm. 'Show me.'

'Look – fuel consumption is incredibly high for the

first hour of my shift, then it comes back to normal for the second hour.'

'It was all over the place during my shift, too,' Eddie said, trying to show mild concern where he felt terrible fear. 'I guess the storm makes everything unpredictable.' Then he asked the question that was tormenting him. 'But do we have enough fuel to get home?' He held his breath.

'Yeah, we have enough,' Mickey said.

Eddie's shoulders slumped with relief. Thank God. At least that worry was over.

'But we've got nothing in reserve,' Mickey added. 'I hope to hell we don't lose an engine.'

Eddie could not worry about such a remote possibility: he had too much else on his mind. 'What's the weather forecast? Maybe we're almost through the storm.'

Mickey shook his head. 'Nope,' he said grimly. 'It's about to get an awful lot worse.'

CHAPTER NINETEEN

NANCY LENEHAN found it unsettling to be in bed in a room with a total stranger.

As Mervyn Lovesey had assured her, the 'honeymoon suite' had bunk beds, despite its name. However, he had not been able to wedge the door open permanently, because of the storm: whatever he tried, it kept banging shut, until they both felt it was less embarrassing to leave it closed than to continue fussing about keeping it open.

She had stayed up as long as possible. She was tempted to sit in the main lounge all night, but it had become an unpleasantly masculine place, full of cigarette smoke and whisky fumes and the murmured laughter and cursing of gamblers, and she felt conspicuous there. In the end there was nothing for it but to go to bed.

They put out the light and climbed into their bunks, and Nancy lay down with her eyes closed, but she did not feel in the least sleepy. The glass of brandy which young Harry Marks had got for her had not helped at all: she was as wide awake as if it had been nine o'clock in the morning.

She could tell that Mervyn was awake too. She heard

every move he made in the bunk above her. Unlike the other bunks, those in the honeymoon suite were not curtained, so her only privacy was the darkness.

She lay awake and thought about Margaret Oxenford, so young and naïve, so full of uncertainty and idealism. She sensed great passion beneath Margaret's hesitant surface, and identified with her on that account. Nancy, too, had had battles with her parents; or, at least, with her mother. Ma wanted her to marry a boy from an old Boston family, but at the age of sixteen Nancy fell in love with Sean Lenehan, a medical student whose father was actually a foreman in Pa's own factory, horrors! Ma campaigned against Sean for months, bringing wicked gossip about him and other girls, snubbing his parents viciously, falling ill and retiring to bed only to get up again and harangue her daughter for selfishness and ingratitude. Nancy had suffered under the onslaught but stood firm, and in the end she had married Sean and loved him with all her heart until the day he died.

Margaret might not have Nancy's strength. Perhaps I was a little harsh with her, she thought, saying that if she didn't like her father she should get up and leave home. But she seemed to need someone to tell her to stop whining and grow up. At her age I had two babies!

She had offered practical help, as well as tough-minded advice. She hoped she would be able to fulfil her promise and give Margaret a job.

That all depended on Danny Riley, the old reprobate who held the balance of power in her battle with her brother. Nancy began to worry at the problem all over again. Had Mac, her lawyer, been able to reach Danny? If so, how had Danny received the story about an inquiry into one of his past misdemeanours? Did he suspect that the whole thing had been invented to put pressure on him? Or was he scared out of his wits? She tossed and turned uncomfortably as she reviewed all the unanswered questions. She hoped she could talk to Mac on the phone at the next stop, Botwood in Newfoundland. Perhaps he would be able to relieve the suspense by then.

The plane had been jerking and swaying for some time, making Nancy even more restless and nervous, and after an hour or two the movement got much worse. She had never been frightened in a plane before, but on the other hand she had never experienced such a storm, and she was scared. She held on to the edges of her bunk as the mighty aircraft tossed in the violent winds. She had faced a lot of things alone since her husband died, and now she told herself to be brave and tough it out. But she could not help imagining that the wings would break off or the engines would be destroyed and they all would plunge headlong into the sea; and she became terrified. She screwed her eyes up tight and bit the pillow. Suddenly the plane seemed to go into free fall. She waited for the fall to stop but it went on and on. She could not suppress a whimper of dread. Then at last there was a bump and the plane seemed to right itself.

A moment later she felt Mervyn's hand on her

shoulder. 'It's just a storm,' he said in his flat British accent. 'I've known worse. There's nothing to fear.'

She found his hand and gripped it tightly. He sat on the edge of her bunk and stroked her hair during the moments when the plane was stable. She was still frightened, but it helped to hold hands during the bumpy bits, and she felt a little better.

She did not know how long they stayed like that. Eventually the storm eased. She began to feel self-conscious, and she released Mervyn's hand. She did not know what to say. Mercifully, he stood up and left the room.

Nancy put on the light and got out of bed. She stood up shakily, put on her electric blue silk robe over her black négligé, and sat at the dressing-table. She brushed her hair, which always soothed her. She was embarrassed about having held his hand. At the time she had forgotten about decorum, and had just been grateful for someone to comfort her; but now she felt awkward. She was glad he was sensitive enough to guess at her feelings and leave her alone for a few minutes to collect herself.

He came back with a bottle of brandy and two glasses. He poured drinks and gave one to Nancy. She held the glass in one hand and gripped the edge of the dressing-table with the other: the plane was still bumping a little.

She would have felt worse if he had not been wearing that comical nightshirt. He looked ridiculous, and he knew it, but he behaved with as much dignity as if he were walking around in his double-breasted suit; and somehow that made him funnier. He was obviously a man who was not afraid to appear foolish. She liked him for the way he wore his nightshirt.

She sipped her brandy. The warm liquor immediately made her feel better, and she drank some more.

'An odd thing happened,' he said conversationally. 'As I was going into the men's room, another passenger came out looking scared to death. When I went inside, the window was broken, and the engineer was stood there looking guilty. He gave me a cock-and-bull story about the glass being smashed by a lump of ice in the storm, but it looked to me as if the two of them had had a fight.'

Nancy was grateful to him for talking about something, just so that they did not have to sit there thinking about holding hands. 'Which one is the engineer?' she said.

'A good-looking lad, about my height, fair hair.'

'I know. And which passenger?'

'I don't know his name. Businessman, on his own, in a pale grey suit.' Mervyn got up and poured her some more brandy.

Nancy's robe unfortunately came only just below her knees, and she felt rather undressed with her calves and her bare feet exposed; but once again she reminded herself that Mervyn was in frenzied pursuit of an adored wife, and he had no eyes for anyone else; indeed, he would hardly notice if Nancy were stark naked. His holding her hand had been a friendly gesture from one human being to another, pure and simple. A cynical voice in the back of her mind said that holding hands with someone else's husband was rarely simple and never pure, but she ignored it.

Searching for something to talk about, she said, 'Is your wife still mad at you?'

'She's as cross as a cat with a boil,' Mervyn replied.

Nancy smiled as she recalled the scene she had found in the suite when she returned from getting changed: Mervyn's wife yelling at him, and the boyfriend yelling at her, while Nancy watched from the doorway. Diana and Mark had quietened down immediately and had left, looking rather sheepish, to continue their row elsewhere. Nancy had refrained from commenting at the time, because she did not want Mervyn to think she was laughing at his situation. However, she did not feel inhibited about asking him personal questions: intimacy had been forced on them by circumstances. 'Will she come back to you?'

'There's no telling,' he said. 'That chap she's with . . . I think he's a weed, but maybe that's what she wants.'

Nancy nodded. The two men, Mark and Mervyn, could hardly have been more different. Mervyn was tall and imperious, with dark good looks and a blunt manner. Mark was an altogether softer person, with hazel eyes and freckles, who normally wore a mildly amused look on his round face. 'I don't go for the boyish type, but he's attractive in his way,' she said. She was thinking, If Mervyn was my husband, I wouldn't exchange him for Mark; but there's no accounting for taste.

'Aye. At first I thought Diana was just being daft, but now that I've seen him, I'm not so sure.' Mervyn looked thoughtful for a moment, then changed the subject. 'What about you? Will you fight your brother off?'

'I believe I've found his weakness,' she said with grim satisfaction, thinking of Danny Riley. 'I'm working on it.'

He grinned. 'When you look like that, I'd rather have you for a friend than an enemy.'

'It's for my father,' she said. 'I loved him dearly, and the firm is all I have left of him. It's like a memorial to him, but better than that, because it bears the imprint of his personality in every way.'

'What was he like?'

'He was one of those men nobody ever forgets. He was tall, with black hair and a big voice, and you knew the moment you saw him that he was a powerful man. But he knew the name of every man who worked for him, and if their wives were sick, and how their children were getting along in school. He paid for the education of countless sons of factory hands who are now lawyers and accountants: he understood how to win people's loyalty. In that way he was old-fashioned – paternalistic. But he had the best business brain I ever encountered. In the depths of the slump, when factories were closing all over New England, we were taking on men because our sales were going up! He understood the power of advertising before anyone else in the shoe industry, and he used it brilliantly. He was interested in psychology, in what makes people tick. He had the ability to throw a fresh light on any problem you brought to him. I miss him every day. I miss him almost as much as I miss my husband.' She suddenly felt very angry. 'And I *will* not stand by and see his life's work thrown away by my good-for-nothing brother.' She shifted in her seat restlessly, reminded of her anxieties. 'I'm trying to put pressure on a key shareholder, but I won't know how successful I've been until—'

She never finished the sentence. The plane flew into the most severe turbulence yet, and bucked like a wild horse. Nancy dropped her glass and grabbed the edge of the dressing-table with both hands. Mervyn tried to brace himself with his feet, but he could not, and when the plane tilted sideways he rolled on to the floor, knocking the coffee-table aside.

The plane steadied. Nancy reached out a hand to help him up, saying, 'Are you all right?' Then the plane tossed again. She slipped, lost her handhold, and tumbled to the floor on top of him.

After a moment he started to laugh.

She had been afraid she might have hurt him, but she was light and he was a big man. She was lying across him, the two of them making the shape of an X on the terracotta carpet. The plane steadied, and she rolled off and sat up, looking at him. Was he hysterical, or just amused?

'We must look daft,' he said, and recommenced laughing.

His laughter was infectious. For a moment she forgot the accumulated tensions of the last twenty-four hours: the treachery of her brother, the near-crash in Mervyn's small plane, her awkward situation in the honeymoon suite, the ghastly row about Jews in the dining room, the embarrassment of Mervyn's wife's anger, and her fear of the storm. She suddenly realized there was also something highly comical about sitting on the floor in her nightclothes with a strange man in a wildly bucking aircraft. She, too, started to giggle.

The next lurch of the plane threw them against one another. She found herself wrapped in Mervyn's arms, still laughing. They looked at one another.

Suddenly she kissed him.

She surprised herself totally. The thought of kissing him had never even crossed her mind. She was not even sure how much she liked him. It seemed like an impulse that came from nowhere.

He was clearly shocked, but he got over it quickly enough, and kissed her back enthusiastically. There was nothing tentative about his kiss, no slow burn: he was instantly aflame.

After a minute she pulled away from him, gasping. 'What happened?' she said foolishly.

'You kissed me,' he said, looking pleased.

'I didn't mean to.'

'I'm glad you did, though,' he said, and he kissed her again.

She wanted to break away, but his grip was strong and her will was weak. She felt his hand steal inside her robe, and she stiffened: her breasts were so small that she was embarrassed, and afraid he would be disappointed. His large hand closed over her small, round breast, and he groaned deep in his throat. His fingertips found her nipple, and she felt embarrassed all over again: she had had enormous nipples since nursing the boys. Small breasts and big nipples – she felt peculiar, almost deformed; but Mervyn showed no distaste, quite the contrary. He caressed her with surprising gentleness, and she gave herself up to the delicious sensation. It was a long time since she had felt this way.

What am I doing? she thought suddenly. I'm a respectable widow, and here I am rolling on the floor of an airplane with a man I met yesterday! What's come over me? 'Stop!' she said decisively. She pulled away and sat upright. Her négligé had ridden up over her knees. Mervyn stroked her bare thigh. 'Stop,' she said again, pushing his hand away.

'Whatever you say,' he said with obvious reluctance. 'But if you change your mind, I'll be ready.'

She glanced at his lap and saw the bulge in his nightshirt made by his erection. She looked away quickly. 'It was my fault,' she said, still panting from the kiss. 'But it was a mistake. I'm acting like a tease, I know. I'm sorry.'

'Don't apologize,' he said. 'It's the nicest thing that's happened to me for years.'

'But you love your wife, don't you?' she said bluntly.

He winced. 'I thought I did. Now I'm a bit confused, to tell you the truth.'

That was exactly how Nancy felt: confused. After ten years of celibacy she now found herself aching to embrace a man she hardly knew.

But I do know him, she thought; I know him quite well. I've travelled a long way with him and we've shared our troubles. I know he's abrasive, arrogant and proud, but also passionate and loyal and strong. I like him despite his faults. I respect him. He's terribly attractive, even in a brown striped nightshirt. And he held my hand when I was frightened. How nice it would be to have someone to hold my hand any time I was frightened.

As if he had read her mind, he took her hand again. This time he turned it up and kissed her palm. It made her skin tingle. After a few moments he drew her to him and kissed her mouth again.

'Don't do this,' she breathed. 'If we start again we won't be able to stop.'

'I'm just afraid that if we stop now we may never start again,' he murmured, and his voice was thick with desire.

She sensed in him a formidable passion, only just kept under control, and that inflamed her more. She had had too many dates with weak, obliging men who wanted her to give them reassurance and security; men who gave up all too easily when she resisted their demands. Mervyn was going to be insistent, powerfully so. He wanted her, and he wanted her now. She longed to surrender.

She felt his hand on her leg beneath her négligé, his fingertips stroking the soft skin on the inside of her thigh. She closed her eyes and, almost involuntarily, parted her legs a fraction. It was all the invitation he needed. A moment later, his hand found her sex, and she groaned. No one had done this to her since her husband, Sean. That thought suddenly overwhelmed her with sadness. Oh, Sean, I miss you, she thought, I never let myself admit how much I miss you. Her grief was sharper than at any time since the funeral. Tears squeezed between her closed lids and ran down her face. Mervyn kissed her and tasted the tears. 'What is it?' he murmured.

She opened her eyes. Through a blur of tears she saw his face, handsome and troubled; and beyond that her négligé pushed up around her waist, and his hand between her thighs. She took his wrist and moved his hand away gently but firmly. 'Please don't be angry,' she said.

'I won't be angry,' he said softly. 'Tell me.'

'No one has touched me there since Sean died, and it made me think of him.'

'Your husband.'

She nodded.

'How long ago?'

'Ten years.'

'It's a long time.'

'I'm loyal.' She gave a watery smile. 'Like you.'

He sighed. 'You're right. I've been married twice, and this is the first time I've come close to being unfaithful. I was thinking of Diana and that chap.'

'Are we fools?' she said.

'Maybe. We should stop thinking about the past, seize the moment, live for today.'

'Perhaps we should,' she said, and she kissed him again.

The plane bucked as if it had hit something. Their

faces were banged together and the lights flickered. The aircraft tossed and bumped violently. Nancy forgot all about kissing and clung on to Mervyn for stability.

When the turbulence eased a little she saw that his lip was bleeding. 'You bit me,' he said with a rueful grin.

'I'm sorry.'

'I'm glad. I hope there's a scar.'

She hugged him hard, feeling a surge of affection.

They lay together on the floor while the storm raged. In the next pause, Mervyn said, 'Let's try and make it to the bunk – we'll be more comfortable than on this carpet.'

Nancy nodded. Getting up on her hands and knees, she crawled across the floor and scrambled up on to her bunk. Mervyn followed her and lay down beside her. He put his arms around her and she snuggled up to his nightshirt.

Each time the turbulence got worse she held him hard, like a sailor tied to the mast. When it lessened she relaxed, and he stroked her soothingly.

At some point she fell asleep.

She was awakened by a knock at the door and a voice calling, 'Steward!'

She opened her eyes and realized she was lying in Mervyn's arms. 'Oh, Jesus!' she said, panicking. She sat up and looked around frenziedly.

Mervyn put a restraining hand on her shoulder and

called out in a loud and authoritative tone, 'Wait a moment, steward.'

A rather frightened voice replied, 'Okay, sir, take your time.'

Mervyn rolled off the bed, stood up, and pulled the bedclothes over Nancy. She smiled gratefully at him then turned away, pretending to be asleep, so that she would not have to look at the steward.

She heard Mervyn open the door and the steward come in. 'Good morning!' he said cheerfully. The smell of fresh coffee wafted into Nancy's nostrils. 'It's nine thirty in the morning British time, four thirty in the middle of the night in New York, and six o'clock in Newfoundland.'

Mervyn said, 'Did you say it's nine thirty in Britain but six o'clock in Newfoundland?'

'Yes, sir. Newfoundland Standard Time is three and a half hours behind Greenwich Mean Time.'

'I didn't know anyone took half hours. It must make life complicated for the people who write the airline timetables. How long until we splash down?'

'We'll be coming down in thirty minutes, just one hour later than scheduled. The delay is because of the storm.' The steward padded out and the door closed.

Nancy turned over. Mervyn pulled up the Venetian blinds. It was daylight. She watched him pour coffee, and the previous night came back to her in a series of vivid images: Mervyn holding her hand in the storm, the two of them falling on the floor, his hand on her breast, her clinging to him while the plane lurched and swayed, the way he had stroked her to sleep. Holy Jesus, she thought, I like this man a lot.

'How do you take it?' he said.

'Black, no sugar.'

'Same as me.' He handed her a cup.

She sipped it gratefully. She suddenly felt curious to know a hundred different things about Mervyn. Did he play tennis, go to the opera, enjoy shopping? Did he read much? How did he tie his tie? Did he polish his own shoes? As she watched him drinking his coffee she found she could confidently guess a great deal. He probably did play tennis, but he did not read many novels and he definitely would not enjoy shopping. He would be a good poker player and a bad dancer.

'What are you thinking?' he said. 'You're eyeing me as if you're wondering whether I'm a good risk for life insurance.'

She laughed. 'What sort of music do you like?'

'I'm tone deaf,' he said. 'When I was a lad, before the war, ragtime was all the rage in the dance halls. I liked the rhythm, although I was never much of a dancer. What about you?'

'Oh, I danced – had to. Every Saturday morning I went to dancing school in a white frilly dress and white gloves, to learn social dancing with twelve-year-old boys in suits. My mother thought it would give me the *entrée* into the uppermost layer of Boston society. It didn't, of course; but fortunately I didn't care. I was more interested in Pa's factory – much to Ma's despair. Did you fight in the Great War?'

'Aye.' A shadow crossed his face. 'I was at Ypres.' He

pronounced it 'wipers'. 'And I swore I'd never stand by and see another generation of young men sent to die that way. But I didn't expect Hitler.'

She looked at him compassionately. He glanced up. They held each other's eyes, and she knew they were both thinking of how they had kissed and petted in the night. Suddenly she felt embarrassed all over again. She looked away, towards the window, and saw land. That reminded her that when they reached Botwood she was hoping for a phone call that would change her life, one way or the other. 'We're almost there!' she said. She sprang out of bed. 'I must get dressed.'

'Let me go first,' he said. 'It looks better for you.'

'Okay.' She was not sure she had a reputation left to protect, but she did not want to say that. She watched him pick up his suit on its hanger, and the paper bag containing the clean clothes he had bought along with his nightshirt in Foynes: a white shirt, black wool socks and grey cotton underwear. He hesitated at the door, and she guessed he was wondering if he would ever kiss her again. She went to him and lifted her face. 'Thank you for holding me in your arms all night,' she said.

He bent down and kissed her. It was a soft kiss, his closed lips on hers. They held it for a long moment, then separated.

Nancy opened the door for him and he went out.

She sighed as she closed it behind him. I believe I could fall in love with him, she thought.

She wondered if she would ever see that nightshirt again.

She glanced out of the window. The plane was gradually losing height. She had to hurry.

She combed her hair quickly at the dressing-table then took her case into the ladies' room, which was right next door to the honeymoon suite. Lulu Bell and another woman were there, but mercifully not Mervyn's wife. Nancy would have liked a bath, but had to make do with a thorough wash at the basin. She had clean underwear and a fresh blouse, navy instead of grey, to go under her red suit. As she dressed she recalled her morning conversation with Mervyn. The thought of him made her feel happy, but beneath the happiness was a strain of unease. Why was that? Once she had asked herself the question, the answer became obvious. He had said nothing about his wife. Last night he had confessed himself 'confused'. Since then, silence. Did he want Diana back? Did he still love her? He had held Nancy in his arms all night, but that did not wipe out a whole marriage, not necessarily.

And what do I want? she asked herself. Sure, I'd love to see Mervyn again, go on dates with him, probably even have an affair with him; but do I want him to abandon his marriage for me? How can I tell, after one night of unconsummated passion?

She paused in the act of applying lipstick and stared at her face in the mirror. Cut the crap, Nancy, she told herself. You know the truth. You want this man. In ten years he's the first you've really fallen for. You're forty years and one day old and you've met Mr Right. Stop kidding around and start nailing his foot to the floor.

She put on Pink Clover perfume and left the room.

As she stepped out she saw Nat Ridgeway and her brother Peter, who had the seats next to the ladies' room. Nat said, 'Good morning, Nancy.' She remembered instantly how she had felt about this man five years ago. Yes, she thought, I might have fallen in love with him, given time; but there wasn't time. And maybe I was lucky: could be he wanted Black's Boots more than he wanted me. After all, he's still trying to get the company, but for sure he's not still trying to get me. She nodded curtly to him and went into her suite.

The bunks had been dismantled and remade as a divan seat, and Mervyn was sitting there, shaved and dressed in his dark grey suit and white shirt. 'Look out of the window,' he said. 'We're almost there.'

Nancy looked out and saw land. They were flying low over a dense pine forest streaked with silver rivers. As she watched, the trees gave way to water – not the deep, dark water of the Atlantic, but a calm grey estuary. On the far side she could see a harbour and a cluster of wooden buildings crowned by a church.

The plane came down rapidly. Nancy and Mervyn sat on the divan with their seat belts fastened, holding hands. Nancy hardly felt the impact when the hull cleaved the surface of the river, and she was not sure they were down until, a moment later, the windows were obscured by spray.

'Well,' she said, 'I've flown the Atlantic.'

'Aye. There's not many can say that.'

She did not feel very brave. She had spent half the trip worrying about her business and the other half holding hands with someone else's husband. She had only thought about the flight itself when the weather was rough and she was scared stiff. What was she going to tell the boys? They would want all the details. She did not even know how fast the plane flew. She resolved to find out all that sort of thing before they got to New York.

When the plane taxied to a halt, a launch came alongside. Nancy put on her coat and Mervyn his leather flying jacket. About half the passengers had decided to get off the plane and stretch their legs. The rest were still in bed, closed in behind the tightly fastened blue curtains of their bunks.

They passed through the main lounge, stepped out on to the stubby sea-wing, and boarded the launch. The air smelled of the sea and of new timber: there was probably a sawmill near by. Near the Clipper's mooring was a fuel barge marked SHELL AVIATION SERVICE, with men in white overalls waiting to refill the plane's tanks. There were also two quite big freighters in the harbour: the anchorage here must be deep.

Mervyn's wife and her lover were among those who had decided to land, and Diana glared at Nancy as the launch headed for the shore. Nancy was uncomfortable and could not meet her eye, although she had less to feel guilty about than Diana herself: after all, Diana was the one who had actually committed adultery.

They landed via a floating dock, a catwalk and a pier. Despite the early hour, there was a small crowd of sightseers. At the landward end of the pier were the Pan American buildings, one large and two small, all made of wood painted green with red-brown trim. Beside the buildings was a field with a few cows.

The passengers entered the large airline building and showed their passports to a sleepy excise man. Nancy noticed that Newfoundlanders spoke fast with an accent more like Irish than Canadian. There was a waiting room, but it attracted no one, and the passengers all decided to explore the village.

Nancy was impatient to speak to Patrick McBride in Boston. Just as she was about to ask for a phone, her name was called: the building had a voice-hailer system like a ship's. She identified herself to a young man in a Pan American uniform.

'There's a telephone call for you, ma'am,' he said.

Her heart leaped. 'Where's the phone?' she asked, looking around the room.

'In the telegraph office on Wireless Road. It's less than a mile away.'

A mile away! She could hardly contain her impatience. 'Then let's hurry, before the connection is broken! Do you have a car?'

The youngster looked as startled as if she had asked for a space rocket. 'No, ma'am.'

'So we'll walk. Lead the way.'

They left the building, Nancy and Mervyn following the messenger. They went up the hill, following a dirt road with no sidewalk. Loose sheep grazed the verges. Nancy was grateful for comfortable shoes – made by Black's, of course. Would Black's still be her company tomorrow night? Patrick McBride was about to tell her. The delay was unbearable.

In ten minutes or so they reached another small wooden building and went inside. Nancy was shown to a chair in front of a phone. She sat down and picked up the instrument with a shaking hand. 'This is Nancy Lenehan speaking.'

An operator said, 'Hold the line for Boston.'

There was a long pause, then she heard, 'Nancy? Are you there?'

It was not Mac, contrary to what she expected, and she took a moment to recognize the voice. 'Danny Riley!' she exclaimed.

'Nancy, I'm in trouble and you have to help me!'

She gripped the phone harder. It sounded as if her plan had worked. She made her voice calm, almost bored, as if the call was a nuisance. 'What sort of trouble, Danny?'

'People are calling me about that old case!'

This was good news! Mac had put the wind up Danny. His voice was panicky. This was what she wanted. But she pretended not to know what he was talking about. 'What case? What is this?'

'You *know.* I can't talk about it on the phone.'

'If you can't talk about it on the phone, why are you calling me?'

'Nancy! Stop treating me like shit! I need you!'

'Okay, calm down.' He was scared enough: now she had to use his fear to manipulate him. 'Tell me exactly what has happened, leaving out the names and addresses. I think I know what case you're talking about.'

'You have all your pa's old papers, right?'

'Sure, they're in my strong room at home.'

'Some people may ask to look through them.'

Danny was telling Nancy the story she herself had concocted. The ploy had worked perfectly so far. Blithely Nancy said, 'I don't think there's anything you need worry about—'

'How can you be sure?' he interrupted frantically.

'I don't know—'

'Have you been through them all?'

'No, there are too many, but—'

'Nobody *knows* what's in there. You should have burned that stuff years ago.'

'I guess you're right, but I never thought . . . Who wants to see the stuff, anyway?'

'It's a Bar inquiry.'

'Do they have the right?'

'No, but it looks bad if I refuse.'

'And it looks all right if I refuse?'

'You're not a lawyer. They can't pressure you.'

Nancy paused, pretending to hesitate, keeping him in suspense a moment longer. Finally she said, 'Then there's no problem.'

'You'll turn them down?'

'I'll do better than that. I'll burn everything tomorrow.'

'Nancy . . .' He sounded as if he might weep. 'Nancy, you're a true friend.'

She felt a hypocrite as she replied, 'How could I do anything else?'

'I appreciate this, God, I really do. I don't know how to thank you.'

'Well, since you mention it, there is something you could do for me.' She bit her lip. This was the delicate bit. 'You know why I'm flying back in such a rush?'

'I don't know, I've been so worried about this other thing—'

'Peter is trying to sell the company out from under me.'

There was a silence at the other end of the line.

'Danny, are you there?'

'Sure, I'm here. Don't you want to sell the company?'

'No! The price is way too low and there's no job for me in the new set-up – of course I don't want to sell. Peter knows it's a lousy deal but he doesn't care so long as he hurts me.'

'Is it a lousy deal? The company hasn't been doing too well lately.'

'You know why, don't you?'

'I guess . . . '

'Come on, say it. Peter is a lousy manager.'

'Okay . . .'

'Instead of letting him sell the company cheap, why don't we fire him? Let me take over. I can turn it around – you know that. Then, when we're making money, we can think again about selling out – at a much higher price.'

'I don't know.'

'Danny, a war has just started in Europe and that means business is going to boom. We'll be selling shoes faster than we can make them. If we wait two or three years we could sell the company for double, three times the price.'

'But the association with Nat Ridgeway would be so useful to my law firm.'

'Forget what's useful – I'm asking you to help me out.'

'I really don't know if it's in your own interests.'

Nancy wanted to say, 'You goddamn liar, it's your interests you're thinking about.' But she bit her tongue and said, 'I know it's the right thing for all of us.'

'Okay, I'll think about it.'

That was not good enough. She was going to have to lay her cards on the table. 'Remember Pa's papers, won't you?' She held her breath.

His voice became lower and he spoke more slowly. 'What are you saying to me?'

'I'm asking you to help me, because I'm helping you. You understand that type of thing, I know.'

'I think I do understand it. Normally it's called blackmail.'

She winced, then she remembered who she was talking to. 'You hypocritical old bastard, you've been doing this sort of thing all your life.'

He laughed. 'You got me there, kid.' But that sparked another thought. 'You didn't *initiate* the damn inquiry yourself, just to have some way of putting pressure on me, did you?'

This was dangerously close to the truth. 'That's what you would have done, I know. But I'm not going to answer any more questions. All you need to know is that if you vote with me tomorrow, you're safe; and if you don't, you're in trouble.' She was bullying him now, and that was the kind of thing he understood; but would he knuckle under, or defy her?

'You can't talk to me like that, I knew you when you wore diapers.'

She softened her tone. 'Isn't that a reason for helping me?'

There was a long pause. Then he said, 'I really don't have a choice, do I?'

'I guess not.'

'Okay,' he said reluctantly. 'I'll support you tomorrow, if you'll take care of that other thing.'

Nancy almost cried with relief. She had done it. She had turned Danny around. Now she would win. Black's Boots was still hers. 'I'm glad, Danny,' she said weakly.

'Your pa said it would be like this.'

The remark came out of nowhere and Nancy did not understand it. 'What do you mean?'

'Your pa. He wanted you and Peter to fight.'

There was a sly note in Danny's voice which made Nancy suspicious. He resented giving in to her, and he wanted to get in a parting shot. She was reluctant to give him that satisfaction but curiosity overcame her caution. 'What the hell are you talking about?'

'He always said the children of rich men were normally bad businessmen because they weren't hungry. He was really worried about it – thought you might throw away everything he'd earned.'

'He never told me he felt that way,' she said suspiciously.

'That's why he set things up so you'd fight one another. He brought you up to take control after his death, but he never put you in place; and he told Peter it would be *his* job to run the company. That way you'd have to fight it out, and the toughest would come out on top.'

'I don't believe this,' Nancy said; but she was not as sure as she sounded. Danny was angry because he had been out-manoeuvred, so he was being nasty to relieve his feelings; but that did not prove he was lying. She felt chilled.

'Believe what you like,' Danny said. 'I'm telling you what your father told me.'

'Pa told Peter he wanted *him* to be chairman?'

'Sure he did. If you don't believe me, ask Peter.'

'If I didn't believe you, I wouldn't believe Peter.'

'Nancy, I first met you when you were two days old,' Danny said, and there was a new, weary note in his voice. 'I've known you all your life and most of mine. You're a good person with a hard streak, like your father. I don't want to fight with you over business, or anything else. I'm sorry I brought this up.'

Now she believed him. He sounded genuinely regretful and that made her think he was sincere. She was shocked by his revelation, and felt weak and a little dizzy. She was silent for a moment, trying to recover her composure.

'I guess I'll see you at the board meeting,' Danny said.

'Okay,' she replied.

'Bye, Nancy.'

'Bye, Danny.' She hung up.

Mervyn said, 'By God, you were brilliant!'

She smiled thinly. 'Thanks.'

He laughed. 'I mean, the way you worked him round

– he never stood a chance! The poor beggar never knew what hit him—'

'Oh, shut up,' she said.

Mervyn looked as if she had slapped him. 'Whatever you say,' he said tightly.

She was sorry right away. 'Forgive me,' she said, touching his arm. 'At the end Danny said something that shocked me.'

'Do you want to tell me about it?' he asked cautiously.

'He says my father set up this fight between me and Peter so that the toughest would end up running the company.'

'Do you believe him?'

'I do, that's the terrible thing. It really rings true. I've never thought about it before but it explains a lot of things about me and my brother.'

He took her hand. 'You're upset.'

'Yeah.' She stroked the sparse black hair on the backs of his fingers. 'I feel like a character in a motion picture, acting out a scenario that was written by someone else. I've been manipulated for years, and I resent it. I'm not even sure I want to win this fight with Peter, now that I know how I was set up.'

He nodded understandingly. 'What would you like to do?'

The answer came to her as soon as he asked the question. 'I'd like to write my own script, that's what I'd like to do.'

CHAPTER TWENTY

Harry Marks was so happy he could hardly move.

He lay in bed remembering every moment of the night: the sudden thrill of pleasure when Margaret had kissed him; the anxiety as he worked up the courage to make a pass at her; the disappointment when she turned him down; and the amazement and delight when she had jumped into his bunk like a rabbit diving into its hole.

He cringed as he remembered that he had come the moment she touched him. This always happened to him the first time with a new girl: he had not owned up to that. It was humiliating. One girl had been scornful and mocked him. Mercifully, Margaret had not been disappointed or frustrated. In a funny way she had been aroused by it. Anyway, she had been happy in the end. So had he.

He could hardly believe his luck. He was not clever, he had no money, and he did not come from the right social class. He was a complete fraud and she knew it. What did she see in him? There was no mystery about what attracted *him* to *her*: she was beautiful, lovable, warm-hearted and vulnerable; and if that were not enough she had the body of a goddess. Anyone would have fallen for her. But him? He was not bad-looking, of course, and he knew how to wear clothes, but he had a feeling that sort of thing did not count much with Margaret. However, she was intrigued by him. She found his way of life fascinating, and he knew a lot of stuff that was strange to her, about working-class life in general and the criminal underworld in particular. He guessed that she saw him as a romantic figure, like the Scarlet Pimpernel, or some kind of outlaw, Robin Hood or Billy the Kid, or a pirate. She was extraordinarily grateful to him for holding her chair in the dining room, a trivial thing he had done without even thinking about it, but it meant a lot to her. In fact he was pretty sure that that was the moment when she had really fallen for him. Girls are peculiar, he thought with a mental shrug. Anyway, it no longer mattered what the original attraction had been: once they took their clothes off it was pure chemistry. He would never forget the sight of her white breasts in the dim, filtered light, her nipples so small and pale they were hardly visible; the riot of chestnut hair between her legs; the scattering of freckles at her throat . . .

And now he was going to risk losing it all.

He was going to steal her mother's jewellery.

It was not something a girl could laugh off. Her parents were awful to her, and she probably believed their wealth should be redistributed anyway, but all the same she would be shocked. Robbing someone was like a slap across the face: it might not do much damage, but it angered people out of all proportion. It could be the end of his affair with Margaret.

But the Delhi Suite was here, on this plane, in the baggage hold, just a few steps from where he lay: the most beautiful jewels in the world, worth a fortune, enough for him to live on for the rest of his life.

He longed to hold that necklace in his hands, feast his eyes on the fathomless red of the Burmese rubies, and run his fingertips over the faceted diamonds.

The settings would have to be destroyed, of course, and the suite broken up, as soon as it was fenced. That was a tragedy, but inevitable. The stones would survive, and end up in another suite of jewellery on the skin of some millionaire's wife. And Harry Marks would buy a house.

Yes, that was what he would do with the money. He would buy a country house, somewhere in America, maybe in the area they called New England, wherever that was. He could see it already, with its lawns and trees, the weekend guests in white trousers and straw hats, and his wife coming down the oaken staircase in jodhpurs and riding-boots—

But the wife had Margaret's face.

She had left him at dawn, slipping out through his curtains while there was no one to see. Harry had looked out of the window, thinking of her, while the plane flew over the spruce forests of Newfoundland and splashed down at Botwood. She had said she would stay on board during the stopover, and snatch an hour's sleep; and Harry said he would do the same, although he had no intention of sleeping.

Now he could see, through his window, a straggle of people in overcoats boarding the launch: about half the passengers and most of the crew. Now, while most people on the plane were still asleep, would be his chance of getting into the hold. Luggage locks would not delay him long. In no time at all he could have the Delhi Suite in his hands.

But he was wondering whether Margaret's breasts were not the most precious jewels he would ever hold.

He told himself to come down to earth. She had spent a night with him, but would he ever see her again after they got off the plane? He had heard people talk of 'shipboard romances' as being notoriously ephemeral: seaplane affairs had to be even more fleeting. Margaret was desperate to leave her parents and live independently, but would it ever happen? A lot of rich girls liked the idea of independence, but in practice it was very hard to give up a life of luxury. Margaret was one hundred per cent sincere, Harry knew, but she had no idea how ordinary people lived and when she tried it she was not going to like it.

No, there was no telling what she would do. Jewellery, by contrast, was completely reliable.

It would have been simpler if he had had to make a straight choice. If the Devil came to him and said, 'You can have Margaret or steal the jewels, but not both,' he would choose Margaret. But the reality was more complicated. He might leave the jewels and still lose Margaret. Or he might get both.

All his life he had been a chancer.

He decided to try for both.

He got up.

He stepped into his slippers and pulled on his bathrobe then looked around. The curtains were still drawn over Margaret's bunk and her mother's. The other three were vacant: Percy's, Lord Oxenford's and Mr Membury's. The lounge next door was empty but for a cleaning woman in a headscarf who had presumably come aboard from Botwood and was sleepily emptying the ashtrays. The outside door was open, and cold sea air blew around Harry's bare ankles. In No. 3 compartment, Clive Membury was talking to Baron Gabon. Harry wondered what they were talking about: waistcoats, perhaps? Further back, the stewards were converting bunks back into divan seats. There was a seedy morning-after air about the whole plane.

Harry went forward and climbed the stairs. As usual, he had no plan of action, no prepared excuses, not the faintest idea what he would do if he should be caught. He found that thinking ahead, and figuring out how things might go wrong, got him so anxious that he was unable to go through with it. Even winging it, like this, he found himself suddenly breathless from tension. Calm down, he said to himself; you've done this a hundred times. If it goes wrong you'll make something up, the way you always do.

He reached the flight deck and looked around.

He was in luck. There was no one there. He breathed easier. What a break!

Glancing forward, he saw a low hatch open under the windsceeen between the two pilots' seats. He looked through it into a big empty space in the bows of the aircraft. A door in the fuselage was open and one of the younger crew members was doing something with a rope. Not so good. Harry pulled his head back in before he was spotted.

He passed quickly along the flight cabin and through the door in the back wall. Now he was between the two cargo holds, underneath the loading hatch which also incorporated the navigator's dome. He picked the left-hand hold, went in and closed the door behind him. He was out of sight now, and he guessed the crew would have no reason to look into the hold.

He examined his surroundings. It was like being in a high-class luggage store. Expensive leather cases were stacked all around and roped to the sides. Harry had to find the Oxenfords' baggage quickly. He went to work.

It was not easy. Some cases were stacked with their name tags underneath, some were covered by other cases which were hard to dislodge. There was no heating in the hold and he was cold in his bathrobe. His hands shook and his fingers hurt as he untied the ropes that prevented the cases shifting in flight. He worked systematically, so that he would not miss any or check pieces twice. He re-tied the ropes as best he could. The names were international: Ridgeway, d'Annunzio, Lo, Hartmann, Bazarov – but no Oxenfords. After twenty minutes he had checked every piece, he was shivering, and he had established that the bags he was looking for must be in the other hold. He cursed under his breath.

He tied the last rope and looked around carefully: he had left no evidence of his visit.

Now he would have to go through the same procedure in the other hold. He opened the door and stepped out, and a startled voice cried, 'Shit! Who are you?' It was the officer Harry had seen in the bow compartment, a cheerful, freckled young man in a short-sleeved shirt.

Harry was equally shocked but he covered it up quickly. He smiled, closed the door behind him, and said calmly, 'Harry Vandenpost. Who are you?'

'Mickey Finn, the assistant engineer. Sir, you're not supposed to be here. You gave me a scare. I'm sorry for swearing. But what are you doing?'

'Looking for my suitcase,' Harry said. 'I forgot my razor.'

'Sir, access to checked baggage is not permitted during the journey, under any circumstances.'

'I thought I couldn't do any harm.'

'Well, I'm sorry, but it's not allowed. I could lend you my razor.'

'I appreciate that, but I kind of like my own. If I could just find my case—'

'Boy, I wish I could do what you want, sir, but I really can't. When the Captain comes back aboard you could ask him, but I know he's going to say the same as me.'

Harry realized with a sinking heart that he was going to have to accept defeat, at least for the present. Putting a brave face on it, he smiled, and said as graciously as he could, 'In that case I guess I'll borrow your razor, and thank you kindly.'

Mickey Finn held the door for him and he stepped into the flight cabin and went down the stairs. What rotten luck, he thought angrily. Another few seconds and I would have been there. God knows when I'll get another chance.

Mickey went into No. 1 compartment and returned a moment later with a safety razor, a fresh blade still in its paper wrapper, and shaving soap in a mug. Harry took them and thanked him. Now he had no choice but to shave.

He took his overnight bag into the bathroom, still thinking about those Burmese rubies. Carl Hartmann, the scientist, was there in his undershirt, washing himself vigorously. Harry left his own perfectly good shaving tackle in his case and shaved hurriedly with Mickey's razor. 'Rough night,' he said conversationally.

Hartmann shrugged. 'I've had rougher.'

Harry looked at his bony shoulders. The man was a walking skeleton. 'I bet you have,' Harry said.

They had no more conversation. Hartmann was not talkative, and Harry was preoccupied.

After he had shaved Harry took out a new blue shirt. Unwrapping a new shirt was one of life's small, intense pleasures. He loved the rustle of the tissue paper and the crisp feel of the virgin cotton. He slipped into it deliciously and tied a perfect knot in his wine-coloured silk tie.

When he returned to his compartment he saw that Margaret's curtains were still closed. He imagined her fast asleep, her lovely hair spread across the white pillow, and he smiled to himself. Glancing into the lounge, he saw the stewards setting out a buffet breakfast that made his mouth water, with bowls of strawberries and jugs of cream and orange juice, and cold champagne in dewy silver ice buckets. Those must be hothouse strawberries, he thought, at this time of year.

He stowed his overnight case; then with Mickey Finn's shaving tackle in his hand he went up the stairs to the flight deck to try again.

Mickey was not there, but to Harry's dismay another crew member was sitting at the big chart table doing calculations on a scratch pad. The man looked up, smiled, and said, 'Hi. Can I help you?'

'I'm looking for Mickey, to return his razor.'

'You'll find him in number one, that's the forward-most compartment.'

'Thanks.' Harry hesitated. He had to get past this guy – but how?

'Something else?' the man said pleasantly.

'This flight deck is unbelievable,' Harry said. 'It's like an office.'

'Incredible, isn't it?'

'Do you like flying these planes?'

'I love it. Uh, look, I wish I had time to talk, but I have to finish these calculations and it's going to take me almost until take-off.'

Harry groaned inwardly. That meant the way to the hold would be blocked until it was too late. He could not think of an excuse to go into the hold. Once again he forced himself to conceal his disappointment. 'Sorry,' he said. 'I'll buzz off.'

'Normally we like to talk to passengers, we meet such interesting people. But right now . . .'

'My fault.' Harry racked his brains for another moment, then gave up. He turned and went back down the stairs, cursing to himself.

His luck seemed to be failing him.

He went forward and gave the shaving kit to Mickey, then returned to his compartment. Margaret still had not stirred. Harry went through the lounge and stepped out on to the sea-wing. He took several deep breaths of the cold, damp air. I'm missing the opportunity of a lifetime, he thought angrily. The palms of his hands itched when he pictured the fabulous jewellery just a few feet over his head. But he had not given up yet. There was one more stop, Shediac. That would be his last chance to steal a fortune.

Part Five

Botwood to Shediac

CHAPTER TWENTY-ONE

Eddie Deakin could feel the hostility of his crew-mates as they went ashore in the launch. None of them would meet his eye. They all knew now how close they had come to running out of fuel and crashing into the stormy ocean. Their lives had been in danger. No one yet knew just why it had happened, but fuel was the engineer's responsibility, so Eddie was to blame.

They must have noticed that he had been behaving oddly. He had been preoccupied the whole flight, he had talked scary to Tom Luther during dinner, and a window had inexplicably broken while he was in the men's room. No wonder the others felt he was not one hundred per cent reliable any more. That kind of feeling spread fast in a tightly knit crew whose lives depended on one another.

The knowledge that his mates no longer trusted him was a bitter pill to swallow. He was proud to be considered one of the most solid guys around. To make matters worse, he himself was slow to forgive others' mistakes, and had sometimes been scornful of people whose performance fell off because of personal problems. 'Excuses don't fly,' he sometimes said, a crack which now made him wince every time he thought of it.

He had tried telling himself he did not give a damn. He had to save his wife and he had to do it alone: he could not ask anyone for help and he could not worry about other people's feelings. He had risked their lives, but the gamble had paid off and that was the end of it. It was all perfectly logical, and none of it made any difference. Engineer Deakin, solid as a rock, had turned into Unreliable Eddie, a guy you had to watch in case he screwed up. He hated people like Unreliable Eddie. He hated himself.

A lot of passengers had stayed on board the plane, as always at Botwood: they were glad of the chance to catch some sleep while the plane was still. Ollis Field, the FBI man, and his prisoner, Frankie Gordino, had also stayed on board, of course: they had not disembarked at Foynes either. Tom Luther was in the launch, wearing a topcoat with a fur collar and a dove-grey hat. As they approached the pier, Eddie got next to Luther and murmured, 'Wait for me at the airline building. I'll take you to where the phone is.'

Botwood was a huddle of wooden houses around a deep-water harbour in the landlocked estuary of the Exploits River. Even the millionaires on the Clipper could never find much to buy here. The village had had telephone service only since June. Such few cars as there were drove on the left, for Newfoundland was still under British rule.

They all went into the wooden Pan American building and the crew made their way to the flight room.

Eddie immediately read the weather reports sent by radio from the big new landplane airport thirty-eight miles away at Gander Lake. Then he calculated the fuel requirement for the next leg. Because this hop was so much shorter, the calculation was not so crucial, but all the same the plane never carried a great excess of fuel, because payload was expensive. There was a sour taste in his mouth as he worked out the arithmetic. Would he ever be able to go through these sums again without thinking of this awful day? The question was academic: after what he was about to do, he would never again be engineer on a Clipper.

The Captain might already be wondering whether to trust Eddie's calculations. Eddie needed to do something towards restoring confidence. He decided to show some implicit self-doubt. He went over his figures twice, then handed his work to Captain Baker, saying in a neutral tone, 'I'd appreciate it if someone would check these.'

'Won't hurt,' the Captain said noncommittally, but he looked relieved, as if he had wanted to propose a double-check but had been reluctant to.

'I'm going to get a breath of air,' Eddie said, and he went out.

He found Tom Luther outside the Pan American building, standing with his hands in his pockets, moodily watching the cows in the field. 'I'll take you to the telegraph office,' Eddie said. He led the way up the hill at a brisk pace. Luther lagged behind. 'Set fire, you,' Eddie said. 'I have to get back.' Luther walked faster. He looked like he did not want to make Eddie angry.

Maybe it was not surprising, after Eddie almost threw him out of the plane.

They nodded to two passengers who appeared to be coming back from the telegraph office: Mr Lovesey and Mrs Lenehan, the couple who had got on at Foynes. The guy wore a flying jacket. Distracted though he was, Eddie noticed that they seemed happy together. People always said he and Carol-Ann looked happy together, he recalled, and he felt a stab of pain.

They reached the office and Luther placed the call. He wrote the number he wanted on a piece of paper: he did not want Eddie to hear him say it. They went into a small private room with a phone on a table and a couple of chairs, and waited impatiently for the call to go through. This early in the morning the lines should not be too busy, but there were probably a lot of connections between here and Maine.

Eddie felt confident that Luther would tell his men to bring Carol-Ann to the rendezvous. That was a big step forward: it meant he would be free to act the moment the rescue was over, instead of continuing to worry about his wife. But what exactly could he do? The obvious thing would be to radio the police immediately; but Luther was sure to think of that, and he would probably smash up the Clipper's radio. Nobody would be able to do anything until help turned up. By then Gordino and Luther would be on land, in a car, speeding away – and no one would even know which country they were in, Canada or the USA. Eddie racked his brains for some way to make it easier for the police to trace Gordino, but he could not think of anything.

And if he were to give the warning beforehand, there was a danger the police would blunder in too early and endanger Carol-Ann – the one risk Eddie was not prepared to take. He began to wonder whether he had achieved anything after all.

After a while the phone rang and Luther picked up the earpiece. 'It's me,' he said. 'There's going to be a change of plan. You have to bring the woman on the launch.' There was a pause, then he said, 'The engineer wants it this way, and he says he won't do it any other way, and I believe him, so just bring the woman, okay?' After another pause he looked at Eddie. 'They want to talk to you.'

Eddie's heart sank. So far Luther had acted like the man in charge. Now it sounded as if he might not have the power to order Carol-Ann brought to the rendezvous. Eddie said edgily, 'Are you telling me this is your boss?'

'I'm the boss,' Luther said uneasily. 'But I have partners.'

Clearly the partners did not like the idea of bringing Carol-Ann to the rendezvous. Eddie cursed. Should he give them the chance to talk him out of it? Was there anything at all to be gained by speaking to them? He thought not. They might bring Carol-Ann to the phone and make her scream, to weaken his resolve . . . 'Tell them to fuck off,' Eddie said. The phone was on the table and he spoke loudly, hoping they could hear him at the other end of the line.

Luther looked scared. 'You can't talk that way to these people!' he said in a high voice.

Eddie wondered if he should be scared too. Maybe he had misread the situation. If Luther was one of the gangsters, what was he frightened of? But there was no time to reassess the position right now. He had to stick to his plan. 'I just want a yes or no,' he said. 'I don't need to talk to the shitheel.'

'Oh, my God.' Luther picked up the phone and said, 'He won't come to the phone – I told you he was difficult.' There was a pause. 'Yes, good idea. I'll tell him.' He turned to Eddie again and held out the earpiece. 'Your wife is on the line.'

Eddie reached for the phone then pulled his hand back. If he talked to her, he would be putting himself at their mercy. But he was desperate to hear her voice. He summoned up every ounce of will-power, thrust his hands deep into his pockets, and shook his head in silent negation.

Luther stared at him for a moment, then spoke into the phone again. 'He still won't speak! He – Get off the line, cunt. I want to talk to—'

Suddenly Eddie had him by the throat. The phone clattered to the floor. Eddie pressed his thumbs into Luther's thick neck. Luther gasped, 'Stop! Let go! Leave me . . .' His voice was choked off.

The red mist cleared from Eddie's eyes. He eased the pressure but retained his grip. He brought his face close to Luther's, so close that Luther blinked. 'Listen to me,' Eddie said. 'You call my wife Mrs Deakin.'

'Okay, okay!' Luther said hoarsely. 'Let me go, for Christ's sake!'

Eddie let him go.

Luther rubbed his neck, breathing hard, then he grabbed the phone. 'Vincini? He just went for me because I called his wife a – a bad word. Says I have to call her Mrs Deakin. Are you getting it now, or do I have to draw you a picture? He'll do anything!' There was a pause. 'I guess I could handle him, but if people see us fighting, what'll they think? It could blow the whole thing!' He was silent for a while. 'Good. I'll tell him. Listen, we're making the right decision, I know it. Hold on.' He turned to Eddie. 'They'll go along with it. She'll be on the launch.'

Eddie made his face a mask to conceal his tremendous relief.

Luther went on nervously, 'But he says I must tell you that if there are any snags, he's going to shoot her.'

Eddie snatched the phone from his hand. 'Get this, Vincini. One: I have to see her on the deck of your launch before I open the doors of the plane. Two: she has to come on board with you. Three: no matter what snags there might be, if she's hurt I'm going to kill you with my bare hands. Just keep that in your mind, Vincini.' Before the man had time to reply he hung up.

Luther looked dismayed. 'What did you do that for?' He lifted the earpiece and jiggled the cradle. 'Hello? Hello?' He shook his head and hung up. 'Too late.' He looked at Eddie with a mixture of anger and awe. 'You really live dangerously, don't you?'

'Go pay for the call,' Eddie snapped.

Luther reached into his inside pocket and took out a roll of bills. 'Listen,' he said. 'Your getting mad doesn't help anyone. I've given you what you ask. Now we have to work together to make this operation a success for both our sakes. Why don't we just try to get along? We're partners now.'

'Fuck you,' Eddie said, and he went out.

He was angrier than ever as he strode along the road back to the harbour. Luther's remark that they were partners had touched a raw nerve. Eddie had done what he could to protect Carol-Ann, but he was still committed to help free Frankie Gordino, who was a murderer and a rapist. The fact that he was being forced into it should have excused him, and in others' minds perhaps it would, but to him it seemed to make no difference: he knew that if he went through with it he would never hold up his head again.

As he walked down the hill to the bay he looked across the water. The Clipper floated majestically on the calm surface. Eddie's career on Clippers was at an end, he knew. He was mad about that, too. There were also two big freighters at anchor and a few smaller fishing boats; and, to his surprise, he saw a US Navy patrol boat tied up at the dock. He wondered what it was doing here in Newfoundland. Something to do with the war? It reminded him of his days in the Navy. Looking back, that seemed like a golden time, when life was simple. Maybe the past always looked attractive when you were in trouble.

He entered the Pan American building. There in the green and white painted lobby was a man in lieutenant's uniform, presumably off the patrol boat. As Eddie walked in the lieutenant turned around. He was a big, ugly man with small eyes too close together and a wart on his nose. Eddie stared at him in amazement and delight. He could not believe his eyes. 'Steve?' he said. 'Is it really you?'

'Hi, Eddie.'

'How in the hell . . .?' It was Steve Appleby, whom Eddie had tried to call from England: his oldest and best friend, the one man above all others he wanted by his side in a tight spot. He could hardly take it in.

Steve came over and they embraced, hitting each other on the back.

Eddie said, 'You're supposed to be in New Hampshire – what the hell are you doing here?'

'Nella said you sounded frantic when you called.' Steve looked solemn. 'Hell, Eddie, I've never known you seem even a little *shook*. You're always such a rock. I knew you had to be in *bad* trouble.'

'I am. I'm—' Suddenly Eddie was overcome with emotion. For twenty hours he had kept his feelings bottled up and tightly corked, and he was ready to explode. The fact that his best friend had moved heaven and earth to come and help him out touched him deeply. 'I'm in bad trouble,' he confessed. Then tears came to his eyes and his throat seized up so he could not speak. He turned away and went outside.

Steve followed. Eddie led him round the corner of the building and through the big open doorway into the empty boat room, where the launch was normally kept. They would not be seen in here.

Steve spoke to cover his embarrassment. 'I can't

count how many favours I've called in to get here. I've been in the Navy eight years, and a lot of people owe me, but today they all paid me back double, and now I owe them. It's going to take me another eight years just to get back to even!'

Eddie nodded. Steve had a natural aptitude for wheeling and dealing. Eddie wanted to say thank you, but he could not stop the tears.

Steve's tone changed and he said, 'Eddie, what the hell is going on?'

'They've got Carol-Ann,' Eddie managed.

'Who has, for Christ's sake?'

'The Patriarca gang.'

Steve was incredulous. '*Ray* Patriarca? The racketeer?'

'They kidnapped her.'

'God Almighty, why?'

'They want me to bring down the Clipper.'

'What for?'

Eddie wiped his face with his sleeve and brought himself under control. 'There's an FBI agent on board with a prisoner, a hoodlum called Frankie Gordino. I figure Patriarca wants to rescue him. Anyway, a passenger calling himself Tom Luther told me to bring the plane down off the Maine coast. They'll have a fast boat waiting, and Carol-Ann will be on it. We swap Carol-Ann for Gordino, then Gordino disappears.'

Steve nodded. 'And Luther was smart enough to realize that the only possible way to get Eddie Deakin to co-operate was to kidnap his wife.'

'Yeah.'

'The bastards.'

'I want to get these people, Steve. I want to fucking crucify them. I want to nail the bastards up, I swear.'

Steve shook his head. 'But what can you do?'

'I don't know. That's why I called you.'

Steve frowned. 'The danger period for them is from when they come aboard the plane until they get back to their car. Maybe the police could find the car and ambush them.'

Eddie was dubious. 'How would the police recognize it? It will just be a car parked near a beach.'

'It might be worth a try.'

'It's not tight enough, Steve. There's too much to go wrong. And I don't want to call in the police – there's no knowing what they might do to endanger Carol-Ann.'

Steve nodded agreement. 'And the car could be either side of the border, so we'd have to call in the Canadian police as well. Hell, it wouldn't stay secret for five minutes. No, the police are no good. That leaves the Navy or the Coast Guard.'

Eddie felt better just for being able to discuss the dilemma with someone. 'Let's talk Navy.'

'All right. Suppose I could get a patrol boat like this one to intercept the launch after the trade, before Gordino and Luther reach land?'

'That might work,' Eddie said, and he began to feel hopeful. 'But could you do it?' It was next to impossible to get naval vessels to move outside their chain of command.

'I think I can. They're out on exercises anyway,

getting all excited in case the Nazis decided to invade New England after Poland. It's just a question of diverting one. The guy who can do that is Simon Greenbourne's father – remember Simon?'

'Sure I do.' Eddie recalled a wild kid with a crazy sense of humour and a huge thirst for beer. He was always in trouble, but he usually got off lightly because his father was an admiral.

Steve continued, 'Simon went too far one day and set fire to a bar in Pearl City and burned down half a block. It's a long story, but I kept him out of jail and his father is eternally grateful. I think he would do this for me.'

Eddie looked at the vessel Steve had come in. It was an SC-class submarine chaser, twenty years old, with a wooden hull, but it carried a three inch, .23 calibre machine-gun and a depth charge. It would scare the pants off a bunch of citified mobsters in a speedboat. But it was conspicuous. 'They might see the boat beforehand and smell a rat,' he said anxiously.

Steve shook his head. 'These things can hide up creeks. Their draught is less than six feet fully loaded.'

'It's risky, Steve.'

'So they spot a Navy patrol boat. It leaves them alone. What are they going to do – call the whole thing off?'

'They might do something to Carol-Ann.'

Steve seemed about to argue, then he changed his mind. 'That's true,' he said. 'Anything might happen. You're the only one who has the right to say we'll take the risk.'

Eddie knew Steve was not saying what he really felt. 'You think I'm running scared, don't you?' he said testily.

'Yeah. But you're entitled.'

Eddie looked at his watch. 'Christ, I'm due back in the flight room.' He had to make up his mind. Steve had come up with the best plan he could, and now it was up to Eddie to take it or leave it.

Steve said, 'One thing you may not have thought of. They could still be planning to double-cross you.'

'How?'

He shrugged. 'I don't know how, but once they're on board the Clipper it's going to be hard to argue with them. They may decide to take Gordino and Carol-Ann too.'

'Why the hell would they do that?'

'To make sure you don't co-operate too enthusiastically with the police for a while.'

'Shit.' There was another reason, too, Eddie realized. He had yelled at these guys and insulted them. They might well be planning some final pay-off to teach him a lesson.

He was cornered.

He had to go along with Steve's plan now. It was too late to do otherwise.

God forgive me if I'm wrong, he thought.

'All right,' he said. 'Let's do it.'

CHAPTER TWENTY-TWO

MARGARET WOKE up thinking, Today I have to tell Father.

It took her a moment to remember what she had to tell him: that she would not be living with them in Connecticut, she was going to leave the family, find lodgings and get a job.

He was sure to throw a tantrum.

A nauseating sensation of fear and shame came over her. It was a familiar feeling. She got it every time she wanted to defy Father. I'm nineteen years old, she thought; I'm a woman. Last night I made passionate love to a wonderful man. Why am I still scared of my father?

It had been like this as long as she could remember. She had never understood why he was so determined to keep her in a cage. He was the same with Elizabeth, but not with Percy. He seemed to want his daughters to be useless ornaments. He was always worst when they wanted to do something practical, like learn to swim or build a tree house or ride bicycles. He never cared how much they spent on gowns but he would not let them have an account at a bookshop.

It was not simply the prospect of defeat that made

her feel sick. It was the way he refused her, the anger and scorn, the mocking jibes and the purple-faced rage.

She had often tried to outwit him by deceit, but that rarely worked: she was so terrified he might hear the scratching of the rescued kitten in the attic, or come across her playing with the 'unsuitable' children from the village, or search her room and find her copy of Elinor Glyn's *The Vicissitudes of Evangeline*, that forbidden delights lost their charm.

She had succeeded in going against his will only with the help of others. Monica had introduced her to sexual pleasure, and he had never been able to take that away from her. Percy showed her how to shoot; Digby the chauffeur taught her to drive. Now perhaps Harry Marks and Nancy Lenehan would help her to become independent.

She already *felt* different. There was a pleasant ache in her muscles, as if she had spent a day at some hard physical work in the fresh air. She lay in her bunk and ran her hands all over her body. For the past six years she had thought of herself as a thing of ungainly bulges and unsightly hair, but now suddenly she liked her body. Harry seemed to think it was wonderful.

From outside her curtained bunk came a few faint noises. People were waking up, she guessed. She peeped out. Nicky, the fat steward, was taking down the opposite bunks, the pair in which Mother and Father had slept, and remaking the divan seat. Harry's and Mr Membury's had already been done. Harry was sitting down, fully dressed, looking out of the window meditatively.

She suddenly felt bashful, and closed the curtain quickly, before he should see her. It was funny: a few hours ago they had been as intimate as two people can possibly be, but now she felt awkward.

She wondered where the others were. Percy would have gone ashore. Father had probably done the same: he generally woke up early. Mother was never very energetic in the morning: she was probably in the ladies' room. Mr Membury was nowhere in sight.

Margaret looked out of the window. It was daylight. The plane was at anchor near a small town in a pine forest. The scene was very still.

She lay back, enjoying the privacy, savouring the memory of the night, recalling the details and storing them away like photographs in an album. She felt as if last night was when she *really* lost her virginity. Previously, with Ian, sexual intercourse had been hurried, difficult, and quick, and she had felt like a guilty child disobediently imitating a grown-up game. Last night she and Harry had been adults taking pleasure in one another's bodies. They had been discreet but not furtive; shy but not embarrassed; uncertain without clumsiness. She had felt like a real woman. I want more of that, she thought; lots more; and she hugged herself, feeling wanton.

She pictured Harry as she had just glimpsed him, sitting by the window in a sky-blue shirt with such a thoughtful look on his handsome face; and suddenly she wanted to kiss him. She sat up, pulled her robe around her shoulders, opened her curtains, and said, 'Good morning, Harry.'

His head jerked round and he looked as if he had been caught doing something wrong. She thought, What were you thinking about? He met her eyes, then smiled. She smiled back, and found that she could not stop. They grinned stupidly at one another for a long minute. Finally Margaret dropped her eyes and stood up.

The steward turned around from fixing Mother's seat and said, 'Good morning, Lady Margaret. Would you care for a cup of coffee?'

'No, thank you, Nicky.' She probably looked a fright, and she was in a hurry to get to a mirror and brush her hair. She felt undressed. She was undressed, whereas Harry had shaved and put on a fresh shirt and looked as bright as a new apple.

However, she still wanted to kiss him.

She stepped into her slippers, remembering how she had indiscreetly left them beside Harry's bunk and retrieved them a split second before Father would have seen them. She put her arms into the sleeves of her robe and saw Harry's eyes drop to her breasts. She did not mind: she *liked* him to look at her breasts. She tied her belt and ran her fingers through her hair.

Nicky finished what he was doing. She hoped he would leave the compartment, so that she could kiss Harry, but instead he asked, 'May I do your bunk now?'

'Of course,' she said, feeling disappointed. She

wondered how long she would have to wait for another chance to kiss Harry. She picked up her bag, shot a regretful look at Harry, then went out.

The other steward, Davy, was laying out a buffet breakfast in the dining room. She stole a strawberry, feeling sinful. She walked the length of the plane. Most of the bunks had now been remade as seats, and a few people were sitting around drinking coffee sleepily. She saw Mr Membury, deep in conversation with Baron Gabon, and wondered what that disparate pair found to talk about so earnestly. Something was missing, and after a moment she realized what: there were no morning newspapers.

She went into the ladies' room. Mother was sitting at the dressing-table. Suddenly Margaret felt dreadfully guilty. How could I have done those things, she thought wildly, with Mother only a couple of steps away? She felt a blush rising to her cheeks. She forced herself to say, 'Good morning, Mother.' To her surprise, her voice sounded quite normal.

'Good morning, dear. You look a little flushed. Did you sleep?'

'Very well,' Margaret said, and she blushed deeper. Then she was inspired, and continued, 'I'm feeling guilty because I stole a strawberry from the breakfast buffet.' She dived into the lavatory to escape. When she came out she ran water into the basin and washed her face vigorously.

She was sorry she had to put on the dress she had been wearing yesterday. She would have liked something fresh. She splashed on extra *eau de toilette.* Harry had told her he liked it. He had even known it was Tosca. He was the first man she had ever met who could identify perfumes.

She took her time brushing her hair. It was her best feature and she needed to make the most of it. I ought to take more trouble over how I look, she thought. She had never cared much until now, but suddenly it seemed to matter. I ought to have dresses that show off my figure, and smart shoes to call attention to my long legs, and colours that look good with red hair and green eyes. The dress she had on was all right: it was a sort of brick red. But it was rather loose and shapeless, and now, looking in the mirror, she wished it had squarer shoulders and a belt at the waist. Mother would never let her wear make-up, of course, so she would have to be satisfied with her pale complexion. At least she had good teeth.

'I'm ready,' she said brightly.

Mother was still in the same position. 'I suppose you're going back to talk to Mr Vandenpost.'

'I suppose I am, since there's no one else there and you're still redecorating your face.'

'Don't be fresh. There's a look of the Jew about him.'

Well, he isn't circumcised, Margaret thought, and she almost said it out of sheer devilment; but instead she started to giggle.

Mother was offended. 'There's nothing to laugh at. I want you to know that I will not permit you to see that young man again after we get off this plane.'

'You'll be happy to know that I don't care tuppence.'

It was true: she was going to leave her parents, so it no longer mattered what they would or would not permit.

Mother threw her a suspicious look. 'Why do I think you're not being quite sincere?'

'Because tyrants can never trust anyone,' Margaret said.

That was quite a good exit line, she thought, and she went to the door; but Mother called her back.

'Don't go away, dear,' Mother said, and her eyes filled with tears.

Did she mean 'Don't leave the room' or 'Don't leave the family'? Could she possibly have guessed what Margaret was planning? She had always had good intuition. Margaret said nothing.

'I've already lost Elizabeth, I couldn't bear to lose you, too.'

'But it's Father's fault!' Margaret burst out, and suddenly she wanted to cry. 'Can't you stop him being so horrid?'

'Don't you think I try?'

Margaret was shocked: Mother had never before admitted that Father might be at fault. 'But I can't help it if he's that way,' she said miserably.

'You could try not to provoke him,' Mother said.

'Give in to him all the time, you mean.'

'Why not? It's only until you're married.'

'If *you* would stand up to him he might not be like this.'

Mother shook her head sadly. 'I can't take your side against him, dear. He's my husband.'

'But he's so wrong!'

'It makes no difference. You'll know that when you're married.'

Margaret felt cornered. 'It's not fair.'

'It's not for long. I'm just asking you to tolerate him a little while longer. As soon as you're twenty-one he'll be different, I promise you, even if you're not married. I know it's hard. But I don't want you to be banished, like poor Elizabeth . . .'

Margaret realized that she would be as upset as Mother if they became estranged. 'I don't want that either, Mother,' she said. She took a step closer to the stool. Mother opened her arms. They embraced awkwardly, Margaret standing and Mother sitting.

'Promise me you won't quarrel with him,' Mother said.

She sounded so sad that Margaret wanted with all her heart to give the promise; but something held her back, and all she would say was, 'I'll try, Mother, I really will.'

Mother let her go and looked at her; and Margaret read bleak resignation in her face. 'Thank you for that, anyway,' Mother said.

There was nothing more to say.

Margaret went out.

Harry stood up when she entered the compartment. She felt so upset that she completely lost all sense of propriety and threw her arms around him. After a moment's startled hesitation he hugged her and kissed the top of her head. She began to feel better right away.

Opening her eyes, she caught an astonished look

from Mr Membury, who was back in his seat. She hardly cared, but she detached herself from Harry and they sat down on the other side of the compartment.

'We've got to make plans,' Harry said. 'This could be our last chance to talk privately.'

Margaret knew that Mother would be back soon, and Father and Percy would return with the other passengers, and after that she and Harry might not be alone again. She was seized by a near-panic as she saw a vision of the two of them parting company at Port Washington and never finding one another again. 'Where can I contact you, tell me quick!' she said.

'I don't know – I don't have anywhere. But don't worry, I'll get in touch with you. What hotel will you be staying at?'

'The Waldorf. Will you telephone me tonight? You must!'

'Calm down, of course I will. I'll call myself Mr Marks.'

Harry's relaxed tone made Margaret see she was being silly . . . and a little selfish, too. She should think of him as well as herself. 'Where will you spend the night?'

'I'll find a cheap hotel.'

She was struck by an idea. 'Would you like to sneak into my room at the Waldorf?'

He grinned. 'Are you serious? You know I would!'

She was happy to have pleased him. 'Normally I'd share with my sister, but now I'll be on my own.'

'Oh, boy. I can't wait.'

She knew how he loved the high life, and she so

wanted to make him happy. What else would he like? 'We'll order scrambled eggs and champagne from room service.'

'I'll want to stay there for ever.'

That brought her back to reality. 'My parents will be moving to my grandfather's place in Connecticut after a few days. Then I'll have to find somewhere to live.'

'We'll look together,' he said. 'Maybe get rooms in the same building, or something.'

'Really?' She was thrilled. They would have rooms in the same building! It was exactly what she wanted. She had been half afraid that he would go over the top and ask her to marry him, and half afraid he would not want to see her again; but this was the ideal: she could stay close to him and get to know him better without making a foolishly hasty commitment. And she would be able to sleep with him. But there was a snag. 'If I work for Nancy Lenehan I'll be in Boston.'

'Maybe I'll go to Boston too.'

'Would you?' She could hardly believe what she was hearing.

'It's as good a place as any. Where is it, anyway?'

'New England.'

'Is that like old England?'

'Well, I've heard that the people are snobbish.'

'It'll be just like home.'

'What sort of rooms will we get?' she said excitedly. 'I mean, how many, and so on?'

He smiled. 'You won't have more than one room, and you'll find it a struggle to pay even for that. If it's anything like the English equivalent, it will have cheap furniture and one window. With luck there might be a gas ring or a hotplate for you to make coffee. You'll share the bathroom with the rest of the house.'

'And the kitchen?'

He shook his head. 'You can't afford a kitchen. Your lunch will be the only hot meal of the day. When you come home you can have a cup of tea and a piece of cake, or you could make toast if you've got an electric fire.'

She knew that he was trying to prepare her for what he saw as unpleasant reality, but she found the whole thing wonderfully romantic. To think of being able to make tea and toast yourself, any time you like, in a little room of your own, with no parents to worry about and no servants to grumble at you . . . It sounded heavenly. 'Do the owners of these places generally live there?'

'Sometimes. It's good if they do, because then they keep the place nice – although they poke their noses into your private life, too. But if the owner lives elsewhere, the building often gets run down: broken plumbing, peeling paint, leaking roofs, that sort of thing.'

It dawned on Margaret that she had an awful lot to learn, but nothing Harry said could dismay her: it was all too exhilarating. Before she could ask any more questions, the passengers and crew who had disembarked arrived back, and at the same moment Mother returned from the ladies' room, looking pale but beautiful. Margaret's elation was punctured. Recalling her conversation with Mother, she knew that the thrill of escaping with Harry would be mingled with heartache.

She did not normally eat a lot in the morning, but today she was ravenous. 'I'd like some bacon and eggs,' she said. 'Quite a lot, in fact.' She caught Harry's eye and realized that she was hungry because she had been making love to him all night. She smothered a grin. He read her mind and looked away hastily.

The plane took off a few minutes later. Margaret found it no less exciting even though this was the third time she had experienced it, but she no longer felt afraid.

She mulled over her conversation with Harry. He wanted to go to Boston with her! Although he was so handsome and charming, and must have had lots of chances with girls just like herself, he seemed to have fallen for her in a special way. It was terribly sudden, but he was being very sensible: not making extravagant vows, but ready to do just about anything to stay with her.

That commitment erased all doubt from her mind. Until now she had not allowed herself to think of a future with him, but suddenly she felt completely confident in him. She was going to have everything she wanted: freedom, independence and love.

As soon as the plane levelled out they were invited to help themselves from the breakfast buffet, and Margaret did so with alacrity. They all had strawberries and cream, except for Percy who preferred cornflakes. Father had champagne with his strawberries. Margaret also took hot rolls and butter.

As Margaret was about to return to the compartment she caught the eye of Nancy Lenehan, who was hovering over the hot porridge. Nancy was as trim and smart as ever, with a navy silk blouse in place of the grey one she had worn yesterday. She beckoned to Margaret and said in a low voice, 'I got a very important phone call in Botwood. I'm going to win today. You can take it that you have a job.'

Margaret beamed with pleasure. 'Oh, thank you!'

Nancy put a small white business card on Margaret's bread plate. 'Just call me when you're ready.'

'I will! In just a few days! Thank you!'

Nancy put a finger to her lips and winked.

Margaret returned to her compartment elated. She hoped Father had not seen the business card: she did not want him asking questions. Fortunately he was too intent on his food to notice anything else.

But as she ate, she realized that he had to be told sooner or later. Mother had begged her to avoid a confrontation, but it could not be done. She had tried to sneak away last time, and it had not worked. This time she had to announce openly that she was leaving, so that the world would know. There must be no secret about it, no excuse to call the police. She must make it clear to him that she had a place to go and friends to support her.

And this plane was surely the place to confront him. Elizabeth had done it on a train and that had worked because he had been obliged to behave himself. Later, in their hotel rooms, he could do anything he liked.

When should she tell him? Sooner rather than later:

he would be in his best mood of the day after breakfast, full of champagne and food. Later, as the day wore on and he had a cocktail or two and some wine, he would become more irascible.

Percy stood up and said, 'I'm going to get some more cornflakes.'

'Sit down,' Father said. 'There's bacon coming. You've had enough of that rubbish.' For some reason he was against cornflakes.

'I'm still hungry,' Percy said, and to Margaret's astonishment he went out.

Father was dumbfounded. Percy had never openly defied him. Mother just stared. Everyone waited for Percy to return. He came back with a bowl full of cornflakes. They all watched. He sat down and began to eat.

Father said, 'I told you not to take more of those.'

Percy said, 'It's not your stomach.' He continued to eat.

Father looked as if he was about to get up, but at that moment Nicky came in from the galley and handed him a plate of sausages, bacon and poached eggs. For a second Margaret thought Father might throw the plate at Percy; but he was too hungry. He picked up the knife and fork and said, 'Bring me some English mustard.'

'I'm afraid we don't carry mustard, sir.'

'No mustard?' Father said furiously. 'How can I eat sausages without mustard?'

Nicky looked scared. 'I'm sorry, sir – no one has ever asked before. I'll make sure we have some on the next flight.'

'That's not much use to me now, is it?'

'I guess not. I'm sorry.'

Father grunted and began to eat. He had taken out his anger on the steward, and Percy had got away with it. Margaret was amazed. This had never happened before.

Nicky brought her bacon and eggs and she tucked in heartily. Could it really be that Father was softening at last? The end of his political hopes, the beginning of the war, his exile, and the rebellion of his elder daughter might have combined to crush his ego and weaken his will.

There would never be a better moment to tell him.

She finished her breakfast, waited for the others to finish theirs. Then she waited for the steward to take away the plates; then she waited while Father got more coffee. Finally there was nothing left to wait for.

She moved to the middle seat of the divan, next to Mother and almost opposite Father. She took a deep breath and began. 'I've got something to tell you, Father, and I hope you won't be cross.'

Mother murmured, 'Oh, no . . .'

Father said, 'What now?'

'I'm nineteen years old and I've never done a stroke of work in my life. It's time I began.'

Mother said, 'For heaven's sake, why?'

'I would like to be independent.'

Mother said, 'There are millions of girls working in factories and offices who would give their eyes to be in your position.'

'I know that, Mother.' Margaret also knew that

Mother was arguing to keep Father out of it. However, it would not work for long.

Mother surprised her by capitulating almost immediately. 'Well, I suppose if you're determined to do it, your grandfather may be able to get you a place with someone he knows—'

'I already have a job.'

That took her by surprise. 'In America? How can you?'

Margaret decided not to tell them about Nancy Lenehan: they might talk to her and try to spoil everything. 'It's all arranged,' she said blandly.

'What sort of a job?'

'An assistant in the sales department of a shoe factory.'

'Oh, for goodness' sake, don't be ridiculous.'

Margaret bit her lip. Why did Mother have to be so scornful? 'It's not ridiculous. I'm rather proud of myself. I got a job, all on my own, without help from you or Father or Grandfather, just on my merits.' Perhaps that was not exactly the way it happened but Margaret was becoming defensive.

'Where is this factory?' Mother said.

Father spoke for the first time. 'She can't work in a factory, and that's that.'

Margaret said, 'I'll be working in the sales office, not the factory. And it's in Boston.'

'That settles it, then,' Mother said. 'You'll be living in Stamford, not Boston.'

'No, Mother, I won't. I'll be living in Boston.'

Mother opened her mouth to speak, then closed it

again, understanding at last that she was confronted with something she could not easily dismiss. She was silent for a moment, then she said, 'What are you telling us?'

'Just that I'm going to leave you and go to Boston, and live in lodgings and go to work.'

'Oh, this is too stupid.'

Margaret flared, 'Don't be so *dismissive.*' Mother flinched at her angry tone, and Margaret immediately regretted it. She said more quietly, 'I'm only doing what most girls of my age do.'

'Girls of your age, perhaps, but not girls of your class.'

'Why should that make any difference?'

'Because there's no point in your working at a silly job for five dollars a week and living in an apartment that costs your father a hundred dollars a month.'

'I don't want Father to pay for my apartment.'

'Then where will you live?'

'I've told you, in lodgings.'

'In squalor! But what is the point?'

'I shall save money until I've got enough for a ticket home, then I'll go back and join the ATS.'

Father spoke again. 'You've no idea what you're talking about.'

Margaret was stung. 'What don't I know, Father?'

Mother, trying to interrupt, said, 'No, don't—'

Margaret overrode her. 'I know I shall have to run errands and make coffee and answer the phone in the office. I know I shall live in a single room with a gas ring, and share the bathroom with other lodgers. I know I shan't like being poor – but I shall love being free.'

'You don't know anything,' he said scornfully. 'Free? You? You'll be like a pet rabbit released in a kennel. I'll tell you what you don't know, my girl: you don't know that you've been pampered and spoiled all your life. You've never even been to school—'

The injustice of that brought tears to her eyes and provoked her into a rejoinder. 'I wanted to go to school,' she protested. 'You wouldn't let me!'

He ignored the interruption. 'You've had your clothes washed and your food prepared, you've been chauffeured everywhere you ever wanted to go, you've had children brought to the house to play with you, and you've never given a thought to how all of it was provided—'

'But I have!'

'And now you want to live on your own! You don't know the price of a loaf of bread, do you?'

'I'll soon find out—'

'You don't know how to wash your own underwear. You've never ridden on a bus. You've never slept in a house alone. You don't know how to set an alarm clock, bait a mousetrap, wash dishes, boil an egg – could you boil an egg? Do you know how?'

'Whose fault is it if I don't?' Margaret said tearfully.

He pressed on remorselessly, his face a mask of contempt and anger. 'What use will you be in an office? You can't make the tea – you don't know how! You've never seen a filing cabinet. You've never had to stay in one place from nine in the morning until five in the afternoon. You'll get bored and wander off. You won't last a week.'

He was giving expression to Margaret's own secret worries, and that was why she was getting so upset. In her heart she was terrified that he might be right: she *would* be hopeless at living alone, she *would* get fired from her job. His mercilessly derisive voice confidently predicting that her worst fears would come true was destroying her dream like the sea washing away a sandcastle. She cried openly, tears streaming down her face.

She heard Harry say, 'This is too much—'

'Let him go on,' she said. This was one battle Harry could not fight for her: it was between her and Father.

Red in the face, wagging his finger, speaking more and more loudly, Father raved on. 'Boston isn't like Oxenford village, you know. People don't help one another there. You'll fall ill and get poisoned by half-breed doctors. You'll be robbed by Jew landlords and raped by street niggers. And as for your joining the army . . .!'

'Thousands of girls have joined the ATS,' Margaret said, but her voice was a feeble whisper.

'Not girls like you,' he said. 'Tough girls, perhaps, who are used to getting up early in the morning and scrubbing floors, but not pampered débutantes. And God forbid that you should find yourself in any kind of danger – you'd turn to jelly!'

She remembered how hopeless she had been in the blackout – scared and helpless and panicked – and she burned with shame. He was right, she had turned to jelly. But she would not always be frightened and defenceless. He had done his utmost to make her powerless and dependent, but she was fiercely determined to be her own person, and she kept that flame of hope flickering even as she cringed under his onslaught.

He pointed his finger at her and his eyes bulged so much they looked as if they would burst. 'You won't last a week in an office, and you wouldn't last a day in the ATS,' he said malevolently. 'You're just too soft.' He sat back, looking self-satisfied.

Harry came and sat beside Margaret. Taking out a crisp linen handkerchief, he dabbed her wet cheeks gently.

Father said, 'And as for you, young fellow-me-lad—'

Harry got up out of his seat in a flash and rounded on Father. Margaret gasped, thinking there was going to be a fight. Harry said, 'Don't dare to speak to me that way. I'm not a girl, I'm a grown man, and if you insult me I'll punch your fat head.'

Father subsided into silence.

Harry turned his back on Father and sat down beside Margaret again.

Margaret was upset but in her heart she felt a sense of triumph. She had told him that she was leaving. He had raged and jeered, and he had reduced her to tears, but he had not changed her mind: she was still going to leave.

All the same, he had succeeded in fostering a doubt. She had already been worried that she might not have the courage to go through with her plans, might be paralysed with anxiety at the last minute. He had inflamed that doubt with his mockery and derision. She had never done anything courageous in her entire life: could she manage it now? Yes, I will, she thought. I'm not too soft, and I'll prove it.

He had discouraged her, but he had failed to make her change course. However, he might not have given up yet. She looked over Harry's shoulder. Father was staring out of the window with a malevolent face. Elizabeth had defied him but he had banished her, and she might never see her family again.

What awful revenge was he planning for Margaret?

CHAPTER TWENTY-THREE

Diana Lovesey was thinking mournfully that true love did not last long.

When Mervyn first fell for her, he had delighted in catering to her every desire, the more capricious the better. At a moment's notice he was ready to drive to Blackpool for a stick of rock, take an afternoon off and go to the cinema, or drop everything and fly to Paris. He was happy to visit every shop in Manchester looking for a cashmere scarf in just the right shade of blue-green, leave a concert half-way through because she was bored, or get up at five in the morning and go for breakfast at a working-men's café. But this attitude had not lasted long after the wedding. He rarely denied her anything, but he soon ceased to take pleasure in gratifying her whims. Delight turned to tolerance and then impatience, and sometimes, towards the end, contempt.

Now she was wondering whether her relationship with Mark would follow the same pattern.

All summer he had been her slave, but now, within days of their running away together, they had had a row. On the second night of their elopement they had been so mad at one another that they had slept apart!

In the middle of the night, when the storm broke and the plane bucked and tossed like a wild horse, Diana had been so frightened that she almost swallowed her pride and went to Mark's bunk; but that would have been too humiliating, so she had just lain still, thinking she was going to die. She had hoped he would come to her, but he had been just as proud, and that made her madder still.

This morning they had hardly spoken. She had woken up just as the plane was coming down at Botwood, and when she got up, Mark had already gone ashore. Now they sat opposite one another in the aisle seats of No. 4 compartment, pretending to eat breakfast. Diana toyed with some strawberries and Mark was breaking up a bread roll without eating it.

She was no longer sure why it had made her so angry to learn that Mervyn was sharing the honeymoon suite with Nancy Lenehan. She just thought Mark should have sympathized with her and supported her. Instead, he had questioned her right to feel that way and implied that she must still be in love with Mervyn. How could Mark say that, when she had given up everything to run away with him?

She looked around. On her right, Princess Lavinia and Lulu Bell were carrying on a desultory conversation. Neither had slept at all because of the storm, and both looked exhausted. To her left, across the aisle, the FBI man, Ollis Field, and his prisoner, Frankie Gordino, ate in silence. Gordino's foot was handcuffed to his seat. Everyone seemed tired and rather grumpy. It had been a long night.

Davy the steward came and took away the breakfast plates. Princess Lavinia complained that her poached eggs had been too soft and her bacon overdone. Davy offered coffee. Diana did not take any.

She caught Mark's eye and tried to smile. He glared at her. She said, 'You haven't spoken to me all morning.'

'Because you seem to be more interested in Mervyn than me!' he said.

Suddenly she felt contrite. Maybe he had a right to feel jealous. 'I'm sorry, Mark,' she blurted out. 'You're the only man I'm interested in, truly.'

He reached out and took her hand. 'Do you mean it?'

'Yes, I do. I feel such a fool. I've behaved so badly.'

He stroked the back of her hand. 'You see . . .' He looked into her eyes, and to her surprise she saw that he was close to tears. 'You see, I'm terrified you'll leave me.'

She had not been expecting that. She was quite shocked. It had never occurred to her that he was frightened of losing her.

He went on, 'You're so lovely, so desirable, you could have any man, and it's hard to believe you want me. I'm scared you'll realize your mistake and change your mind.'

She was touched. 'You're the most lovable man in the world, that's why I fell for you.'

'You really don't care for Mervyn?'

She hesitated, only for a moment, but it was enough.

Mark's face changed again, and he said bitterly, 'You do care for him.'

How could she explain? She was no longer in love with Mervyn, but he still had some kind of power over her. 'It's not what you think,' she said desperately.

Mark withdrew his hand. 'Then set me straight. Tell me how it is.'

At that moment Mervyn entered the compartment.

He looked around, located Diana, and said, 'There you are.'

She immediately felt nervous. What did he want? Was he angry? She hoped he would not make a scene.

She looked at Mark. His face was pale and tense. He took a deep breath and said, 'Look here, Lovesey – we don't want another row, so maybe you should just get out of here.'

Mervyn ignored him and spoke to Diana. 'We've got to talk about this.'

She studied him warily. His idea of a conversation could be one-sided: a 'talk' sometimes turned out to be a harangue. However, he did not look aggressive. He was trying to keep his face expressionless, but she had a notion he was feeling sheepish. That made her curious. Cautiously she said, 'I don't want any fuss.'

'No fuss, I promise.'

'All right, then.'

Mervyn sat down beside her. Looking at Mark, he said, 'Would you mind leaving us alone for a few minutes?'

'Hell, yes!' Mark said vociferously.

They both looked at her. She would have to decide. On balance she would have liked to be alone with Mervyn, but if she said that she would hurt Mark, she knew. She hesitated, afraid to side with one or the other. Finally she thought, I've left Mervyn, and I'm with Mark; I should take his side. With her heart pounding, she said, 'Say your piece, Mervyn. If you can't say it in front of Mark, I don't want to hear it.'

He looked shocked. 'All right, all right,' he said irritably; then he composed himself and became mild again. 'I've been thinking about some of the things you said. About me. How I became cold towards you. How miserable you've been.'

He paused. Diana said nothing. This was not like Mervyn. What was coming?

'I want to say that I'm really sorry.'

She was astonished. He meant it, she could tell. What had brought about this change?

He went on, 'I wanted to make you happy. When we were first together, that was all I wanted to do. I never wanted you to be miserable. It's wrong that you should be unhappy. You deserve happiness because you give it. You make people smile just by walking into a room.'

Tears came to her eyes. She knew it was true, people did love to look at her.

'It's a sin to make you sad,' Mervyn said. 'I shan't do it any more.'

Was he going to promise to be good? she wondered with a sudden stab of fear. Would he beg her to come back to him? She did not want him even to ask. 'I'm not coming back to you,' she said anxiously.

He took no notice of that. 'Does Mark make you happy?' he said.

She nodded.

'Will he be good to you?'

'Yes, I know he will.'

Mark said, 'Don't talk about me as if I'm not here!'

Diana reached across and took Mark's hand. 'We love each other,' she said to Mervyn.

'Aye.' For the first time, the hint of a sneer appeared on his face, but it passed quickly. 'Aye, I think you do.'

Was he going soft? This was not like him at all. How much did the widow have to do with the transformation? 'Did Mrs Lenehan tell you to come and speak to me?' Diana said suspiciously.

'No – but she knows what I'm going to say.'

Mark said, 'I wish you'd hurry up and say it.'

Mervyn looked scornful. 'Don't push it, lad – Diana's still my wife.'

Mark stood his ground. 'Forget it,' he said. 'You have no claim on her, so don't try to make one. And don't call me lad, Grandpa.'

Diana said, 'Don't start that. Mervyn, if you've got something to say, come out with it, and stop trying to throw your weight around.'

'All right, all right. It's just this.' He took a deep breath. 'I'm not going to stand in your way. I've asked you to come back to me and you've turned me down. If you think this chap can succeed where I've failed, and make you happy, then good luck to you both. I wish you well.' He paused, and looked from one to the other of them. 'That's it.'

There was a moment's silence. Mark was about to say something, but Diana got in first. 'You bloody hypocrite!' she said. She had seen in a flash what was really going on in Mervyn's mind, and she surprised herself with the fury of her reaction. 'How dare you?' she spat.

He was startled. 'What? Why . . .?'

'What rubbish, saying you won't stand in our way. Don't you condescend to wish us luck, as if you were making some kind of sacrifice. I know you only too damn well, Mervyn Lovesey. The only time you ever give something up is when you don't want it any more!' She could see that everyone in the compartment was listening avidly, but she was too riled to care. 'I know what you're up to. You had it off with that widow last night, didn't you?'

'No!'

'No?' She watched him carefully. She thought he was probably telling the truth. 'It was close, though, wasn't it?' she said; and she could see by his face that she had guessed right this time. 'You've fallen for her, and she likes you, and now you don't want me any more – that's the truth of the matter, isn't it? Now admit it!'

'I'll not admit any such thing—'

'Because you haven't got the courage to be honest. But I know the truth and everyone else on the plane suspects it. I'm disappointed in you, Mervyn. I thought you had more guts.'

'Guts!' That stung him.

'That's right. But instead you had to make up a pitiful story about not standing in our way. Well, you *have* gone soft – soft in the head. I wasn't born yesterday and you can't fool me so easily!'

'All right, all right,' he said, holding up his hands in a defensive gesture. 'I've made a peace offering and you've spurned it. Please yourself.' He stood up. 'From the way you talk, anybody would think I was the one who had run off with a lover.' He went to the doorway. 'Let me know when you get wed. I'll send you a fish slice.' He went out.

'Well!' Diana's blood was still up. 'The nerve of the man!' She looked around at the other passengers. Princess Lavinia looked away haughtily, Lulu Bell grinned, Ollis Field frowned disapprovingly and Frankie Gordino said, 'Attagirl!'

Finally she looked at Mark, wondering what he had thought of Mervyn's performance and her outburst. To her surprise he was grinning broadly. His smile was infectious, and she found herself grinning back. 'What's so funny?' she said with a giggle.

'You were magnificent,' he said. 'I'm proud of you. And I'm pleased.'

'Why pleased?'

'You just stood up to Mervyn for the first time in your life.'

Was that true? She thought it was. 'I suppose I did.'

'You're not scared of him any more, are you?'

She thought about it. 'You're right, I'm not.'

'Do you know what that means?'

'It means I'm not scared of him.'

'It means more than that. It means you don't love him any more.'

'Does it?' she said thoughtfully. She had been telling herself that she stopped loving Mervyn ages ago, but now she looked into her heart and saw that it was not so. All summer, even while she was deceiving him, she had remained in his thrall. He had retained some kind of hold over her, even after she left him, and on the plane she had been full of remorse and had thought of going back to him. But not any longer.

Mark said, 'How would you feel if he went off with the widow?'

Without thinking, she said, 'Why should I care?'

'See?'

She laughed. 'You're right,' she said. 'It's over at last.'

CHAPTER TWENTY-FOUR

As the Clipper began its descent to Shediac Bay in the St Lawrence Gulf, Harry was having second thoughts about stealing Lady Oxenford's jewels.

His will had been weakened by Margaret. Just to sleep with her in a bed at the Waldorf Hotel, and wake up and order breakfast from room service, was worth more than jewels. But he was also looking forward to going to Boston with her, and living in lodgings; helping her to become independent, and getting to know her really well. Her excitement was infectious, and he shared her thrilled anticipation of their simple life together.

But all that would change if he robbed her mother.

Shediac was the last stop before New York. He had to make up his mind quickly. This would be his last chance to get into the hold.

He wondered again if he could find a way to have Margaret and the jewels both. First of all, would she ever know that he had stolen them? Lady Oxenford would discover the loss when she opened her trunk, presumably at the Waldorf. But no one would know whether the jewels had been taken on the plane, or before, or since. Margaret knew Harry was a thief, so she would certainly suspect him; but if he denied it, would she believe him? She might.

Then what? They would live in poverty in Boston while he had a hundred thousand dollars in the bank! But that would not be for long. She would find some way of returning to England and joining the women's army, and he would go to Canada and become a fighter pilot. The war might last a year or two, maybe longer. When it was over, he would take his money out of the bank and buy that country house; and perhaps Margaret would come and live there with him . . . and then she would want to know where the money had come from.

Whatever happened, sooner or later he would have to tell her.

But later might be better than sooner.

He was going to have to give her some excuse for staying on the plane at Shediac. He could not tell her he felt ill, for then she would want to stay on board with him, and that would spoil everything. He had to make sure she went ashore and left him alone.

He glanced at her across the aisle. At that moment she was fastening her seat belt, pulling her stomach in. In a vivid flash of imagination he saw her sitting there naked, in the same pose, with her bare breasts outlined by the light from the low windows, a tuft of chestnut hair peeping out from between her thighs, and her long legs stretched across the floor. Would he not be a fool, he thought, to risk losing her for the sake of a handful of rubies?

But it was not a handful of rubies, it was the Delhi

Suite, worth a hundred grand, enough to turn Harry into what he had always wanted to be, a gentleman of leisure.

Nevertheless he toyed with the idea of telling her now. 'I'm going to steal your mother's jewels, I hope you don't mind?' She might say, 'Good idea, the old cow never did anything to deserve them.' No, that would not be Margaret's reaction. She thought herself radical, and she believed in redistribution of wealth, but that was all theoretical: she would be shocked to the core if he actually dispossessed her family of some of their riches. She would take it like a body blow, and it would change her feelings about him.

She caught his eye and smiled.

He smiled back, guiltily, then looked out of the window.

The plane was coming down to a horseshoe-shaped bay with a scattering of villages along its edge. Behind the villages was farmland. As they came closer, Harry made out a railway line snaking through farms to a long pier. Close to the pier were moored several vessels of different sizes and a small seaplane. To the east of the pier were miles of sandy beaches, with a few large summer cottages dotted among the dunes. Harry thought how nice it would be to have a summer house on the edge of the beach in a place like this. Well, if that's what I want, that's what I'll have, he said to himself; I'm going to be rich!

The plane splashed down smoothly. Harry felt less tension: he was an experienced air traveller now.

'What time is it, Percy?' he asked.

'Eleven o'clock, local time. We're running an hour late.'

'And how long do we stay here?'

'One hour.'

At Shediac a new method of docking was in operation. The passengers were not landed by launch. Instead, a vessel that looked like a lobster boat came out and towed the plane in. Hawsers were attached to both ends of the plane and it was winched in to a floating dock connected to the pier by a gangway.

This arrangement solved a problem for Harry. At previous stops, where the passengers had been landed by launch, there had been only one chance to go ashore. Harry had consequently been trying to think of some excuse for staying on board throughout this stopover without letting Margaret stay with him. Now, however, he could let Margaret go ashore and tell her he would follow in a few minutes, and she was less likely to insist on staying with him.

A steward opened the door and the passengers started putting on their coats and hats. All the Oxenfords got up. So did Clive Membury, who had hardly spoken a word all through the long flight – except, Harry now recalled, for one rather intense conversation with Baron Gabon. He wondered again what they had been talking about. Impatiently, he brushed the thought aside and concentrated on his own problems. As the Oxenfords were going out, Harry whispered to Margaret, 'I'll catch you up.' Then he went into the men's room.

He combed his hair and washed his hands, just to

have something to do. The window had been broken in the night, somehow, and there was now a solid screen fixed to the frame. He heard the crew come down the stairs from the flight deck and pass the door. He checked his watch and decided to wait another two minutes.

He guessed almost everyone would get off. A lot of them had been too sleepy at Botwood, but by now they wanted to stretch their legs and get some fresh air. Ollis Field and his prisoner would stay on board, as always. It was odd that Membury went ashore, though, if he was supposed to keep an eye on Frankie. Harry was still intrigued by the man in the wine-red waistcoat.

The cleaners would be coming aboard almost immediately. He listened hard: he could hear no sound from the other side of the door. He cracked it an inch and looked out. All was clear. Cautiously, he stepped out.

The kitchen opposite was empty. He glanced into No. 2 compartment: empty. Looking towards the lounge, he saw the back of a woman with a broom. Without further hesitation he went up the staircase.

He trod lightly, not wanting to advertise his approach. At the turn of the stairs he paused and scrutinized as much of the floor of the flight cabin as he could see. No one was there. He was about to go on when a pair of uniformed legs came into view, walking across the carpet away from him. He ducked back around the corner, then peeped out. It was the assistant engineer, Mickey Finn, the one who had caught him last time. The man paused at the engineer's station and turned. Harry pulled his head back again, wondering where the crewman was headed. Would he come down the stairs? Harry listened hard. The footsteps went across the flight deck and became silent. Last time, Harry recalled, he had seen Mickey in the bow compartment, doing something with the anchor. Was the same thing happening now? He had to take a chance on it.

He went on up silently.

As soon as he was high enough he looked forward. His guess appeared to have been right: the hatch was open and Mickey was nowhere to be seen. Harry did not stop to look more closely, but hurried across the flight deck and passed quickly through the door at the rear end into the hold area. He closed the door softly behind him and breathed again.

Last time he had searched the starboard hold. This time he went into the port side.

He knew immediately that he was in luck. In the middle of the hold was a huge steamer trunk in green-and-gold leather with bright brass studs. He felt sure it belonged to Lady Oxenford. He checked the tag: there was no name, but the address was The Manor, Oxenford, Berkshire.

'Bingo,' he said softly.

It was secured by one simple lock which he snapped with the blade of his penknife.

As well as the lock, it had six brass clasps which were fastened without keys. He undid them all.

The trunk was designed to be used as a wardrobe in a stateroom on board a liner. Harry stood it on end and opened it up. It divided into two spacious cupboards. On one side was a hanging rail with dresses and coats, and a small shoe compartment at the bottom. The other contained six drawers.

Harry went through the drawers first. They were made of light wood covered in leather, and were lined with velvet. Lady Oxenford had silk blouses, cashmere sweaters, lace underwear and crocodile belts.

On the other side, the top of the trunk lifted like a lid, and the hanging rail slid out to make it easier to get at the dresses. Harry ran his hands up and down each garment and felt all around the sides of the trunk.

Finally he opened the shoe box. There was nothing in it but shoes.

He was crestfallen. He had been so sure that she would have her jewels with her; but maybe there was a flaw in his reasoning.

It was too soon to give up hope.

His first inclination was to look for the rest of the Oxenford family's luggage, but he thought again. If I were going to transport priceless jewellery in checked baggage, he thought, I would try to conceal them somehow. And it would be easier to make a hiding-place in a big trunk than in a regular suitcase.

He decided to look again.

He started with the hanging compartment. He put one arm inside the trunk and one outside and tried to gauge the thickness of the sides: if they seemed abnormal there might be a hidden compartment. But he found nothing unusual. Turning to the other side, he pulled all the drawers completely out—

And found the hiding-place.

His heart beat faster.

A large manila envelope and a leather wallet were taped to the back of the trunk.

'Amateurs,' he said, shaking his head.

With growing excitement he began detaching the tapes. The first item to come loose was the envelope. It felt as if it contained nothing but a wad of papers, but Harry ripped it open anyway. Inside were about fifty sheets of heavy paper with elaborate printing on one side. It took him a while to figure out what they were, but eventually he decided they were bearer bonds, each worth a hundred thousand dollars.

Fifty of those added up to five million dollars, which was a million pounds.

Harry sat staring at the bonds. A million pounds. It was almost too much to take in.

Harry knew why they were there. The British government had brought in emergency exchange control regulations to stop money leaving the country. Oxenford was smuggling his bonds out, which was a criminal offence, of course.

He's just as much of a crook as I am, Harry thought wryly.

Harry had never stolen bonds. Would he be able to cash them? They were payable to the bearer: that was stated plainly on the front of each certificate. But they were also individually numbered, so that they could be identified. Would Oxenford report them stolen? That might mean admitting he had smuggled them out of England. But he could probably think of a lie to cover that.

It was too dangerous. Harry had no experience in the field. If he tried to cash the bonds he would be caught. Reluctantly, he put them aside.

The other hidden item was a tan leather folder like a man's pocketbook but somewhat larger. Harry detached it.

It looked like a jewellery wallet.

The soft leather was fastened with a zip. He opened it out.

There, lying on the black velvet lining, was the Delhi Suite.

It seemed to glow in the gloom of the baggage hold like stained glass in a cathedral. The profound red of the rubies alternated with the rainbow sparkle of the diamonds. The stones were huge, perfectly matched, and exquisitely cut, each one set on a gold base and surrounded by delicate gold petals. Harry was awestruck.

He picked up the necklace solemnly and let the gems run through his fingers like coloured water. How strange, he thought bemusedly, that something should look so warm and feel so cold. It was the most beautiful piece of jewellery he had ever handled, perhaps the most beautiful ever made.

And it would change his life.

After a minute or two he set down the necklace and

examined the rest of the suite. The bracelet was like the necklace, with alternating rubies and diamonds, although the stones were proportionately smaller. The earrings were particularly dainty: each had a ruby stud with a drop of alternating small diamonds and rubies on a gold chain, each stone on a tiny version of the same gold petal setting.

Harry imagined the suite on Margaret. The red and gold would look stunning on her pale skin. I'd like to see her wearing nothing but this, he thought, and the vision gave him an erection.

He was not sure how long he had sat on the floor gazing at the precious stones when he heard someone coming.

The first thought that flashed through his mind was that it was the assistant engineer again; but the footsteps sounded different: intrusive, aggressive, authoritarian . . . official.

Suddenly he was taut with fear, his stomach tight, his teeth clenched, his fists balled.

The steps came rapidly closer. In a sudden frenzy of activity Harry replaced the drawers, threw in the envelope containing the bonds, and closed up the trunk. He was stuffing the Delhi Suite into his pocket when the door to the hold opened.

He ducked behind the trunk.

There was a long moment of silence. He had a dreadful feeling he had not got down fast enough, and the guy had seen him. He heard moderately hard breathing, like that of a fat man who has hurried up stairs. Was the guy going to come right inside and look around, or what? Harry held his breath. The door closed.

Had the man gone? Harry listened hard. He could no longer hear breathing. He stood up slowly and looked out. The man had gone.

He sighed with relief.

But what was going on?

He had a notion those heavy footsteps and hard breathing belonged to a policeman. Or maybe a customs officer? Perhaps this had only been a routine check.

He went to the door and cracked it. He could hear muffled voices from way off in the flight cabin, but there seemed to be no one right outside. He stepped out and stood by the door to the flight cabin. It was ajar, and he could hear two male voices.

'The guy ain't on the plane.'

'He has to be. He didn't get off.'

The accents were a muted American that Harry recognized as Canadian. But who were they talking about?

'Maybe he sneaked off after everyone else.'

'So where has he gone? He's nowhere around.'

Had Frankie Gordino made his escape? Harry wondered.

'Who is he, anyway?'

'They say he's an "associate" of this hoodlum they got on the plane.'

So Gordino himself had not got away, but one of his gang had been on board, had been discovered, and had made his escape. Which of the respectable-looking passengers could it have been?

'It ain't a crime to be an associate, is it?'

'No, but he's travelling on a false passport.'

A chill struck Harry. He was travelling on a false passport himself. Surely they could not be looking for him?

'Well, what do we do now?' he heard.

'Report back to Sergeant Morris.'

After a moment the scary thought dawned on Harry that he *could* be the one they were looking for. If the police had learned, or guessed, that someone on board was going to try to rescue Gordino, they would naturally run a check on the passenger list – and they would soon discover that Harry Vandenpost had reported his passport stolen in London two years ago; and then they would only have to call at his home to learn that he was not on the Pan American Clipper but sitting in the kitchen eating his cornflakes and reading the morning paper, or something. Knowing that Harry was an impostor, they would naturally assume he was the one who was going to try to rescue Gordino.

No, he told himself, don't jump to conclusions. There could be some other explanation.

A third voice joined in the conversation. 'Who are you guys looking for?' It sounded like the assistant engineer, Mickey Finn.

'Guy's using the name of Harry Vandenpost, but he ain't him.'

That settled it. Harry felt stunned with shock. He had been found out. The vision of the country house with the tennis court faded like an ageing photograph, and instead he saw blacked-out London, a court, a prison cell, and then, eventually, an army barracks. This was the worst luck he had ever heard of.

The engineer was saying, 'You know, I found him sneaking around here, while we were at Botwood.'

'Well, he ain't up here now.'

'Are you sure?'

Shut up, Mickey, Harry thought.

'We looked all over.'

'Did you check the mechanics' stations?'

'Where are they?'

'In the wings.'

'Yeah, we looked in the wings.'

'But did you crawl along? There are places to hide in there that you couldn't see from here in the cabin.'

'We better look again.'

These two policemen sounded kind of dumb, Harry thought. He doubted whether their sergeant would trust them very far. If he had any sense he would order one more search of the plane. And next time they would surely look behind the steamer trunk. Where could Harry hide?

There were several little hiding-places, but the crew would know them all. A thorough search was bound to take in the bow compartment, the toilets, the wings, and the shallow void in the tail. Any other place Harry could find would surely be known to the crew.

He was stuck.

Could he leave? He might sneak off the plane and

get away along the beach. It was a slim chance, but better than giving himself up. But even if he could get out of this little village undetected, where could he go? He could talk his way out of anything in a city, but he had a feeling he was an awfully long way from any cities. In the countryside he was a dead loss. He needed crowds, alleyways, railway stations and shops. He had an idea that Canada was a pretty big country, most of it trees.

He would be all right if only he could get to New York.

But where could he hide in the meantime?

He heard the policemen come out of the wings. For safety he ducked back into the hold—

And found himself staring straight at the answer to his problem.

He could hide in Lady Oxenford's trunk.

Could he get inside? He thought so. It was about five feet high and two feet square: if it had been empty you could have got two people into it. It was not empty, of course: he would have to make room in it by taking out some of the clothes. Then what would he do with them? He could not leave them lying around. But he could cram them into his own half-empty suitcase.

He had to hurry.

He crawled over the piled luggage and grabbed his own case. Working feverishly, he opened it and stuffed Lady Oxenford's coats and dresses into it. He had to sit on the lid to close it again.

Now he could get into the trunk. He found he could

close it from the inside easily enough. Would he be able to breathe when it was shut? He would not be inside for long: it might get stuffy but he would live.

Would the cops notice if the clasps were undone? They might. Could he close them from inside? That looked difficult. He studied the problem for a long moment. If he made holes in the trunk near the clasps, he might be able to poke his knife through and manipulate the clasps through the holes. The same holes would bring him air, too.

He took out his penknife. The trunk was made of wood covered with leather. The dark green-brown leather was imprinted with a pattern of gold-coloured flowers. Like all penknives, his had a pointed implement for getting stones out of horses' hooves. He set the point in the middle of one of the flowers and pushed it in. It penetrated the leather easily enough, but the wood was harder. He worked it in and out. The wood was about a quarter of an inch thick, he guessed. It took a minute or two but eventually he got through.

He pulled the point out. Because of the pattern, the hole could hardly be seen.

He got inside the trunk. With relief he found that he could close and open the clasp from inside.

There were two clasps on top and three down the side. He went to work on the top ones first as they were most visible. He had just finished them when he heard footsteps again.

He got inside the trunk and closed it.

Somehow it was not so easy to close the clasps this

time. Standing with his legs bent he found it difficult to manoeuvre. But he managed it at last.

His position was painfully uncomfortable after a couple of minutes. He twisted and turned but got no relief. He would just have to suffer.

His own breathing sounded very loud. Noises from outside were muffled. However, he could hear footsteps outside the hold, probably because there was no carpet there and vibrations were transmitted through the deck. There were now at least three people out there, he guessed. He could not hear doors opening and closing but he suddenly felt a much nearer step and knew someone had come into the hold.

The voice came suddenly from right next to him. 'I don't see how the bastard got away from us.'

Don't look at the side clasps, please, Harry thought fearfully.

There was a knock on the top of the trunk. Harry stopped breathing. Maybe the guy just leaned his elbow on it, he thought.

Someone else spoke from a distance.

'No, he ain't on this plane,' the man replied. 'We've looked everywhere.'

The other party spoke again. Harry's knees hurt. For God's sake, he thought, go and chat somewhere else!

'Oh, we'll catch him all right. He ain't gonna walk a hundred and fifty miles to the border without somebody sees him.'

A hundred and fifty miles! It would take him a week to walk that far. He might hitch a ride, but in this wilderness he would surely be remembered.

There was no speech for a few seconds. At last he heard receding footsteps.

He waited a while, hearing nothing.

He took out his knife and poked it through one of the holes to undo the clasp.

This time it was harder still. His knees hurt so much that he could hardly stand, and would have fallen if there had been room. He became impatient, and poked the blade through the hole again and again. A panicky claustrophobia seized him and he thought, I'm going to suffocate in here! He tried to be calm. After a moment he was able to blank his mind to the pain while he carefully worked the blade through the hole so that it engaged the catch. He pushed the blade. It lifted the brass loop, then slipped. He gritted his teeth and tried again.

This time the catch came undone.

Slowly and painfully he repeated the process with the other catch.

At last he was able to push the two halves of the trunk apart and stand upright. The pain in his knees became excruciating as he straightened his legs, and he almost cried out; then it eased.

What was he going to do?

He could not get off the plane here. He was probably safe until they reached New York, but what then?

He would have to stay in hiding on the plane and then slip out at night.

He might get away with it. He had no alternative, anyway. The world would know that he had stolen Lady Oxenford's jewels. More importantly, Margaret would know. And he would not be around to talk to her about it.

The more he contemplated this possibility, the more he hated it.

He had known that stealing the Delhi Suite put his relationship with Margaret at risk, but he had always imagined that he would be around when she discovered what he had done, so that he could try to make it all right with her. Even so he had still been uncomfortable. Now, however, it might be days before he reached her; and if things went wrong, and he got arrested, it would be years.

He could guess what she would think. He had befriended her, made love to her, and promised to help her find a new home; and it had all been a sham, for he had stolen her mother's jewellery and left her high and dry. She would think the jewels had been all he wanted right from the start. She would be heart-broken, then she would come to hate and despise him.

The idea made him feel sick with misery.

Until this moment he had not fully realized what a difference Margaret had made to him. Her love for him was genuine. Everything else in his life had been faked: his accent, his manners, his clothes – his entire way of life was a disguise. But Margaret had fallen in love with the thief, the working-class boy with no father, the real Harry. It was the best thing that had ever happened to him. If he threw it away, his life would always be what it was now, a matter of pretending and dishonesty. But she had made him want something more. He still hoped for the country house with the tennis courts, but it would not please him unless she were there.

He sighed. Harry boy was not Harry boy any more. Perhaps he was becoming a man.

He opened Lady Oxenford's trunk. He took from his pocket the tan leather wallet containing the Delhi Suite.

He opened the wallet and took out the jewels once again. The rubies glowed like banked fires. I may never see anything like this again, he thought.

He replaced the jewels in their wallet. Then, with a heavy heart, he put the wallet back in Lady Oxenford's trunk.

CHAPTER TWENTY-FIVE

Nancy Lenehan sat on Shediac's long plank pier, at the shoreward end, outside the air terminal. This was a building like a seaside cottage, with flowers in window-boxes and sunshades over the windows; but a radio mast beside the house and an observation tower rising from its roof gave away its true function.

Mervyn Lovesey sat beside her in another striped canvas deck-chair. The water shushed against the pier in a soothing way, and Nancy closed her eyes. She had not slept much. A faint smile twitched the corners of her mouth as she recalled how she and Mervyn had misbehaved in the night. She was glad she had not gone all the way with him. It would have been too sudden. And now she had something to look forward to.

Shediac was a fishing village and a seaside resort. To the west of the pier was a sunlit bay, on which floated several lobster boats, some cabin cruisers and two planes, the Clipper and a little seaplane. To the east was a wide sandy beach that seemed to go on for miles, and most of the passengers from the Clipper were sitting among the dunes or strolling along the edge of the shore.

The peace of the scene was disturbed by two cars which screeched up the pier and disgorged seven or eight policemen. They went into the flight building in a hurry, and Nancy murmured to Mervyn, 'They looked like they were planning to arrest someone.'

He nodded and said, 'I wonder who?'

'Frankie Gordino, perhaps?'

'They can't – he's already arrested.'

They came out of the building a few moments later. Three went on board the Clipper, two set off along the beach and two followed the road. They looked as if they were searching for someone. When one of the Clipper's crew emerged, Nancy said, 'Who are the cops after?'

The man hesitated, as if he was not sure he should reveal anything; then he shrugged and said, 'The guy's calling himself Harry Vandenpost, but that's not his real name.'

Nancy frowned. 'That was the boy sitting with the Oxenford family.' She had an idea Margaret Oxenford was developing a crush on him.

Mervyn said, 'Aye. Did he get off the plane? I didn't see.'

'I'm not sure.'

'I thought he looked a bit of a wide boy.'

'Really?' Nancy had taken him for a young man from a good family. 'He's got beautiful manners.'

'Exactly.'

Nancy smothered a smile: it seemed characteristic that Mervyn would dislike men with beautiful manners.

'I think Margaret was quite interested in him. I hope she doesn't get hurt.'

'Her parents will be grateful for a narrow escape, I imagine.'

Nancy could not be happy for the parents. She and Mervyn had witnessed the crass behaviour of Lord Oxenford in the dining room of the Clipper. Such people deserved everything they got. However, Nancy felt sorry for Margaret if she had fallen for a bounder.

Mervyn said, 'I'm not normally the impulsive type, Nancy.'

She was suddenly alert.

He went on, 'I met you only a few hours ago, but I feel completely certain that I want to know you for the rest of my life.'

Nancy thought, You can't be *certain,* you idiot! But she was pleased all the same. She said nothing.

'I've been thinking about leaving you in New York and going back to Manchester, and I don't want to do it.'

Nancy smiled. This was just what she wanted him to say. She reached out and touched his hand. 'I'm so glad,' she said.

'Are you?' He leaned forward. 'The trouble is, soon it will be next to impossible to cross the Atlantic, for anyone other than the military.'

She nodded. The problem had occurred to her, too. She had not thought about it very hard, but she felt sure they would be able to find a solution if they were determined enough.

Mervyn went on, 'If we split up now, it may be years, literally, before we can see one another again. I can't accept that.'

'I feel the same.'

Mervyn said, 'So will you come back to England with me?'

Nancy stopped smiling. 'What?'

'Come back with me. Move into a hotel, if you like, or buy a house, or a flat – anything.'

Nancy felt resentment rise up inside her. She gritted her teeth and tried to stay calm. 'You're out of your mind,' she said dismissively. She looked away from him. She was bitterly disappointed.

He looked hurt and puzzled by her reaction. 'What's the matter?'

'I have a home, two sons and a multi-million-dollar business,' she said. 'You're asking me to leave them all to move into a hotel in Manchester?'

'Not if you don't want to!' he said indignantly. 'Live with me, if that's what you want.'

'I'm a respectable widow with a place in society – I'm not going to live like a kept floozie!'

'Look, I think we'll get married, I'm sure we will, but I don't imagine you're ready to commit yourself to that, are you, after just a few hours?'

'That's not the point, Mervyn,' she said, although in a way it was. 'I don't care what arrangements you envisage, I just resent the casual assumption that I'm going to give up everything and follow you to England.'

'But how else could we be together?'

'Why didn't you ask that question, instead of assuming the answer?'

'Because there is only one answer.'

'There are three. I could move to England; you could move to America; or we could both move, to somewhere like Bermuda.'

He was nonplussed. 'But my country is at war. I have to join the fight. I may be too old for active service but the air force is going to need propellers by the thousand, and I know more about making propellers than anyone else in the country. They need me.'

Everything he said seemed to make it worse. 'Why do you assume that my country doesn't need me?' she said. 'I make boots for soldiers, and when the US gets into this war there are going to be a lot more soldiers needing good boots.'

'But I've got a business in Manchester.'

'And I've got a business in Boston – a much bigger one, by the way.'

'It's not the same for a woman!'

'Of course it's the same, you fool!' she yelled.

She regretted the word *fool* right away. A look of stony fury settled on his face: she had offended him mortally. He got up from his chair. She wanted to say something to stop him walking away in a snit, but she could not think of the right words, and a moment later he had gone.

'Damn,' she said bitterly. She was angry with him and furious with herself. She did not want to drive him away – she liked him! Years ago she had learned that nose-to-nose confrontation was not the right approach when dealing with men: they would accept aggression from one another but not from women. In business she had always tempered her combative spirit, softened her tone, and got her way by manipulating people, not quarrelling with them. Now, just for a moment, she had stupidly forgotten all that, and in consequence she had had a fight with the most attractive man she had come across in ten years.

I'm such a fool, she thought; I know he's proud, that's one of the things I like about him, it's part of his strength. He is tough, but he hasn't suppressed all his emotions the way tough men often do. Look at the way he followed that runaway wife half across the world. See how he stood up for the Jews when Lord Oxenford blew his top in the dining room. Remember how he kissed me . . .

The irony of it was that she felt very ready to think about a change in her life.

What Danny Riley had told her about her father had cast a new light over her entire history. She had always assumed that she and Peter quarrelled because he resented her being cleverer. But that kind of sibling rivalry normally faded away in adolescence: her own two boys, having fought like cat and dog for almost twenty years, were now the best of friends and fiercely loyal to one another. By contrast, the hostility between her and Peter had stayed alive into middle age, and she could now see that Pa was responsible.

Pa had told Nancy that she was to be his successor, and Peter would work under her; but he had told Peter the opposite. In consequence, both of them thought they were intended to run the company. But it went back farther than that. Pa had always refused to lay down clear rules or define areas of responsibility, she could now see. He would buy toys they had to share, then refuse to adjudicate the inevitable disputes. When they were old enough to drive he had bought a car for them both to use: they had fought over it for years.

Pa's strategy had worked for Nancy: it had made her strong-willed and smart. But Peter had ended up weak, sly and spiteful. And now the stronger of the two was about to take control of the company, in accordance with Pa's plan.

And that was what disturbed Nancy: it was all *in accordance with Pa's plan.* The knowledge that everything she did had been foreordained by someone else spoiled the taste of victory. Her whole life now seemed like a school assignment set by her father: she had got an 'A', but at forty she was too old to be at school. She had an angry wish to set her own goals and live her own life.

In fact, she had been in just the right mood to have an open-minded discussion with Mervyn about their future together. But he had offended her by assuming that she would drop everything and follow him half across the world, and instead of talking him round she had bawled him out.

She had not expected him to go down on his knees and propose, of course, but . . .

She realized that in her heart she felt he really *should* have proposed. She was not a Bohemian, after all; she was an American woman from a Catholic family, and if a man wanted a commitment from her there was only one kind of commitment he was entitled to ask for, and that was her hand in marriage. If he could not do that he should not ask for anything.

She sighed. It was all very well to be indignant, but she had driven him away. Perhaps the rift would not be permanent. She hoped so with all her heart. Now that she was in danger of losing Mervyn she understood how much she wanted him.

Her thoughts were interrupted by the arrival of another man she had once driven away: Nat Ridgeway.

He stood in front of her, took off his hat politely, and said, 'It seems you've defeated me – again.'

She studied him for a moment. He could never have started a company and built it up as Pa had built Black's Boots: he did not have either the vision or the drive. But he was very good at running a big organization: he was clever, hard-working and tough. 'If it's any consolation, Nat,' said Nancy, 'I know I made a mistake five years ago.'

'A business mistake, or a personal one?' he said, and there was an edge to his voice that betrayed underlying resentment.

'Business,' she said lightly. His departure had ended a romance that had hardly begun: she did not want to talk about that. 'Congratulations on your marriage,' she said. 'I saw a picture of your wife – she's very beautiful.' It was not true: she was attractive at best.

'Thank you,' he said. 'But to revert to business, I'm

rather surprised that you've resorted to blackmail to get what you want.'

'This is a takeover, not a tea-party. You said that to me yesterday.'

'*Touché.*' He hesitated. 'May I sit down?'

Suddenly she was impatient with formality. 'Hell, yes,' she said. 'We worked together for years, and for a few weeks we dated too; you don't have to ask permission to sit down, Nat.'

He smiled. 'Thanks.' He took Mervyn's deck-chair and moved it round so that he could look at her. 'I tried to take over Black's without your help. That was dumb, and I failed. I should have known better.'

'No argument here.' That sounded hostile, she realized. 'And no hard feelings, either.'

'I'm glad you said that – because I still want to buy your company.'

Nancy was taken aback. She saw that she had been in danger of underestimating him. Don't let your guard down! she told herself. 'What did you have in mind?'

'I'm going to try again,' he said. 'Of course, I'll have to make a better offer next time. But more important, I want you on my side – before and after the merger. I want to come to terms with you, and then I want you to become a director of General Textiles and sign a five-year contract.'

She had not expected this, and she did not know how she felt about it. To gain time she asked a question. 'A contract? To do what?'

'To run Black's Boots as a division of General Textiles.'

'I'd lose my independence – I'd be an employee.'

'Depending on how we structure the deal, you might be a shareholder. And while you're making money, you'll have all the independence you want – I don't interfere with profitable divisions. But if you lose money, then yes, you'll forfeit your independence. I fire failures.' He shook his head. 'But you won't fail.'

Nancy's instinct was to turn him down. No matter how he sugared the pill, he still wanted to take the company away from her. But instant refusal was what Pa would have wanted, and she had resolved to stop living her life by her father's programme. However, she had to say something, so she prevaricated. 'I might be interested.'

'That's all I want to know,' he said, standing up. 'Think about it and figure out what kind of deal would make you comfortable. I'm not offering you a blank cheque, but I want you to understand that I'll go a long way to make you happy.' Nancy was faintly bemused: his technique was persuasive. He had learned a lot about negotiating in the last few years. He looked past her, towards the land. 'I think your brother wants to talk to you.'

She looked over her shoulder and saw Peter coming. Nat put on his hat and walked away. This looked like a pincer movement. Nancy stared resentfully at Peter. He had deceived her and betrayed her, and she could hardly bring herself to speak to him. She would have liked to mull over Nat Ridgeway's surprising offer, and think about how it fitted in with her new feelings about her life, but Peter did not give her time. He stood in front of her, put his head on one side in a way that reminded her of his boyhood, and said, 'Can we talk?'

'I doubt it,' she snapped.

'I want to apologize.'

'You're sorry for your treachery now that it's failed.'

'I'd like to make peace.'

Everyone wants to do a deal with me today, she thought sourly. 'How could you possibly make up for what you've done to me?'

'I can't,' he said immediately. 'Never.' He sat down in the chair vacated by Nat. 'When I read your report, I felt such a fool. You were saying I couldn't run the business, I'm not the man my father was, my sister could do it better than me, and I felt so ashamed because in my heart I knew it was true.'

Well, she thought, that's progress.

'It made me mad, Nan, that's the truth.' As children they had called each other Nan and Petey, and his use of the childhood name brought a lump to her throat. 'I don't think I knew what I was doing.'

She shook her head. That was a typical Peter excuse. 'You knew what you were doing.' But she was sad, now, rather than angry.

A group of people stopped near the door to the airline building, chatting. Peter looked irritably at them and said to Nancy, 'Come and walk along the shore with me?'

She sighed. He was, after all, her little brother. She got up.

He gave her a radiant smile.

They walked to the landward end of the pier then

stepped across the railroad track and descended to the beach. Nancy took off her high-heeled shoes and walked along the sand in her stockings. The breeze tossed Peter's fair hair, and she saw, with a little shock, that it was receding from his temples. She wondered why she had not noticed that before, and realized that he combed his hair carefully to conceal it. That made her feel old.

There was nobody near by now, but Peter said no more for a while, and eventually Nancy spoke. 'Danny Riley told me a weird thing. He said Pa deliberately set things up so you and I would fight.'

Peter frowned. 'Why would he do that?'

'To make us tougher.'

Peter laughed harshly. 'Do you believe it?'

'Yes.'

'I guess I do too.'

'I've decided I'm not going to live the rest of my life under Pa's spell.'

He nodded, then said, 'But what does that mean?'

'I don't know, yet. Maybe I'll accept Nat's offer, and merge our company into his.'

'It's not "our" company any more, Nan. It's yours.'

She studied him. Was this genuine? She felt mean, being so suspicious. She decided to give him the benefit of the doubt.

He looked sincere as he went on, 'I'm not cut out for business, so I'm going to leave it to people like you who are good at it.'

'But what will you do?'

'I thought I might buy that house.' They were passing

an attractive white-painted cottage with green shutters. 'I'm going to have lots of time for holidays.'

She felt rather sorry for him. 'It's a pretty house,' she said. 'Is it for sale, though?'

'There's a board on the other side. I was poking around earlier. Come and see.'

They walked around the house. It was locked up, and the shutters were closed, so they could not look into the rooms, but from the outside it was appealing. It had a wide veranda with a hammock. There was a tennis court in the garden. On the far side was a small building without windows, which Nancy guessed was a boat-house. 'You could have a boat,' she said. Peter had always liked sailing.

A side door to the boat-house stood open. Peter went inside. She heard him exclaim, 'Good God!'

She stepped through the doorway and peered into the gloom. 'What is it?' she said anxiously. 'Petey, are you all right?'

Peter appeared beside her and took her arm. For a split second she saw a nasty, triumphant grin on his face, and she knew she had made a terrible mistake. Then he jerked her arm violently, pulling her farther in. She stumbled, cried out, dropped her shoes and handbag, and fell to the dusty floor.

'Peter!' she cried out furiously. She heard him take three rapid steps, then the door banged and she was in darkness. 'Peter?' she called, fearful now. She got to her feet. There was a scraping sound and then a knock as if something was being used to jam the door. She yelled out, 'Peter! Say something!'

There was no reply.

Hysterical fear bubbled up in her throat and she wanted to scream in terror. She put her hand to her mouth and bit the knuckle of her thumb. After a moment the panic began to recede.

Standing there in the dark, blind and disoriented, she realized he had planned this all along: he had found the empty house with its convenient boat-house, lured her here and locked her in, so that she would miss the plane and be unable to vote at the board meeting. His regrets, his apology, his talk of giving up business and his painful honesty had all been faked. He had cynically evoked their childhood to soften her. Once again she had trusted him; once again he had betrayed her. It was enough to make her weep.

She bit her lip and considered her situation. As her eyes became accustomed to the darkness she was able to see a line of light under the door. She walked towards it, holding both hands out in front of her. When she reached the door she felt the wall on both sides of it and found a switch. She turned it and the boat-house was flooded with light. She found the handle of the door and tried, without any real hope, to push it open. It did not budge: he had jammed it well. She put her shoulder to the door and heaved with all her might, but it would not move.

Her elbows and knees hurt where she had fallen, and her stockings were torn. 'You pig,' she said to the absent Peter.

She put on her shoes, picked up her handbag and looked around. Most of the space was taken up by a big sailing boat on a wheeled dolly. Its mast hung in a cradle from the ceiling, and its sails were folded in neat bundles on the deck. At the front of the boat-house was a wide door. Nancy examined it and found, as she expected, that it was securely locked.

The house was set back from the beach a little, but there was a chance that passengers from the Clipper, or even someone else, might meander past. Nancy took a deep breath and shouted at the top of her voice, 'HELP! HELP! HELP!' She decided to yell at one-minute intervals, so that she would not get hoarse.

Both the front and side doors were stout and well-fitting, but she might be able to break them open with a crowbar or something. She looked around. The owner was a neat man: he did not keep his gardening tools in his boat-house. There were no shovels or rakes.

She shouted for help again, then climbed on to the deck of the boat, still looking for a tool. There were several closets on deck but all had been locked shut by the tidy owner. She looked around the place again from up on the deck, but she saw nothing new. 'Damn, damn, damn!' she said aloud.

She sat on the raised centreboard and brooded despondently. It was quite cold in the boat-house, and she was glad of her cashmere coat. She continued to call for help every minute or so but, as time passed, her hopes diminished. The passengers would be back on board the Clipper by now. Soon it would take off, leaving her behind.

It struck her that losing the company might be the least of her worries. Suppose nobody came by this boat-house for a week? She could die here. Panicking, she began to yell loudly and continuously. She could hear a note of hysteria in her own voice, and that scared her even more.

After a while she just got tired, and that calmed her. Peter was wicked but he was not a murderer, he would not leave her to die. He probably intended to place an anonymous call to the Shediac police department and tell them to let her out. But not until after the board meeting, of course. She told herself she was safe, but she still felt deeply uneasy. What if Peter was more wicked than she thought? What if he should forget? What if he should fall ill, or suffer some sort of accident? Who would save her then?

She heard the roar of the Clipper's mighty engines sounding out across the bay. From panic her mood switched to total despair. She had been betrayed and defeated, and she had even lost Mervyn, who would be on board the plane by now, waiting to take off. He might wonder idly what had happened to her, but since her last words to him had been 'You fool!' he probably figured she was through with him.

It had been arrogant of him to assume she would follow him to England, but to be realistic about it, any man would have made the same assumption, and she had been silly to get mad about it. Now they had parted angrily and she would never see him again. She might even die.

The roar of the distant engines rose to a crescendo. The Clipper was taking off. The noise persisted at high volume for a minute or two, then began to fade as, Nancy presumed, the plane climbed into the distant sky. That's it, she thought; I've lost my business and I've lost Mervyn, and I'm probably going to starve to death here. No, she would not starve, she would die of thirst, raving and screaming in agony . . .

She felt a tear on her cheek, and wiped it away with the cuff of her coat. She had to pull herself together. There must be a way out of here. She looked around yet again. She wondered if she could use the mast as a battering ram. She reached up to the sling. No, the mast was much too heavy to be moved by one person. Could she cut through the door somehow? She recalled stories of prisoners in medieval dungeons scratching the stones with their fingernails year after year in a vain attempt to dig a way out. She did not have years, and she would need something stronger than fingernails. She looked in her bag. She had a small ivory comb, a bright red lipstick almost used up, a cheap powder compact the boys had given her for her thirtieth birthday, an embroidered handkerchief, her cheque book, a five-pound note, several fifty-dollar bills, and a small gold pen: nothing she could use. She thought of her clothes. She was wearing a crocodile belt with a gold-plated buckle. It occurred to her that the point of the buckle might be used to gouge away the wood of the door around the lock. It would be a long job; but she had all the time in the world.

She climbed off the boat and located the lock on the big front door. The wood was quite stout, but perhaps she would not need to scratch all the way through: when she had made a deep groove it might then break. She shouted for help again. No one answered.

She took off her belt. Her skirt would not stay up without it, so she took that off, folded it neatly, and draped it over the gunwale of the boat. Although no one could see her, she felt glad she was wearing pretty panties with a lacy trim and a matching garter belt.

She scratched a square mark all around the lock and then began to make it deeper. The metal of her buckle was not very strong, and after a while the prong bent. Nevertheless she carried on, stopping every minute or so to shout. Slowly the mark became a groove. Sawdust trickled out and drifted to the floor.

The wood of the door was soft, perhaps because of the damp air. The work went more quickly and she began to think she might get out soon.

Just as she was becoming hopeful, the prong snapped off.

She picked it up from the floor and tried to continue, but without the buckle the prong on its own was hard to handle. If she dug deep it slipped from her fingers, and if she scratched lightly she made the groove no deeper. After dropping it five or six times she cursed aloud, cried tears of rage, and hammered uselessly on the door with her fists.

A voice called, 'Who's there?'

She shut up and stopped hammering. Had she really heard it? She shouted, 'Hello! Help!'

'Nancy, is that you?'

Her heart leaped. It was a British accent and she recognized the voice. 'Mervyn! Thank God!'

'I've been searching for you. What the devil happened to you?'

'Just let me out, will you?'

The door shook. 'It's locked.'

'Come around the side.'

'On my way.'

Nancy crossed the boat-house, skirting the sailing boat, and went to the side door. She heard him say, 'It's wedged – just a minute . . .' She realized she was standing there in her stockings and underwear, so she pulled her coat around her to cover her nakedness. A moment later the door flew open and she flung herself into Mervyn's arms. 'I thought I was going to die in here!' she said, and to her embarrassment she began to cry.

He hugged her and stroked her hair, saying, 'There, there.'

'Peter locked me in,' she said tearfully.

'I guessed he'd done something sly. That brother of yours is a right bastard, if you ask me.'

Nancy did not care about Peter, she was too glad to see Mervyn. She looked into his eyes through a haze of tears, then kissed his face all over: eyes, cheeks, nose and finally lips. She suddenly felt powerfully aroused. She opened her mouth and kissed him passionately. He put his arms around her and squeezed her tight. She pressed herself against him, hungry for the feel of his body. He ran his hands down her back inside her coat and stopped, startled, when he felt her panties. He drew back and looked at her. Her coat had fallen open. 'What happened to your skirt?'

She laughed. 'I tried to cut through the door with the prong of my belt buckle, and my skirt wouldn't stay up without the belt, so I took it off . . .'

'What a nice surprise,' he said thickly, and he stroked her bottom and her bare thighs. She felt his penis grow erect against her stomach. She reached down and stroked it.

In a moment they were both mad with desire. She wanted to make love now, here, and she knew he felt the same. He covered her small breasts with his big hands, and she gasped. She pulled open the buttons of his fly and reached inside. All the time, in the back of her mind, she was thinking I might have died, I might have died, and the thought made her desperate for satisfaction. She found his penis, squeezed it, and pulled it out. They were both breathing like sprinters now. She stood back and looked down at the big cock in her small white hand. Giving in to an irresistible urge, she bent over and took it in her mouth.

It seemed to fill her up. There was a mossy smell in her nostrils and a salty taste in her mouth. She groaned: she had forgotten how much she liked doing this. She could have gone on for ever, but eventually he drew her head up, moaning, 'Stop, before I burst.'

He bent in front of her and slowly drew her panties down. She felt shy and inflamed at the same time. He kissed her pubic hair. He pulled her panties down to her ankles and she stepped out of them.

He straightened up and embraced her again, and then at last his hand closed over her sex, and a moment later she felt his finger slide easily inside. All the while they kissed wetly, lips and tongues in a frantic tangle, pausing only to gasp for breath. After a while she drew away from him, looked around, and said, 'Where?'

'Put your arms round my neck,' he said.

She reached up and clasped her hands behind his neck. He put his hands under her thighs and lifted her effortlessly off the ground. Her coat swung behind her. As he lowered her, she guided him inside, then wrapped her legs around his waist.

For a moment they were still, and she savoured the feeling she had been without so long, the comforting sense of utter closeness that came from having a man inside her and mingling two bodies so intimately. It was, she now recalled, the best feeling in the world, and she thought she must have been mad to go without it for ten years.

Then she began to move, pulling herself to him and pushing away. She heard him groan deep in his throat, and the thought of the pleasure she was giving him inflamed her more. She felt shameless, making love in this bizarre position with a man she hardly knew. At first she wondered whether he could take her weight; but she was petite and he was a big man. He grasped the globes of her bottom and moved her, lifting her up and down. She closed her eyes and savoured the feeling of his penis going in and out and her clitoris pressing against his belly. She forgot to worry about his strength and concentrated intensely on the sensations in her groin.

After a while she opened her eyes and looked at him. She wanted to tell him that she loved him. Somewhere in the back of her mind a sentinel of common sense told her it was too soon; but all the same she felt it. 'You're very dear,' she whispered to him.

The look in his eyes told her that he understood. He murmured her name and began to move faster.

She closed her eyes again and thought only of the waves of delight emanating from the place where their bodies met. She heard her own voice, as if at a distance, giving small cries of pleasure each time she sank down on him. He was breathing hard, but he held her weight without any sign of strain. Now she sensed him holding back, waiting for her. She thought of the pressure building up inside him with every rise and fall of her hips, and that image pushed her over the top. Her whole body thrilled with pleasure and she cried aloud. She felt him surge and jerk, and she rode him like a bucking horse as the climax shook them both. At last the pleasure eased, Mervyn became still, and she slumped on his chest.

He hugged her hard and said, 'By heck, is it always like that for you?'

She laughed breathlessly. She loved a man who could make her laugh.

Eventually he lowered her to the floor. She stood shakily on her feet, still leaning on him, for a few minutes. Then, reluctantly, she put her clothes back on.

They smiled at one another a lot, but did not speak, as they went out into the mild sunshine and walked slowly along the beach towards the pier.

Nancy was wondering if perhaps it was her destiny to live in England and marry Mervyn. She had lost her battle for control of the company: there was no way she could get to Boston in time for the board meeting, so Peter would outvote Danny Riley and Aunt Tilly, and carry the day. She thought of her boys: they were independent now, she did not need to live her life according to their needs. And she had now discovered that as a lover Mervyn was everything she longed for. She still felt dazed and a little weak after their love-making. But what would I do in England? she thought. I can't be a housewife.

They reached the pier and stood looking over the bay. Nancy wondered how often trains ran from here. She was about to propose making enquiries when she noticed Mervyn staring hard at something in the distance. 'What are you looking at?' she said.

'A Grumman Goose,' he said thoughtfully.

'I don't see any geese.'

He pointed. 'That little seaplane is called a Grumman Goose. It's quite new – they've only been out for a couple of years. They're very fast, faster than the Clipper . . .'

She looked at the seaplane. It was a modern-looking twin-engined monoplane with an enclosed cabin. She realized what he was thinking. In a seaplane she could get to Boston in time for the board meeting. 'Could we charter it?' she asked hesitantly, hardly daring to hope.

'That's what I was thinking.'

'Let's ask!' She hurried along the pier to the airline building, and Mervyn followed, his long stride easily keeping up with her. Her heart was pounding. She might yet save her company. But she kept her elation bottled up: there might be a snag.

They entered the building, and a young man in a Pan American uniform said, 'Hey, you guys missed your plane!'

Without preamble, Nancy said, 'Do you know who the little seaplane belongs to?'

'The Goose? Sure do. A mill owner called Alfred Southborne.'

'Does he ever rent it?'

'Yeah, whenever he can. You want to charter it?'

Nancy's heart leaped. 'Yes!'

'One of the pilots is right here – came to look at the Clipper.' He stepped back and called into an adjoining room. 'Hey, Ned? Someone wants to charter your Goose.'

Ned came out. He was a cheerful man of about thirty in a shirt with epaulettes. He nodded politely and said, 'I'd like to help you folks, but my co-pilot ain't here and the Goose needs a crew of two.'

Nancy's heart sank again.

Mervyn said, 'I'm a pilot.'

Ned looked sceptical. 'Ever flown a seaplane?'

Nancy held her breath.

Mervyn said, 'Yes – the Supermarine.'

Nancy had never heard of a Supermarine, but it must have been a competition plane, for Ned was impressed. 'Do you race?' he asked.

'I did when I was young. Now I just fly for pleasure. I have a Tiger Moth.'

'Well, if you've flown a Supermarine you won't have any trouble being co-pilot on the Goose. And Mr Southborne is away until tomorrow. Where do you want to go?'

'Boston.'

'Cost you a thousand dollars.'

'No problem!' Nancy said excitedly. 'But we need to leave right away.'

The man looked at her in mild surprise: he had assumed the man was in charge. 'We can be gone in a few minutes, ma'am. How would you pay?'

'I can give you a personal cheque, or you can bill my company in Boston, Black's Boots.'

'You work for Black's Boots?'

'I own it.'

'Hey, I'm wearing your shoes!'

She looked down. He had the $6.95 toecapped Oxford in black, size nine. 'How do they feel?' she said automatically.

'Great. They're good shoes. But I guess you know that.'

She smiled. 'Yes,' she said. 'They're good shoes.'

Part Six

Shediac to the Bay of Fundy

CHAPTER TWENTY-SIX

MARGARET WAS frantic with worry as the Clipper climbed over New Brunswick and headed for New York. Where was Harry?

The police had found out that he was travelling on a false passport: that much was common knowledge among the passengers. She could not imagine how they had found out, but it was an academic question. More important was what they would do to him if they caught him. Presumably he would be sent back to England, where he would either go to jail for stealing those wretched cufflinks or be conscripted into the army; and then how would she ever find him?

As far as she knew, they had not caught him yet. The last time she saw him, he had gone to the men's room as she was disembarking at Shediac. Was that the beginning of some escape plan? Had he known then that he was in trouble?

The police had searched the plane without finding him, so he must have got off at some point; but where had he gone? Was he even now walking along a narrow road through the forest, trying to thumb a lift? Or had he perhaps talked his way on to a fishing vessel and left by sea? Whatever he had done, the same question tortured Margaret: would she ever see him again?

She told herself again and again she must not be discouraged. Losing Harry hurt, but she still had Nancy Lenehan to help her.

Father could not stop her now. He was a failure and an exile, and he had lost his power to coerce her. However, she was still frightened that he might lash out, like a wounded animal at bay, and do something terribly destructive.

As soon as the plane reached cruising height, she unfastened her seat belt and went aft to see Mrs Lenehan.

The stewards were preparing the dining room for lunch as she passed through. Farther back, in No. 4 compartment, Ollis Field and Frank Gordino were sitting side by side, handcuffed together. Margaret went all the way to the rear and knocked on the door of the honeymoon suite. There was no reply. She knocked again, then opened it. It was empty.

Cold fear touched her heart.

Perhaps Nancy was in the ladies' powder room. But, then, where was Mr Lovesey? If he had gone to the flight deck or the men's room, Margaret would have seen him pass through No. 2 compartment. She stood in the doorway, frowning and staring around the suite as if they might be hiding somewhere; but there was nowhere to hide.

Nancy's brother Peter and his companion were sitting right next to the honeymoon suite, across the aisle from the powder room. Margaret said to them, 'Where's Mrs Lenehan?'

Peter replied, 'She decided to leave the flight at Shediac.'

Margaret gasped. 'What?' she said. 'How do you know?'

'She told me.'

'But why?' Margaret said plaintively. 'What made her stay behind?'

He looked offended. 'I guess I don't know,' he said frostily. 'She didn't say. She simply asked me to inform the Captain that she would not be joining the plane for the last leg of the trip.'

Margaret knew it was rude to interrogate him but she had to persist. 'Where did Nancy go?'

He picked up a newspaper from the seat beside him. 'I have no idea,' he said, and began to read.

Margaret was desolate. How could Nancy do this? She knew how much Margaret was relying on her for help. Surely she would not have left the flight without saying anything, or at least leaving some kind of message?

Margaret stared hard at Peter. She thought he had a shifty look. He was a little too touchy about being questioned, too. On impulse she said, 'I don't believe you're telling me the truth.' It was a very insulting thing to say and she held her breath as she waited for his reaction.

He looked up at her, reddening. 'You have inherited your father's bad manners, young lady,' he said. 'Please go away.'

She was crushed. Nothing could be more hateful to her than to be told she was like Father. She turned away without another word, feeling close to tears.

Passing through No. 4 compartment she noticed Diana Lovesey, Mervyn's beautiful wife. Everyone had been riveted by the drama of the runaway wife and the pursuing husband, and amused when Nancy and Mervyn had been obliged to share the honeymoon suite. Now Margaret wondered whether Diana might know what had happened to her husband. It would be embarrassing to ask, of course, but Margaret was too desperate to worry about that. She sat down next to Diana and said, 'Excuse me, but do you know what happened to Mr Lovesey and Mrs Lenehan?'

Diana looked surprised. 'Happened? Aren't they in the honeymoon suite?'

'No – they're not on board.'

'Really?' Diana was obviously shocked and mystified. 'How come? Did they miss the plane?'

'Nancy's brother says they decided not to finish the flight, but I don't think I believe him.'

Diana looked cross. 'Neither of them said anything to me.'

Margaret looked in enquiry at Diana's companion, the mild-mannered Mark. 'They certainly didn't confide in me,' he said.

In a different tone of voice Diana said, 'I hope they're all right.'

Mark said, 'What do you mean, honey?'

'I don't know what I mean. I just hope they're all right.'

Margaret nodded agreement with Diana. 'I don't trust the brother. I think he's dishonest.'

Mark said, 'You may be right, but I guess there's

nothing we can do about it while we're in mid-air. Besides—'

'He's not my concern any more, I know,' Diana said irritably. 'But he was my husband for five years and I'm worried about him.'

'There will probably be a message from him waiting when we get to Port Washington,' Mark said soothingly.

'I hope so,' Diana said.

Davy the steward touched Margaret's arm. 'Lunch is ready, Lady Margaret, and your family are at table.'

'Thank you.' Margaret had no interest in food. However, these two could tell her no more.

As Margaret stood up to leave, Diana said, 'Are you a friend of Mrs Lenehan's?'

'She was going to give me a job,' Margaret said bitterly. She turned away, biting her lip.

Her parents and Percy were already seated in the dining room, and the first course was being served: lobster cocktail made with fresh lobsters from Shediac. Margaret sat down and said automatically, 'I'm so sorry to be late.' Father just glared at her.

She toyed with her food. She felt like laying her head on the table and bursting into tears. Harry and Nancy had both abandoned her without warning. She was back at square one, with no way to support herself and no friends to help her. It was so unfair: she had tried to be like Elizabeth and plan everything, but her careful scheme had fallen apart.

The lobster was taken away and replaced by kidney soup. Margaret took one sip and put down her spoon. She felt tired and irritable. She had a headache and no appetite. The super-luxurious Clipper was beginning to feel like a prison. They had now been *en route* for almost twenty-seven hours, and she had had enough. She wanted to get into a real bed, with a soft mattress and lots of pillows, and go to sleep for a week.

The others were also feeling the strain. Mother was pale and tired. Father was hung over, with bloodshot eyes and bad breath. Percy was unsettled and nervy, like someone who has drunk too much strong coffee, and he kept throwing hostile looks at Father. Margaret had a feeling he was going to do something outrageous before long.

For the main course they had a choice: fried sole with cardinal sauce, or fillet steak. She did not want either but she chose the fish. It came with potatoes and Brussels sprouts. She asked Nicky for a glass of white wine.

She thought about the dreary days ahead. She would stay with Mother and Father in the Waldorf, but Harry would not sneak into her room: she would lie in bed alone and long for him. She would have to accompany Mother on shopping trips for clothes. Then they would all go on to Connecticut. Without asking her, they would enrol Margaret in a riding club and a tennis club, and she would be invited to parties. Mother would construct a whole social round for them in no time at all, and before long there would be 'suitable' boys coming for tea or cocktails or bicycle rides. How could she enter into all that when England was at war? The more she thought about it, the more depressed she felt.

For dessert there was apple tart with cream, or ice

cream with chocolate sauce. Margaret ordered ice cream and ate it all.

Father asked for brandy with his coffee, then cleared his throat. He was about to make a speech. Could it be that he would apologize for the frightful scene at dinner yesterday? Impossible.

'Your mother and I have been discussing you,' he began.

'As if I were a disobedient parlourmaid,' Margaret snapped.

Mother said, 'You're a disobedient child.'

'I'm nineteen years old, and I've been menstruating for six years – how could I be a child?'

'Hush!' Mother was shocked. 'The very fact that you can use such words in front of your father shows that you're not yet adult.'

'I give up,' Margaret sighed. 'I can't win.'

Father said, 'Your foolish attitude just confirms everything we've been saying. You can't yet be trusted to lead a normal social life among people of your own class.'

'Thank heaven for that!'

Percy laughed out loud, and Father glared at him, but spoke to Margaret. 'We've been trying to think of somewhere to send you, a place where you will have the minimum opportunity to cause trouble.'

'Did you consider a convent?'

He was not used to her cheeking him, but he controlled his anger with an effort. 'This kind of talk won't make things any better for you.'

'Better? How could things be better for me? My

loving parents are determining my future, with only my best interests at heart. What more could I want?'

To her surprise, her mother shed a tear. 'You're very cruel, Margaret,' she said, wiping it away.

Margaret was touched. The sight of her mother weeping destroyed her resistance. She became meek again. 'What do you want me to do, Mother?'

Father answered the question. 'You're going to live with your aunt Clare. She has a place in Vermont. It's in the mountains, rather remote; there will be nobody near by for you to embarrass.'

Mother added, 'My sister Clare is a wonderful woman. She never married. She's the backbone of the Episcopalian Church in Brattleboro.'

Cold rage gripped Margaret, but she kept herself under control. 'How old is Aunt Clare?' she asked.

'In her fifties.'

'Does she live alone?'

'Apart from the servants, yes.'

Margaret was shaking with anger. 'So this is my punishment for trying to live my own life,' she said in an unsteady voice. 'I'm exiled to the mountains to live alone with a mad spinster aunt. How long do you expect me to stay there?'

'Until you've calmed down,' Father said. 'A year, perhaps.'

'A year!' It seemed a lifetime. But they could not make her stay there. 'Don't be so stupid. I shall go mad, kill myself or run away.'

'You're not to leave without our consent,' Father said. 'And if you do . . .' He hesitated.

Margaret looked at his face. My God, she thought, even he is ashamed of what he's about to say. What on earth can it be?

He pressed his lips together in a determined line, then said, 'If you run away, we will have you certified insane and committed to a lunatic asylum.'

Margaret gasped. She was speechless with horror. She had not imagined him capable of such cruelty. She looked at her mother, but Mother would not meet her eyes.

Percy stood up and flung down his napkin. 'You bloody old fool, you've gone off your rocker,' he said, and he walked out.

If Percy had spoken like that a week ago there would have been hell to pay, but now he was ignored.

Margaret looked again at Father. His expression was guilty, defiant and obstinate. He knew he was doing wrong, but he would not change his mind.

At last she found the words to express what she felt in her heart.

'You've sentenced me to death,' she said.

Mother started to cry quietly.

Suddenly the engine note changed. Everyone heard it and all conversation stopped. There was a lurch, and the plane began to go down.

CHAPTER TWENTY-SEVEN

When both port engines cut out at the same time, Eddie's fate was sealed.

Until that moment he could have changed his mind. The plane would have flown on, no one knowing what he had planned. But now, whatever happened, it would all come out. He would never fly again, except maybe as a passenger: his career was over. He fought down the rage that threatened to possess him. He had to stay cool and get this job done Then he would think about the bastards who had ruined his life.

The plane had to make an emergency splashdown now. The kidnappers would come aboard and rescue Frankie Gordino. After that anything could happen. Would Carol-Ann be safe and unhurt? Would the Navy ambush the gangsters as they headed for shore? Would Eddie go to jail for his part in the whole thing? He was a prisoner of fate. But if he could just hold Carol-Ann in his arms, alive and well, nothing else would matter.

A moment after the engines cut out he heard the voice of Captain Baker in his headphones. 'What the hell is going on?'

Eddie's mouth was dry with tension and he had to swallow twice before he could speak. 'I don't know yet,' he replied; but he did. The engines had stopped because they were getting no fuel: he had cut the supply.

The Clipper had six fuel tanks. The engines were supplied by two small feeder tanks in the wings. Most of the fuel was kept in four large reserve tanks located in the hydrostabilizers, the stubby sea-wings that the passengers stepped on to as they got on and off the plane.

Fuel could be dumped from the reserve tanks, but not by Eddie, because the control was at the second pilot's station. However, Eddie could pump fuel from the reserve tanks up to the wings and back down again. Such transfers were controlled by two large handwheels to the right of the engineer's instrument panel. The plane was now over the Bay of Fundy about five miles from the rendezvous, and in the last few minutes he had drained both the wing tanks. The starboard tank had fuel for a few more miles. The port tank had now run dry, and the port engines had stopped.

It would be a simple matter to pump fuel back up from the reserves, of course. However, while the plane was in Shediac Eddie had come aboard on his own and tampered with the handwheels, moving the dials so that when they said 'Pump' they were in fact off, and when they said 'Off' they were pumping. Now the dials indicated that he was trying to fill the wing tanks when in fact nothing was happening.

He had been using the pumps with the wrong settings for the first part of the flight, of course; and another engineer might have noticed that and wondered what the hell was going on. Eddie had worried every second that the off-duty assistant engineer, Mickey Finn, would come upstairs; but he stayed fast asleep in No. 1 compartment, as Eddie had expected: at this stage of the long flight, off-duty crew always slept.

There had been two nasty moments in Shediac. The first had come when the police announced they had learned the name of Frankie Gordino's accomplice aboard the plane. Eddie assumed they were talking about Luther, and for a while he thought the game was up, and racked his brains for some other way of rescuing Carol-Ann. Then they had named Harry Vandenpost, and Eddie almost jumped for joy. He had no idea why Vandenpost, who appeared to be an amiable young American from a wealthy family, should be travelling with a false passport; but he was grateful to the man for deflecting attention from Luther. The police looked no farther, Luther escaped notice, and the plan could go ahead.

But all this had been too much for Captain Baker. Even while Eddie was still recovering from the scare, Baker had dropped a bombshell. The fact that there really had been an accomplice on board meant that someone was serious about rescuing Gordino, he said, and he wanted Gordino off the plane. That too would have ruined everything for Eddie.

There had been a stand-up row between Baker and Ollis Field, with the FBI man threatening to have the Captain charged with obstruction of justice. In the end Baker had called Pan American in New York and dumped the problem on them; and the airline had decided to let Gordino fly on; and once again Eddie was relieved.

He had got one more piece of good news in Shediac. A cryptic but unmistakable message from Steve Appleby had confirmed that a US Navy cutter would be patrolling the coast where the Clipper was going to come down. It would stay out of sight until the splashdown, then intercept any vessel that made contact with the downed plane.

That made all the difference to Eddie. Knowing the gangsters would be caught afterwards, he could with a clear conscience make sure the plan went off without a hitch.

Now the deed was almost done. The plane was close to the rendezvous and flying on two engines only.

Captain Baker was at Eddie's side in a moment. Eddie said nothing to him at first. With a shaky hand he switched the engine feed so that the starboard wing tank was fuelling all engines, and restarted the port engines. Then he said, 'The port wing tank ran dry and I can't fill it.'

'Why not?' the Captain snapped.

Eddie pointed to the handwheels. Feeling like a traitor, he said, 'I've switched the pumps on but nothing's happening.'

Eddie's instruments did not show either fuel flow or fuel pressure between the reserve tanks and the feeder tanks, but there were four glass sights at the rear of the control cabin for visual checking of the fuel in the pipes. Captain Baker looked at each in turn. 'Nothing!' he said. 'How much is left in the starboard wing tank?'

'It's almost dry – a few miles.'

'How come you've only just noticed?' he said angrily.

'I thought we were pumping,' Eddie said feebly.

It was an inadequate answer and the Captain was furious. 'How could both pumps go at the same time?'

'I don't know – but thank God we have a hand pump.'

Eddie seized the handle next to his table and began to operate the hand pump. This was normally used only when the engineer was draining water from the fuel tanks in flight. He had done this immediately after leaving Shediac, and he had deliberately omitted to reset the F-valve which allowed the water to escape overboard. In consequence, his vigorous pumping action was not filling the wing tanks, but just dumping fuel overboard.

The Captain did not know this, of course, and it was not likely that he would notice the setting on the F-valve; but he could see that no fuel was moving through the sight gauges. 'It's not working!' he said. 'I don't understand how all three pumps could fail at the same time!'

Eddie looked at his dials. 'The starboard wing tank is almost dry,' he said. 'If we don't splash down soon we're going to fall out of the sky.'

'Prepare for emergency splashdown, everybody,' Baker said. He pointed a finger at Eddie. 'I don't like your role in this, Deakin,' he said with ice-cold fury. 'I don't trust you.'

Eddie felt rotten. He had good reason to lie to his

captain, but just the same he hated himself. All his life he had dealt honestly with people, and scorned men who used trickery and deceit. Now he was acting in a way he despised. You'll understand in the end, Captain, he thought; but he wished he could say it.

The Captain turned to the navigator's station and bent over the chart. The navigator, Jack Ashford, shot a puzzled look at Eddie, then put a finger on the chart and said to the Captain, 'We're here.'

The whole plan relied on the Clipper coming down in the channel between the coast and Grand Manan island. The gangsters were betting on that, and so was Eddie. But in emergencies people did strange things. Eddie decided that if Baker irrationally chose another location, he would speak up and point out the advantages of the channel. Baker would be suspicious, but he would have to see the logic of it; and then *he* would be the one behaving oddly if he landed somewhere else.

However, no interference was necessary. After a moment Baker said, 'Here. In this channel. That's where we'll come down.'

Eddie turned away so that no one could see his expression of triumph. He was another step closer to Carol-Ann.

As they all went through the procedure for emergency splashdown, Eddie looked out of the window and tried to gauge what the sea was like. He saw a small white vessel like a sports fishing boat bobbing on the swell. The surface was choppy. The landing would be rough.

He heard a voice that stopped his heart. 'What's the emergency?' It was Mickey Finn coming up the stairs to investigate.

Eddie stared at him in horror. Mickey would guess in a minute that the F-valve on the hand-pump had not been reset. Eddie had to get rid of him, quickly.

But Captain Baker beat him to it. 'Get out of here, Mickey!' he snapped. 'Off-duty crew must be strapped in during an emergency splashdown, not wandering around the aircraft asking stupid questions!'

Mickey was gone like a shot, and Eddie breathed easy again.

The plane lost height rapidly: Baker wanted to be close to the water in case they ran out of fuel earlier than expected.

They turned west so as not to overfly the island: if they ran out of fuel over land they were all dead. A few moments later they were above the channel.

There was a big swell, about four feet, Eddie estimated. The critical wave height was three feet: above that it was dangerous to land the Clipper. Eddie gritted his teeth. Baker was a good pilot, but it was going to be dicey.

The plane came down fast. Eddie felt the hull touch the top of a high wave. They flew on for a moment or two then it touched again. The second time there was a stronger impact, and his stomach lurched as the huge aircraft bounced up into the air.

Eddie was afraid for his life: this was how flying boats crashed.

Although the plane was airborne now, the impact

had reduced its airspeed, so that it had very little lift; and instead of sliding into the water at a shallow angle, it would come down hard. It was the difference between a smooth racing dive and a painful belly-flop; except that the belly of the plane was made of thin aluminium which could burst like a paper bag.

He froze, waiting for the impact. The plane hit the water with a terrific bang which he felt all the way up his spine. Water covered the windows. Facing sideways as he was, he was thrown to his left, but managed to stay in his seat. The radio operator, who faced forward, banged his head on his microphone. Eddie thought the plane was breaking up. If it dipped a wing that would be the end.

A second passed, then another. The cries of terrified passengers floated up the staircase. The plane lifted again, coming partly out of the water and moving forward with the reduction in drag; then it sank back, and Eddie was thrown sideways again.

But the plane stayed level, and Eddie began to hope they would make it. The windows cleared and he glimpsed the sea. His engines were still roaring: they had not been submerged.

The plane slowed gradually. Second by second Eddie felt safer, until at last the plane was stationary, rising and falling on the waves. In his headphones Eddie heard the Captain say, 'Jesus, that was rougher than I expected,' and the rest of the crew laughed with relief.

Eddie stood up and looked out through all the windows, searching for a boat. The sun was shining but there were rainclouds in the sky. Visibility was fair, but he could not see any other vessels. Perhaps the launch was behind the Clipper, where he could not see it.

He took his seat again and shut down the engines. The radio operator broadcast a Mayday. The Captain said, 'I'd better go and reassure the passengers.' He went down the stairs. The radio operator got a reply, and Eddie hoped it was from the people who were coming for Gordino.

He could not wait to find out. He went forward, opened the hatch in the cockpit, and climbed down the ladder into the bow compartment. The forward hatch opened downward, forming a platform. Eddie stepped outside and stood on it. He had to hold the door frame to keep his balance in the swell. The waves were coming over the sea-wings, and some were high enough to splash his feet as he stood on the platform. The sun was going behind the clouds intermittently, and there was a stiff breeze. He looked carefully at the hull and wings: he could see no damage. The great aircraft appeared to have survived unscathed.

He released the anchor, then stood surveying the sea all around, hunting for a vessel. Where were Luther's buddies? What if something had gone wrong? What if they did not turn up? But then at last he saw a motor launch in the distance. His heart missed a beat. Was this it? And was Carol-Ann on board? Now he worried that it might be some other vessel, coming to look at the downed plane out of curiosity, which would interfere with the plan.

It came in fast, riding up and down the waves. Eddie was supposed to return to his station on the flight deck, having dropped anchor and checked for damage, but he could not move. He stared hypnotically at the launch as it grew larger. It was a big, fast boat with a covered wheelhouse. He knew it was racing at twenty-five or thirty knots, but it seemed painfully slow. There was a group of figures on deck and soon he could count them: four. He noticed that one was much smaller than the others. The group began to look like three men in dark suits and a woman in a blue coat. Carol-Ann had a blue coat.

He thought it was her but he was not sure. The waiting was unbearable. The woman had fair hair and a slight figure, just like her. She was standing apart from the others. All four were at the rail, looking at the Clipper. Then the sun came out from behind a cloud and the woman raised her hand to her face to shield her eyes. Something about the gesture pulled at Eddie's heartstrings, and he knew it was his wife.

'Carol-Ann,' he said aloud.

A surge of excitement seized him, and for a moment he forgot about the perils they both still faced, and gave in to the joy of seeing her again. He raised his arms and waved happily. 'Carol-Ann!' he yelled. 'Carol-Ann!'

She could not hear him, of course, but she could see him. She started with surprise, hesitated as if she was not sure whether it was him, then waved back, timidly at first and then vigorously.

If she could wave like that she must be all right. He felt as weak as a baby with relief and gratitude.

He remembered that it was not over yet. He had

more to do. He gave one more wave then, reluctantly, went back inside.

He emerged on to the flight deck just as the Captain was coming up from the passenger deck. 'Any damage?' Baker said.

'Nothing at all, as far as I can see.'

The Captain turned to the radio operator, who reported, 'Our Mayday has been answered by several ships, but the nearest vessel is a pleasure boat now approaching on the port side. You can probably see her.'

The Captain looked out of the windows and saw the launch. He shook his head. 'She's no use. We have to be towed. Try to raise the Coast Guard.'

'The people on the launch want to come aboard,' the radio operator said.

'Nix to that,' said Baker. Eddie was dismayed. They had to come aboard! 'It's too dangerous,' the Captain went on. 'I don't want a boat tied up to the plane: it could damage the hull. And if we try to transfer people in this swell, someone's sure to fall in the goddamn drink. Tell them we appreciate their offer, but they can't help us.'

Eddie had not anticipated this. He put on an unconcerned look to mask his sudden anxiety. The hell with damage to the plane, Luther's gang were coming aboard! But they would have a hard time without help from the inside.

Even with help, it would be a nightmare to try to board through the normal doors, he realized. The waves were washing over the sea-wings and half-way up the doors: no one could stand on the sea-wing without a rope to hold, and water would pour into the dining room while the door was open. This had not occurred to Eddie before because the Clipper normally landed only on the calmest of seas.

Then how could they board?

They would have to come through the forward hatch in the bow compartment.

The radio operator said, 'I've told them they can't board, Captain, but they don't seem to take any notice.'

Eddie looked out. The launch was circling the plane.

'Just ignore them,' the Captain said.

Eddie stood up and went forward. As he stepped on to the ladder leading down into the bow compartment, Captain Baker snapped, 'Where are you going?'

'I need to check on the anchor,' Eddie said vaguely, and went on without waiting for a reply.

He heard Baker say, 'That guy is *through.*'

I knew that already, he thought with a heavy heart.

He got out on to the platform. The launch was thirty or forty feet from the nose of the Clipper. He could see Carol-Ann standing at the rail. She had on an old dress and flat shoes, just what she would have been wearing for housework. She had thrown on her best coat over her work clothes when they took her. He could see her face now. She looked pale and drained. Eddie felt anger boil deep inside him. I'll get them for this, he thought.

He raised the collapsible capstan, then waved to the launch, pointing to the capstan and miming throwing a rope. He had to do it several times before the men on deck understood. He guessed they were not experienced sailors. They certainly looked out of place on a boat, in their double-breasted suits, holding their fedoras on their heads in the wind. The guy in the wheelhouse, presumably the skipper of the launch, was busy with his controls, trying to keep the boat steady relative to the plane. At last one of the men made a gesture of acknowledgement and picked up a rope.

He was no good at throwing it, and it took four tries before Eddie was able to catch it.

He secured it to the capstan. The men on the launch hauled their craft closer to the plane. The boat, being so much lighter, rose and fell more on the swell. Tying the launch to the plane was going to be difficult and dangerous.

Suddenly he heard Mickey Finn's voice behind him, saying, 'Eddie, what the hell are you doing?'

He turned round. Mickey was in the bow compartment, looking up at him with a concerned expression on his open, freckled face. Eddie yelled, 'Stay right out of this, Mickey! I'm warning you, if you interfere, people are going to get hurt!'

Mickey looked scared. 'Okay, okay, whatever you say.' He retreated towards the flight deck, his face showing that he thought Eddie had gone mad.

Eddie turned back to face the launch. It was quite close now. He looked at the three men. One was very young, no more than eighteen. Another was older but short and thin, with a cigarette dangling from a corner of his mouth. The third, wearing a black suit with a chalk stripe, looked like he was in charge.

They were going to need two ropes, Eddie decided, to hold the launch steady enough. He put his hands to his mouth to make a megaphone and shouted, 'Throw another rope!'

The man in the striped suit picked up a rope in the bow, next to the one they were already using. That was no good: they needed one at each end of the launch, to make a triangle. 'No, not that one,' Eddie called. 'Throw me a stern rope.'

The man got the message.

This time Eddie caught the rope the first time. He took it inside the plane and tied it to a strut.

With a man hauling on each rope the launch came rapidly closer. Suddenly its engines were cut and a man in overalls came out of the wheelhouse and took over the rope work. This guy was obviously a seaman.

Eddie heard another voice from behind him, coming from within the bow compartment. This time it was Captain Baker. He said, 'Deakin, you're disobeying a direct order.'

Eddie ignored him and prayed that he would keep out of the way for a few moments more. The launch was as close as it could come. The skipper wound the ropes around the deck stanchions, leaving just enough slack to allow the boat to rise and fall with the waves. To board the Clipper, the men would have to wait until the swell brought the deck level with the platform, then jump from one to the other. To steady themselves they could hold on to the rope that ran from the stern of the launch to the inside of the bow compartment.

Baker barked, 'Deakin! Get back in here!'

The seaman opened a gate in the rail and the gangster in the striped suit stood ready to jump across. Eddie felt Captain Baker's hand clutch at his jacket from behind. The gangster saw what was happening and reached inside his coat.

Eddie's worst nightmare was that one of his crew-mates would decide to be a hero and get himself killed. He wished he could tell them about the Navy cutter Steve Appleby had sent – but he was afraid that if he did that one of them might accidentally let it out and forewarn the gangsters. So he just had to try and keep the situation under control.

He turned to Baker and yelled, 'Captain! Get out of the way! These bastards have guns!'

Baker looked shocked. He stared at the gangster, then ducked out of sight. Eddie turned round to see the man in the striped suit stuffing a pistol back into his coat pocket. Jesus, I hope I can stop these guys shooting people, he thought fearfully. If someone dies it will be my fault.

The boat was on the crest of a wave, its deck a little above the level of the platform. The gangster grabbed the rope, hesitated, then jumped on to the platform. Eddie caught him, steadying him.

'You Eddie?' the man said.

Eddie recognized the voice – he had heard it over the phone. He recalled the man's name: Vincini. Eddie had insulted him. Now he regretted it, for he needed his co-operation. 'I want to work with you, Vincini,' he said. 'If you want things to go smoothly, with no snags, let me help you.'

Vincini gave him a hard look. 'Okay,' he said after a moment. 'But make one false move and you're dead.' His tone was brisk and businesslike. He showed no sign of resentment: no doubt he had too much on his mind to think about past slights.

'Step inside and wait right there while I bring the others over.'

'Okay.' Vincini turned to the launch. 'Joe – you next. Then Kid. The girl comes last.' He stepped down into the bow compartment.

Looking inside, Eddie saw Captain Baker climbing the ladder that led to the flight deck. Vincini pulled out his gun and said, 'Stay there, you.'

Eddie said, 'Do what he says, Captain, for God's sake, these guys are serious.'

Baker stepped off the ladder and raised his hands in the air.

Eddie turned back. The runty man called Joe was standing at the rail of the launch looking scared to death. 'I can't swim!' he said in a rasping voice.

'You won't have to,' Eddie said. He reached out a hand.

Joe jumped, caught his hand, and half stepped, half fell into the bow compartment.

The young one was last. Having seen the other two make the transfer safely, he was over-confident. 'I can't swim either,' he said with a grin. He jumped too soon, landed on the very edge of the platform, lost his balance, and tipped backwards. Eddie leaned out, holding thc rope with his left hand, and grabbed the boy by the waistband of his pants. He pulled him on to the platform.

'Gee, thanks!' the boy said, as if Eddie had merely given him a hand, instead of saving his life.

Now Carol-Ann was standing on the deck of the launch, looking across at the platform with fear on her face. She was not normally timid, but Eddie could tell that Kid's near-disaster had unnerved her. He smiled at her and said, 'Just do what they did, honey. You can make it.'

She nodded and took hold of the rope.

Eddie waited with his heart in his mouth. The swell brought the launch up level with the platform. Carol-Ann hesitated, missed her chance, and looked more fearful. 'Take your time,' Eddie called, making his voice calm to hide his own fear. 'Whenever you're ready.'

The launch went down and rose again. Carol-Ann's face wore an expression of forced resolution, her lips pressed together, her forehead creased in a frown. The launch drifted a foot or two away from the platform, making the gap rather too big. Eddie called, 'Maybe not this time – ' but he was too late. She was so determined to be brave that she had jumped already.

She missed the platform completely.

She let out a scream of terror and swung from the rope, her feet scrabbling in mid-air. Eddie could do nothing as the launch slipped down the slope of the wave and Carol-Ann fell away from the platform. 'Hold tight!' he yelled frantically. 'You'll come up!' He got ready to jump into the sea to save her if she should let go.

But she clung fiercely to the rope as the swell took her down then brought her up again. When she drew level she stretched out one leg towards the platform but it did not reach. Eddie went down on one knee and made a grab for her. He almost overbalanced and fell in the water, but he could not quite touch her leg. The swell took her down again, and she gave a cry of despair.

'Swing!' Eddie yelled. 'Swing to and fro as you come up!'

She heard. He could see her gritting her teeth against the pain in her arms, but she managed to swing backwards and forwards as the swell lifted the launch. Eddie knelt down, reaching out. She came level and swung with all her might. Eddie grabbed and caught her ankle. She had no stockings on. He pulled her closer and got hold of the other ankle, but her feet still did not reach the platform. The launch crested the wave and began to fall. Carol-Ann screamed as she felt herself going down. Eddie still held on to her ankles. Then she let go of the rope.

He held on like grim death. As she fell, he was pulled forward by her weight and almost toppled into the sea; but he was able to flop on to his belly and stay on the platform. Carol-Ann swung upside-down from his hands. In this position he could not lift her, but the sea did the job. The next wave submerged her head but lifted her towards him. He let go of one ankle, freeing his right hand, and got his arm around her waist.

He had her safe. He rested for a moment, saying, 'It's okay, baby, I've got you,' while she choked and spluttered. Then he hauled her up on to the platform.

He held her hand while she turned and stood up, then he helped her inside.

She fell into his arms, sobbing. He pressed her dripping head against his chest. He felt tears come but he forced them back. The three gangsters and Captain Baker were looking at him expectantly, but he ignored them for a few moments more. He held Carol-Ann tightly as she shook violently.

At last he said, 'Are you okay, honey? Did these bastards hurt you?'

She shook her head. 'I'm okay, I guess,' she said through chattering teeth.

He looked up and caught the eye of Captain Baker. Baker looked from him to Carol-Ann and back again, then said, 'Jesus Christ, I'm beginning to understand this . . .'

Vincini said, 'Enough talk, we got work to do.'

Eddie released Carol-Ann. 'Okay. I think we should deal with the crew first, get them calmed down and out of the way. Then I'll take you to the man you want. Is that all right?'

'Yeah, but let's get on with it.'

'Follow me.' Eddie crossed to the ladder and went up it. He came out on to the flight deck first and began speaking right away. In the few seconds before Vincini caught up with him he said, 'Listen, guys, please don't anybody try to be a hero. *It isn't necessary.* I hope you've understood me.' He could not risk more than that hint.

A moment later Carol-Ann, Captain Baker and the three hoodlums came up through the hatch. Eddie went on, 'Everybody keep calm and do what you're told. I don't want any shooting, I don't want anybody to get hurt. The Captain is going to tell you the same thing.' He looked at Baker.

'That's right, men,' Baker said. 'Don't give these people any reason to use their guns.'

Eddie looked at Vincini. 'Okay, let's go. Come with us please, Captain, to calm the passengers. Then Joe and Kid should take the crew to No. 1 compartment.'

Vincini nodded assent.

'Carol-Ann, will you go with the crew, honey?'

'Yes.'

Eddie felt good about that. She would be away from the guns, and she could also explain to his crew-mates why he was helping the gangsters.

He looked at Vincini. 'Do you want to put your gun away? You'll scare the passengers—'

'Fuck you,' said Vincini. 'Let's go.'

Eddie shrugged. It had been worth a try.

He led the way down the stairs to the passenger deck. There was a hubbub of loud talk, some semi-hysterical laughter, and the sound of one woman sobbing. The passengers were all in their seats, and the two stewards were making heroic efforts to look calm and normal.

Eddie went along the plane. The dining room was a mess, with smashed crockery and broken glass all over the floor; although fortunately there was not much spilt food because the meal had been almost over and everyone had been having coffee. People went quiet when they saw Vincini's gun. Behind Vincini, Captain Baker was saying, 'I apologize for this, ladies and gentlemen, but please remain seated and try to keep calm and it will all be over shortly.' He was so smoothly reassuring that Eddie almost felt better himself.

He passed through No. 3 compartment and entered No. 4. Ollis Field and Frankie Gordino were sitting side by side. This is it, Eddie thought; this is where I set free a murderer. He pushed the thought aside, pointed to Gordino, and said to Vincini, 'There's your man.'

Ollis Field stood up. 'This is FBI agent Tommy McArdle,' he said. 'Frankie Gordino crossed the Atlantic on a ship that reached New York yesterday, and he is now in jail in Providence, Rhode Island.'

'Jesus Christ!' Eddie exploded. He was thunderstruck. 'A decoy! I went through all that for a goddamn decoy!' He was not going to free a murderer after all; but he could not feel glad, because he was too scared of what the gangsters might do now. He looked fearfully at Vincini.

Vincini said, 'Hell, we ain't after Frankie. Where's the Kraut?'

Eddie stared at him, flabbergasted. They were not after Gordino? What did it mean? Who was the Kraut?

Tom Luther's voice came from No. 3 compartment. 'He's in here, Vincini. I've got him.' Luther stood in the doorway holding a gun at the head of Carl Hartmann.

Eddie was mystified. Why the hell would the

Patriarca gang want to kidnap Carl Hartmann? 'What do you guys want with a scientist?' he said.

Luther said, 'He's not just a scientist. He's a nuclear physicist.'

'Are you guys Nazis?'

Vincini said, 'Oh, no. We're just doing a job for them. Matter of fact, we're Democrats.' He laughed coarsely.

Luther said coldly, 'I am no Democrat. I am proud to be a member of the Deutsch-Amerikaner Bund.' Eddie had heard of the Bund: it was supposed to be a harmless German-American friendship league, but it was funded by the Nazis. Luther went on, 'These men are just hired hands. I received a personal message from the Führer himself, requesting my help in apprehending a runaway scientist and returning him to Germany.' He was proud of this honour, Eddie realized: it was the greatest thing that had ever happened to him. 'I paid these people to help me. Now I am going to take Herr Doktor Professor Hartmann back to Germany, where his presence is required by the Third Reich.'

Eddie caught Hartmann's eye. The man looked sick with dread. Eddie was stricken with guilt. Hartmann was going to be taken back to Nazi Germany, and it was Eddie's fault. Eddie said to him, 'They had my wife . . . what could I do?'

Hartmann's face changed immediately. 'I understand,' he said. 'We are used to this sort of thing in Germany. They make you betray one loyalty for the sake of another. You had no choice. Don't blame yourself.'

Eddie was astonished that the man could find it in his heart to console *him* at a moment like this.

He caught the eye of Ollis Field. 'But why did you bring a decoy on to the Clipper?' he said. 'Did you *want* the Patriarca gang to hijack the plane?'

'Not at all,' Field said. 'We got information that the gang wanted to *kill* Gordino to stop him squealing. They were going to hit him as soon as he reached America. So we let it out that he was flying on the Clipper, but sent him on ahead by ship. Round about now, the news will be on the radio that Gordino is in jail and the gang will know they've been fooled.'

'Why aren't you guarding Carl Hartmann?'

'We didn't know he was going to be on this flight – nobody told us!'

Was Hartmann completely unprotected? Eddie wondered. Or did he have a bodyguard who had not yet revealed himself?

The little gangster called Joe came into the compartment with his gun in his right hand and an opened bottle of champagne in his left. 'They're quiet as lambs, Vinnie,' he said to Vincini. 'Kid's back there in the dining room, he can cover the whole front part of the plane from there.'

Vincini said to Luther, 'So where's the fuckin' submarine?'

Luther answered, 'It will be here at any moment, I'm sure.'

A submarine! Luther had a rendezvous with a U-boat right here off the coast of Maine! Eddie looked out of the windows, expecting to see it rising from the water like a steel whale, but he saw nothing but waves.

Vincini said, 'Well, we've done our bit, gimme the money.'

Keeping Hartmann covered, Luther stepped back to his seat, picked up a small case, and handed it to Vincini. Vincini opened it. It was packed tight with wads of bills.

Luther said, 'A hundred thousand dollars, all in twenties.'

Vincini said, 'I better check it.' He put his gun away and sat down with the case on his knee.

Luther said, 'It'll take you for ever—'

'What do you think I am, green?' Vincini said in a tone of exaggerated patience. 'I'll check two bundles, then I'll count how many bundles there are. I've done this before.'

Everyone watched Vincini count the money. The passengers in the compartment – Princess Lavinia, Lulu Bell, Mark Alder, Diane Lovesey, Ollis Field and the Frankie Gordino impostor – looked on. Joe recognized Lulu Bell. 'Hey, ain't you in the movies?' he said. Lulu looked away, ignoring him. Joe drank from his bottle, then offered it to Diana Lovesey. She paled and shrank away from him. 'I agree, this stuff is overrated,' Joe said, then he reached out and poured champagne over her cream-and-red spotted dress.

She gave a cry of distress and pushed his hand away. The wet dress clung to her bosom revealingly.

Eddie was appalled. This was the kind of thing that could lead to violence. He said, 'Knock it off, you.'

The man took no notice. 'Great jugs,' he said with a leer. He dropped the bottle and grabbed one of her breasts, squeezing hard.

She screamed.

Her boyfriend, Mark, was struggling with his safety belt, saying, 'Don't touch her, you cheap hood—'

With a surprisingly quick movement, the hoodlum hit him in the mouth with his gun. Blood spurted from Mark's lips.

Eddie said, 'Vincini, for Christ's sake, put a stop to this!'

Vincini said, 'Girl like that, hell, if she ain't had her tits felt by her age, it's about time.'

Joe thrust his hand down the front of Diana's dress. She struggled to avoid his grasp, but she was strapped in her seat.

Mark got his seat belt undone, but as he was rising to his feet the man hit him again. This time the butt of the gun hit the corner of his eye. Joe used his left fist to punch Mark in the stomach, then hit him across the face with the gun a third time. Now blood from his wounds got into Mark's eyes and blinded him. Several women were screaming.

Eddie was appalled. He had been determined to avoid bloodshed. Joe was about to hit Mark again. Eddie could stand it no longer. Taking his life in his hands, he grabbed the little gangster from behind, pinning his arms.

Joe struggled, trying to point his gun at Eddie, but

Eddie held on tight. Joe pulled the trigger. The bang was deafening in the confined space, but the gun was pointing down and the bullet went through the floor.

The first shot had been fired. Eddie had a horrified, scary feeling that he was losing control of the situation. If that happened there could be a bloodbath.

At last Vincini intervened. 'Knock it off, Joe!' he yelled.

The man became still.

Eddie let him go.

Joe gave him a venomous look but said nothing.

Vincini said, 'We can go. The money's all here.'

Eddie saw a ray of hope. If they would leave now at least the bloodshed had been limited. Go, he thought, for God's sake, go!

Vincini went on, 'Bring the cunt with you if you want, Joe. I might prong her myself – I like her better than the engineer's skinny wife.' He stood up.

Diana screamed, 'No, no!'

Joe undid her seat belt and grabbed her by the hair. She struggled with him. Mark got to his feet, trying to wipe the blood from his eyes. Eddie grabbed Mark, restraining him. 'Don't get yourself killed!' he said. Lowering his voice, he said, 'It'll be okay, I promise you!' He wanted to tell Mark that the gang's launch was going to be stopped by a US Navy cutter before they would have time to do anything to Diana, but he was afraid of being overheard by Vincini.

Joe pointed his gun at Mark and said to Diana, 'You come with us or your boyfriend gets it right between the eyes.'

Diana became still and started to sob.

Luther said, 'I'm coming with you, Vincini. My submarine hasn't made it.'

'I knew it wouldn't come,' Vincini said. 'They can't get this close to the USA.'

Vincini did not know anything about submarines. Eddie could guess the real reason why the U-boat had not appeared. The U-boat commander had seen Steve Appleby's Navy cutter patrolling the channel. He was probably now waiting near by, listening to the cutter's radio chatter, hoping it would go away and patrol some other stretch of water.

Luther's decision to flee with the gangsters, instead of waiting for the submarine, raised Eddie's spirits. The gangsters' launch was headed for Steve Appleby's trap, and if Luther and Hartmann were on the launch, Hartmann would be saved. If this whole thing could end with nothing worse than a few stitches in Mark Alder's face, Eddie would rejoice.

'Let's go,' Vincini said. 'Luther first, then the Kraut, then Kid, then me, then the engineer – want you close to me until I get off this crate – then Joe with the blonde. Move!'

Mark Alder began to struggle in Eddie's arms. Vincini said to Ollis Field and the other agent, 'You want to hold this guy down, or you want Joe to shoot him?' They grabbed Mark and held him still.

Eddie filed out behind Vincini. Passengers stared wide-eyed at them as they passed through No. 3 compartment and into the dining room.

As Vincini entered No. 2 compartment, Mr Membury pulled a gun and said, 'Stop!' He aimed directly at Vincini. 'Everybody keep still or I shoot your boss!'

Eddie took one step back to get out of the way.

Vincini went white and said, 'All right, boys, nobody move.'

The one they called Kid swung round and fired twice.

Membury fell.

Vincini yelled furiously at the boy, 'You cocksucker, he might have killed me!'

'Didn't you hear his voice?' Kid replied. 'He's an Englishman.'

'So fuckin' what?' Vincini screamed.

'I seen every movie ever made, and nobody ever gets shot by an Englishman.'

Eddie knelt down beside Membury. The bullets had entered his chest. His blood was the same colour as his waistcoat. 'Who are you?' Eddie said.

'Scotland Yard, Special Branch,' Membury whispered. 'Assigned to protect Hartmann.' So the scientist had not been completely unguarded, Eddie thought. 'Bloody failure,' Membury said hoarsely. His eyes closed and he stopped breathing.

Eddie cursed. He had vowed to get the gangsters off the plane without anyone being killed, and he had come so close to succeeding! Now this brave policeman was dead. 'So unnecessary,' Eddie said aloud.

He heard Vincini say, 'How come you're so sure nobody needs to be a hero?' He looked up. Vincini was staring at him with suspicion and hostility. Jesus Christ, I think he'd like to kill me, Eddie thought. Vincini went on, 'Do you know something the rest of us don't?'

Eddie had no answer, but at that moment the seaman from the launch came rushing down the stairs and into the compartment. 'Hey, Vinnie, I just heard from Willard—'

'I told him not to use that radio except for emergency!'

'This is an emergency – there's a Navy ship going up and down the shore, just like they're looking for someone.'

Eddie's heart stopped. He had not thought of this possibility. The gang had a sentry on shore, keeping watch, with a short-wave radio so he could talk to the launch. Now Vincini knew about the trap.

It was all over, and Eddie had lost.

'You double-crossed me,' Vincini said to Eddie. 'You bastard, I'll kill you for this.'

Eddie caught Captain Baker's eye and saw understanding and a surprised respect in his face.

Vincini pointed his gun at Eddie.

Eddie thought, I did my best, and everyone knows it. I don't care if I die now.

Then Luther said, 'Vincini, listen! Do you hear something?'

They were all silent. Eddie heard the sound of another plane.

Luther looked out of the window. 'It's a seaplane, coming down right near by!'

Vincini lowered his gun. Eddie felt weak at the knees.

Vincini looked out, and Eddie followed his gaze. He saw the Grumman Goose that had been moored at Shediac. As he watched, it splashed down on the long side of a wave and came to rest.

Vincini said, 'So what? If they get in our way we'll shoot the bastards.'

'Don't you see?' Luther said excitedly. 'This is our escape! We can fly over the goddamn Navy and get away!'

Vincini nodded slowly. 'Good thinking. That's what we'll do.'

Eddie realized they were going to get away. His life was saved, but he had failed after all.

CHAPTER TWENTY-EIGHT

NANCY LENEHAN had found the answer to her problem as she flew along the Canadian coast in the chartered seaplane.

She wanted to defeat her brother, but she also wanted to find some way of escaping from the tramlines of her father's plans for her life. She wanted to be with Mervyn, but she was afraid that if she left Black's Boots and went to England she would become a bored housewife like Diana.

Nat Ridgeway had said he was willing to make a higher offer for the company, and give Nancy a job in General Textiles. Thinking about that, she had remembered that General Textiles had several factories in Europe, mostly in Britain; and that Ridgeway was not going to be able to visit them until the war was over, which might be years. So she was going to offer to become the European manager of General Textiles. That way she could be with Mervyn and still be in business.

The solution was remarkably neat. The only snag was that Europe was at war and she might get killed.

She was reflecting on that distant but chilling possibility when Mervyn turned round in his co-pilot's seat and pointed out of the window and down; and she saw the Clipper floating on the sea.

Mervyn tried to raise the Clipper by radio, but he got no response. Nancy forgot about her own troubles as the Goose circled the downed plane. What had happened? Were the people on board all right? The plane appeared undamaged, but there was no sign of life.

Mervyn turned to her and shouted over the roar of the engines, 'We have to go down and see if they need help.'

Nancy nodded vigorously in agreement.

'Strap in and hold tight. It may be a rough splashdown, because of the swell.'

She fastened her safety belt and looked out. The sea was choppy and there were long rollers. The pilot, Ned, brought the seaplane down in a line parallel with the crests of the waves. The hull touched water on the back of a swell, and the seaplane rode the wave like a Hawaiian surf-rider. It was not as rough as Nancy had feared.

There was a motor launch tied up to the Clipper's nose. A man in dungarees and a cap appeared on the deck and beckoned to them. Nancy gathered he wanted the Goose to tie up alongside the launch. The bow door of the Clipper was open, so presumably they would board that way. Nancy could see why: the waves were washing over the sea-wings, so it would be difficult to board through the normal door.

Ned edged the seaplane towards the launch: Nancy could tell it was a tricky manoeuvre in this sea. However, the Goose was a high-winged monoplane, and its wing was well above the superstructure of the launch, so they were able to draw alongside, with the hull of the plane bumping against the row of rubber tyres on the side of the boat. The man on deck tied the plane to his vessel fore and aft.

While Ned shut down the engines of the seaplane, Mervyn came aft, opened the door, and broke out the gangway.

'I ought to stay with my plane,' Ned said to Mervyn. 'You'd better go and find out what's going on.'

'I'm coming too,' said Nancy.

Because the seaplane was roped to the launch, the two vessels rose and fell together on the waves, and the gangway shifted relatively little. Mervyn disembarked first and held out a hand to Nancy.

When they were both on deck, Mervyn said to the man on the launch, 'What happened?'

'They had fuel trouble and had to splash down,' he replied.

'I couldn't get them on the radio.'

The man shrugged. 'You'd better go aboard.'

Getting from the launch to the Clipper involved a little jump, from the deck of the launch on to the platform made by the open bow door. Once again Mervyn went first. Nancy took off her shoes and stuffed them inside her coat, then followed suit. She was a little nervous but in fact it was easy.

In the bow compartment was a young man she did not recognize.

Mervyn said, 'What happened here?'

'Emergency landing,' the young man said. 'We were fishing, saw the whole thing.'

'What's wrong with the radio?'

'Dunno.'

The youngster was not very bright, Nancy decided. Mervyn must have had the same thought, for he said impatiently, 'I'd better speak to the Captain.'

'Go this way – they're all in the dining room.'

The boy was not very sensibly dressed for fishing, in his two-tone shoes and yellow tie, Nancy thought with amusement. She followed Mervyn up the ladder to the flight deck, which was deserted. That explained why Mervyn had been unable to raise the Clipper on the radio. But *why* were they all in the dining room? It was odd that the entire crew should leave the flight deck.

She began to feel uneasy as she went down the stairs to the passenger deck. Mervyn led the way into No. 2 compartment and stopped suddenly.

Looking past him, Nancy saw Mr Membury lying on the floor in a pool of blood. She put her hand to her mouth to stifle a cry of horror.

Mervyn said, 'Dear God, what's been happening here?'

Behind them, the young man in the yellow tie said, 'Keep moving.' His voice had become harsh.

Nancy turned to him and saw that he had a gun in his hand. 'Did you do this?' she said angrily.

'Shut your fuckin' mouth and keep moving!'

They stepped into the dining room.

Three more men with guns were standing in the room. There was a big man in a striped suit who looked as if he might be in charge. A little man with a mean face was standing behind Mervyn's wife, casually fondling her breasts: when Mervyn saw this he let out a curse. The third gunman was a passenger, Mr Luther: he was pointing his gun at another passenger, Professor Hartmann. The Captain and the engineer were also there, looking helpless. Several passengers were seated at tables, but most of the dishes and glassware had fallen to the floor and smashed. Nancy caught a glimpse of Margaret Oxenford, pale and frightened; and in a sudden flash she recalled the conversation in which she had glibly told Margaret that regular people did not need to worry about gangsters because they only operated in the slums. How stupid.

Mr Luther was speaking. 'The gods are on my side, Lovesey. You have arrived in a seaplane just when we need one. You can fly me and Mr Vincini and our associates over the Navy cutter that the treacherous Eddie Deakin has summoned to trap us.'

Mervyn looked hard at him and said nothing.

The man in the striped suit spoke up. 'Let's get moving, before the Navy starts to feel impatient and comes along to investigate. Kid, you take Lovesey. His girlfriend can stay here.'

'Okay, Vinnie.'

Nancy was not sure what was going on, but she knew she did not want to be left behind: if Mervyn was in trouble she would rather be by his side. But no one was asking what she preferred.

The man called Vincini continued giving instructions. 'Luther, you take the Kraut.'

Nancy wondered why they were taking Carl Hartmann. She had assumed this was all something to do with Frankie Gordino, but he was nowhere in sight.

Vincini said, 'Joe, bring the blonde.'

The little man pointed his gun at Diana Lovesey's bosom. 'Let's go,' he said. She did not move.

Nancy was horrified. Why were they kidnapping Diana? She had a dreadful feeling she knew the answer.

Joe poked the barrel of the gun into Diana's soft breast, prodding her hard, and she gasped with pain.

'Wait a minute,' Mervyn said.

They all looked at him.

'All right, I'll fly you out of here, but there's a condition.'

Vincini said, 'Shut up and move. You can't make no fuckin' conditions.'

Mervyn spread his arms wide. 'So shoot me,' he said.

Nancy let out a cry of fear. These were the kind of men who would shoot someone who dared them; didn't Mervyn understand that?

There was a moment of silence, then Luther said, 'What condition?'

Mervyn pointed at Diana. 'She stays.'

Joe, the little man, gave Mervyn a killing look.

Vincini said, 'We don't need you, shithead. There's a whole bunch of Pan American pilots up front – any one of them can fly that seaplane as well as you.'

'And any one of them will make the same condition,' Mervyn said. 'Ask them – if you've got time.'

Nancy realized that the gangsters did not know there was another pilot in the Goose. Not that it made much difference.

Luther said to Joe, 'Leave her behind.'

The little man went red with anger. 'Hell, why—'

'Leave her behind!' Luther shouted. 'I paid you to help me kidnap Hartmann, not rape women!'

Vincini intervened. 'He's right, Joe. You can pick up another cunt later.'

'Okay, okay,' Joe said.

Diana began to cry with relief.

Vincini said, 'We're running out of time, let's get out of here!'

Nancy wondered whether she would ever see Mervyn again.

From outside came the sound of a klaxon. The skipper of the launch was trying to get their attention.

The one they called Kid spoke up from the next room. 'Holy shit, boss, look out the fuckin' window!'

Harry Marks was knocked out when the Clipper splashed down. On the first bounce he fell headlong across the piled suitcases; then, just as he was getting to his hands and knees, the plane flopped into the sea and he was flung against the forward wall. He banged his head and was out cold.

When he came round he wondered what the hell was going on.

He knew they had not arrived at Port Washington: they were only about two hours into a five-hour flight. This was an unscheduled stop, then; and it had seemed like an emergency splashdown.

He sat upright, feeling his injuries. Now he knew

why planes had seat belts. His nose was bleeding, his head hurt like hell, and he was bruised just about everywhere; but nothing was actually broken. He wiped his nose with his handkerchief and considered himself lucky.

There were no windows in the baggage hold, of course, so he had no way of finding out what was going on. He sat still for a while and listened for clues. The engines were shut down, and there was a long period of quiet.

Then he heard a shot.

Firearms meant gangsters, and if there were gangsters on board they were probably after Frankie Gordino. More importantly, gunplay meant confusion and panic, and in those circumstances Harry might be able to get away.

He had to take a look outside.

He opened the door a crack. He saw no one.

He stepped out into the corridor and went forward to the door that led to the flight deck. He stood behind it, listening hard. He heard nothing.

Gently and silently, he eased the door open and peeped through.

The flight deck was deserted.

He stepped over the high threshold, treading softly, and went to the top of the staircase. He could hear men's voices raised in argument, but he could not make out the words.

The cockpit hatch was open. Looking through, he could see daylight in the bow compartment. He went closer and saw that the bow door was open.

He stood up and looked through the window, and saw a motor launch tied up to the nose of the aircraft. There was a man on deck in rubber boots and a cap.

Harry realized he could be very close to escape.

Here was a fast boat that could take him to a lonely spot on the coast. There appeared to be only one man on board. There had to be a way Harry could get rid of him and take the boat.

He heard a footstep right behind him.

He spun around, his heart pounding.

It was Percy Oxenford.

The boy stood in the rear doorway, looking as shocked as Harry felt.

After a moment Percy said, 'Where have you been hiding?'

'Never mind that,' Harry said. 'What's going on down there?'

'Mr Luther is a Nazi who wants to send Professor Hartmann back to Germany. He's hired some gangsters to help him and he gave them a hundred thousand dollars in a briefcase!'

'Blimey,' said Harry, forgetting to do his American accent.

'And they killed Mr Membury. He was a bodyguard from Scotland Yard.'

So that was what he was. 'Is your sister all right?'

'So far. But they want to take Mrs Lovesey with them because she's so pretty – I hope they don't notice Margaret . . .'

'God, what a mess,' said Harry.

'I managed to sneak away and come up through the trapdoor next to the ladies' room.'

'What for?'

'I want Agent Field's gun. I saw Captain Baker confiscate it.' Percy pulled open the drawer under the chart table. Inside was a compact revolver with a short barrel, just the kind of thing an FBI man might carry under his jacket. 'I thought so – it's a Colt Thirty-eight Detective Special,' Percy said. He picked it up, broke it open expertly and spun the cylinder.

Harry shook his head. 'I don't think that's such a great idea. You'll get yourself killed.' He grabbed the boy's wrist, took the gun from him, put it back and closed the drawer.

There was a loud noise from outside. Harry and Percy both looked out of the windows and saw a seaplane circling the Clipper. Who the hell was this? After a moment it started to descend. It splashed down, riding a wave, and taxied towards the Clipper.

'Now what?' said Harry. He turned round. Percy had disappeared. The drawer was open.

And the gun had gone.

'Damn,' Harry said.

He went through the rear door. He dashed past the holds, under the navigator's dome and across a low compartment, then looked through a second door.

Percy was scampering along a crawlway through a space that got lower and narrower as it approached the tail. The plane's structure was bare here, with struts and rivets visible and cables trailing along the floor.

The space was obviously a redundant void above the rear half of the passenger deck. There was light at the far end, and Harry saw Percy drop down through a square hole. He remembered seeing a ladder on the wall next to the ladies' room, with a trapdoor above it.

He could not stop Percy now: it was too late.

He recalled Margaret saying they could all shoot, it was a family obsession; but the boy knew nothing about gangsters. If he got in their way they would gun him down like a dog. Harry liked the boy, but his own feelings did not concern him so much as Margaret's. Harry did not want her to see her brother killed. But what the hell could he do?

He returned to the flight deck and looked out. The seaplane was tying up to the launch. Either the people from the seaplane would come aboard the Clipper, or vice versa: in any event someone would soon be passing through the flight cabin. Harry had to get out of the way for a few moments. He went out through the rear door, leaving it open a crack so he could hear what went on.

Soon someone came up the stairs from the passenger deck and went through to the bow compartment. A few minutes later a number of people, two or three, came back. Harry listened to their footsteps going down the stairs, then came out.

Had they brought help, or reinforcements for the gangsters? Harry was in the dark again.

He went to the top of the stairs. There he hesitated. He decided to risk going part way down to listen.

He went to the bend in the staircase and peeked

around the corner. He could see the little kitchen: it was empty. What would he do now, if the seaman from the launch decided to come aboard the Clipper? I'll hear him coming, Harry thought, and slip into the men's room. He went on down, one slow step at a time, pausing and listening on each step. When he reached the bottom he heard a voice. He recognized Tom Luther's voice, a cultured American accent with a trace of something European underneath. 'The gods are on my side, Lovesey,' he was saying. 'You have arrived in a seaplane just when we need one. You can fly me and Mr Vincini and our associates over the Navy cutter that the treacherous Eddie Deakin has summoned to trap us.'

That answered the question. The seaplane was going to enable Luther and Hartmann to get away.

Harry crept back up the stairs. The thought of poor Hartmann being taken back to the Nazis was heartbreaking; but Harry might have let it happen – he was no hero. However, young Percy Oxenford would do something stupid any moment now, and Harry could not stand aside and let Margaret's brother get himself killed. He had to get in first, create a diversion, somehow put a spoke in the gang's wheel, for her sake.

Looking into the bow compartment, he saw a rope tied to a strut, and he was inspired.

He suddenly saw a way he could create a diversion and maybe get rid of one of the gangsters as well.

First he had to untie the ropes and set the launch adrift.

He went through the hatch and down the ladder.

His heart beat faster. He was scared.

He did not think about what he would say if someone caught him now. He would just make something up, as he always did.

He crossed the compartment. As he had thought, the rope came from the launch.

He reached up to the strut, undid the knot, and dropped the rope on the floor.

Looking out, he saw that there was a second rope running from the bow of the launch to the nose of the Clipper. Damn. He would have to get out on to the platform to reach it, and that meant he might be seen.

But he could not give up now. And he had to hurry. Percy was back there like Daniel in the lions' den.

He stepped up on to the platform. The rope was tied to a capstan sticking up from the nose of the aircraft. He untied it rapidly.

He heard a shout from the launch. 'Hey, you, what are you doing?'

He did not look up. He hoped the guy did not have a gun.

He detached the rope from the capstan and threw it in the sea.

'Hey, you!'

He turned round. The skipper of the launch was standing on deck shouting. He was not armed, thank God. The man picked up his end of the other rope and pulled. The rope snaked out of the bow compartment and fell in the water.

The skipper ducked into the wheelhouse and started his engine.

The next part was more dangerous.

It would only take a few seconds for the gangsters to notice that their launch had come adrift. They would be puzzled and alarmed. One of them would come to investigate and to tie the launch up again. And then—

Harry was too scared to think about what he was going to do then.

He dashed up the ladder and across the flight deck and concealed himself in the cargo area once again.

He knew it was deadly dangerous to fool around like this with gangsters, and he felt cold at the thought of what they would do to him if they caught him.

For a long minute nothing happened. Come on, he thought, hurry up and look out of the window! Your launch is adrift – you have to notice it before I lose my nerve.

At last he heard footsteps again, heavy ones, hurrying, coming up the stairs and through the flight cabin. To his dismay it sounded like two men. He had not anticipated having to deal with two.

When he judged that they must have descended into the bow compartment he looked out. It was all clear. He crossed the cabin and looked through the hatch. Two men with guns in their hands were staring out of the bow door. Even without the guns Harry would have guessed they were crooks by their flashy clothes. One was an ugly little guy with a mean look; the other was very young, about eighteen.

Maybe I should go back and hide, Harry thought.

The skipper was manoeuvring the launch, still with the seaplane tied to its side. The two gangsters would have to tie the launch up to the Clipper again, and they could not do that with guns in their hands. Harry waited for them to put their firearms away.

The skipper shouted something Harry could not make out, and a few moments later the two hoods stuffed the guns into their pockets and stepped out on to the platform.

With his heart in his mouth, Harry went down the ladder into the bow compartment.

The men were trying to catch a rope that the skipper was throwing to them, and all their attention was directed outwards, so they did not see him at first.

He sidled across the compartment.

When he was half-way, the young one caught the rope. The other man, the little one, half turned – and saw Harry. He put his hand in his pocket and got his gun out just as Harry reached him.

Harry felt sure he was about to die.

Desperately, without thinking, he stooped, grabbed the little man's ankle, and heaved.

A shot rang out, but Harry felt nothing.

The man staggered, almost fell, dropped his gun, and seized hold of his buddy for support.

The younger man lost his balance and let go of the rope. For an instant they swayed, clutching at one another. Harry still had hold of the little man's ankle, and he jerked it again.

Both men fell off the platform and plunged into the heaving sea.

Harry let out a whoop of triumph.

They sank below the waves, came up again, and

began to struggle. Harry could tell that neither of them could swim.

'That's for Clive Membury, you bastards!' Harry shouted.

He did not wait to see what became of them. He had to know what happened on the passenger deck. He dashed back across the bow compartment, scrambled up the ladder, emerged into the flight cabin, then tiptoed down the staircase.

On the bottom step he stopped and listened.

Margaret could hear her own heartbeat.

It sounded in her ears like a kettledrum, rhythmic and insistent, and so loud that she fancied other people must be able to hear it too.

She was more frightened than she had ever been in her life. And she was ashamed of her fear.

She had been frightened by the emergency splash-down, the sudden appearance of guns, the bewildering way people such as Frankie Gordino, Mr Luther and the engineer kept changing their roles, and the casual brutality of these stupid thugs in their awful suits; and most of all she was frightened because quiet Mr Membury was lying on the floor dead.

She was too frightened to move, and that made her ashamed.

For years she had been talking about how she wanted to fight Fascism, and now the opportunity had arrived. Right here in front of her, a Fascist was kidnapping Carl Hartmann to take him back to Germany. But she could do nothing about it because she was paralysed by fear.

Perhaps there was nothing she *could* do, anyway; perhaps she would only get herself killed. But she ought to try, and she had always said she was willing to risk her life for the cause and for the memory of Ian.

Her father had been right to pour scorn on her pretensions of bravery, she realized. Her heroism was all in her imagination. Her dream of being a motorcycle courier on the battlefield was mere fantasy: at the first sound of gunfire she would hide under a hedge. When there was real danger she was completely useless. She sat frozen still while her heart pounded in her ears.

She had not spoken a word while the Clipper splashed down, the gunmen came aboard, and Nancy and Mr Lovesey arrived in the seaplane. She remained silent when the one called Kid saw the launch drifting away, and the one called Vincini sent Kid and Joe to help tie it up again.

But when she saw Kid and Joe drowning she screamed.

She had been staring fixedly out of the window, looking at but not seeing the waves, when the two men drifted into view. Kid was trying to keep afloat, but Joe was on Kid's back, pushing his friend under as he tried to save himself. It was a horrible sight.

When she screamed, Luther rushed to the window and looked out. 'They're in the water!' he yelled hysterically.

Vincini said, 'Who – Kid and Joe?'

'Yes!'

The skipper of the launch threw a rope, but the

drowning men did not see it: Joe was thrashing around in a blind panic and Kid was being held underwater by Joe.

'Do something!' Luther said. He was on the verge of panic himself.

'What?' said Vincini. 'There ain't nothing we can do. Crazy bastards don't have the smarts to save themselves!'

The two men drifted nearer to the sea-wing. If they had kept calm they could have climbed on to it and been saved. But they did not see it.

Kid's head went under and did not come up again.

Joe lost contact with Kid and breathed a lungful of water. Margaret heard one hoarse scream, muffled by the Clipper's soundproofing. Joe's head went under, came up, and went under again for the last time.

Margaret shuddered. They were both dead.

'How did this happen?' Luther said. 'How come they fell in?'

'Maybe they were pushed,' said Vincini.

'Who by?'

'There must be someone else on this fuckin' airplane.'

Margaret thought, Harry!

Was it possible? Could Harry still be on board? Had he hidden somewhere, while the police were searching for him, and come out after the emergency splash-down? Was it Harry who had pushed the two gangsters into the sea?

Then she thought of her brother. Percy had disappeared after the launch tied up to the Clipper and

Margaret had assumed he had gone to the men's room and then decided to stay out of the way. But that was not characteristic. He was more likely to seek out trouble. She knew he had found an unofficial way up to the flight deck. What was he up to now?

Luther said, 'This whole thing is falling apart! What are we going to do?'

'We're leaving on the seaplane, just like we planned – you, me, the Kraut and the money,' said Vincini. 'If anyone gets in the way, put a bullet in his belly. Calm down and let's go.'

Margaret had a dreadful premonition that they would meet Percy on the stairs, and he would be the one to get a bullet in his belly.

Then, just as the three men were leaving the dining room, she heard Percy's voice coming from the back of the plane.

At the top of his voice he shouted, 'Stop right there!'

To Margaret's astonishment he was holding a gun – and pointing it right at Vincini.

It was a short-barrelled revolver, and Margaret guessed immediately that it must be the Colt that had been confiscated from the FBI agent earlier. Now Percy held it in front of him, straight-armed as if he were aiming at a target.

Vincini turned around slowly.

Margaret was proud of Percy even while she was afraid for his life.

The dining room was crowded. Behind Vincini, right

next to where Margaret was sitting, were Luther and Hartmann, Luther holding his gun to Hartmann's head. On the other side of the compartment stood Nancy, Mervyn Lovesey, Diana Lovesey, and the engineer and the Captain. And most of the seats were occupied.

Vincini looked at Percy for a long moment, then said, 'Get out of here, kid.'

'Drop your gun,' Percy said in his cracked adolescent voice.

Vincini moved with surprising speed. He ducked to one side and raised his gun. There was a shot. The bang deafened Margaret: she heard a distant scream and realized it was her own voice. She could not tell who had shot whom. Percy seemed all right. Then Vincini staggered and fell, blood spurting from his chest. He dropped his briefcase and it burst open. Blood splashed the bundles of money.

Percy dropped the gun and stared, horrified, at the man he had shot. He looked as if he was about to burst into tears.

Everyone looked at Luther, the last of the gang, and the one person who still held a gun.

Carl Hartmann made a sudden move, breaking free of Luther's grasp while the man was distracted, and flung himself on the floor. Margaret was terrified Hartmann would be killed; then she thought Luther would shoot Percy; but what actually happened took her completely by surprise.

Luther grabbed *her*.

He pulled her out of her seat and held her in front of himself with his gun at her head, just as he had held Hartmann before.

Everyone froze.

She was too terrified to move, to speak, even to scream. The barrel of the gun dug painfully into her temple. Luther was shaking: he was as frightened as she. In the silence he said, 'Hartmann. Go to the bow door. Go on board the launch. Do as you're told or the girl gets it.'

Suddenly she felt a dreadful calm descend over her. She could see, with hideous clarity, that Luther had been brilliantly cunning. If he had merely pointed his gun at Hartmann, Hartmann might have said, 'Shoot me – I'd rather die than go back to Germany.' But now it was her life at stake. Hartmann might have been prepared to give his own life, but he would not sacrifice a young girl.

Slowly, Hartmann got up from the floor.

Everything was up to her, Margaret understood with icy, fearful logic. She could save Hartmann by sacrificing herself. It's not fair, she thought, I wasn't expecting this, I'm not ready for it, I can't do it!

She caught her father's eye. He looked horrified.

In that awful moment she recalled how he had taunted her, saying she was too soft to fight, she would not last a day in the ATS.

Was he right?

All she had to do was move. Luther might kill her, but the other men would jump on him before he could do anything else, and Hartmann would be saved.

Time passed as slowly as in a nightmare.

I can do it, she thought with the same awful frozen composure.

She took a deep breath and thought, Goodbye, everyone.

Suddenly she heard Harry's voice behind her. 'Mr Luther, I think your submarine has arrived.'

Everyone looked through the windows.

Margaret felt the pressure of the gun barrel at her temple ease a fraction: Luther was momentarily distracted.

She ducked her head and wriggled out of his grasp.

There was a shot, but she felt nothing.

Everyone moved at once.

The engineer, Eddie, flew past her and fell on Luther like a tree.

Margaret saw Harry grab Luther's gun hand and tear the weapon from his grasp.

Luther crashed to the floor with Eddie and Harry on top of him.

Margaret realized she was still alive.

She suddenly felt as weak as a baby, and she sank helplessly into a seat.

Percy dashed to her. She hugged him. Time stood still. She heard herself say, 'Are you all right?'

'I think so,' he said shakily.

'You're so brave!'

'So are you!'

Yes, I was, she thought; I was brave.

All the passengers began to shout at once, then Captain Baker yelled, 'Quiet, everybody, please!'

Margaret looked around.

Luther was still on the floor, face down, pinned and harmless with Eddie and Harry on top of him. The danger from within the aircraft was over. She looked outside. The submarine floated on the water like a great grey shark, its wet steel flanks gleaming in the sunshine.

The Captain said, 'There's a naval cutter nearby and we're going to radio it right away and tell them about the U-boat.' The crew had come through from No. 1 compartment, and now the Captain addressed the radio operator. 'Get on the horn, Ben.'

'The submarine commander may hear our radio message and run for it.'

'All the better,' the Captain growled. 'Our passengers have seen enough danger.'

The radio operator went up the stairs to the flight deck.

Everyone kept looking out at the U-boat. Its hatch stayed shut. Its commander must be waiting to see what would happen.

Captain Baker went on, 'There's one gangster we haven't caught, and I'd like to bring him in: the skipper of the launch. Eddie, go to the bow door and lure him aboard – tell him Vincini wants him.'

Eddie got off Luther and went away.

The Captain spoke to the navigator. 'Jack, collect up all these damn guns and take the ammunition out.' The Captain realized he had cursed, and added, 'Pardon my language, ladies.'

They had heard so much foul language from the

gangsters that Margaret laughed at him apologizing for a 'damn'; and the other passengers nearby laughed too. He was taken aback at first, and then saw the joke, and he smiled.

The laughter was a sign that they were out of danger, and some of the passengers began to relax. Margaret still felt peculiar: she was shivering as if she was freezing cold.

The Captain nudged Luther with the toe of his shoe and spoke to another crewman. 'Johnny, stick this guy in No. 1 compartment and keep a close watch on him.'

Harry got off Luther and one of the crew took the man away.

Harry and Margaret looked at one another.

She had imagined he had abandoned her; she had thought she would never see him again; she had been sure she was about to die. Suddenly it seemed unbearably wonderful that they were both alive and together. He sat down next to her, and she threw herself into his arms. They hugged one another tight.

After a while he murmured in her ears, 'Look outside.'

The submarine was slowly slipping beneath the waves.

Margaret smiled up at Harry and then kissed him.

CHAPTER TWENTY-NINE

When it was all over, Carol-Ann would not touch Eddie.

She sat in the dining room, sipping hot milky coffee prepared by Davy the steward. She was pale and shaky, but she kept saying she was all right. However, she flinched every time Eddie put his hand on her.

He sat close, looking at her, but she would not meet his eyes. They spoke in low voices about what had happened. She told him obsessively, again and again, how the men had burst into the house and dragged her out into their car. 'I was standing there bottling plums!' she kept saying, as if that was the most outrageous aspect of the whole episode.

'It's all over now,' he would say each time, and she would nod her head vigorously, but he could tell she did not believe it.

At last she looked at him and said, 'When will you have to fly next?'

Then he understood. She was frightened about how she would feel the next time he left her alone. He felt relieved: he could reassure her about that, easily. 'I won't be flying any more,' he told her. 'I'm resigning right away. They'd have to fire me otherwise: they can't employ an engineer who's deliberately brought a plane down the way I did.'

Captain Baker overheard part of the conversation, and interrupted him. 'Eddie, there's something I have to say to you. I understand what you did. You were put in an impossible position and you handled it the best you could. More than that: I don't know another man that would have handled it so well. You were brave and you were smart, and I'm proud to fly with you.'

'Thank you, sir,' Eddie said, and there was a lump in his throat. 'I can't tell you how good that makes me feel.' Out of the corner of his eye he spotted Percy Oxenford, sitting alone, looking shocked: 'Sir, I think we all should thank young Percy: he saved the day!'

Percy heard him and looked up.

'Good point,' said the Captain. He patted Eddie on the shoulder and went over to shake the boy's hand. 'You're a brave man, Percy.'

Percy brightened instantly. 'Thank you!' he said.

The Captain sat down to chat with him, and Carol-Ann said to Eddie, 'If you're not flying, what will we do?'

'I'll start that business we've been talking about.'

He could see the hope in her face, but she did not really believe it yet. 'Can we?'

'I've got enough money saved to buy the airfield, and I'll borrow what I need to get started.'

She was visibly cheering by the second. 'Could we run it together?' she said. 'Maybe I could keep the books and answer the phone while you do repairs and refuelling?'

He smiled and nodded. 'Sure, at least until the baby comes.'

'Just like a Mom and Pop store.'

He reached out and took her hand, and this time she did not flinch, but squeezed his hand in return. 'Mom and Pop,' he said, and at last she smiled.

Nancy was hugging Mervyn when Diana tapped him on the shoulder.

Nancy had been lost in joy and relief, overwhelmed by the pleasure of being alive and with the man she loved. Now she wondered if Diana would cast a cloud over this moment. Diana had left Mervyn indecisively, and she had shown signs of regretting it, off and on, ever since. He had just proved that he still cared for her by bargaining with the gangsters to save her. Was she about to beg him to take her back?

Mervyn turned and gave his wife a guarded look. 'Well, Diana?'

Her face was wet with tears, but she had a determined expression. 'Will you shake hands?' she said.

Nancy was not sure what this meant, and Mervyn's wary manner told her that he, too, was uncertain. However, he offered his hand, saying, 'Of course.'

Diana held his hand in both of hers. New tears came, and Nancy felt sure she was about to say, 'Let's try again,' but instead she said, 'Good luck, Mervyn. I wish you happiness.'

Mervyn looked solemn. 'Thank you, Di. I wish you the same.'

Then Nancy understood: they were forgiving one another for the hurt that had been done. They were still going to split up, but they would part friends.

On impulse, Nancy said to Diana, 'Will you shake hands with me?'

The other woman hesitated only for a fraction of a second. 'Yes,' she said. They shook hands. 'I wish you well,' Diana said.

'And I you.'

Diana turned round without saying any more and went aft along the aisle to her compartment.

Mervyn said, 'But what about us? What are we going to do?'

Nancy realized she had not yet had time to tell him of her plan. 'I'm going to be Nat Ridgeway's European manager.'

Mervyn was surprised. 'When did he offer you the job?'

'He hasn't – but he will,' she said, and she laughed happily.

She heard the sound of an engine. It was not one of the Clipper's mighty engines, but a smaller one. She looked out of the window, wondering if the Navy had arrived.

To her surprise, she saw that the gangsters' motor launch had been untied from the Clipper and from the little seaplane and was pulling rapidly away.

But who was driving it?

*

Margaret opened the throttle wide and steered the launch away from the Clipper.

The wind blew her hair off her face, and she gave a whoop of sheer exhilaration. 'Free!' she yelled. 'I'm free!'

She and Harry had been standing in the aisle of the Clipper, wondering what to do next, when Eddie the engineer brought the skipper of the launch down the stairs and put him in No. 1 compartment with Luther; and both of them had been struck by the identical thought.

The passengers and crew were too busy congratulating one another to take much notice of Margaret and Harry as they slipped into the bow compartment and boarded the launch. The engine was idling. Harry had untied the ropes while Margaret figured out the controls, which were just like Father's boat in Nice, and they were away in seconds.

She did not think they would be chased. The naval cutter summoned by the engineer was in hot pursuit of a German submarine, and could not be expected to take an interest in a man who had stolen a pair of cufflinks in London. When the police arrived they would be investigating murder, kidnapping and piracy: it would be a long time before they worried about Harry.

Harry rummaged in a locker and found some maps. After studying them for a while he said, 'There are lots of charts of the waters around a bay called Black's Harbour, which is right on the border between the

USA and Canada. I think we must be near there. We should head for the Canadian side.'

A little later he said, 'There's a big place about seventy-five miles north of here called St John. It has a railway station. Are we heading north?'

She looked at the compass. 'More or less, yes.'

'I don't know anything about navigating, but if we keep in sight of the coast I don't see how we can go wrong. We should get there around nightfall.'

She smiled at him.

He put the charts down and stood beside her at the wheel, staring at her hard.

'What?' she said. 'What is it?'

He shook his head as if in disbelief. 'You're so beautiful,' he said. 'And you like me!'

She laughed. 'Anyone would like you, if they knew you.'

He put his arm around her waist. 'This is a hell of a thing, sailing along in the sunshine with a girl like you. My old ma always said I was lucky, and she was right, wasn't she?'

'What will we do when we get to St John?' she said.

'We'll beach the launch, walk into town, get a room for the night and take the first train out in the morning.'

'I don't know what we're going to do for money,' she said with a little frown of worry.

'Yes, that is a problem. I've only got a few pounds, and we'll have to pay for hotels, rail tickets, new clothes . . .'

'I wish I'd brought my overnight case, like you.'

He looked mischievous. 'That's not my case,' he said. 'It's Mr Luther's.'

She was mystified. 'Why did you bring Mr Luther's case?'

'Because it's got a hundred thousand dollars in it,' he said, and he started to laugh.

AFTERWORD

THE GOLDEN age of the flying boats was very short.

Only twelve Boeing B-314's were built, six of the first model and six more of a slightly modified version called the B-314A. Nine were handed over to the US military early in the war. One of these, the *Dixie Clipper*, carried President Roosevelt to the Casablanca Conference in January 1943. Another, the *Yankee Clipper*, crashed at Lisbon in February 1943 with twenty-nine casualties, the only crash in the history of the aircraft.

The three planes Pan American did not give to the US military were sold to the British, and were also used to carry VIPs across the Atlantic: Churchill flew on two, the *Bristol* and the *Berwick*.

The point of flying boats was that they did not need expensive long concrete runways. During the war, however, long runways were built in many parts of the world to accommodate heavy bombers, and the advantage of the flying boats disappeared.

After the war the B-314 was uneconomic, and one by one the planes were scrapped or scuttled.

There are now none left anywhere in the world.

ACKNOWLEDGEMENTS

I THANK the many people and organizations who helped me research this book, especially:

In New York: Pan American Airlines, most particularly their librarian Liwa Chiu;

In London: Lord Willis;

In Manchester: Chris Makepeace;

In Southampton: Ray Facey of Associated British Ports and Ian Sinclair of RAF Hythe;

In Foynes: Margaret O'Shaughnessy of the Flying Boat Museum;

In Botwood: Tip Evans, the Botwood Heritage Museum, and the hospitable people of Botwood;

In Shediac: Ned Belliveau and his family, and Charles Allain and the Moncton Museum;

Former Pan American crew and other employees who flew on the Clipper: Madeline Cuniff, Bob Fordyce, Lew Lindsey, Jim McLeod, States Mead, Roger Wolin and Stan Zedalis;

For finding most of the above: Dan Starer and Pam Mendez.